Patricia Burns was born in █████████████████████, she
decided to train as a teacher, which she combines with writing
novels.

She is now happily single and lives in Essex with her three
children, a cat and a delinquent tortoise. *Packards* is her fourth
novel. Her previous three, *Trinidad Street*, *Cinnamon Alley* and
Keep Safe for Me are all available in Arrow paperback.

Also by Patricia Burns

Trinidad Street
Cinnamon Alley
Keep Safe for Me

PACKARDS

Patricia Burns

ARROW

Published by Arrow Books in 1997

1 3 5 7 9 10 8 6 4 2

Copyright © Patricia Burns 1997

The right of Patricia Burns to be identified as the author
of this work has been asserted by her in accordance
with the Copyright, Designs and Patents Act, 1988

First published in 1997 by
Century Books,
Random House UK Limited
20 Vauxhall Bridge Road, London SW1V 2SA

Random House Australia (Pty) Limited
16 Dalmore Drive, Scoresby, Victoria 3179, Australia

Random House New Zealand Limited
18 Poland Road, Glenfield
Auckland 10, New Zealand

Random House South Africa (Pty) Limited
Endulini, 5a Jubilee Road, Parktown 2193, South Africa

Random House UK Limited Reg. No. 954009

A CIP catalogue record for this book
is available from the British Library

Papers used by Random House UK Limited
are natural, recyclable products made from wood grown in
sustainable forests. The manufacturing processes conform to
the environmental regulations of the country of origin

ISBN 0 09 960901 0

Printed and bound in Germany by
Elsnerdruck, Berlin

To Marianne, Nicholas and Daniel
who keep my feet on the ground

1

'Home at last!' Amelie said.

She stood at the top of the steps at the entrance to Victoria Station and breathed in the familiar London smell of smoke, horses, petrol fumes and human beings.

'Aren't you going to find it a trifle dull after America?' her brother Perry asked.

'Chicago was wonderful, but this is home,' Amelie said.

Around her, people flowed in and out of the station, new motor cabs and outmoded hansoms put down and picked up passengers, porters toted mountains of luggage and cleaners swept the steps, while newspaper boys, flower girls and hot chestnut men cried their wares. Amelie took it all in, absorbing the sights and sounds she had been away from for the last three months, trying to pinpoint just what it was that entranced her. Then it came to her.

'London voices,' she said. 'Do you know, I'd forgotten how nice it is to hear them.'

'Even cockney?' Perry asked, amused.

'Especially cockney. Americans might speak the same language as us – almost – but it sounds different. This is where I belong. Be a darling, Perry, and go and get me some violets from that girl.'

'Violets! Oh really, Mel, how common,' Perry grumbled, but he did as he was asked, and was rewarded with a flirtatious smile from the flower girl.

Nobody looking at them could have failed to recognise that the Amberleys were brother and sister. Both had very fair skins with a tendency to freckle, blue eyes, and thick fair hair with a reddish tinge that framed handsome regular faces with straight noses and mobile mouths. They were of a height, making Amelie tall for a girl, but while Perry, at twenty-one, was already gaining weight, Amelie was unfashionably slim, a result of boundless energy and a love of sport. Both were dressed in the height of fashion, Perry in a long overcoat with an astrakhan collar, his glossy top hat set at a jaunty angle, and Amelie in a loose travelling coat over a tailor-made skirt and jacket, with a velvet hat trimmed with feathers. They looked like children of the nobility, but in fact they were not of the old order, but of London's new and successful shopocracy.

A Rolls-Royce Silver Ghost glided to a halt at the foot of the steps, stately amongst the vulgar scurrying of the cabs. Amelie gave a cry of delight.

'Grandfather's sent his motor! Oh the darling!'

She ran down the steps as fast as her restricting layers of clothes would allow, greeted the chauffeur, who stood smartly to attention as he held the door open for her, climbed inside and sat back on the maroon leather upholstery with a sigh of pleasure. She might have known that her grandfather would not have forgotten that she was arriving home today. After the excitement of coming into port at Southampton, she had been rather hurt to find that only Perry had come to meet her, especially as she guessed he had been given the task because he had nothing better to do with his time.

'He remembered me, then,' she said to Perry as he sat down beside her.

'Remembered! It's all he's talked about this past week. He's missed you, Mel.'

'I've missed him,' Amelie said, tears unexpectedly pricking her eyes. When the chauffeur finished supervising the loading of her luggage she picked up the speaking tube to talk to him.

'Would you drive back via Oxford Street, please, Brightman? I want to take a little peek at the store.'

Perry protested, but Amelie overruled him.

'I must just see that it's still there.'

The Rolls pulled out into Buckingham Palace Road to join the slow-moving stream of drays, delivery vans, carts, cabs and omnibuses. Amelie leant forward, gazing out of the window and commenting on everything they passed.

'Isn't it odd how you expect everything to be different when you come back from a holiday? I've been away three months and so much has happened, and yet everything's very much the same.'

'They're hardly likely to pull it all down and build it up again while your back's turned,' Perry said.

'They do in Chicago. They're building all the time there, higher and higher.'

'Sounds most frightfully vulgar.'

'Rubbish, it's exciting.'

The motor swept round the palace and accelerated into the Mall. Here the commercial traffic gave way to the shining motor cars and horse-drawn carriages of the rich.

'How beautiful it is – look, snowdrops under the trees in St James's Park. Spring's on the way already here. There's still five feet of snow on the ground in Chicago.'

'Still dashed cold, though,' Perry complained.

'Cold! This is nothing. This is warm. You should feel the wind when it comes down off Lake Michigan. It shrivels the skin off your face.'

'You know, old thing, if you keep on with all these traveller's tales, you're going to become the most dreadful bore,' her brother told her.

'You're the bore if you can't be interested in anything other than yourself,' Amelie retorted.

They bickered amicably the length of St James's and Bond Street, but when they reached Oxford Street Amelie was distracted. Amongst all the array of shops from small specialist establishments to big stores, there was just one that she wanted to see.

'There it is!'

'Just where you left it,' said Perry.

Amelie ignored him. For there it indeed was – Packards, Suppliers to the Nation. A solid edifice of Portland stone with eighteen display windows, five entrances, four selling floors and ninety-eight departments. A glow of possessive pride started within her and spread over her whole body. Nothing in London, from the Crown Jewels to the Zoological Gardens could compare to the splendour of Packards.

'The greatest store in the whole world!' Amelie declared.

'What, better than the ones in Chicago?' Perry teased.

'Infinitely,' Amelie maintained.

The stores on State Street might be building up to eleven

storeys and have air conditioning and escalators, but Packards had something that they did not. Her family name. Or rather, her grandfather's family name. There were times when she almost forgot she was an Amberley. She had always been far more of a Packard.

The chauffeur took the motor car right round the island site, giving Amelie time to peer at the windows and assess the flow of customers into the store. She gazed enviously at the people going through the doors.

'Oh I wish I could just have a little look round,' she said.

'Best not, old girl. Mama will be waiting for us, you know.'

'I know, but – oh, look at those hats!' Amelie grabbed the speaking tube and told the chauffeur to stop. Ignoring Perry's protests yet again, she scrambled out to look more closely at the display of hats mounted on narrow columns of varying heights. The window was a feast for the eyes, a winter garden of velvet and silk creations adorned with feathers or bows or rosettes or artificial flowers with the occasional practical tweed cap for contrast. But looking at the window was not enough. Amelie yearned to go inside.

Unable to leave his sister unescorted in a public street, Perry joined her on the pavement.

'Come on, old thing.'

'Don't you think I should just call on Grandfather and let him know I'm back? Especially as he sent the motor for me.'

'Mama's expecting us. We're already late, and you know what she's like about punctuality.'

The euphoria of homecoming deflated just a little. Amelie knew all too well what her mother was like about punctuality.

'Yes, yes,' she agreed, reluctantly turning away.

'Anyway, it's only the store. It will still be here tomorrow,' Perry pointed out.

'*Only* the store – !' Amelie began. But she did not bother to finish. Perry did not understand. Neither would he understand her ambitions. They would have to wait until she managed to see her grandfather.

They both stepped back into the motor and the chauffeur headed south into Mayfair. Dusk was falling and lights were coming on in a few of the white stuccoed houses in the elegant

4

eighteenth-century terraces and squares. Many of them were unoccupied at present, as their aristocratic owners were away on their country estates. Mayfair would not come properly alive until the Season got under way in late spring. Amelie tried not to think of the Season.

The motor pulled up in front of the Amberley's house in Bruton Street. It was a four-storey building in a terrace of identical houses, each with a semi-basement, a pillared porch, and three pairs of well-proportioned windows decreasing in height with each floor. Home. The home that her grandfather paid for and her mother considered not large enough.

Amelie jumped out of the car and ran up the steps, her hand out to grasp the knocker, but before she could reach it the door opened to reveal the butler.

'Welcome home, Miss Amelie. I trust you had an enjoyable trip?'

She greeted him with real pleasure. 'Very enjoyable, thank you, Nichols. You're well, I hope?'

'In excellent health, I thank you, Miss Amelie.'

The footman took her travel coat and hat, and Nichols opened the door into the drawing room.

'Miss Amelie, madam.'

Warmth enveloped her. As always, the room was unusually well heated for a London house. Across a blue and fawn room set with elegant walnut furniture, Winifred Amberley sat on a chintz-covered sofa. She did not smile to see her only daughter.

'So here you are at last. You're late. I was expecting you half an hour ago.'

Amelie felt a spurt of irritation. How typical. She had been away for three months, then travelled from Chicago by train, steamer and train again, and the first thing her mother did was to accuse her of being half an hour late.

'Yes, here I am, Mama, turned up again like the bad penny,' she said.

Winifred was dressed in an oyster-coloured silk tea gown trimmed with layers of ruffles and lace, which went some way to disguising the fact that now she was over forty she was putting on a considerable amount of weight. Her once pretty face had a decided double chin and her fair hair was fading to grey, but her eyes were still as blue as Amelie's.

'Well, come here, child.'

She extended a chubby hand and offered her cheek to be kissed. Amelie walked over and bent to give her a light peck. Her mother's skin felt soft and downy, like an overripe peach.

'Hello, Mama. How are you? You're looking well.'

'Tolerably well, thank you.'

Winifred's eyes raked over her daughter. Despite the fact that she was now eighteen, had left school and been all the way to the United States and back, Amelie found herself holding her breath as she used to as a child when Nanny brought the three of them – herself, Perry and their older brother Edward – down at six o'clock each evening to meet their parents. Her father, if he was there, was always delighted to see them, asking after what they had been doing and ready to initiate guessing games or hide and seek. But their mother was quite different. First would come the inspection, when both the children and Nanny would tremble least a ribbon should be unevenly tied or a sock not quite pulled up. Then there would be the inquisition. Had they been for their walk? Eaten up all their meals? Learnt their lessons? Finally some sort of performance was expected, the repeating of a list of facts or a times table, or the recitation of a poem, or the playing of a piano piece. Amelie and Edward competed to shine at these tests. Both had quick brains and the will to apply them. They achieved faultless feats of memory and precision. But somehow, it was never quite good enough. Their father would clap and cry 'Bravo!' but their mother would merely nod. Perversely, it was Perry who gained her smiles. Perry found learning a trial, so did not bother himself too much with it. He muddled his way through and fell back on charm, and to Edward and Amelie's disgust, it usually worked. With a laugh and a joke and a self-deprecatory smile, Perry could win through to the well-hidden softer side of Winifred's nature.

Now, Amelie waited for her mother's comment. She hoped allowances would be made for the fact that she had not been able to change since leaving the liner at midday.

Winifred gave a nod. There was grudging approval in her face. Amelie let out her breath. Evidently her fawn and brown travelling outfit with its military-style frogging and braid had passed muster.

'I had hoped you might have gained a little more distinction to your figure while you were away, but even so, you do seem to look rather less gawky than you did. Yes, a definite improvement. Come and sit down. I think there might be time for some tea before the dressing bell.'

Winifred's days were divided not by meals, but by the need to wear the correct clothing at any given time. She could change anything up to five times between getting up and going to bed, and would no more think of wearing a morning gown after twelve noon than she would consider carrying a parcel or preparing a meal. Her personal maid was kept fully employed seven days a week making sure she always presented an immaculate appearance to the world. So naturally the rigours of dressing for dinner must take precedence over greeting a daughter who had been away for three months.

'And what manner of establishment do the Schneiders keep?' she enquired. 'I failed to form more than a very vague impression from the brief letters you sent me.'

'I wrote every week, Mama,' Amelie protested. 'And I thought I told you a great deal about them. They are very kind and generous people.'

She launched into a long description of the people she had been staying with, the family of one of her schoolfriends, meat packers of a wealth and influence that her mother would have envied, if only it had come from a respectable source. But though Winifred was mildly impressed by the tales of dazzling social events given by the Schneiders and actually surprised to find that they funded a host of cultural activities in Chicago, nothing could shift the faintly patronising expression in her face and voice. Amelie knew exactly why. In her mother's eyes, the Schneiders were really nothing more than glorified butchers. It gave her a very satisfying feeling of superiority. Winifred lived with the mortifying knowledge that polite society, the only people who mattered, would always look on her as the daughter of a shopkeeper. A very successful shopkeeper, but none the less, tainted by the smell of Trade. Winifred had managed to marry into Society by capturing Bertie Amberley, youngest son of an impoverished baron. The two of them and their three children had lived on Packards' money ever since. But Winifred despised Packards and all it stood for. She wanted only to be accepted into her husband's world.

'I'm sure it's been a very pleasant holiday for you,' she said at last, breaking into Amelie's account of the ball the Schneiders had held the week before she left. 'But after all, they are not really the sort of people one wants to cultivate. Tomorrow you shall come with me when I am paying calls, and start leaving your card. To be sure, society is very thin at the moment, but there are a few families in Town for one reason or another.'

Amelie knew better than to disagree outright at this early stage, but she knew just what she was going to do tomorrow. She was going to visit her grandfather at the store.

2

At half-past ten the next morning, Amelie won the first round in what she knew was going to be a battle royal with her mother. Fortunately, she had courtesy and family ties on her side.

'Grandfather would be so disappointed if I didn't call on him today,' she said. 'And I could go this morning. You won't be visiting your friends till this afternoon, will you?'

This was all patently true, so even though Winifred did not want her daughter to be running off to the store practically the first moment she was home, she could not refuse.

'Perhaps I shall accompany you,' she said.

Amelie tried not to let the dismay show on her face. That was the very last thing she wanted. It was essential that she spoke to her grandfather alone.

'That would be lovely,' she lied.

'Well – maybe another day. We shall all be meeting at the family dinner, after all,' Winifred said.

Amelie carefully let out a sigh of relief, and offered to make any purchases her mother might need.

Ten minutes later, she set off, escorted only by the footman walking a discreet half-step behind her. She marched at a brisk pace along the streets, her steps matching the determination in her heart. She had to get her grandfather on her side, or she was lost. She knew that what she wanted to do was unconventional, and that her mother would be utterly opposed to it, but then again she was her grandfather's favourite, which must count for quite a lot. Added to that was the practical point that she really did have something to offer the store. Three months in Chicago had shown her that London stores, even her own wonderful Packards, were very out of date. She had lots of ideas that would put them well ahead of all their rivals.

By the time she got to Oxford Street, her cheeks were glowing from her fast walk. She slowed down then, looking critically at the display windows as she passed, until she came to a halt outside Packards. The windows were the first thing on her list of innovations. Three months ago, Amelie would have thought that they looked perfect, but after viewing the ones on State Street, she knew better. Like every other London department store, Packards crowded each window with as many goods as possible, each clearly labelled with a neat price ticket. Amelie gazed critically at an array of silver-mounted glassware. There was a dazzling selection. Row upon row of preserve jars, celery glasses, ice pails, decanters, jugs, vases, flower bowls, salt cellars, butter dishes, pickle bottles, sugar basins . . . all of the most beautiful cut or engraved glass, of every imaginable pattern from the ornate to the restrained, all sparkling and gleaming. Whatever your taste, there was something there to appeal, if you could see it. That was the problem. There was just too much. In America, they had very different ways of setting out the goods.

For the umpteenth time, Amelie wondered how her grandfather would take to the idea. In the past, he had always been ready to try something new. That was one of the reasons he had managed to build a huge store from one tiny shop in fewer than thirty years, why he had gone on expanding and competing successfully with the other great names in London shopping. But Thomas Packard was seventy-four now, and even he was becoming a little set in his ways. What she needed, Amelie knew, was something that would catch his imagination. Nothing as sweeping as changing the whole way they displayed their goods. That would come later. First, she had to present something small-scale but clever. The trouble was, she was not entirely clear as to what it should be.

She turned from the glassware and walked to the main entrance and in through the tall revolving doors to stop in the spacious red marble vestibule. The deep familiar thrill of it coursed through her. The most exciting place in the world. Packards.

The store had been built in the 1870s, before the days of electric lighting, so its main feature was a huge central dome of glass that let light into the middle of the building. Under this dome, a magnificent marble staircase curved upwards from floor to floor, leading the shopper ever onwards to more and more departments. The whole place had an air of inviting opulence. 'Come in,' the shop seemed to say. 'Look about you, feast your eyes, enjoy . . . and perhaps you might care to buy something?'

Amelie surrendered willingly. She made her way through Fancy Stationery to Grocery to Ladies' Gloves and Umbrellas, unable to resist a pretty notebook with a marbled paper cover and a pair of crocheted lace gloves. Her quick eyes noted that no customer was kept waiting, that floorwalkers discreetly directed proceedings, that shopmen and girls were polite and efficient. On up the stairs, through Jewellery and Drapery and Infants' Cots, through China and Glass and Ladies' Underwear. Everything you might need in life, from a pound of cheese to a Persian carpet, from a baby's layette to a mourning ring, could be got at Packards. The profusion and variety was infinite.

Floorwalkers, men who had known her from infancy, treated her like visiting royalty. Amelie knew most of them by name.

'Good morning, Mr Ames. Business looks very brisk in here. How are the new patent bootstretchers selling?'

'Mr Patterson – how is your back? It seems rather quiet in Books this morning.'

All of them addressed her as Miss Packard. The fact that her mother had married an Amberley carried no weight here. At the store, all Thomas Packard's descendants were Packards.

Up again and into Toys. Her department, as she liked to think of it, for she had suggested it to her grandfather. One day, when about six years old, she had been processing through the store with her hand in his, looking at the marvels it held and listening to him talking to the staff and pointing things out to her. They had stopped for rather a long time in the linen section of Drapery and she had begun to get bored. Sheets and tablecloths and bolts of plain white fabric were not very exciting for a small child. She knew better than to try to distract her grandfather when he was speaking to a buyer, so she stood fidgeting from foot to foot and wishing for something to play with. Then it had come to her, the realisation that her darling grandpa's wonderful store was actually lacking in something. The moment he had finished, she tugged urgently at his hand.

'Grandpa – why haven't you any toys? All the things here are for grown-ups, except for the cots and prams.'

The grandfather had stared at her for a moment, frowning. She had been afraid, thinking she had said something to offend him. But then he had burst out laughing and picked her up in his strong arms.

'By George, the child's a genius! Browning –' he called to the man he had just been speaking to, who came hurrying anxiously over. 'Browning, do you know what this little girl of mine has just done? She's invented a whole new department. Toys! Why didn't I think of it? We'll have it open in time for Christmas.'

True to his word, he had put the new project in hand, and she had been the one to open the toy department, cutting the pink ribbon with a pair of silver scissors and making the first purchase, a beautiful Noah's Ark. Her brother Edward had been beside himself with jealousy, she remembered, and had given her a Chinese burn that had hurt for days afterwards.

Now, she wandered happily round. A couple, grandparents at a guess, were choosing a box of wooden bricks. A boy of about ten and his uncle were debating the relative merits of box and lozenge-shaped kites. A small girl with her mother was looking with round-eyed longing at a wheeled horse and brightly painted dairy cart complete with churn, can and filler.

'Don't you want to come and look at the dolls?' the mother asked.

But the child stayed stubbornly gazing at the sturdy little horse with its flowing mane and tail and real leather harness.

'No.'

She put out a finger and stroked the creature's curved neck. Amelie recognised the depth of the child's desire. She wanted in just the same way. The difference was that she wanted the whole store.

She watched as an elderly shopman asked if he might be of assistance. The mother gave the little girl's arm a sharp tug.

'No thank you. We're just looking.'

She dragged the reluctant child away, but the girl still looked back, fixing the toy with a fierce stare, as if willing it not to be sold to anyone else. Amelie silently wished her luck. Maybe she had a fond grandfather whom she could appeal to, one who would buy it for her birthday.

On the fourth floor the bulky goods that people did not buy very often were situated. Amelie wandered through Carpets and admired the new selection of Turkish kelims in the company of the buyer. Basking pleasantly by now in the feeling of belonging, she could believe that her ambition was easily within reach. After all, what could be more natural than that she should take her place in the management of the store?

In Furniture, she came upon a very good reason why not. Her brother Edward. He was a commanding figure, six feet tall and very dark, his impeccably tailored jacket covering the muscled shoulders of a fearless rugger player. Many of Amelie's friends had declared him to be deliciously handsome. To Amelie he was simply her deadly childhood rival, the big brother who would go to any lengths to prove himself the best. He was not going to like the idea of her taking any of the power that he stood to inherit at Packards.

Edward did not notice her standing by the walnut bedroom suites, for he was taking the floorwalker to task. Sales were down and the floorwalker was to blame. The unfortunate man was red in the face with humiliation, for the whole department could hear what was being said, from the senior salesman to the brown-aproned delivery men. Amelie could see two youthful shopmen drinking in the whole scene, their expressions a mixture of horror and delight that would have been comical had the situation not been so painful. Indignation boiled inside her. Edward had no right to give the man a public dressing-down like this. He should have called him into his office, not exposed him to the sniggers of his underlings.

Without stopping to think, she snapped into action. Walking forward with a big delighted smile on her face, she interrupted Edward's flow.

'Edward! How delightful to see you again. I was just coming to visit you in your office, and here you are.'

'Melly – what a surprise.'

Edward switched from dissatisfied boss to affable brother with admirable ease. He kissed Amelie on the cheek. 'I hadn't expected to see you here so soon.'

'Just try to keep me away!' Amelie returned the kiss, then smiled at the floorwalker. 'And good morning to you, Mr Green. Forgive me for interrupting. It's very naughty of me, I know, but I haven't seen my brother for three months.'

Mr Green could only make an assenting noise in his throat. He was looking at her as if she were an angel come down from heaven to save him.

Amelie smiled beguilingly up at Edward. 'Now, it was very bad of you not to come and welcome me home, you know. Perry travelled all the way to Southampton to meet me off the boat.'

'Good for Perry,' Edward said. They both knew that Perry had nothing better to do with his time. 'Now, Mel, I'm delighted to see you, but I am rather busy at the moment. Why don't you trot off and visit Grandfather?'

'But it was Grandfather whom I wanted to talk to you about,' Amelie said, wondering as she did so just what she was going to say when challenged. She made a quick movement with her eyes towards Mr Green and back, trying to indicate that this was a private family concern.

'I'm sure it will wait till later,' Edward said.

'Not really,' Amelie insisted. She put on a tone of great reasonableness. 'But if you wish I shall wait here until you have finished speaking to Mr Green. It will be interesting to learn just what is going on in Furniture.'

She planted herself ready to listen to every word of the exchange. She was fairly sure that Edward would not want her witnessing what he said, and almost definitely sure that he would not want to wrangle further with her in front of company employees. She was right.

'Very well,' he agreed. He looked at the unfortunate floorwalker. 'I shall return to continue our conversation.'

Mr Green swallowed and nodded. Amelie threaded her arm through her brother's, and was immediately aware of his anger beneath the suave front he maintained. Determined not to be cowed having got this far, she smiled at everyone and swept out of the department with him.

They stopped on the landing leading to one of the echoing

service staircases. Edward extricated his arm and turned to face her.

'Well? It had better be really important, Amelie. I do have work to do, you know, and I do not appreciate being dragged away from important matters by some silly whim of yours.'

'It isn't a silly whim. And aren't you the littlest bit pleased to see me?'

Edward's mouth hardened with barely controlled irritation. 'Save the pretty little girl air for Grandfather, it doesn't wash with me. What was it you wanted to say?'

Amelie thought as she went along.

'Well, as I said, it's about Grandfather. You work with him every day, Edward, so you know better than any of us how he is. Do you think it's all getting too much for him? He's not a young man any longer, but he's so stubborn, and I'm sure he wouldn't admit to not being able to cope like he used to.'

It should have worked. She knew that Edward wanted their grandfather to retire. It was his dearest wish, though he had never openly admitted it to anyone.

'So that's it, is it? That's what could not wait until later?' Clearly Edward was not taken in.

'But I had to speak to you before I went to see Grandfather,' Amelie maintained.

'Why? So that you could single-handedly persuade him to retire? I think not. You were just trying to interfere, weren't you? You've not been home twenty-four hours and already you're waltzing in here throwing your weight around.'

Amelie held his eyes, but inside a quake of fear started. Edward's anger was not to be taken lightly. She tried to temporise.

'Oh, come on, Edward, I had to do it. That poor man. You were humiliating him in front of his whole staff.'

'That was none of your business. You know nothing of the circumstances.'

A thousand fights from childhood onwards should have taught her to keep control, but instead Amelie snapped.

'I do know that you shouldn't dress him down like that in public! You were enjoying it, weren't you? You liked seeing him squirm. You're revolting!'

Edward gave her a look of contempt. 'And you are a silly little girl who knows nothing of how business is conducted.'

'I know that it's not right to expose people to ridicule!' Amelie shouted.

Edward shook his head, an unpleasant smile on his handsome face. 'Neither is it wise to butt in where it is not your place to do so. You realise, I hope, that had you been sensible enough to wait until I had finished, Green would only have suffered a dressing-down, which would have had the desired effect of making him pull his socks up. As it is, I may find that I have to dismiss him.'

Amelie was horrified. 'Edward, you can't! You don't mean it.'

'Oh but I do mean it. Now that you have undermined my authority, it may be my only possible course of action.'

Appalled, Amelie stared at him. She knew her brother was quite capable of carrying out the threat. Mr Green would be thrown out, and it would be all her fault.

'But that's a terrible thing to do. He might not get another position. He'll starve, and all his family with him.'

'Sentiment, my dear sister. The man's private life is of no concern to me. All that matters is that he is a good servant of Packards. If he is not, then he has to go.'

'I don't think Grandfather would approve if I told him,' Amelie warned.

Was she imagining things, or did a flicker of wariness cross Edward's face? If it did, then it was soon gone.

'Sentiment again, Mel. You might think of Grandfather as the kind old man who doted on you when you were a golden-haired little girl, but the reality of it is that he's as tough as old boots. He would never have built the business up in the first place if he were not. I shouldn't go bothering him with the woes of the staff if I were you.'

Amelie definitely did not want to start her campaign for a place in the store by involving her grandfather in a squabble with Edward, especially over a member of staff. But still she felt horribly responsible for Mr Green's fate. She was sure he would think that having a strip torn off him in public was nothing to being dismissed.

'And I shouldn't go sacking people out of hand if I were you, you're not in charge yet,' she retorted.

Edward merely gave a smile of quiet confidence. 'No, but I shall be,' he stated.

Before she could stop herself, Amelie said, 'That's what you think, but you're not the only one, you know. There's Perry and me as well.'

Edward laughed. 'Perry's an idiot and you're a female. Now run along, Melly, there's a good girl. Some of us do have work to do.' And he strolled off in the direction of the furniture department.

Amelie was left fuming.

'Stupid, stupid, stupid,' she said out loud, thumping the wall with her fist.

She had lost that round, and what was more she had lost it on behalf of Mr Green. The only way she could think of to save him was to go to her grandfather, but she would have to approach him carefully, far more carefully than the way in which she had tackled Edward. In fact, she had to think and plan everything more slowly if she were to achieve her aims. The last thing she had wanted to do this morning was to have a row with Edward the moment she saw him. She had meant to be very sweet and friendly, and keep on the right side of him for as long as possible. She had certainly not intended to let out the fact that she had her sights set on a place at the store.

She took several deep breaths, and recalled that Edward had not appeared to take her seriously when she had said that she and Perry had equal rights to Packards. So maybe she had not put him on his guard. The churning anger and frustration subsided a little as she began to think clearly again. If she was going to see Grandfather, then she must be amusing and winsome. That was her one big advantage over Edward. He always rubbed the old man up the wrong way, whereas she knew just how to get him round her little finger. There were some advantages to being a girl.

She made her way to the ladies' rest room, checked her appearance, pinned up a few stray hairs, smiled at herself in the glass. Yes, she looked fine. Grandfather would think so, anyway. To calm herself further, she went for a walk round Sports and

Games. A freckle-faced shopman, obviously new to the store since he did not recognise her, asked if he might be of assistance.

'Oh – yes – I'm looking for a mackintosh cape to wear when cycling in wet weather,' she said, knowing full well that she would not find one there.

'I'm sorry, madam. You'll have to go down to Ladies' Outerwear.'

'Really? Well, do you do tennis blouses?'

The youth looked nonplussed. 'Er – no – that would be the ladies' department as well.'

'Outerwear?'

'Well – no – Daywear, I think –'

By this time, the floorwalker had spotted her and come over. He gave the unfortunate youth a withering look.

'Good morning, Miss Packard. I'm afraid Briggs is new to the job. How can I help you?'

'Briggs is doing very well,' Amelie said quickly. One dismissal on her conscience was enough for one morning. 'I was just wondering why clothing for sport was not sold in this department.'

'That's the way it has always been arranged, Miss Packard. We sell the equipment here. The clothing is elsewhere.'

'Yes –' Amelie could feel an idea brewing. 'Thank you. Good day to you. You have been most helpful.'

She walked on, frowning to herself as the idea took shape. What if she wanted to take up, say, golf? She would have to go to Ladies' Tailoring for a tweed skirt and jacket, then to Gloves, and Footwear, and Millinery, and finally here to Sports and Games to buy a set of clubs. And even here there was not such a wide selection for ladies as there was for men. It was the same for other pursuits – archery, for instance, or cycling. For cycling one needed good strong knickers as well as a veiled hat for dry weather and waterproofs for rain. A knot of excitement gathered inside her. This was it, the idea to present to her grandfather. She just knew it was right, and that she could make it work. All she needed to do was to put it to him the right way.

came. A bucket... to shop... made vaults for... at first were not... his three reptile list, asked if he might have it loaded... Halloween. But looking for a reason because so were... that coming... way well for... she had charming... all forth and his... would not had one direct... c... of him... he hub... a... company... c... sale for it left on... company me hay. You'll be it at the... hay... looking...

3

Thomas James Packard sat behind his vast mahogany desk and stared at the drawings on the green papered wall opposite. He knew every detail by heart, but he never tired of looking at them, for they were the floor plans of the store that bore his name, showing the position and size of every department. Mostly they gave him a great sense of satisfaction. Not bad for one man's life's work. Pretty good, in fact, considering that that man had arrived in London at the age of fifteen with just three shillings in his pocket. Three shillings, and the dream of becoming a Somebody. He certainly was a Somebody now. His was a household name. Every day, hundreds of people said, 'We could get it at Packards,' whatever 'it' might be. People arranged to meet at Packards. People gave directions with Packards as a reference point. The store was an essential part of the London scene.

Today, as he looked at the plans, niggling doubts in his mind subsided. His store was more than a match for this man Selfridge. Thomas was certain that Packards was superior to any other London establishment. It was brighter and more attractive than the Army and Navy, catered for a wider range of customers than Harrods, had more departments than Marshall and Snelgrove or Debenham and Freebody. Nothing this American upstart could build could possibly be superior. And besides, whoever heard of anyone building a large store straight off like Selfridge was doing? All the other big names had started the same way as he had, with one small shop. Harrods had been a grocers, John Lewis started with a job lot of silks, Dickens and Jones were linen drapers. Packards had begun as a tiny place selling a bargain line in fire-damaged mourning apparel. It had been a daring investment at the time. He had put all his savings into the enterprise and taken out a loan. But it had paid off. Hard work, an ability to forecast what people wanted and the courage to take risks had turned that one shop into a row of seven in just six years.

Looking back, even the hard times seemed exciting. The years after he moved the store to its present site in Oxford Street were the most knife-edge of all. Several times he had been on the verge of bankruptcy, but always he had succeeded in turning things around, often at the very last minute. It was a good thing he had been able to keep the real state of affairs from his wife. If there was one thing that Margaret liked, it was security. If she had known what risks he was taking, how close they often were to ruin, his home life would not have been worth living.

All the time this was going on, he had been buying the properties adjacent to the store, his mind fixed on acquiring the entire island site. And just when he had signed the deal on the last row of houses, disaster struck. A fire started in the drapery department and gutted the entire shop. Thomas turned to the side wall of the office, where a print from the *Illustrated London News* showed the spectacular blaze. New visitors to his room often asked why he should want to keep a souvenir of such a terrible event.

'To remind me not to get above myself,' he invariably answered.

It was a complete lie. Thomas Packard had always aimed to get above himself, and still did. The truth was that the old, piecemeal store had been very well insured. So well, in fact, that there had been suspicious whispers at the time. Thomas ignored them all. Let lesser folk say what they liked about arson. He had great plans. A new, magnificent, purpose-built store rose phoenix-like from the ashes, and Packards was on the way to spectacular success.

Success still had to be fuelled, though. Thomas took up the copy of the last six months' sales figures, covering the late summer and autumn of 1907 through to the start of 1908. He looked through them again, though he knew the various totals off by heart. Not as good as he expected. Something had to be done. And even though he was not afraid of this Selfridge man setting up just a few blocks down Oxford Street, still he did have to be taken into consideration. By next year, Selfridge's store would be yet another rival for custom.

Thomas's eyes focused on the hands that held the papers, hands that were swelling with the onset of arthritis. That was another thing. He was not getting any younger. He had tried to ignore this fact, but increasingly it was brought home to him that his body was not as reliable as it used to be. His brain was still as sharp as ever, thank God, but he ached and creaked and got tired so quickly. No longer could he work a sixteen-hour day and keep a wife and a succession of mistresses happy. Just six hours at the store now and he was near to his limit. And what was more, young Edward knew this.

There was a knock at the door, and his secretary put his head round the door.

'Mr Edward to see you, sir.'

'Thank you, Archer. Show him in.'

Thomas was immediately every inch the captain of his ship. He waved his grandson to a seat across the desk from him.

'Ah – Edward – you're good and prompt. Sit down.'

Edward folded his powerful frame onto the upright chair. He opened his mouth to speak, but Thomas got in first, keeping control of the interview.

'I've been reading these figures. I'm not very happy.'

The inference was: *I'm not very happy with your performance.* Edward did not rise to it.

'I agree with you, sir. Christmas was reasonable and the Sales showed a fairly healthy return, but the percentage increase month by month over last year is very low. Very low indeed, in some cases. In fact, in the furniture department –'

'Thank you. I can see that for myself. The question is, what are we going to do about it? I take it you have some views?'

'I do, sir. I think we need to take some action.'

Thomas sat back and laced his fingers over his stomach. 'And what action would you propose, then?' he asked, carefully bland.

'I think it is time to review just how we use our space. We're all going to have our ideas shaken up when Selfridge opens with his American ways of doing things. Why not be prepared here at Packards, be one jump ahead of him?'

It was resonable enough, but Thomas merely nodded.

'So?'

'So I've been comparing the sales figures not only with this time last year but with the previous five years. And one department stands out as consistently under-performing. Furniture.'

Edward paused for a reaction. Thomas gave none.

Edward continued, 'When you consider the amount of square yardage taken by Furniture, that space could be far more profitably used for departments that show a higher turnover.'

'So your solution is to scrap Furniture altogether?'

'At its most extreme, yes. At the very least, we should go through the figures in detail and see whether a contracted department might work.'

'Either we have a furniture department, or we don't. Packards always stock the best selection of everything. A small department would not be able to do that.'

'In that case I think we should do away with it. That way we would have almost three-quarters of a floor to devote to other goods.'

'And what about our claim to provide everything the British family needs?'

Edward gave a slight shrug, brushing aside the reputation that Thomas had spent so many years building. *Whatever it is – you'll find it at Packards.* That had been the store's claim since the new building opened, and he had always made sure that it was true. Nobody went away from Packards unsatisfied.

'I hardly think that's important.'

'You don't?'

A slight flush crept up Edward's neck. When he spoke, it was with only partly disguised patience.

'No, sir, I don't. What matters is that the store should show a growing level of profit from year to year. Anything –'

It had gone quite far enough. Thomas slammed his fist down on the desktop, making the gold pens quiver.

'What matters is service! First, last and foremost. Service to our customers. That is what a department store is about, providing what our customers need, and one of the things they need is furniture for their homes. Packards is not merely a machine to make money.'

Edward's voice rose as well, and took on an edge of

contempt. 'If it ceases to make money, then it ceases to exist. We are not running a charity.'

'*We* are not running anything. I am,' Thomas shouted. He watched the frustration show in his grandson's eyes. He might be getting old, but he was not done yet, and the boy had better realise it. He brought his anger under control.

'If the furniture department is not performing well enough, then it must be improved. Is the stock the type and design that people want? Are the prices competitive? Is the advertising effective?' He looked at Edward from under his bushy eyebrows. 'That can be your special responsibility. Look into it and report back to me this time next week. I shall want a full plan of action, ready to be implemented immediately.'

Edward stood up. He planted his knuckles on the desktop and leant forward. To anyone but Thomas the effect would have been intimidating.

'I think you're making an expensive mistake,' he stated.

Thomas continued to look steadily back at him. 'No, it is you who is making the mistake. I suggest you go and set about your new task. Now.'

With extreme reluctance, Edward straightened up. He turned and marched out of the office without a further word, leaving the door swinging open behind him. Thomas was left savouring a painful victory.

A bald head appeared round the door, attached to a birdlike man of indeterminate age.

'Cup of tea, sir? Or can I pour you a whisky?'

For a moment, Thomas hesitated. He would really have liked a whisky, but to have one would be to admit that his grandson had upset him.

'Tea, please, Archer.'

'Coming right up.'

Thomas still employed a male secretary. Not that he was prejudiced against women in offices. Far from it. The typists employed by Packards were all female. He would dearly have liked to have an attractive young woman to stand guard over his outer office and be his personal assistant. But Archer had been with him for twenty-four years now and was loyal right to his back teeth. With Thomas, loyalty counted for a lot. He would not get rid of Archer even for the pleasure of having a pretty girl bringing him his tea.

Tea arrived, best Assam as available from Grocery, served in porcelain as sold in Glass and China.

'You know, Archer, young Mr Edward Packard grows more like my late father every day.'

'Is that so, sir?'

It was, and Thomas did not like it. His father had been a tyrant. When Thomas left home, he had felt as if he were escaping from slavery. He had returned but once, to his mother's funeral. He did not want to leave Packards to a man like that.

And yet – what was the alternative? The one thing he had failed to do in all these years of empire-building was to procreate a dynasty from which to select a successor. His marriage to Margaret had produced just one child, Winifred. Winifred had done her duty and brought forth two boys and a girl, but nobody in their right mind would leave anything but a sleeping interest in the store to Perry. If he were to keep Packards under family control Thomas's successor had to be Edward. He sighed, reviewing the other possibilities that had occurred to him over the years. There was plenty of talent within the management. A team of the brightest and best could be appointed to run the store. But family was family, and Packards without a Packard at the helm did not seem right. He would have to concentrate on taming Edward before he relinqushed control to him.

For a while Thomas became immersed in administration, dictating some letters and speaking to the head of staffing. That done, he allowed himself to rest his thoughts on his third grandchild: Amelie, his favourite. The dear girl had come home at last. This afternoon he would indulge himself and leave work early to pay a call at Winifred's house. He could not wait any longer before seeing his Amelie again. It seemed like an age since he had last basked in her sparkling smile or heard her cheerful voice. The world was a dull place without her.

As if summoned by thought, her laughter came to him from the outer office. At first he fancied he had imagined it, but then he clearly caught her words as she spoke to his secretary.

'Oh come along, Archer, don't be so stuffy. You know Mr Packard will always see me.'

And then the door burst open and there she was, dressed in an outfit of yellow trimmed with pale green and looking like a breath of spring.

'Grandpa!'

She ran across the room, flung her arms round him and planted a smacking kiss on his cheek.

'How are you, you old darling? I've come to thank you for sending the motor for me yesterday. It was absolutely sweet of you.'

Thomas kissed her back, then stood to hold her at arm's length and look at her.

'You look prettier than ever. How are you, my dear?'

'I couldn't be better. Oh, Grandpa, I've had such a marvellous time. America is an amazing place. It's just bursting with new ideas. You would love it, I'm sure. But it's lovely to be home again, too.'

'And it's good to see you,' Thomas said, with wild understatement. 'I didn't expect you'd be here today.'

'Just try to keep me away! Mama wants me to go visiting her boring friends with her later on, but I persuaded her that I should come here this morning.'

'Quite right, too,' Thomas agreed.

Archer brought more tea, and set chairs in front of the fireplace. Amelie sat on the edge of hers, telling her grandfather all about her trip. He listened avidly, interested in everything she said, just because she was saying it. But when she started talking about shops he took a professional interest as well.

'You should see the stores on State Street, Grandpa! Some of them are eleven storeys high, and so beautiful, they're like palaces. People go and spend the day at Marshall Field's, there's so much to see. And the windows – you should see the windows, Grandpa. They are like works of art. Instead of crowding everything in like we do, they display only a few items so that they look really inviting. People come just to see the effect.'

'Ah, but do they go into the store once they've looked?' Thomas asked.

'Oh yes. The goods look so beautiful, people just have to go in and see what else is on offer. You should try it, Grandpa, you really should.'

Thomas smiled, unconvinced. 'We'll see. And what did you think of Packards as you walked through? Is the old place still up to scratch after all these wonders you've seen?'

'Of course it is, Grandpa. It's still the best store in the world. Now tell me, how is everything? How did the Sales go this year? Is the new tea room a success?'

Thomas gave her a résumé of everything that had been going on while she had been away. Amelie fixed her bright eyes on his face and drank in all he said, nodding and adding a comment or question from time to time. Thomas had not had such a receptive audience since she went away. He found himself telling her all about the disappointing sales figures and his set-to with Edward.

'Oh dear.' Amelie looked anxious. 'That was something I wanted to speak to you about, Grandpa. Now you know I don't like to interfere, but I was just walking through the furniture department on my way to see you, and I ran into Edward . . .' She told the tale, ending up with, 'So you see I just have to ask you to stop him from dismissing poor Mr Green. He's been with us for years, and I'm sure it's not all his fault that the sales are down in Furniture.'

Thomas gave her a serious look. 'You think I should countermand Edward, do you?'

Amelie got up and sat on the arm of his chair, stroking the top of his head.

'I know it's a lot to ask, Gramps darling, but Edward was being so beastly, I just had to stick up for poor Mr Green. You will say you'll let him stay, won't you?'

'I'll think about it,' Thomas promised, deciding then and there to take steps without delay.

'Darling Gramps! And now let me tell you about the wonderful idea I've just had. This will improve your sales figures, I'm sure. I've invented a whole new department, and I'm sure it could be a very successful one.'

She outlined her plan for Ladies' Sportswear. As she spoke, Thomas realised that she could have hit on a good original idea. He started to question her about what stock might be carried, how big she envisaged the department, where she thought would be the best place to advertise.

'I haven't really thought about the details yet. It only popped into my head this morning as I was walking round the store,' Amelie admitted. 'But we could start with a corner of Ladies' Outerwear and maybe two or three shopgirls, and we'd stock clothing for every sort of sport that women do these days. You'd be amazed how many there are, Grandpa! Tennis, croquet, bathing, horseriding, golf, archery, hockey, cycling, skating – and motoring, though I don't really count that as a sport. We'd have all the things a woman might need for any sport from underwear to gloves, all in one department. That way they'd be sure to buy the whole outfit from Packards, and it would be so convenient that any woman wanting anything to do with sports would automatically come to us rather than go from department to department in one of the other stores. And just think what an up-to-date thing it would be, Grandpa. Packards would be catering for the modern woman. We don't want the store to be all stuffy and old-fashioned, do we?'

'We certainly do not,' Thomas agreed.

She gave his shoulders a little squeeze.

'And of course you'll let me run it, won't you?'

'*What?*'

This really was a shock. Thomas looked at her closely, trying to work out whether she was joking. Amelie's face was deadly serious.

'You'll let me run it,' she repeated. 'I'd be very good at it, Grandpa, I'm certain of it. After all, you've always said that I'm a chip off the old block. Shopkeeping runs in my blood, whatever Mama might say.'

'Crafty little minx,' Thomas said.

He could see through what she was trying to do. She was using Winifred's snobbish attitude to the source of the family money as a way to get round him. The idea did have a certain appeal. He mulled over the consequences. If he gave Amelie the authority to start up and run her new department, Winifred would indeed be highly incensed, which would be amusing, if nothing else. Over the years he had paid out thousands of pounds supporting her and her ne'er-do-well husband, because

27

he could not bear to see his daughter and her children living in less than the manner to which they wanted to be accustomed. It had rankled that Winifred did her best to forget just where that money came from.

More important than that, it would bring young Edward up short. He would no longer be able to assume that he was the sole heir to the Packards empire. Some healthy competition would make him toe the line.

Most important of all, it would be giving Amelie something she wanted, and that was always a great source of pleasure to him. But it would not do. Reluctantly, he patted her hand.

'Now I know you could make a splendid job of it, my dear, but you won't have the time, will you? You're to come out this Season. You'll be spending all your days visiting and going to parties.'

It hurt to see the disappointment in her face.

'Grandpa! You know I don't want to be a beastly debutante. It's all Mother's stupid idea. You don't want me married off to some lordling with not a sensible idea in his head, now do you?'

'Of course not, darling. But you do have to get married, and your mother knows the best way to go about it. Running a department certainly isn't going to put you in the way of suitable young men.'

'But you can't give my department to somebody else! It would be too unfair after I thought it up. Please – darling Gramps – to please me?'

Thomas just could not resist. He compromised.

'You can set it up. Get it going before the Season starts, and then you can leave it in the hands of the head of Ladies' Outerwear and come in whenever you can to keep an eye on it. How does that sound?'

'We-ell – it's better than nothing, I suppose. Thank you, Gramps.'

Thomas frowned at her in mock severity. 'This isn't a game, mind. I shall expect your department to make a profit. If it doesn't, then that's an end to it.'

Amelie's voice lost its girlish tone and took on a new edge. 'Don't you worry, Grandpa. It will make a profit all right. I shall see to that.'

4

So many people, and all so happy, so confident. Isobel Norton found herself shrinking from them. They had such loud voices, such a lordly way of carrying themselves. The men were glossy and well-tailored, the women corseted and elaborately coiffured and dressed in layers of silk, fur and finest wool. None of them with anything more pressing on their minds than which pair of gloves to buy and what to wear that evening.

After only a week in London, Isobel found it hard to believe that she had once been as pampered and carefree as they. Just four months ago she had been Mama and Papa's darling daughter, enjoying the round of teas and dinners and card parties and small private dances, idly visiting the shops, just like these people all around her now, in search of a pretty length of ribbon or a spray of silk flowers. Now her feet throbbed, her whole body ached with weariness, a tearing anxiety pulled at her heart. Now she had only enough money to pay for her room till the end of the week. Now she was going to the shops not to buy, but to seek employment. The trouble was, she had been totally unsuccessful so far. Nobody wanted a young woman with no previous experience and no character references and who, what was more, had obviously not done a serious day's work in her life.

Isobel stopped and gazed at the nearest shop window. An array of blouses crowded the space, displayed on wire frames, blouses of silk or muslin or nun's veiling, all elaborately trimmed with tucks and frills and lace, all neatly ticketed with a price. How her dearest mama would have enjoyed such a wonderful selection.

'One can never have enough pretty blouses,' she used to say, when selecting yet another. 'Such a useful addition to the wardrobe. So very feminine.'

Blinking back tears, Isobel looked to find the name of the

shop. Packards. Dearest Mama had always been enthusiastic about Packards.

'Such a genteel establishment, and such a profusion of departments. When we go to London, my dear, we shall treat ourselves to a trip to Packards.'

But the long-promised expedition had never come to be. Dearest Mama lay in the churchyard next to Papa, and Isobel was in London all alone, cold, frightened and nearly destitute. She moved on till she came to the main entrance, and once again hesitated, trying to steel herself to face another possible rejection. The warmth and light of the store beckoned. Isobel swallowed and squared her shoulders. She still looked perfectly respectable. She could enter without danger of being escorted out by a floorwalker. She went inside.

She knew what to do by now. No wandering about pretending she was just another customer, because the longer she did that, the more her courage oozed away. She found the lifts. If Packards was like the other stores she had been to, then she probably needed the very top floor. Her good intentions were undermined by the lift attendant mentioning the restaurant and the tea room. She was desperate for a cup of tea. But she knew just how little money she had in her purse. It was essential that she thought three times about every penny. No, no tea. But when the ladies' rest room was called out, she succumbed to temptation. The one thing she wanted most, even more than a cup of tea, was simply to sit down. She stepped out at the third floor.

Packards' ladies' rest room was a haven of warmth and comfort. There were soft carpets, pink-shaded lamps, a tasteful arrangement of flowers. Rows of dressing tables and looking-glasses were built along two of the pink-papered walls and upholstered benches on the others. Isobel sank on to one of these with a sigh of relief. She had to get her strength back, she told herself in justification, or she would not be able to face the interview, always supposing she got as far as an interview. She closed her eyes, trying not to think of anything, trying to cut out the last dreadful week, trying even harder not to remember the terrifying events that had led to her running away, but as always when she relaxed for a moment, the images came flooding back. The policeman announcing Papa's death, his partner telling them of the pile of debts, Mama's last illness, the look in her brother-in-law's eyes ... Isobel pulled herself together at this point. She must not think of that or she would be physically sick. With shaking knees, she walked across the room and sat at one of the dressing tables.

A pale-faced girl with dark shadows under her bluebell eyes stared back at her from the looking-glass. She raised weary arms to take off her hat and pin up escaping strands of blonde hair. That was where her new poverty was already showing itself. Her clothes were good. The black costume with its braid trim had been newly made for her during the week following her father's death. But managing long hair and styling it into fashionable piles of smooth curls without any help was well-nigh impossible. Isobel had opted for neatness and simplicity. At least it was clean. She had had to pay extra for warm water and shiver for hours in her unheated hotel room waiting for it to dry, but it had been worth it to see it glossy again, free of London dirt.

Around her, women chatted to friends about what they had bought, where they should go next, what they should provide for the next supper party. Not for the first time, Isobel considered going back to Tillchester, the pleasant cathedral city that had been her home all her life. But to go back would mean admitting to what had driven her away, and she could never, ever tell anyone about that. So there was only one thing to do. She stood up and made her way to the top floor to ask if there were any vacancies.

Carpets and inviting displays gave way to lino and plain cream walls. A clerk of indeterminate age and colourless face sat behind a desk at the staffing office. He addressed her as 'Madam'. Slight surprise registered when he heard what Isobel had come for. His pale eyes flicked over her, not quite tying up her appearance and accent with her request.

'You're applying for a job behind the counter?'

Isobel swallowed. 'Yes.'

His entire attitude changed. She was an inferior, and one who needed something from him. He pushed a form towards her.

'Fill this in, give it back to me, then take a seat in the waiting room through there. You're in luck, miss. They're interviewing today.'

At dear Papa's office, men like him had treated her with the utmost respect, as mere clerks should do when the senior partner's daughter dropped by. Now this one was addressing her with barely disguised insolence. Isobel bit her lip. She must not mind it. At least she had got over the first hurdle. She looked around and saw a table at which she could fill in the form.

Name, Date of Birth, Address, Religion. She dipped the pen in the inkwell and filled in her details in an elegant hand, substituting the name 'Brand' for her own. After that, it became more difficult.

Name and address of previous employer. Nature of previous employment. She left both blank. It seemed better than writing 'None'.

Reasons for wishing to obtain employment with Packards. At least she could write something in here. The question was, what exactly should she put? The truth? 'Because I am desperate and nearly destitute and need a position and somewhere to live.' Not really suitable. Isobel frowned over the question, then wrote, 'My late mother always spoke in the highest terms of Packards, so I know it to be an establishment of integrity.'

Will you require living-in accommodation? A firm 'Yes' to this one.

Please attach two character references. Perhaps the most difficult one of all. She blotted the ink and handed the form back to the clerk. He glanced at it with undisguised disdain.

'You don't stand a cat's chance, miss. Character references?'

Isobel experienced a brief burst of anger. It was at the tip of her tongue to tell him to keep his opinions to himself. But she swallowed it down. After all, he could refuse to forward the form to the next person on the grounds that it would be wasting company time. Instead she stammered, 'I – I don't have them about my person just now.'

The clerk shrugged. 'Then you really don't have a cat's chance. I shouldn't bother staying if I was you.'

If only she could just take his advice and go. He was sure to be right. Nobody in their right mind was going to employ her. Her mother would not have considered for one moment taking on even a daily cleaning woman without a character reference. But she had no choice. She had to try.

'J-Just pass on that form to whom it concerns, if you please,' she said, and made her way through the inner door.

The waiting room was full of young men and women, all stiffly seated on wooden chairs placed around the walls. Silence fell the moment Isobel went in, and two dozen pairs of eyes looked at her, weighing up the chances of her getting the job they wanted. Some looked away almost immediately, others stared at her. Isobel felt a flush spread up her neck and into her face. She glanced round the room. There was just one chair unoccupied, between two men. With the greatest reluctance, she sat on it, trying to shrink her body so that no part of it touched one of her neighbours. A low murmur of conversation started up again.

The minutes dragged by. Every so often a worn-looking middle-aged man appeared at the far door and barked a name, and another hopeful applicant went in for an interview. Some came out looking pleased, more were disappointed. Though she knew it was most impolite to eavesdrop, Isobel could not help overhearing some of the talk around her.

'I been with my place in Bristol three years. Done haberdashery, baby linens and stationery.'

'I started on haberdashery and all. They say you got a better chance here if you're a girl. Some places don't hardly take no girls.'

'Look at him over there. One what looks like he's got all the cares of the world on his shoulders. He won't get nothing if he don't liven up a bit. You got to be a bit eager, ain't you?'

'Prob'ly got a wife and seven kids at home all hoping he'll get this job. Mind you, I bet he's a churchgoer. They like churchgoers, this lot. S'pose they think they're more honest.'

Everyone seemed to know what they were doing, except for her. Isobel sat with her back straight and her feet together and her hands clasped in her lap, and prayed.

'Miss Brand!'

For a moment, Isobel didn't realise it was she who was being called. She still was not used to her alias.

'Miss Brand not here?'

'Oh yes – I'm sorry –'

Flustered, Isobel jumped to her feet, dropped her gloves, felt the blood rush to her head as she stooped to pick them up. The man at the door tutted impatiently.

'Come along, come along.'

With a sinking sense of failure, Isobel followed him into his office and sat down on the chair in front of the polished oak desk. A brass nameplate declared the owner of it to be Mr R. Mason, Staff Manager. Neat piles of application forms filled the in- and out-baskets on each side of the desk and, on the blotter in the middle, Isobel recognised her own effort, with its glaring blank spaces. Mr Mason settled wire-rimmed spectacles on his nose and read through the form before sighing and looking across at Isobel.

'No previous experience and no character references?'

'Er – no,' Isobel admitted.

'And why is that?'

'Well – I – I have not needed to take paid employment in the past.'

'So you have not worked at all?'

'I have assisted at charity bazaars.'

'Charity bazaars. I see. I think you would find Packards a rather different kettle of fish.'

The interview was taking an all-too-familiar path. Isobel tried to assure him that she was not afraid of hard work.

'Well yes, but I'm sure I –'

'I see you have put down that you would like to live in?'

'Yes.'

'And you are currently residing at a hotel?'

'Yes.'

'So where is your home address?'

'I –'

She did not want to reveal that. It was essential that she covered her tracks. They were sure to come after her.

'Eastbourne,' she said. She had happy memories of the resort. They had spent a holiday there, her parents and herself, the summer before last.

'Eastbourne,' Mr Mason repeated, scepticism plain in his face.

'So no doubt there are persons in that town to whom you could apply for a reference?'

All hope ran out then. Isobel opened her mouth to answer. She even started to stand up and leave, since there was no point in staying. But at that moment the outer door opened and a young woman came breezing in, dressed in the height of fashion in a cherry-red walking dress and a delightful little hat trimmed with velvet flowers.

The staff manager jumped to his feet.

'Miss Packard –'

'Oh Mr Mason, I'm so sorry I'm late. I had to do beastly afternoon calls. A card here and a card there and fifteen minutes' stupid small talk. You cannot think how tedious. But here I am now, and I shall take over. Thank you so much for all you have done. I really am most grateful.'

The all-powerful staff manager, the man who held Isobel's fate in his hands, was cheerfully dismissed by a girl no older than Isobel herself. She gave a friendly smile and sat down behind the desk.

'Good afternoon.' She adopted a businesslike manner that sat uneasily on her glowing face and frivolous outfit. 'I'm Amelie Amberley Packard, and I'm looking for people to work in my new department, Ladies' Sportswear. Tell me, Miss – er –' she glanced at the form '– Brand, do you by any chance play any sports?'

Isobel blinked at her, not quite believing what she was hearing. One of the Packard family was personally interviewing her, and she was asking about her hobbies. One thing was sure, it was better than being grilled about her lack of references.

'Well – yes, yes I do,' she said. 'I'm very fond of lawn tennis, and croquet.'

Miss Amberley Packard beamed at her. 'How absolutely splendid. Do you know you are the first person I've spoken to who knows the least thing about it. What about golf?'

'I have played clock golf,' Isobel told her.

'Not quite the same thing, but it's a start, and heaps better than anyone else I've interviewed. It's so important you see, that I should have somebody who really knows what she is talking about when she serves the customers. I want to build a reputation for excellent advice as well as first-class merchandise. Now tell me, if I were to come to you and ask to see tennis outfits, how would you advise me?'

Isobel thought. 'Well – I would recommend a dress rather than a skirt and blouse, as a blouse does tend to ride up when one takes a swing at the ball –'

Miss Packard nodded encouragingly.

'– with a hemline on the short side, to allow for easy running around, and not too tight, so that you can reach for the ball and breathe easily.'

'Bravo! You have it exactly.'

For the first time in weeks, Isobel found herself smiling naturally. Hope stirred painfully once more inside her. She very much wanted, not just any position, but one with this vital and friendly girl. On impulse, she decided to forestall the inevitable questions about her past experience.

'I've never worked in a shop before,' she admitted. 'In fact, I've never worked anywhere. My parents both died very recently and I find myself in very reduced circumstances. I'm not really qualified to do anything, but I'm more than willing to learn and I'm quick with figures.'

Miss Packard was instantly sympathetic. 'How dreadful for you. And now you're quite on your own? That explains this then,' she nodded at the form. 'Well, I'm more than happy to offer you a position in my department. The only trouble is, I do have to ask you for a reference. Company policy, you see. Now, surely there is somebody who would vouch for you? Your vicar or minister perhaps?'

Isobel could have wept with frustration. At last, a job was within her reach, a job with a roof over her head and food to eat and money at the end of each week. But what was this nice girl going to say when she explained the next bit?

'There – there is – I mean, the vicar would be very willing, I'm sure – it's just – well – when I came to London, I wanted to make a new start where nobody knows me, so I changed my name.'

Miss Packard nodded. 'Of course, yes, I can see it would be very embarrassing to have all your old friends knowing you were now serving in a department store. But surely you could depend upon your vicar to be discreet about it?'

Isobel almost laughed. The whole of Tillchester could talk about her working in a department store for all she cared. What mattered was that her brother-in-law should never ever find out where she was living.

'I suppose so,' she said.

'Well then, that's easily settled, isn't it? If you could let me have some proof of your real name and address, then I can write for a testimonial and it can all be put away in your file and nobody but you and I will know anything about it.'

Isobel had to take a chance on it. It was that or lose the job, and she couldn't bear that, not after getting so close. She reached into her pocket and took her very last visiting card out of its case. On the back she wrote her vicar's name and address.

'Splendid. I'm sure that together we shall build the most successful department in the store. This is very important to me, you know. We shall only be a small team and we have ourselves to prove, but we shall be successful, shall we not?

'Now, terms and conditions. You will be given bed and board at one of our houses in Trent Street and dinner and tea here at the staff dining room. As you will be employed as a junior sales girl, your wages will be seven shillings and sixpence per week. Hours are from half-past eight till half-past six in the winter and seven in the summer, with a half-day on Saturday, when we close at two. After your first year, you are entitled to five days' holiday a year. You must wear a plain black skirt and white blouse to work in, and I am having a badge designed for the people in my department, with a tennis racquet and "Ladies' Sportswear" on it. Now, is that all clear?'

Her head spinning, Isobel nodded. She would have agreed to almost anything if it meant work and safety.

'Good. Well, I shall have to send for this reference, but I'm sure that will be all right, so I take it you are free to start work on Monday week?'

'Y—Yes.'

'Then you should report to Trent Street on Sunday afternoon. I'll make sure somebody knows you will be coming. Good afternoon, Miss Brand.'

It was over. Miss Packard was standing up and holding out her hand. Isobel stood as well, shook hands, stammered her thanks and tottered out. She stood for fully half a minute in the waiting room without seeing or hearing anything. Then suddenly her legs gave way and she collapsed into the nearest chair. Tears slid down her face.

There was an arm round her shoulders, and a voice somewhere near.

'Never mind, ducks. Plenty of other places, eh?'

Isobel shook her head, tried to speak through the tears.

'I got it. I got a place. Oh it's so wonderful. I can't believe it. Now I shall be safe.'

5

'I still don't see why you got to go and live in,' Daisy's mum complained. 'What's the matter with your own home? Ain't it good enough for you?'

Daisy sighed. They had been through all this a hundred times before.

'It ain't that, Mum. I told you, it's just that it'll be nearer. Just five minutes' walk away from the shop. If I stopped at home, it'd take me ages each day on the bus, and cost me a fortune and all.'

They were sitting in the tiny back room that served as kitchen, scullery, eating and living room of the Phippses' house. It was early Sunday morning, so not everybody was up. Those who had been out drinking last night would probably not make an appearance till gone midday.

'Cost you a fortune living in, more like. You won't have hardly nothing left.'

That was the real core of the matter. Money. Of the twelve members of the Phipps family, only four were working. Daisy's dad had injured his back in a dock accident five years ago. He was still able to do his bit towards creating more little Phippses, but it had finished his chances of permanent employment. The two eldest boys both had jobs, but one was about to get married and take his income to his future mother-in-law's place. All six smaller children were still too young for full-time jobs, though they were expected to earn what they could out of school hours, which left Daisy, who had been slaving all hours at a small draper's in Poplar, and her sister Nell, who worked in a local factory. Naturally, they gave their pay packets to their mother each week, and she doled out their pocket money. But it still did not leave much for Mrs Phipps to feed all those mouths, and now that Daisy was leaving home, there was going to be even less.

'I'll send you a postal order each week,' Daisy promised.

Her mother sniffed. 'I should hope so too, after I worked my fingers to the bone all these years bringing you up.'

'Dot'll be twelve in July. She'll be able to work then,' Daisy pointed out.

'That's as maybe, but what about Billy, and Ivy?' Mrs Phipps demanded.

Daisy tried hard not to feel guilty. It wasn't her fault that the strength in the family seemed to run out about halfway down the line of children. Not that any of the older ones were particularly fine specimens. Like Daisy, they were small and thin with pinched features and a colourless look to them. But at least they were tough and could stand the long hours and hard conditions they had to endure at work. The younger Phippses were poor things by comparison. They suffered from weak chests, or wasted limbs, or worst of all in two cases, were simple in the head. They were sitting at the table now, listening to the conversation with open mouths and vacant eyes. It was a terrible burden for Mrs Phipps to bear.

'At least there'll be more room with me out of the way,' Daisy pointed out. 'Two of the little 'uns can share my bit of the bed with Nell. You won't have to pay Aunty Aggie to have them round at her place.'

'There's that, I suppose,' her mother conceded.

But she was not convinced, and Daisy knew it. What was more, she knew that Nell, inspired by her own break for freedom, was considering leaving home as well. Not for the first time, she wavered. Good daughters stayed at home and helped their mums by bringing in a pay packet and lending a hand with all the many chores. If Daisy did what was expected of her, she would earn the approval of her parents and the respect of all the neighbours. And she would marry some boy from nearby and end up just like her mother. Daisy did not want that.

'Don't you want me to better myself, Mum?' she asked. She might have saved her breath.

'Better y'self! Who do you think you are, for Gawd's sake? Running off to this fancy shop in the West End. They'll see right through you, my girl. Lot of stuck-up snobs, that lot. All la-di-da and thinking they're something special. You'll be back with your tail between your legs, you mark my words.'

That was just what Daisy was most worried about. The other shopgirls had all seemed such superior creatures. She was afraid they would look down on her. But she was not going to let her mother know of her fears.

'I'm just as good as what they are any day. Miss Packard herself give me a job, didn't she? So I must be. And anyway, Mum, whatever you say, I'm going to give it a go.'

Mrs Phipps folded her arms across her skinny chest. 'Well, don't say as I didn't warn you, my girl.'

Daisy picked up her carpetbag. It had seen better days, but she loved it, for ever since she had bought it from a second-hand stall it had been her symbol of escape. She, Daisy Phipps, was going to leave the Isle of Dogs with its filth and noise and drudgery and go to live in the magical world of Oxford Street. Now the moment had come, and it suddenly felt like a very big step indeed. She dropped the bag again and flung her arms round her mother.

'I'll miss you all, Mum, I really will!'

For a moment her mother was stiff and resistant. Then she gave way, and hugged her back.

'You be a good girl, mind.'

'I will, Mum, I promise.'

Nell appeared with a shawl round the shift she had slept in. She gave Daisy a hug and a kiss.

'Keep smiling, Sis.'

'Thanks, Nell. Look after y'self, and Mum and the kids.'

The younger ones flocked round her then. Daisy brushed them off as quickly as possible. They mostly had runny noses and dirty fingers, and she was wearing her best dress. Sniffs and wails started up.

'Oh Gawd, that's all I need. I'm not going to the blooming North Pole, you know,' Daisy said, trying to turn it into a joke. 'I'll be back to see you before you know I've gone.'

She finally managed to get away from the clinging hands. She crept through the front room where her two older brothers were snoring on the Put-u-up, and stepped outside.

The street that had been home to her for all of her eighteen years was wrapped in its Sunday morning quiet. Only the Catholic families were up, getting ready for early Mass. A thin drizzle started, emphasising the drabness of the place, with its two rows of mean terraced houses facing each other across a narrow stretch of dirty cobbles. Later on in the day, it would come to life with children playing and women gossiping, but now it just looked dead and depressed. There was nothing here to keep Daisy from wanting to go. Nothing except a short lifetime of ties and memories. Here lived her friends, her school pals, her relatives, even a couple of past sweethearts. Tears pricked behind Daisy's eyes. She blinked them back. She must not cry. She was off on her great adventure. Squaring her thin shoulders, she set off.

It was a slow journey through London, for though there were none of the weekday traffic jams, neither were there many buses. The East End was slowly coming to life as she left it, but the City was dead and the West End still asleep. The churches and chapels she passed on the way had people going in or out, but otherwise most of London seemed to be taking a well-earned rest.

Daisy stepped down from the new motor bus in Oxford Street and stood as it rumbled away. She looked across the road, and there it was – her Eldorado, Packards. It rose to a majestic five storeys, topped by its noble glass dome. Even in the gloom of a wet March morning, its windows gleamed. Daisy gazed at it. Tomorrow, she was going to be working there, in that fairytale palace filled with light and warmth and beautiful things. It was just too good to be true. She crossed the road and walked slowly all round the shop, looking in every window, veering between apprehension and wonder.

She had just come back to the front again when she was confronted by a whiskered policeman. He stared down at her with obvious disapproval.

'Move along, miss.'

Daisy gaped at him. 'What?'

'I said, move along, miss. We don't have your sort hanging about here. Not that you're likely to get much custom at this time of day.'

Daisy was enraged. 'Who do you think I am? Flaming cheek! Do I look like a prossie? Do I? I'm a respectable girl, I am. I'll have you know I'm starting work right here at this shop tomorrow.'

The policeman had the grace to look chastened. 'Just doing my duty, miss.'

'Well you better look a bit harder at people before you go accusing them,' Daisy told him.

She was just about to flounce off when it struck her that she had been a long time in getting here.

'Here,' she said, 'if you're so keen on duty, you can tell us the time.'

The man consulted his watch. 'Two minutes past ten, miss.'

'Blimey!' Daisy squealed. She was supposed to have been at the staff hostel at ten o'clock.

'Looking for Trent Street, miss?' the policeman asked.

'Yes,' Daisy admitted.

'First left, second right.'

Daisy set off at a trot, the carpetbag weighing heavily on her arm. As she turned the corner, she saw the policeman still looking at her. She waved.

'Thanks, mate.'

She arrived at Trent Street red-faced and breathless, and looked down the road. She was once again in a street of terraced houses, but very different from the one she had left earlier that morning. The two rows of dwellings were three storeys high, plus dormered attics, and set over semi-basements. The brickwork was sooty, but the doors and railings were newly painted, the windows were clean and the steps scrubbed. Some of the area sills even sported windowboxes filled with crocuses and daffodils. The whole place had a well-cared-for look. Daisy was overwhelmed. To think that she was going to live somewhere like this. She walked up the street, looking at the numbers.

At number twenty-four, she stopped. This was it: her new home. Her heart thudded painfully in her chest and her mouth felt dry. Then from inside came the sound of laughter, and someone started singing 'The Boy I Love is Up in the Gallery'. Daisy's courage returned. She marched up the steps and banged the shiny brass knocker.

The door was opened by a girl a year or two older than

herself with a mass of frizzy dark hair. There was a smell of polish overlaid by that of fried bacon. Daisy's stomach growled.

'Yes? Oh – you must be the other new girl. One's come already. Is that all you've got?' She nodded at Daisy's bag.

Daisy responded instantly to the whiff of contempt. ''Course not. The rest's following later. You going to let us in, then?'

The other girl shrugged and stood aside. She called into the depths of the house.

'Mrs Drew! New girl's come.'

There was the sound of heavy footsteps ascending, and a middle-aged woman dressed entirely in black appeared from the direction of the basement stairs. Her grey hair was scraped back into a tightly controlled bun and her mouth was set in a line. Her sharp eyes looked Daisy over.

'You'll be Miss Phipps?'

Daisy gulped. Nobody had ever called her that before. Her family and friends called her Daisy or Daise, or sometimes Daisy Belle after the song, and at the draper's she was called Phipps. But never Miss Phipps.

'I am Mrs Drew. I am the housekeeper for here and number twenty-six. I am responsible for the good conduct of these houses, so I trust you do know how to behave?'

Daisy drew breath to say something indignant, met the grey eyes and thought the better of it. One of the teachers at her old school had had a look just like that, able to quell a riot at a glance.

'Er – yes,' she said.

Mrs Drew nodded. 'I hope so. Follow me and I'll show you to your room.'

'Oh – er – thanks,' Daisy muttered.

They went up the first flight of stairs, the treads of which were covered with highly polished linoleum.

'You are in room 1A in the attic, with the other new girl,' the housekeeper said.

On the landing, a door opened and a face poked round, gave Daisy the once-over and popped back in again. An explosion of giggles came from inside the room. Mrs Drew gave a disapproving snort.

'Foolish child.'

44

Up another flight, and then the stairs got narrower and steeper as they went up into the roof. In the dim light at the top, Daisy could just make out the metal numbers on the cream-painted doors. Mrs Drew knocked on 1A and went in without waiting for an answer.

'Miss Brand, this is your roommate, Miss Phipps.'

She turned to Daisy. 'The house rules are behind the door. Read them. You can fetch hot water from the kitchen if you need it. The lavatory is on the first floor. Dinner is at one o'clock sharp.'

With which she was gone.

Daisy was left standing in the middle of the room. It was painted a uniform cream colour and was spotlessly clean. The ceiling sloped on both sides, but it was still higher than any of the rooms in the Phipps house. A dormer window with green flowered curtains let in the spring light and the floor was covered with polished linoleum in a fawn and green fern pattern. There were two iron bedsteads with green coverlets, two rows of pegs, two plain deal chests of drawers and a washstand with a plain white basin and ewer. All this was remarkable enough, and normally would have left Daisy breathless, had it not been for the other inhabitant of the room. For she was quite simply the most lovely thing Daisy had ever seen.

'Blimey,' she said. 'You're like something off a soap advertisement.'

She had known girls who had something attractive about them, pretty eyes, maybe, or curling hair. Jinny Blaire down her street had all the boys after her because of her big breasts and come-hither smile. But mostly the combination of poor health, inadequate diet and bad living conditions had bred a plain lot down her way. Nothing like the women who got their pictures in the papers, the music-hall stars and society beauties. They might just as well have been a different race. But here she was looking at someone who looked as if she belonged to that other world. She had flawless pink and white skin, glossy blonde hair and wide blue eyes, straight nose and cupid's-bow mouth in a perfect oval face. And she was looking at Daisy in astonishment.

'Th-thank you. That's very kind of you,' she said.

Even her voice was different. It was gentle and cultured.

Daisy flushed. Her mother had been right. These people were going to look down on her.

'I'm Daisy Phipps,' she said, rather too loudly. 'I'm from Dog Island. Take it or leave it.'

The other girl smiled and held out her hand. 'I'm Isobel Brand. How do you do?'

To her surprise, Daisy found herself shaking hands. Isobel's was soft with well-kept nails.

'I hope you don't mind, but I've already started unpacking and I've put my things on that side,' Isobel said. 'It's a little Spartan here, but it's very clean.'

There was a deliberate brightness in her voice, as if she were trying to keep cheerful.

'Yeah –' Daisy said. The fact that this was her room, with only one other person to share it with, was gradually sinking in. Her room. All this space. A whole bed to herself. And a washstand, a real washstand. 'Blimey –' she breathed. 'Just wait till I tell 'em about this back home. They'll never believe me.'

She walked round, touching everything, just to prove that she really could. She sat down on the bed. It gave deliciously. The coverlet looked practically new. She tweaked it back a little at the top and found white cotton sheets and a pillow in a real pillowcase, crisp and white and ironed. It was like being a princess. She looked at her new roommate, who was taking a dress out of a big leather portmanteau. A beautiful dress of soft blue wool with yellow ribbon trimmings. She hung it up on one of the rows of pegs, alongside two dark skirts and a black tailor-made costume. Daisy glanced down at her scruffy carpetbag. When she got out the clothes she had inside there, they were going to look just exactly what they were – cheap and second-hand. Were all the girls here as elegant and expensive-looking as this Isobel? But then she remembered the frizzy-haired girl who had let her in. She might have tried to be snooty about Daisy's bag, but she was only an ordinary working girl. So were the rest of the people at Packards.

'What's someone like you doing here?' she blurted out.

Isobel's lovely face took on a closed look. 'Settling in, just like you.'

That was not quite what Daisy meant.

'But – you're the sort what buys things at Packards, not sells them,' she said.

'I need to support myself. Packards offered me a position.'

'But why are you living in? Ain't you got no family?'

'Why are you living in?' Isobel countered.

'It's more nearer here. And there ain't enough room for us all at home,' Daisy said. She did not add the most pressing reason, that she wanted to escape. She wasn't going to give away everything yet.

'Do you have a large family?' Isobel asked.

'Yeah, loads of us.' Daisy found herself distracted. She reeled off their names. 'You?'

'No – none.'

Daisy stared at her. 'What – nobody?'

'No. I'm an orphan.'

Isobel turned her back and started taking underwear out of her portmanteau and folding it neatly into one of the chests of drawers. But she did not hide her face quite well enough. Daisy realised that she was biting her lip, trying to fight back tears. At once her heart was melted. Here was not a posh lady with expensive clothes and a snooty accent, but a girl in trouble. She went over and put an arm round Isobel's shoulders.

'You poor love. You all on your own in the world, then?'

Isobel nodded. Her chin wobbled and the tears spilled over. 'I'm sorry – I don't mean to – it's just –'

'There, there,' Daisy soothed. 'You have a good old cry, then. Do you good.'

She guided Isobel over to her bed and held her, patting her back and stroking her head, while she sobbed on her shoulder. She had done the same many a time for her brothers and sisters. The big difference was, Isobel smelt sweet.

'There,' she said, as Isobel subsided into sniffs and hiccups. 'That better now?'

Isobel nodded. 'I'm so sorry, you must think I'm very foolish. The thing is, it's not only losing my parents, it's all this –' She indicated the room with a slight wave of the hand. 'I don't know whether I'm going to be able to do it.'

'Well, I ain't never been away from home before neither,'

Daisy admitted. 'Tell you what, we'll look out for each other, eh? I'll stick up for you and you stick up for me. Mates, like. What d'you think?'

Isobel gave a watery smile.

'I think I should like that very much, Daisy. Thank you.'

6

The Thomas Packards' house in Hill Street, Mayfair, was all lit up and ready for a family dinner party. The seating in the green and gilt drawing room was arranged to accommodate the guests, the long polished table in the dining room was set out with silver and Royal Doulton and Waterford crystal, and down in the kitchens a meal of regal proportions was within half an hour of perfection. These family gatherings took place once a month. Thomas, in his role of head of the family, insisted that everyone should attend, and because they were all dependent on him, everyone came.

Whether they wanted to come was another matter. In the drawing room of their house, Bertie Amberley was complaining to Winifred.

'Dashed nuisance, these dinners at your pa's. Always seem to be when there's something particularly good on at the theatre.'

'Well, don't think that I enjoy them,' Winifred retorted. 'But family is family and duty is duty, after all.'

Bertie grunted and helped himself to a generous measure of brandy and soda.

'Don't see why the old boy has to have them so often. I mean to say, once every two or three months is enough to keep up the old family ties, surely? We don't dine with my folks more often than that.'

'No, we don't,' Winifred agreed petulantly.

She would have liked to have dined with Bertie's family far more often. But she knew, to her chagrin, that she and Bertie were only invited the very minimum amount for form's sake. Bertie's mother and father were glad Winifred had taken him off their hands and provided for him, since the Amberley fortunes were low and Bertie showed no inclination to do anything to support himself. But they were old-fashioned in their attitude to money and trade. The Prince of Wales might make friends of

49

bankers and shopkeepers, but the Amberleys could never fully admit them to their circle.

'At least they can be relied upon to provide a decent dinner,' Bertie conceded.

'I'm happy you'll find something to enjoy in the evening,' Winifred said, glancing at his paunch.

'Be able to keep an eye on me, won't you, old girl?' Bertie pointed out. 'Can't do anything but behave m'self, can I?'

Winifred compressed her lips and said nothing. He was right, of course. While he was sitting at the family table, he could not be out chasing actresses. That was something to be glad of. She looked at the ormolu clock on the mantelpiece.

'What can those children be doing? They should have been down five minutes ago.'

Half a mile or so across town at his bachelor's rooms, Edward was flinging his second spoilt bow tie on the floor. He also disliked the family dinners. He saw quite enough of his grandfather at work, and had left home in order to get away from a father he despised and a mother who irritated him. However, there was one advantage to this evening's gathering, which was that it would give him a chance to work out just how strongly his mother was against this ridiculous plan of Amelie's to run her own department within the store. This was one instance when he and his mother were of the same mind, though for different reasons, and he meant to take advantage of it.

At the third try, he managed a perfect knot in his tie. He picked up his evening cape, his silk scarf, his gloves and his top hat and, every inch the debonair man about town, went downstairs to call a cab.

At Hill Street, Thomas was listening to his wife, Margaret's, complaints with half an ear.

'. . . and then I caught her laying the dessert spoons and forks round the wrong way. It is really quite impossible to get a decently trained servant these days, and without them these dinner parties are so difficult . . .'

'It is only a family dinner,' Thomas pointed out.

'That's as may be, but it still has to be done properly when there's that creature of Winifred's looking down his nose at us all the time,' Margaret told him.

'Well, if you don't think you can manage, my dear –' Thomas said.

'Manage! Of course I can manage! Oh, I know what you're thinking. You'd like to get rid of me and have some flighty young creature for your wife –'

'Nonsense,' Thomas said, thinking longingly of his mistress. She never made scenes like this. To distract Margaret, he said, 'What have you ordered for dinner tonight?'

'Consommé julienne, then fillets of sole Coburg and devilled oysters, then saddle of mutton, honey-glazed ham, various vegetables and salad, then iced pudding and apple charlotte, then dessert,' Margaret reeled off, not without a note of satisfaction. They both knew that this was a very acceptable meal.

'Sounds delicious,' Thomas said.

From downstairs came the sound of a knock at the door. The evening had begun.

For the first hour or so, nothing was said that had not been said a hundred times before. Healths were enquired into, the current state of the store dissected, the latest doings at court commented on. Edward, bored, was reduced to viewing his family as an outsider might. They were an impressive lot, he had to admit. His grandfather, though he had never been tall and was now shrinking with age, was still blessed with abundant white hair that, together with his air of authority, gave him quite the look of the patriarch. Edward's grandmother was definitely an old lady now, the lines on her face emphasising the discontented twist to her mouth, but she was very expensively dressed in claret-coloured silk embellished by pearls and garnets set in gold. His father was fast losing his looks, but nobody could mistake that lazy drawl, that air of total confidence that marked the member of the upper classes. His mother and his sister were both stunningly dressed, the one in a gown of peach-coloured embroidered chiffon over satin, the other in palest green net with sequins over white, and even Edward had to admit that Amelie had grown into a very pretty girl. And then there was his brother. Perry, like the rest of the men impeccably turned out in evening dress, looked just what he was – the spoilt younger son with too much time on his hands. All in all, they were a handsome bunch, and their prosperity glowed from them.

Everything about the meal spoke money as well. There was enough food for twice as many people, all cooked to perfection and artistically presented. The servants, despite Margaret's complaints, were swift and unobtrusive in handing round food and removing plates. There was sherry to accompany the soup, followed by champagne and claret with the other courses. And all provided by Packards. The store that Winifred and the Amberleys despised was the source of the whole family's extravagant way of life.

Not for the first time it struck Edward that the best thing about his family was that compared with most others it was exceedingly small. There were no uncles or cousins with a claim on the store. It had to come to him. With this comfortable thought in mind, he began to listen to the conversation again.

Talk was centred round one of the perennial family topics – the purchase of a country estate. Edward was convinced that his grandfather liked to trail it before the others every now and again just to stir them up. If that was his intention, it worked every time.

'I did hear that the Maynards are having to give up their place in Wiltshire,' Winifred was saying. 'So dreadful for them, poor things. I believe it's been in the family for over two hundred years. Of course, it's not their main property. They still have Archforth. But so sad to have to part with family land. Such a pretty place, too, so I hear.'

'Archforth's a monstrosity. I don't know why they don't get rid of that and keep the Wiltshire house. It's much nicer,' Perry said.

Winifred pounced on this. 'Have you been there, then, darling?'

'Two or three times, I suppose.'

'You never told me.'

'Oh well – you know how it is. You go here and you go there for Saturday-to-Mondays and forget where you've been half the time,' Perry said vaguely.

Edward could well believe this. His brother seemed to have invitations from half the Top Ten Thousand of England. He never could work out how, but Perry just seemed to have the knack of making himself agreeable.

'Wiltshire, eh? Very pretty part of the world,' Thomas said. Predictably, Winifred snatched at this.

'Oh it is indeed, Father. One of the prettiest counties in England. And I believe the Maynards' house is quite delightful. Isn't that so, Perry? What did you think of it? What is it like?'

'Very neat little place. You know the sort of thing – mullioned windows, panelled hall with a minstrels' gallery, lot of fireplaces you could roast an ox in. Nice lake, too. Full of fish. Went for a boating party on the lake, all rigged out with Chinese lanterns and rugs and champagne and that. Rowed across to the little island and wound the gramophone up and danced. Very jolly.'

It was quite clear to Edward that Perry could have been talking about any of the country houses he had visited, but their mother seemed to be taken in.

'Oh, it sounds just perfect. You know how you enjoy fishing, Father.'

'Wiltshire's a long way from London,' Thomas said.

'Not these days. Great Western would get you there in no time,' Edward said, just to annoy him.

Having his grandfather safely out of the way in the country would suit him down to the ground, but he knew there was no chance. The old boy was wedded to the store.

'Could work up a very decent shoot down there too, I shouldn't wonder,' Bertie put in.

Edward glanced at his father. It wasn't the shooting that really attracted him. That was just the excuse. What Bertie liked was a supply of bored and available married women, and shooting parties provided them in abundance.

'It would be so nice for Amelie to have a little country retreat in the family, now that she's about to come out,' Winifred said.

Which was clever, Edward had to admit. If there was anything that might sway Thomas, it was the thought of providing something for Amelie.

'It's not really possible to launch a girl properly without a country property somewhere in the background, is it?' he put in.

Winifred shot him a grateful look.

'Well, of course one *can*, but there's no doubt that property does matter. There are so many of these dreadful American girls coming over here with quite vulgar amounts of money behind them, so it really does count for a great deal that an English girl should have some solid landed property in her family.'

Amelie had been unusually silent, though she had been getting more and more agitated as the conversation progressed. Now her pale skin was flushed red with annoyance.

'Why don't you just take out an advertisement in the paper: *Marriageable girl, large fortune, country property, any offers?*'

'Amelie!' Winifred was genuinely shocked.

But Thomas laughed. 'That's right. Anyone would think the child's got buck teeth or warts or something. Pretty girl like our Amelie will have all the young fellows running after her.'

'Yes, but will they be the right sort of young fellows?' Winifred retorted.

'We certainly don't want some fortune-hunter after her money,' said Margaret, with a meaningful look at Bertie.

Bertie gazed at the bubbles in his glass of champagne. 'Our little girl has breeding, on one side at least. She doesn't need anything else,' he said.

'For heaven's sake!' Amelie burst out. 'Will you please all stop talking about me as if I wasn't here? Have any of you considered that I might not want to come out?'

'That's right. Our Melly's a New Woman, aren't you, Mel?' Perry said.

'Nonsense,' said Winifred.

'Oh but she is, Mama. She's going to wear a stiff collar and tie and she's going to earn her own living.'

Amelie glared at him. 'It's all just a joke to you, isn't it, Perry?'

'I think we have heard quite enough of this silly talk,' their mother snapped. 'Of course Amelie is going to come out. Anyone would think she was some clerk's daughter from Clapham wanting to become a typist.'

'Instead of which I'm a shopkeeper's granddaughter from

Mayfair wanting to help run the store. And I'm going to, aren't I, Grandpa?'

There was a moment's loaded silence as everybody waited for everybody else's reaction. Edward's glance flicked from his mother to his grandfather. Then he noticed that Amelie was looking at him. The little minx. She was getting the old man to fight her battles for her. And hoping, no doubt, to stir her big brother into public opposition. But Edward was not going to play her game. He composed his face into a bland smile as her eyes locked briefly with his, and waited for their mother to lay down the law.

But Thomas got in first. 'You are indeed, my flower.'

Winifred exploded. 'Really, Father, what are you thinking of? How can a debutante possibly be seen to be playing at being a shopgirl? It's absolutely unheard of. Who is going to send her invitations if that sort of thing got about?'

Thomas gave one of his dangerously sweet smiles. 'Well, my dear, if our Amelie's breeding is as impeccable as Bertie here assures us, on his side of course, I'm sure she can have very little to be afraid of. You'll have eligible young men beating a path to your door.'

'I shall be a laughing stock!'

Winifred had gone too far. At the head of the table, Thomas's expression was pure ice. Edward moved to dissociate himself from her.

'Steady on, Mother. Don't exaggerate. This is the twentieth century now, remember. Young girls are doing all sorts of extraordinary things. I'm sure all your friends will think it quite original of Mel.'

Amelie threw him a puzzled look, affording him passing amusement.

Thomas took a long breath through his nose. He fixed Winifred with his penetrating blue eyes.

'Anyone who considers it laughable to be concerned with honest work at Packards need not bother to sit at this table.'

'I —'

It was the first time Edward could remember ever having seen his mother lost for words. Come to that, it was the first time she had ever really let slip to Thomas how she felt about being connected with the store. She had made a very serious mistake, and she knew it. But while Edward was still considering whether it would benefit him to act as peacemaker, Amelie stepped in.

'I'm sure Mama did not mean it like that, Grandpa. Did you, Mama? She was just thinking of what her silly friends might say, not saying what she thinks herself.'

'Quite,' Winifred managed to say.

'As if the opinion of a bunch of overbred ne'er-do-wells mattered,' Edward said, with feeling.

He had suffered terribly when he first went to school from young sprigs of the aristocracy who looked down on one whose family fortune came from trade. He had retaliated with his fists, gradually silencing them by giving out more black eyes and bloody noses than he received. By the time he left, he had earned their grudging respect by becoming captain of both the rugger team and the cricket first eleven. But he had never ceased to resent them, the ones who were born to power and influence.

'It matters to your mother, it seems,' Thomas said.

Winifred recovered a little of her self-control. 'It matters if one is to move in their circles, and that is what Amelie is going to do if she is to come out properly and be presented at court,' she said with admirable dignity.

Amelie looked rebellious but had the sense to keep her mouth shut.

'After all,' Winifred went on, 'to see her daughter marry well must be the proper concern of every mother. I'm sure you would agree with me, Mother.' She smiled sweetly at Margaret, who indeed could only agree.

'I'm sure we all want the best for Mel,' Edward said.

'Did anyone see that piece in the paper about Jerry Benson's balloon?' Perry enquired.

Margaret took the hint and called for the dessert to be served. Silver dishes piled high with out-of-season fruits, bonbons, sugared almonds and *petits fours* were placed on the table, and a yellow sweet wine was poured. Conversation limped doggedly along the path Perry had opened, for everyone had something to say about the craze for ballooning.

It was not until the very end of the evening that the subject of Amelie's interest in the shop was raised again, and then only furtively. They were in the hall preparing to leave when Winifred grabbed Edward's sleeve.

'I thought you at least might have been on my side,' she hissed.

'No good ever comes of rubbing the old boy up the wrong way,' Edward said, wishing he would listen to his own good advice at times. He patted his mother on the shoulder. 'You concentrate on keeping her busy and I'll see to it that it's just a passing phase,' he said. 'Don't worry. She'll soon get bored with it when she finds that it's actually hard work. Then she'll be only too glad to dress up and go to parties.'

'I hope you're right,' Winifred said.

So did Edward. If Amelie didn't give up of her own accord, then she would have to be persuaded.

7

'This is going to be our part of the floor,' Miss Packard said.

With a sweep of the arm, she indicated the space that had been cleared in the far corner of Ladies' Outerwear. Already her individual touch was clear. She had had the area partially fenced off with two rows of the standard Packard drawer units that faced inwards into the new department, with an archway of garden trellis constructed between them, making a distinctive entrance. This was going to be very much her own kingdom.

'I am going to have tennis racquets and golf clubs and croquet mallets fixed to the arch,' she explained, 'and a wax figure on either side, each wearing one of our outfits. Then all along the top of the drawers here we can display hats and small items of clothing.'

Daisy, Isobel and the rest of the staff of the new department nodded and made small noises of admiration. This was Miss Packard's project. It was not their place to comment. Daisy was still living in a state of constant wonder at being part of this Aladdin's cave. After the stuffy, crowded little premises in Poplar with its limited range of inferior goods, this was a palace. She loved handling the beautiful things and dealing with all the amazing variety of people who came into the store. She and Isobel had done two weeks in Mantles and Underwear respectively, learning the ropes. They now knew how to speak to customers, wrap purchases, and work the overhead wires that sent money to and from the central counting house. They were ready to help Miss Packard set up Ladies' Sportswear.

'Now, we have plenty to do before we open on Thursday,' Miss Packard said. 'But before we start, I want to talk to you all.'

She led the way under the arch. The space inside looked sad and dull. The counters were bare, the ranks of glass-fronted drawers empty. Packing cases of clothing and equipment were piled in the middle of the floor. A heap of wire body forms lay jumbled in a corner. But Miss Packard was glowing with enthusiasm.

'This is going to be the most successful department in the store. I expect you have heard others saying that it's sure to fail. It's certainly been said to me. But please take no notice. I am convinced that it is a good idea. We have been given a window on Oxford Street and I have placed advertisements in the papers and ladies' journals. Now I am asking you people to help me make it a success. We are going to show the doubting Thomases that they are wrong. We have lots of stock, we are going to have very pretty displays and it is the right time of year now to start, when everyone is looking forward to summer. So – are you all with me?'

'Oh yes!' Daisy cried.

The others turned to look at her. Daisy flushed with embarrassment, but Miss Packard smiled.

'Thank you, Miss Phipps. And what about the rest of you?'

Isobel, the two other girls, Maisie and Dot, and Miss Higgs, the senior saleswoman, all nodded and murmured.

Miss Packard turned to the nearest counter and opened a box which was lying there.

'So that we are just a little different, and a little better than everyone else, I have had badges made for you all to wear. I hope you like them.'

Daisy looked at the silver brooch that Miss Packard handed her. It was shaped like a tennis racquet lying at an angle with the distinctive P for Packards across it. She smoothed it with her thumb. It was quite the nicest thing that anyone had ever given her. She could tell just by the weight of it in her hand that it was a quality item. But more than that, it made her feel as if she really belonged in her new world. Miss Packard had given it to her, so she must think she was good enough. She pinned it onto her white blouse.

'Now, we are all in this together,' Miss Packard declared, patting her own brooch. 'Let's start making this look like the best department in the store. Miss Higgs, if I tell you where I want everything to go, then you can direct the girls.'

Miss Higgs nodded. She was a tall, rawboned woman in her early thirties who had been with Packards for fourteen years.

The grapevine had it that she was an excellent saleswoman who had been overlooked for promotion up till now because she did not get on with the floorwalkers and buyers who were, without exception, men.

Daisy and Dot were told to start unpacking a box of gloves, Isobel and Maisie some underwear. But then Miss Packard had another idea. Isobel was to write the labels that slipped into the brass holders on the front of each dark oak drawer.

'Miss Brand has a very clear hand. I remember it from her application form,' said Miss Packard. 'I think perhaps she should write all our labels for us.'

Daisy happened to be looking at Miss Higgs as this was said. The senior saleswoman's mouth compressed into a hard line. She was not happy. After a moment's hesitation, she spoke up.

'With respect, Miss Packard, don't you think it would be best if we get everything packed away first, then write the labels. We are sure to change things around before we get it just how we want it, so it will be a waste of time to do it now.'

Miss Packard considered this, frowning. Then she smiled. 'Yes, you're right, Miss Higgs. I might well change my mind about exactly how things should be arranged. Please carry on.'

The senior saleswoman was satisfied. But the smooth running of the operation was hard to achieve with Miss Packard around. She kept swooping on the girls as they worked.

'Now, just look at these golfing gloves. Do you see how they are made? A flexible leather back so that the hands can move easily, a nice warm lining for cold days, and this knitted underside to give a good grip. This is the sort of thing you need to be able to make clear to our customers . . . Oh, you have the cycling knickers. These are very practical. They're made of cashmere so they are very light to wear, and there are these in the grey mixture or black thin ones for summer, and these heavier ones in fancy mixtures for winter. Or if you have a lady who wants ankle length rather than knee length, then we have these home-knit ones in black. Very cosy on a chilly day. These would be suitable for golf as well. And of course they all come in four sizes.'

Daisy was charmed by her. Apart from the customers she had been allowed to serve since she came to the store, she had never before been in contact with a member of the upper classes. Everything about Miss Packard was fascinating, her accent, her beautiful clothes, her elaborately styled hair. Isobel was different enough, but Miss Packard had something more. Isobel was timid and self-effacing, whereas Miss Packard exuded confidence. When the floorwalkers or buyers gave orders, you could always hear the command in their voices. Miss Packard did not need to sound bossy. She just knew that when she asked for something to be done, then it would be done. On top of all that, there was her enthusiasm. It was irresistible. By the end of the morning even Dot, who had been sulking about being moved from the frothy delights of Millinery, could see something to admire in a lightweight corset.

'Do look at everything carefully before you fold it up,' Miss Packard kept telling them. 'It's very important that you know all about everything in our department. When ladies come in here to buy, I want them to feel that they are talking to staff who can really give them good advice. Of course, this applies to you especially, Miss Higgs, and I know you understand that, but I want you to see that the girls know what they are doing as well. If you are already serving a customer, they won't be able to refer to you immediately.'

By dinner time, Daisy felt as if her head were overflowing with new information. Prices, qualities, special functions – it was like being at school, but very much more interesting. Miss Higgs sent Maisie and Dot off for first sitting in the staff dining room and the remaining four continued unpacking the boxes.

'Oh, here are my new tennis blouses,' Miss Packard exclaimed, cutting the string on a large case and diving in. She took out the first garment and held it up for Miss Higgs, Isobel and Daisy to admire. At first sight it was just a pretty blouse, made of fine lawn with tucks down the front and a ruffle at the neck, but then Miss Packard displayed its unique feature.

'You see this long tail here at the back? This goes right underneath the body and does up at the bottom of the front of the blouse with these two buttons, so that when you take a smash at the ball, the blouse does not ride up out of the skirt, but stays neatly tucked in. And as well as the tail, they are all cut full across the back, with pleats or gathers along the yoke, to allow for ease of movement. They will be a real boon to anyone who wants to really play hard. A lot of people just want to play pat-ball, of course, but for those who are very keen on tennis, and want to play winning shots without looking like a hoyden, these blouses are the answer. There are lots of styles – see – neat plain shirt collars that you could wear with a bow or a tie, or fancy ones with broderie anglaise yokes, or insertion work down the sleeves. The women who wear these can enjoy tennis and still look feminine.'

To Daisy's surprise, Isobel actually ventured an opinion.

'That is such a good idea. I'm sure they will be very popular.'

Miss Packard gave one of her dazzling smiles. 'I do hope you are right. Oh, it's so exciting, isn't it? Look at how much we have done this morning. It's already beginning to look like a proper shop in here. How I wish I could stay here all day working with you. I want to start selecting things to put out on display – these blouses for a start – but I have to go home. My mother insists that I go with her to a tea party this afternoon. It's sure to be deadly dull. Nothing but tedious small talk. But I shall make use of my time away from here, and tell everyone about our new department and make sure they tell their friends, and then they will all wonder what it is about and come and buy something on opening day.'

Dot and Maisie arrived back promptly at half-past twelve, and Daisy and Isobel were sent for their dinner. They clattered up the service stairs to the fifth floor, hurrying to get a good place in the queue.

'That Miss Packard, she's corker, ain't she? I never known nobody like her.'

'She's certainly very original,' Isobel agreed. 'But I must admit I don't understand her at all. She has every advantage of fortune and family, she is to be presented at court, and yet she chooses to work! It is very odd.'

'Must be lovely not to work, if you got the money for it. I wonder what you do all day?' Daisy said.

She had always worked, ever since she was old enough to mind a baby or run an errand. While she was still at school, there were chores to be done morning and evening for her mother, and the day she was twelve she had been sent to labour six days a week at a grocer's shop. The idea of having endless time on her hands simply to enjoy herself was totally alien.

'You'd be surprised how the days fill up. There are visits that have to be paid, and shopping to do, and charitable works to perform. It is all so pleasant.'

There was longing in Isobel's voice. Daisy still wasn't used to the fact that what had been a huge step up for her was an even larger step down for her roommate. It was difficult to understand that Isobel might not appreciate how amazing it was to have three solid meals every day and a clean bed to go to each night.

They arrived at the huge staff dining room to be met by a wall of steamy heat and the inevitable queue. The dining room performed wonders every day, providing hot dinners for three thousand staff in three sittings, but it was still a problem to get in, find a seat, eat and get out again all in half an hour. Daisy ran an eye down the line. Already she was beginning to find out the best way of organising the time.

'Look, why don't you go to the lav while I queue, then you can keep my seat for me while I go?' she suggested.

Isobel looked relieved. 'Oh yes, that's a good idea.'

Daisy waited, grateful for the chance to lean on the polished rail while she did so. The morning's work had not been as tiring as serving behind the counter, but still she had been on the go without a break since half-past eight. The girl in front of her struck up a conversation and Daisy answered carefully. She had realised early on that most of the shopgirls had two accents, their own and a heavily genteel one used for customers, but though they were all working class like herself, her particular brand of East End was considered common. The only person she had met who spoke correctly, apart from Miss Packard, was Isobel, and she sounded so attractive that it was her accent and grammar that Daisy was trying to pick up. It was a difficult task to break herself of the speech habits of a lifetime, and she knew that at the moment she just sounded odd, or worse, pretentious.

'Oo, 'ark at you!' some of the girls had mocked. 'Trying to sound like Lady Muck, are we?'

She got to the head of the queue. As it was Monday, it was sausage, mash and cabbage followed by syrup pudding. The dinners followed a strict rota of menus that never varied, summer or winter. Tuesday was steak and kidney pudding and plum crumble; Wednesday, shepherd's pie and rice pudding; Thursday, Irish stew and apple pie; Friday, baked fish and spotted dick; Saturday, bacon roll and bread-and-butter pudding. It was all steaming hot and plenty of it. Daisy relished every crumb. There had been many times in her life when she had known real hunger, and now she was making up for all those lost and inadequate meals.

Isobel appeared at her side and they took a loaded plate in each hand, picked up their cutlery and surveyed the crowded long tables for two seats together. The dining room was divided into two unequal areas by a barrier of wrought iron. Men occupied the larger part while the women, still the smaller part of the workforce, stayed in the other. Fraternisation between the sexes was frowned upon by the management, which of course made the young people all the more eager to get to know each other. The most popular places in the room were naturally those adjoining the barrier, and it was there that Daisy spotted two girls about to leave.

'Come on, I can see some places,' she said to Isobel, and marched across the room to claim them.

They were over halfway there before Isobel realised just where she was heading for.

'Oh – do we have to go there? Isn't there anywhere else?' she asked, looking anxiously around.

'Not together. Come on, quick, or someone else'll get them,' Daisy said.

She fairly ran round the packed tables, squeezed between the seated rows of shopgirls and plonked her plate down on the coveted place. She looked back to see Isobel still hesitating three tables away, trying to locate some alternative seats. She waved at her.

'Come on, Iz, move y'self!'

Very reluctantly, Isobel complied.

Almost before Isobel had sat down, there was interest from the other side of the barrier. Two young men were giving them the once-over.

'Aye aye, what've we got here, then? You girls new?'

Daisy gave them a withering look. 'What's it to you?'

They were rather nice, she decided. They were both in their early twenties. The one who had spoken to them had a snub nose, freckles and a cheeky grin, the other was darker, with a strong square face. For just a moment, their eyes met and in that moment Daisy knew that nothing was going to tear her from her seat now. Going to the lav would have to wait.

'Just being friendly,' the darker one said. 'Who's your friend?'

'Who's yours?' Daisy countered.

They introduced themselves. The snub-nosed one was Arthur Grigg from Men's Gloves.

'And I'm Johnny Miller, Carpets.'

Johnny Miller. Something about the name made her heart beat a little faster.

'Come on,' Arthur said. 'You know ours, now who are you?'

Daisy told them.

'Pleased to meet you, Miss Brand, Miss Phipps.'

Isobel gave the briefest of nods without actually looking at them, then gave her full attention to her meal, though she only picked at it and pushed the food around her plate.

'What department are you?' Arthur asked.

'Ladies' Sportswear,' Daisy told him.

'Oh – Miss Packard's special, eh?' Johnny said. 'And what about you, Miss Brand?'

Isobel said nothing.

'She's in Ladies' Sportswear and all.'

'Like it there, do you?'

'Oh yeah. Miss Packard, she's right there working with us, unpacking stuff and that. And she give us these badges –' Daisy pulled at hers, displaying it. The two young men leant forward.

'Very nice. Don't have them in Carpets. You got one and all, Miss Brand?' Johnny asked.

Isobel nodded.

'You like working with Miss Packard, do you? What's she like?'

'Miss Packard is a very friendly and clever young lady,' Isobel said, still not looking directly at the men. Her tone indicated that this was all she had to say on the subject.

Johnny Miller did not take the hint.

'Not often you get one of the Family grafting alongside of us lot, is it? Must be a bit odd, like, isn't it?'

Isobel did not reply. Daisy could not understand her. Why was she giving these two the cold shoulder? Or was it a trick to get more of their attention? If so, it was certainly working. They were both looking intently at Isobel, waiting for a reaction from her.

'Not all of us is up to it,' Daisy said loudly. 'You got to be special to work in Ladies' Sportswear.'

'I'd like to see the Kaiser behind the counter in Men's Gloves,' Arthur said.

'The Kaiser?' Daisy asked.

'Yeah. Mr Edward.'

'That what you call him?'

'That's what everyone calls him, when the floorwalkers ain't listening, that is.'

'But why?'

'It's obvious, ain't it? You only got to see him walking round or talking to someone.'

'I think I've seen him just a couple of times,' Daisy said.

'How long you been working here?'

'A fortnight.'

'You really are new, ain't you? No wonder we ain't seen you before.'

'You new here and all, Miss Brand?' Johnny asked.

Isobel nodded once more.

'Living over in Trent Street, are you?'

Daisy's heart leapt. They were interested. She put on a heavily casual tone. 'Yeah, that's right, number twenty-four.'

Isobel stood up. Her face was pink, her hands, as she steadied herself by leaning on the table top, were trembling.

'I'll see you at the department,' she said to Daisy, and walked away, leaving a half-eaten first course and untouched pudding.

Daisy and both young men were left staring after her.

'Blimey,' Arthur said. 'I think I been put in my place.'

Johnny watched Isobel until she left the canteen. Then he looked at Daisy.

'Your friend, what's she doing working here?'

A hot wave of jealousy swept over Daisy. It was Isobel he fancied. Isobel with her pretty face and her la-di-da ways.

'She's just earning a crust, like what we all are,' she said sharply.

She stood up herself. Somehow, her usual ravenous appetite seemed to have deserted her.

'I got to go. Ta-ta,' she said.

She picked up the plates and threaded her way towards the exit. All of the shine had gone out of the day.

8

Amelie awoke with a start. This was it, the big day. She switched on the bedside lamp and peered at the clock beneath it. Five to six. For a moment she lay listening to the sounds of the house. All was quiet on her floor, but faintly, from down below, could be heard the footsteps and voices of the lower servants. She had asked to be called at seven, intending to be at the store before the staff arrived at half-past eight, but now she was wide awake and so full of energy and excitement that she could not stay in bed a minute longer. She flung back the covers, slid out of bed, pulled on her dressing gown and padded out along the silent landing to the bathroom.

The Amberleys' house had every modern convenience, thanks to Thomas's generosity. There were electric lights, bathrooms with hot and cold running water, flush lavatories, and, down in the basement, a kitchen with a huge gas cooker and all the latest devices. There was even talk of buying one of the new vacuum cleaners, though Winifred was not convinced about that, maintaining that it would only make the servants lazy. This morning, Amelie was extra glad of the huge white bathroom since it meant that she did not have to wait for water to be brought up to her, but she did not turn the hot tap, as the pipes made a terrible noise and the last thing she wanted to do was to wake her mother.

By a quarter to seven she was dressed and ready but for her hair. She had thought long and hard about what she should wear. The shopgirls had to wear plain black skirts and white blouses. Women employed in offices often wore stiff-collared shirt blouses with ties. She wanted to look businesslike, but not dull. She hated looking dull. So in the end she settled on a dark green tailor-made costume of fine wool and velvet with a bolero jacket, over a lacy blouse. She pinned on her tennis racquet brooch and stood back to look at the finished effect. Yes, very good, or at least it was going to be when her hair was up. The head parlourmaid who had been assigned to look after her since she was not allowed her own personal lady's maid, did not get up till seven. Only underservants rose before then. So Amelie rang for her breakfast to be served in her room.

When the parlourmaid deigned to appear she was most disapproving.

'Does your mother know you're up and planning to go out at this time of day?' she asked, as she brushed and pinned Amelie's hair into place.

'She knows I'm going to the store today, yes,' Amelie hedged.

The woman pursed her lips. Amelie knew just what she was thinking. Servants were such snobs. It was not the way she expected a young lady of 'her' family to behave, rushing off at the crack of dawn to work.

'We New Women are doing all sorts of things these days, you know, Parker,' she said.

Parker was not convinced. 'I'm not at all sure I shouldn't go and tell your mother right now,' she said. 'If I let you go there'll be trouble, sure as eggs is eggs.'

'If there is, then I'll take the blame. Don't you worry about that,' Amelie assured her.

It was half-past seven before she was ready, and then Parker insisted on walking with her. The thought of Miss Amelie Amberley going out in London by herself was totally scandalous. Parker simply would not hear of it. Amelie sighed and gave in. It was a small point, and it prevented the maid from going to her mother.

The windows were being cleaned and redressed when she arrived in Oxford Street. Amelie paused to admire hers. In contrast to all the others, which as usual were being packed with as many items as they could hold, her window was hung with green drapes, and contained just three lifelike wax dummies, one dressed in a golfing outfit, one in a tennis dress and the third in a riding habit. They really did look very effective. A notice on the floor of the window stated 'Ladies' Sportswear – exclusive to Packards.' All it needed now was the one that said 'Opening Today.'

'There, isn't that splendid? It really makes you stop and look, doesn't it?' she said.

Parker sniffed. 'Very nice, I'm sure.'

Amelie had no patience with the woman. 'It's this place that pays your wages, you know,' she said. 'Now, you've delivered me to the door, so you can go back. I'm quite safe here. My grandfather and my brother are around to see I don't get into any trouble.'

The sense of pride as she entered the doors was even stronger than usual. Her store. Truly hers now that she was working here. Ladies' Sportswear might be only one small department, but it was hers, and she was going to make it a huge success.

She hurried through the first floor and gazed at her archway, adorned with sporting equipment. Today, people would be coming through it to buy. She passed underneath, ready to admire once again the arrangements she had supervised. Instead, she stopped short. The glow of ownership drained away, leaving a chill of disbelief. Water was trickling down one of the walls, round a counter and spreading into a puddle on the floor.

'No!' she cried.

For a long moment she stared at it, hoping that what she was seeing was not true. Then she ran forward, trying to make out where the water was coming from. All the plaster down the wall was soaked. She could only guess that a pipe had burst. She opened the drawers nearest to the wet wall. The contents were soaking. It was a disaster. Even if it could be fixed and the mess cleared up, the floor where the water was lying would look wet and stained. Her beautiful new department! And on opening day, too. She thought of all the people she had tried to talk into coming today. She was going to be made to look a fool in front of them. She thought of her mother and how pleased she would be to find the scheme ruined. And Edward – he would be delighted. Despite the fact that he had changed his tune lately, she was sure he still resented her gaining a foothold in the store. Dismay hardened into resolution. They were not going to get the better of her. She was not going to delay her opening. She ran to the little office cuddy belonging to the buyer for Ladies' Outerwear, lifted the internal phone and asked for Maintenance. Then she got to work taking all the wet stock out of the drawers.

When the plumber arrived he couldn't understand it.

'Whole blooming pipe's cracked. Shouldn't of gone like that, miss. Never seen nothing like it in my life, I ain't. Not indoors like this. It's not as if it's frozen, now is it?'

'Can you fix it?' was all Amelie wanted to know.

'Well yes, I can fix it –'

'How soon?'

'Take an hour so so.'

'Then do it.'

The water had been turned off so at least it wasn't running down the wall. But her lovely department looked a mess. A heap of soggy garments now lay beside the puddle on the floor. If she hadn't been so cross, Amelie could have cried. Instead, she started taking out the wet drawers and piling them up. Miss Higgs arrived, closely followed by the four girls. They all gazed in dismay. Amelie realised that she had to act.

'You clear this lot up. I'm going to find something to cover the damp,' she said, and set off.

At first she did not even know what she was going to do. She headed for the fittings workshop in the lower basement. Then in the lift going down, it came to her. Grass.

'Grass?' the fittings storekeeper repeated.

'Yes, artificial grass, the sort of thing they have in Greengrocery to display the fruit and vegetables. You must have plenty of it in stock.'

'Well, I suppose so, Miss Packard. It's just that I ain't never been asked for it by another department, that's all.'

'I'm asking for it now. So will you please fetch it for me, and quickly?'

The man disappeared, and Amelie telephoned Maintenance again to ask for two men with scissors, hammers and nails to be sent to Ladies' Sportswear. They were there by the time she arrived back with a lad from Fittings carrying the roll of greengrocer's grass. There was a certain amount of head scratching and sucking in of breath from the men, but in the end Amelie convinced them that she really was serious in wanting grass on the floor and covering the ugly wet patch on the wall.

'It will still dry out underneath it, and it will look simply splendid. I don't know why I didn't think of it before. It's like bringing the outdoors into the department,' she said.

Her staff, who were becoming used to her odd ideas now, were enthusiastic.

'That looks really pretty, Miss Packard,' Daisy Phipps said.

'You could even pin small items to the piece on the wall. Gloves, perhaps, or handkerchefs,' Isobel Brand suggested.

'Oh yes! That's a very good idea,' Amelie cried. 'We shall not let anything spoil our opening day. Miss Higgs, has the "Opening Today" notice been placed in the window?'

'Not yet, Miss Packard. I wasn't sure whether we were still going to open.'

'Of course we are! See to it at once.'

Just as Maisie was sent scurrying off with the notice, Edward came strolling through the archway.

'Good morning, Amelie. How – Good heavens! What is going on here?'

Amelie explained. Edward was all concern.

'I can't think how that could have happened.'

'Neither can the plumber.'

'Somebody is evidently at fault. Don't worry, Mel, I'll see to it that I find out who was responsible. At the very best, it amounts to gross negligence. What a pity, though, on your opening day. You were so looking forward to it, weren't you? It must be very disappointing for you.'

Amelie still couldn't make him out. He seemed to be genuinely sympathetic. His attitude had changed remarkably since the last family dinner. He had been really helpful over the department and had made some very sensible suggestions. It was all a bit too good to be true.

'It would have been, but we're opening as planned. As you can see, I'm covering up the damage,' she said, waving an arm towards the artificial greenery.

'Yes – well – it's certainly unusual. Very – original.'

His eyes strayed round the department, lingered for a moment on Isobel Brand, then turned back to Amelie.

'Are you sure you can manage, Mel? You can't have customers in here when the workmen are still about their business. I think it might be wiser to postpone the opening.'

So — just as she had suspected, he was seizing on this opportunity to spoil her big day. Amelie gave him her brightest smile.

'Don't worry, Brother dear. The men will soon be done and the plumber's working under the floorboards of the next floor, so he won't bother us at all. And in any case, who is going to come in here and buy a yachting outfit before ten o'clock at the very earliest? We've plenty of time.'

Edward looked doubtful. 'If you have any problems, Mel, just call for me and I'll come and see what I can do.'

'Thank you, Edward. I'll remember that,' Amelie said, thinking as she did so that if anything else were to go wrong, he was the last person she would turn to.

By mid-morning, she was beginning to realise that at least something of what she had said to him was only too true: nobody was buying sportswear at that time of day. Not one penny had been sent whizzing over the wires from her department to the floor's counting office. The workmen had gone, the ruined stock and cabinets had been replaced from Stores, everything had been dusted, polished, tidied and retidied, but not one customer had come under the archway. Amelie was fairly bursting with frustration.

Her grandfather came processing through the store as he always did at eleven o'clock, and came to see how she was doing.

'Good morning, Amelie my dear. I heard about your problem, but Edward said it was all being seen to. Everything fixed up now? Looks very pretty in here, I must say. Very unusual. How's business?'

'Well — we're not run off our feet yet, but I'm very satisfied,' Amelie lied.

'Good, good. Staff satisfactory?' His sharp glance took everything in, including the girls standing alert and ready for the nonexistent customers. 'Now, you just keep me in touch with everything that happens, won't you? Must be getting along now. Good luck, my dear.'

As if he had bestowed a magic touch, a lady in her thirties wandered in not two minutes after he had left. Amelie sailed forward to meet her.

'Good morning. Welcome to Ladies' Sportswear. How may I help you?'

The woman gave her a puzzled look. 'Oh – er – you're working here, are you?'

'That's right. Can I show you anything?'

'Well yes. I need a raincape for cycling in bad weather.'

Amelie was delighted. 'Certainly. We have a large selection. Miss Phipps! Cycling raincapes for this lady, please.'

She hovered by the woman while Daisy spread out half a dozen stout waterproofs, all of them guaranteed to keep out the very worst of the English weather. The customer dithered, tried a couple on, looked unconvinced.

'No – I don't think they're quite what I want, thank you.'

Amelie fumed. She wanted to point out that the woman wouldn't find anything better anywhere in town, but she remembered her grandfather's maxim: never browbeat a customer into buying something they really don't want. You might make one sale, but you'll lose their future custom.

'I'll swear she never meant to buy anything in the first place. She was just wasting our time,' she said to Miss Higgs.

The supervisor was philosophical. 'Very likely, Miss Packard. You get them all the time – tabbies, you know, women with time on their hands. She'll most likely do that in a dozen different departments before she buys something.'

'How very frustrating,' Amelie said. 'How do you stand it?'

'All part of the job, Miss Packard. But she'll be back, and perhaps next time she'll bring a friend and they'll both buy something. At least she knows we're here now.'

It struck Amelie that she had never actually stayed in one department for a whole morning before. You got a very different view of the store from when you swanned around just looking at what was going on. The morning was a very long time when nothing much happened.

By eleven fifteen she was beginning to despair of anyone ever coming near them, when a mother and her grown-up daughter walked in.

'Look – how charming!' the daughter was saying.

Amelie warmed to her immediately.

She was thinking of taking up archery, the girl explained.

Could Amelie advise as to what she would need? Amelie was in her element. This was just the sort of customer she wanted. The shopgirls ran about, producing leather gloves, bracer, belt and a jaunty Robin Hood hat with a clutch of pheasant's feathers.

'Oh, how wickedly charming!' the girl remarked at this last item.

She tried them all on, and emerged from the changing room well pleased. Yes, she would have them all.

'We have bows and arrows and quivers as well,' Amelie said.

She demonstrated the virtues of the different bows, and the girl chose the most expensive one, plus a quiver full of arrows.

'Of course, to look really the thing, you need a dress of Lincoln green,' Amelie told her. 'You can wear your ordinary clothes, of course, and many ladies do, but myself I think nothing looks so charming as the proper green.'

The girl dithered for a while, consulted her mother, and wondered what her friends might be wearing. Amelie sent Daisy to fetch a couple of bolts of fabric, which were unrolled with a flourish and bunched into artistic drapes.

'It looks a picture against a tree-lined meadow,' Amelie said. 'Let me show you some fashion plates –'

They were won over. The chief dressmaker was sent for from Ladies' Gowns, and the girl and her mother handed over to her for the first measurements and consultations on style. Amelie could have kissed them. This must be a portent of future success.

By now it was well into the fashionable time for ladies to go shopping. If the people Amelie had been working on were going to come, then they must start to appear soon.

People did begin to flow into the department. Many of them were mere lookers, like the cycling cape woman, but a fair number bought at least a small item. Three even vouchsafed the opinion that a department solely for ladies' sportswear was a good idea. Amelie hoped fervently that they would tell their friends about it. As her grandfather often said, advertising was good, but word of mouth was better.

As ill luck would have it, Edward turned up again just when the department was empty of customers. Even more unfortunate, the rest of the ladies' clothing departments were buzzing with women who seemed to be buying as if for a siege. It was nearly midday. Another hour, and everyone who was anyone would be changing for luncheon.

'Never mind, Mel. It often takes a while for a department to establish itself,' he said, patting her kindly on the shoulder. Amelie could have bitten him.

'We have been really busy. We've sold heaps of stuff,' she exaggerated.

'Yes, of course you have,' Edward said, glancing round at the shopgirls, who were once again needlessly tidying shelves and drawers.

For one awful moment, Amelie thought he was going to suggest that some of them might be better employed in another department.

'We're just having a little lull at the moment. We've been rushed off our feet up till now,' she told him.

'Of course you have,' Edward repeated. 'Now, I do hope you're not doing too much, Mel. We all know how much effort you have put into setting up the department. It doesn't mean that you have to be here all the time, you know. Miss Higgs and her girls will run it for you.'

'But I like being here!' Amelie said.

Edward ignored this. 'I'm sure that when Grandfather took up your idea, he did not mean you to act as a glorified floorwalker, supervising everything that was going on for every minute of the day.'

'But I'm not –' Amelie began, then stopped, for out of the corner of her eye she saw movement in the archway.

She turned to look properly and saw two of her old schoolfriends with one of their mothers in tow. Smiling broadly, she went to greet them.

'Here we are, Melly. So this is your shop? It's simply sweet!'

'Yes, awfully jolly. I do like the way you've done the entrance. So clever. Isn't she clever, Mother?'

They had hardly got over their first transports before more young ladies arrived, ones whom Amelie had met in the course of the social round her mother had taken her on when she would much rather have been buying stock. When her mother was not listening, she had told all of them about her venture and invited them to the opening day. Now it looked as if they were taking up the suggestion. She stole a look at Edward as she went about greeting the new arrivals. Now he would see what a success her idea was.

Before long, the department began to resemble a party. The ladies stood around chatting to each other, Amelie circulated and the shopgirls ran about serving those who decided they might actually make a purchase. Once one or two had stock laid out for them to look at, then others became interested. Soon they were encouraging each other.

'Will you look at this sweet boater –'

'My dear, it's just you. You must have it.'

'Have you seen these clever tennis blouses? You play tennis, don't you? They're such a good idea.'

'Didn't I hear you saying the other day that you needed a motoring coat?'

And then, in the midst of the crush, there was her mother. Smiling serenely, she wove her way round the groups of women, speaking to everyone. Amelie could not understand it. Her mother had been utterly against her project from the start, so what was she doing here now? Then she came within Amelie's earshot, and it became perfectly clear what she was doing.

'So kind of you to come to Amelie's little gathering. Yes, I'm as surprised as you. You never know what these girls are going to get up to next, do you? No, I know, in our day we did not have opinions of our own, did we? We took advice from our elders. But these modern girls are all so busy. Of course, dear Amelie has always been such an active girl, she likes to have her little hobbies. Oh no, she doesn't *run* the department. Dear me no, you didn't think I would let her *work* here? The idea! No, it's a nice interest for her. Far preferable to joining those dreadful suffragettes, don't you think?'

Winifred was indefatigable. As long as there were any of her social acquaintances in the department, she was there, talking to them, giving them to understand that her daughter was merely amusing herself playing at shops, that it was no more real Trade than setting up a charity bazaar. Only when the last ladies had trailed off to luncheon did she turn her attention to Amelie.

Even then she did not speak to her directly. Instead she told one of the girls to fetch Miss Amberley's hat.

'But, Mother –' Amelie started.

'But nothing. You are coming home with me this minute.'

Edward appeared, a concerned smile on his face.

'Yes, off you go, Amelie. It's been a long morning for you. I'll see to everything here, don't you worry.'

Winifred rounded on him. 'Things should never have been allowed to get this far. I should have been informed.'

'If you remember, Mother, I did inform you. It was Grandfather who encouraged this foolishness.'

'Foolishness!' Amelie cried. 'I –'

'Quiet!' her mother hissed, with such force that Amelie found herself obeying.

Winifred was addressing Edward. 'Yes, your grandfather. I shall be speaking with him at the earliest opportunity.'

Amelie's big day was crumbling around her. She found herself marched out to where the motor was waiting at one of the side entrances. Once inside, she tried to protest.

'I hope you're satisfied now, Mother. You've made me look a complete idiot in front of my staff.'

Try as she might, she could not quite keep the squeak of tears out of her voice. Furious, she brushed her sleeve across her eyes.

Winifred did not look at her. Her voice, by contrast, was icily controlled.

'They are not your staff, Amelie, they are your grandfather's staff. And as for what I have done, I have saved you from social disgrace. I suppose I cannot hope for you to be grateful right at this very moment, but believe me, in time you will be. As for this shop nonsense, I trust that you have now got it out of your system.'

9

Isobel tidied away a pile of motoring caps, veils, goggles and gloves. Another fruitless half-hour. Once again, it was brought home to her that she was not very good at her job. She glanced at Miss Higgs, hoping that she had not noticed. A vain hope, of course, since Miss Higgs knew everything that was going on in the department. She was just completing a sale, but even so, she was sure to be aware of Isobel's lack of success. Daisy would not have let that last customer go without at least selling her a pair of gloves, if not a whole motoring outfit. She could hear her now, extolling the virtues of a gymslip of a particularly ugly shade of brown.

'It's really the only thing to wear for proper exercise, madam. I know some ladies do wear long skirts for cricket, but for someone like you what's a *serious* player – yes, it's ever so respectable and ladylike, madam. You don't have to wear it knee-length like what schoolgirls do, you can have it right down to your calves – would you like to try it on? I'll find you a pretty blouse to go underneath, so's you get the effect – how about this one? The changing rooms are over here, madam. Do you need any help?'

That one would not get away empty-handed, either, Isobel decided. Daisy was by far the best saleswoman in the team, Miss Higgs excepted. Isobel hated pressing people who seemed not to want what the department had to offer. It went against all her early training, the rules of polite behaviour drummed into her by her mother. But Daisy had no such problems. If a lady did not like one thing, Daisy was quick to offer an alternative. Not only that, but she was so enthusiastic about the stock. Her genuine delight in the quality, colour, shape or sheer brand-newness of even the most utilitarian pair of cycling knickers communicated itself to her customers. Once Daisy was in full flow, she was irresistible.

Dear Daisy. What would Isobel have done without her these

last few weeks? A girl whom her dear mama would probably not have considered employing as a tweeny had become her closest friend and support. Isobel was fascinated and horrified by the glimpses Daisy gave of her home life, of shared beds and second-hand clothes and weeks of cold and hunger. No wonder that the hostel that Isobel found Spartan seemed like a palace to Daisy. It had taken her a month to get over the wonder of the flush lavatories. With Daisy's help, Isobel found her present life bearable. She was permanently tired, often bored, frequently frustrated by the pettiness of the customers and Miss Higgs, but the rules and routines of the store and the hostel gave a point and a pattern to her life, giving her security. As long as she did not look forwards or backwards, she was all right. Or would have been, if it were not for those two dreadful young men.

They had been at the front door of number twenty-four Trent Street this morning. They tried to give the impression that they had just happened to be passing, but Isobel suspected they had been hanging about waiting for Daisy and herself to come out.

"Morning, girls! Well, here's a nice surprise. Going our way?' Arthur Griggs had cried.

'Oo, hark at him! Going our way, indeed. As if he don't know,' Daisy responded, echoing Isobel's thoughts. Except that Daisy made it sound teasing.

The weeks of solid food had worked a change in Daisy. Her face had lost its pinched look and started to acquire a fashionable roundness. Now, flushed and excited, she looked almost pretty. Arthur Griggs gave one of the cheery grins that Isobel found so grating.

'Mind if we walk along of you, then?'

Daisy stuck her nose in the air with mock disdain. 'Don't see as we can stop you.'

While this exchange was going on, Isobel was studiously ignoring Johnny Miller. This ought to have been signal enough that she did not wish to speak with him. After all, it was up to the lady to show that she wished to acknowledge an acquaintance. But Johnny Miller was not a gentleman. He took a step closer to her.

'Good morning, Miss Brand. Keeping well, are you?'

Of the two, he was the better. He was not so brash, and he took off his hat when he spoke to her. But still Isobel did not like being forced into conversation with him.

'Yes, thank you,' she said, not meeting his eyes. She edged away from him, and nearer to Daisy.

'. . . stand here bandying words with you. We got to get to work,' Daisy was saying.

To Isobel's relief, Daisy grabbed her arm and started walking up the street. The pavement was crowded with Packards employees, all going the same way, all in a hurry, all shouting out greetings to each other as they met. More flooded out of each door as they went along. But the crowd did not save them from Arthur and Johnny. They stayed doggedly close, dodging round trees and people in order to keep up the lop-sided conversation.

'How's it going in Ladies' Sportswear, then? Enjoying it?' Johnny asked. He addressed the question to Isobel, but Daisy answered.

'Oh, it's lovely. We're doing ever so well. Miss Packard, she's ever so pleased with us. When she comes in, that is. Her mum, she don't want her in the shop, but Miss Packard comes anyway. Right card, she is.'

'Chip off of the old block, she is, then. Old Mr Packard, he's all right, and all. If he's pleased, he comes and tells you himself,' Johnny said.

'Knows most of the names, he does. Amazing, it is, when you think how many people work at the store,' Arthur said. 'I was putting some stuff out the other day when he come round and he looks straight at me and he says, "Untidy shelf, there, Griggs. See to it." You could of knocked me down with a feather, you could. I jumped to it good and proper, I can tell you.'

'Has Mr Packard spoken to you?' Johnny asked Isobel.

'No, never,' she said.

Old Mr Packard seemed a pleasant man, from what she had seen of him, and very fond of his granddaughter. Mr Edward Packard was a different matter. She had disliked him on sight, feeling obscurely threatened by him.

'I'll bet he's noticed you, though. Pretty girl like you.'

Isobel flushed and looked away. There was only one thing to

be done, and that was to ignore him, and to thank God that it was not very far to the store. Daisy had been unaccountably cool with her when they arrived.

Now, Isobel looked to where Daisy's customer was emerging from the changing rooms, a little red about the cheeks, but looking pleased.

'Yes, it looks very nice. Very workmanlike,' she was saying. 'I'll have the blouse as well.'

'Certainly, madam. And how about a nice new boater to complete the outfit? We have a number of ladies' models –'

Just as Isobel predicted, the sales mounted. By the time the customer left, there was a generous pile of goods lying on the counter ready to be packed and delivered. Daisy earned a nod of approval from Miss Higgs and a summons to serve the next customer. Isobel was directed to wrap and label the last one's purchases. Isobel did as she was bid. At least she knew she could make a good job of that.

The pair of them were sent off to early dinner. Daisy was not her usual chatty self. In fact, Isobel got the distinct impression that she was cross with her about something. She could not for the life of her think what. There was none of the coveted seats by the barrier available, to Isobel's relief, so Daisy plumped down in the first they came to and began eating in sulky silence. Isobel tried to make allowances. Perhaps she was tired. Perhaps it was her monthlies. Whatever it was, she couldn't have it out with her here, in public. It would have to wait until the end of the day. In the meantime, one of the other girls on the table started a conversation, which Daisy joined in with alacrity. Isobel poked at her food. The monotony of the menu and the stodginess of the cooking depressed her. She ate a few mouthfuls, but did not feel hungry. Unlike Daisy, she had lost weight since she came to Packards.

'. . . she sent me down the stockroom, and I skipped off round by Turnery and there he was,' the other girl's story went on and on, every detail of conversation retold. Isobel glanced at Daisy. She was not looking happy. By the time they were ploughing their way through the pudding, Daisy had obviously had enough.

'So what happened?' she asked, interrupting the flow.

'Well – he asked me if me and my pal'd like to go walking with him and his mate on Sunday!' The other girl gave a self-satisfied smile and patted her hair, then affected an air of patronising kindness.

'Yours asked you out yet, has he?'

'Lots of times,' Daisy said.

Isobel wondered what on earth she was talking about.

'What's the matter, don't you fancy him?'

'I ain't throwing myself at him, if that's what you mean.'

'You saying I am, then?'

Daisy shrugged. 'If the cap fits . . .'

'You little cow!'

The other girl pushed her chair back and stood up. She glared down at Daisy, then addressed the rest of the table.

'You hear what she said to me? She said –'

'Oh shut up,' someone else said.

'No, you shut up. She's got a cheek, she has. Just because she works in Miss Packard's department, she thinks she's one up on us.'

'Yeah, stuck-up lot, acting all la-di-da –'

Isobel was terrified. There was real venom in the faces around them. She tried to catch Daisy's attention.

'Er – Daisy – I think we had better leave now. We only have five minutes –'

'Eoh yes, Ai think we had better leave now,' one of the girls said, savagely mimicking her accent.

'Hark at her! Lady Muck with her little tennis bat badge.'

'What's the matter, your ladyship, ain't we good enough for you?'

Isobel stood up. She was shaking so much she could hardly pick up her plates. She tottered from the canteen and stopped outside, leaning on the green-painted wall for support. To her surprise, she found Daisy right behind her.

'Those dreadful girls –' she said.

Daisy rounded on her, hot-eyed. 'It's all your fault.'

'Mine? But –'

'Yes, yours! Don't act all Miss Innocent with me. Leading them on.'

Isobel was bewildered. 'Leading who on? Those girls? I didn't say a word –'

'Not them, stupid! Johnny –'

'Oh –' Light began to dawn. 'Is it those young men? Is that the trouble? But, Daisy, I have hardly spoken a word to them. I don't speak to them at all unless I'm actually forced to.'

'That's what I mean!' Daisy cried. 'Giving them the cold shoulder like that. Leading them on. Don't tell me you don't know what you're doing.'

'But – but I –'

Isobel felt sick. That was what *he* had said, her brother-in-law. That she had led him on.

'Daisy, I – that was the last thing I wanted to do. I hate it when they hang round us. This morning, when they were there at the door, I was horrified. You must have noticed that.'

Daisy's lower lip trembled. 'I tell you what I noticed, mate. I noticed Johnny hanging on every word what you let him drag from you. I noticed the way what he looked at you. That's what.'

The fear clutched at Isobel with sharp talons.

'What do you mean, looking at me?'

But she knew. She knew what it meant, too. It started with looks and smiles and compliments and it ended with them tearing at you. The nightmare closed in on her, the fear and the guilt. *Your fault – your fault – you led me on* – She doubled over, arms hugging her body in feeble defence.

'Stop it,' she wailed. 'Stop it. Please –'

An arm touched her shoulder. She flinched and gasped. He was trying to get her.

'No – no –'

Then Daisy's voice came through to her, sharp with anxiety. 'Isobel, what's the matter?'

The pounding in her head receded. She was in a corridor. There were people coming past them. Some of them stopped.

'What's up? She all right?'

'She's poorly,' Daisy's voice told them. 'She'll be all right in a minute. Come on, Izzy, come out of the way. That's it.'

It was cooler. There was an echoing space round her and the smell of humanity had gone. Isobel took a shuddering breath, the fear subsiding. She realised she was out on one of the service stairways. Daisy's face swam into view, pale with concern.

'What is it, Izzy? What happened?'

But she couldn't explain. Not even to Daisy.

'Nothing. I felt – faint. That's all. Faint. I'm all right now.'

'You sure? You look awful.'

'I'm all right,' Isobel repeated, though nothing could be further from the truth.

'Look – was it something I said?' Daisy asked.

'No, no, nothing.' She did not want to talk about it. She had managed to keep it bottled up inside her so far and inside was where it was going to stay. It was safer there. She could contain it. And nobody would know her shame. She took a shuddering breath, tried to make her voice sound normal.

'I think – hadn't we better get back? We'll be late.'

'If you're sure . . .' Daisy said reluctantly.

The department suddenly seemed like a haven of security. There was no danger of Johnny Miller appearing. He would be confined to Carpets. The only men who came in were those accompanying their womenfolk and they were safe on the other side of the counter. You didn't even have to look at them.

'I'm sure,' she said.

The afternoon stretched out in front of her, hours of standing and smiling and being obliging. Isobel went through the motions, producing stock, taking money, putting up with indecision and time-wasting and rudeness.

Miss Packard swept in with her other brother in tow, the one who looked like her. The whole atmosphere of the department changed, became charged with excitement. She looked into every corner, questioned Miss Higgs at length, then spoke to each of the shopgirls. Isobel answered as best she could.

'Oh, it's so frustrating, not being able to be here with you all,' Miss Packard complained. 'Here you are, doing so well, and I'm forced to go to beastly dress fittings. I only escaped here today because Perry's supposed to be in charge of me. Now, Miss Higgs, I must tell you about the summer lines I've ordered. My dear brother here is going to take me out to the factories this afternoon, so that I can see for myself exactly what they are doing. They have promised me some simply charming bathing dresses, so once the holiday season is upon us, we must make a display of them. And then there is the yachting wear as well. I thought we could have seaside things in the archway and the walls – lifebelts and nets and that sort of thing –'

Isobel found herself envying Miss Packard. Not her wealth or her position, but her enthusiasm and confidence. Miss Packard was not afraid of life. She watched her as she talked and moved about the department, then realised she was staring and looked away, only to find her eyes meeting those of Miss Packard's brother. She blushed and looked away again. Men. There were men everywhere. There was no getting away from them. But at least this one was a gentleman. He did not try to speak to her when he had not been introduced. For that she had to be grateful.

Dot sidled up to her after the Packards had gone.

'Don't often see Mr Perry Packard in here, do we? Handsome, ain't he? Most of the girls prefer Mr Edward. They like 'em tall and dark. But me, I like Mr Perry. He's more sort of gentle.'

Isobel didn't have a preference for either of them. All she asked was that they leave her alone. But an answer seemed to be expected of her, so she said, 'Yes.'

'He was giving you the eye, wasn't he?'

Isobel shuddered. Not again, please. She couldn't stand it.

'I sincerely hope not,' she said.

'Oo, you are a funny one! If he gave me the eye, I'd be pleased as Punch. He'd give you a real good time, I bet. Nights out, presents, everything.'

To Isobel's infinite relief, Miss Higgs intervened.

'No gossiping. You should know that by now. Miss Brand, those drawers need tidying.'

Isobel diligently folded, stacked and lined up the offending merchandise, grateful for the mindlessness of the occupation. By the time she had finished, she felt a little calmer, and just about able to attend to the customer that Miss Higgs directed her to serve. The lady concerned kept her busy fetching this and showing that, dithered over the choice of divided skirts, declined to try any on and in the end went out without buying anything. Isobel had just finished putting all the things she had asked for away again when a movement just the other side of the archway caught her eye.

She looked, and went cold. It couldn't be. She was seeing things. It was a result of having that turn at dinner time. Her heart hammering in her chest, she looked again at the man now standing on the threshold of the department. A sick certainty crawled over her. Everything about him was horribly familiar, from the shape of his head to the way he planted his feet. It was him, and he had come looking for her. She flung herself to the floor and huddled as close to the counter as she could get.

Feet stopped beside her.

'Whatever's the matter?' Daisy's voice hissed down.

Isobel pressed against her. Daisy would save her. Daisy was brave.

'Don't let him see me.'

'Who? Don't let who see you?'

Oh God, if he saw Daisy talking to her, he would come over.

'Don't say anything. Pretend I'm not here.'

She squeezed her eyes shut, put her arms over her head, willing him to go away. But she knew that he wouldn't. He was stronger than her. She'd been a fool to think she could escape from him.

Miss Higgs's voice broke in, strident with irritation. 'Where is Miss Brand?'

'She – she's picking some things up, Miss Higgs.'

'From the floor? How very clumsy. Well, help her. Don't just stand there.'

Daisy's arm was about Isobel's shoulders, her voice close to her ear.

'Izzy, what's up? You been acting like you're off of your head. What are you afraid of?'

Isobel tried to explain, but couldn't. 'There – there's a man –'

'For God's sake, Iz! What man?'

'Out there – by the archway.'

The department no longer felt like a haven. It had become a trap. The only way out was through the arch.

There was a movement as Daisy straightened up, then bent down again.

'Iz, there ain't no men in the department at all. There's two young ladies buying bicycling skirts, a mother and daughter looking at the motoring hats and an older lady asking for golfing jackets, and Miss Higgs is looking this way and if you don't get up right now there's going to be big trouble.'

Isobel did not move. Miss Higgs was nothing to the terror that clawed at her.

'I can't.'

'What *is* going on here?'

Daisy leapt to defend her. 'Oh Miss Higgs, Miss Brand ain't feeling well. Faint. Yes – she feels faint. It's her monthlies, you see.'

Miss Higgs tutted with impatience. 'If she's not well, she had better go home. This is a shop, not a sickroom.'

Home! That would mean leaving the store. By herself. And *he* was out there somewhere waiting for her. Isobel got to her feet. She felt sick and clammy. But Daisy was right – he was not in the department. She clutched at the counter, trembling.

'I – I think I'll be all right, Miss Higgs.'

The senior saleswoman eyed her with suspicion. 'Are you sure? I can't have you fainting in front of customers. It gives a very bad impression.'

'I won't, I promise.'

The rest of the afternoon passed in a haze of fear. Isobel could not concentrate on anything. She dropped things, failed to hear what was said to her, forgot what she was supposed to be doing. Her eyes were continually straying to the archway, watching each new person that entered. But he did not come back. She began to wonder if she really had seen him. Perhaps it was just her imagination. She desperately hoped so.

10

'Really, Mel, this place is appalling,' Perry complained. 'The smell!'

He took out a large linen handkerchief and held it to his nose.

Amelie was rather inclined to agree with him. The smell coming in through the motor car windows was horrible. Their surroundings were horrible too – filthy tenement buildings crowded both sides of the narrow street. Hawkers cried their wares in raucous voices and ragged children played in the gutters. Pale men and women with hopeless eyes stared at them from doorways. Amelie suppressed a shudder. A world away in Mayfair, spring was filling squares and parks and gardens with colour and scent. Trees were in blossom, tulips and wallflowers bright in the flowerbeds. Here the sunshine seemed only to emphasise the poverty and dirt.

'Cheer up, Perry, it will make you all the more grateful for your dinner tonight.'

'I still don't see why you had to come here in person. Surely you could have telephoned?'

'Telephoned? Perry, they've hardly heard of the telephone in this part of the world.'

'You could have written, then. Or asked the man to come and see you.'

'I've no office in which to receive him, Perry. I can't just speak to him in the middle of the department.'

'There's going to be no end of a song and dance made of it if Mother finds out. We're supposed to be making calls,' Perry pointed out.

'I know, but you don't want to do that, do you? It's so utterly boring.'

'I don't think coming to the East End is particularly amusing.'

'Nonsense, you'll be able to make no end of funny stories out of it for your friends. I'm sure they don't even know where it is.'

'I'm not sure that I want to,' Perry said.

'Well, I'm very grateful to you for coming with me, Brother dear. I'll make it up to you one day, I promise.'

They had to stop to ask the way several times, attracting knots of onlookers, most of them fascinated, but some openly resentful of such a display of wealth.

'They'd better not touch my motor,' Perry said, glaring at the filthy hands stretching out towards the shiny metalwork.

At last they arrived outside a three-storey building of blackened brick. Perry then had to decide whether to do the right thing and go in with his sister to protect her against whatever dangers might await her, or stay outside and guard his beautiful motor car.

'Oh for heaven's sake, stay with your toy, do,' Amelie told him. 'I shall be perfectly all right.'

Perry glanced up at the small sign above the door, 'Y. Baum & Sons, Clothing Manufacturers', then at the grubby children that were already gathering in a circle round them.

'Very well, then,' he agreed. His lovely yellow Renault was not brand-new, but he had only bought it two weeks ago from a friend who was in financial difficulties, and he loved it like a baby.

Amelie pushed open the door and was confronted with a steep flight of bare wooden stairs. A smell hung over the place that she couldn't identify, and there was the sound of voices and a continual heavy rumbling that got louder as she went upwards. At the top of the stairs was a landing crowded with packing cases, and two doors with windows in them. One led to an office, in which two men were conferring, the other to the factory floor. Amelie stared through this second window, fascinated. The rumbling came from the rows of sewing machines which were packed so close together that the young boys carrying pieces of half-completed work from one part of the room to another could hardly squeeze between them. Pale, tired-looking women and girls were bent over the machines, guiding the fabric under the stabbing needles while under the tables their legs treadled away, powering the whirring wheels. The ones nearest the small windows could work by daylight, but further away they peered at the racing seams by the smeary glare of gaslamps. As she watched, a thickset man in his shirtsleeves picked up a piece that one girl had just finished, inspected it and began shouting and brandishing it under her nose. The girl at first looked frightened, then argued back, but Amelie could not make out what they were saying above the racket from the machines.

'Can I help you?'

Startled, Amelie turned round. She had been so engrossed in watching the drama unfolding that she had lost sight of what she had come for. A dark young man stood before her, dressed in a well-cut jacket and trousers, but with the exotic addition of a skull cap set at the back of his head. He was looking at her with just as much interest as she was looking at his factory.

'Oh – yes – I am Miss Packard. I have come to speak to Mr Baum.'

Now it was his turn to look startled. 'Miss Packard? *The* Miss Packard? From Packards' store?'

'Yes. I wanted to see to the order for bathing dresses personally.'

'This is a great honour, Miss Packard. I am Nathan Baum. Come into the office, please, and meet my father.'

He ushered her into a small room crowded with desk, shelves, filing cabinets, a big new typewriter and piles of samples. He spoke rapidly in a language that sounded something like German but wasn't, to a small middle-aged man with long greying hair falling in thin curls on either side of his face, then introduced him to Amelie as his father, Yitzak Baum.

'You are very welcome, Miss Packard. Please to sit down,' the older Mr Baum said. His thick accent was a surprise after his son's pure cockney.

Amelie was offered tea, which was brought by a pretty dark girl about her own age. The two Baums consulted rapidly in the Germanic language again, for which Nathan apologised, telling her that his father's English was not very good. He then explained that they were especially surprised to see her as they had thought that the order had been cancelled. Amelie could not understand it.

'It's certainly nothing of my doing,' she said. 'Do you have the letter?'

Nathan produced an invoice, stamped across in red with 'Packards: Cancelled'.

'We received this yesterday. We were about to enquire into it.'

'That's very odd indeed. I shall look into it myself,' Amelie said. 'But it is most clearly a mistake. I was very pleased with your samples, but I have some ideas on how to make them even better. Now –'

She outlined her ideas for bathing dresses that were lighter and easier to move in but still preserved a woman's modesty. The Baums produced fabric samples and the girl, who turned out to be Nathan's sister, was called back again to sketch variations on the original design. When they had decided on the exact lines of collars and sleeves and skirts, the details of trim had to be agreed. Braids and buttons were laid out for Amelie to look at. Colour and quality was debated in two languages. Three designs with variations of colour and trim were finally decided upon. Then came the question of cost. The chief cutter, an uncle, was called in, and rapid calculations were made.

'Now, you understand that this is only a rough estimate,' Nathan said, then named a price that took Amelie's breath away.

'That's nearly twice as much as your other samples,' she objected.

'Ah, but these are top quality, and we shall be making them exclusively for Packards,' Nathan pointed out.

'That's as maybe, but even rich ladies aren't going to pay that much for something they won't actually be seen in. They walk straight down the bathing machine steps and into the sea,' Amelie said. She tried not to look too regretfully at the designs. They really were wonderful, and she was sure she could sell them, but not at that price.

Then she realised that this was all part of the game. The Baums were just trying her out. The bargaining began.

Amelie finally emerged from the building exhausted but elated. Nathan escorted her down to the motor and shook hands.

'It has been a great pleasure to do business, Miss Packard.'

'Thank you, Mr Baum. I think I can say the same. Now

remember, only take any notice of letters or orders that have my own signature on them.'

'Right you are.'

He handed her in beside a furiously impatient Perry, and obligingly swung the starter handle of the Renault.

As they chugged off down the street, Perry complained even more vociferously than on the way out.

'What have you been doing in there, Mel? You've been two hours! I was never so bored in my life. We're sure to be late now. God knows what Mother's going to say.'

Amelie hardly listened, and laughed off what she did hear. What did it matter what Mother said? She had had a very successful afternoon.

It gave her strength to face the rest of the day. The Season was now getting under way, and days were filling with a round of entertainment that required constant changes of clothes, all of them highly corseted and uncomfortable, a great deal of waiting about and the making of polite but meaningless conversation to people whom Amelie mostly found extremely uninteresting. That evening, they were due to go to a dinner, then on to a dance.

Winifred, fortunately, did not get in till six. She looked in on Amelie to make sure she was resting before the rigours of the evening and to inspect her choice of dress, which met with her approval.

'Did you make all your calls?' she asked

'Perry squired me around very ably,' Amelie evaded, crossing her fingers.

Winifred nodded. She was in a good humour, having been introduced to an aristocratic lady of the old school with whom she had longed to be on calling terms.

'Very good. Now remember to be ready by half-past seven. You must start getting changed at least an hour beforehand.'

'Yes, Mama.'

Amelie breathed a sigh of relief and submitted to the lengthy process of preparing for public display. Her mother's maid came in and dressed her hair in elaborate rolls and curls, pinning it up over pads to get the required shape. Then everything she had worn during the day from stockings outwards had to be changed. Layers of underwear went on, followed by a raspberry pink crepe-de-Chine dinner dress trimmed with falls of cream-coloured lace. Shoes, elbow-length gloves, jewellery, flowers, hair ornaments and a fan then had to be chosen, but of course not a breath of makeup. Pale girls had to resort to a quick biting of the lips and pinching of the cheeks to raise a little colour before entering a room.

Her mother looked her over critically when she entered the drawing room.

'Mmm. You will pass,' she said. 'I wasn't sure about that colour on you, but I think you can get away with it.'

Her father smiled approvingly. 'Very pretty, my dear. Very pretty indeed.'

A short carriage ride brought them to the house of the Wyatts, a family whom Winifred had been cultivating for some time. Sixteen people assembled in the drawing room and made desultory conversation. Amelie found herself in a group with one of the Misses Wyatt and a young married lady, neither of whom was interested in anything other than clothes.

'Do either of you bathe?' Amelie asked, her afternoon's business still fresh in her mind.

'I've tried it, but I was rather frightened. One's clothes seem to pull one under the water, and it does sting the eyes so,' the married lady complained.

'Ah well, you need one of my new bathing dresses,' Amelie told her, and began to describe them in detail.

She had almost succeeded in convincing them that they both needed one when the butler announced that dinner was served. The son of the house paraded up to Amelie to take her in to dinner. Amelie looked at his pudgy face and pompous expression and wished that it was Nathan Baum who was offering her his arm. Nathan, she was sure, would make an amusing dinner companion, whereas Herbert Wyatt had nothing of interest to say at all. She smiled to herself as she went down the stairs to the dining room, thinking of what her mother would say if she were to be escorted into dinner by an East End clothing manufacturer, and a Jewish immigrant to boot.

The dinner was everything that was expected of such an

occasion. A choice of two soups was followed by two fish, three entrées, two removes, three sorts of game, five sweets, two ices and four types of fruit. Herbert Wyatt turned out to be obsessed with fishing and polo, which he could, and did, talk about at length. Polo he did not play, but watched with a devotion that enabled him to remember shots from matches three years in the past. Amelie felt her eyes glazing over like those of the many fish he described to her. It was with relief that she turned to the gentleman on her other side, a short man called Orton, of indeterminate age and intense gaze.

'Tell me, Miss Amberley, are you aware of the theory of eugenics?' he asked her.

Amelie's heart sank. She seemed to be doomed to an evening of fanatics.

'No,' she said, 'but I have a feeling that I soon shall be.'

This rolled right off his back.

'It's a very serious matter, one that concerns each and every one of us. The very future of our great British race is at stake.'

'Indeed?' Amelie said, hesitating between curried eggs, mushrooms and sweetbreads, and vol-au-vent à la financière.

'Oh yes. Did you know that of all the recruits presenting themselves for our armed forces, nearly half of them have to be rejected because of their poor physique?'

'Really?' She decided on the vol-au-vent, but only had a very tiny helping, as her corset was digging cruelly into her.

'The poor are becoming degenerate, you see. Just think of the feats performed by the British private soldier, and even the British workman in the past. Waterloo, Balaclava, our great bridges and our railways. None of that could be achieved today by the specimens you see about you.'

Amelie thought of the people she had seen that very afternoon, the tired women bending over the sewing machines, the ragged children in the street.

'Could that be because they don't have enough to eat, or enough of the right food to eat?'

'No, no, you are quite mistaken. A common misconception, but wrong nevertheless.' Mr Orton took a generous portion of curried eggs. 'It's a question of selective breeding, you see. You are acquainted with the work of Mr Charles Darwin?'

'Of course,' Amelie said, not wanting to have the theory of natural selection explained to her.

'Then you will understand how it happens. The very poorest and most degenerate people gravitate towards each other, and because they have not the same control over their animal instincts as the better type of person, then they breed the most, and produce copius offspring feeble in both mind and body. The process therefore perpetuates itself. How many brothers and sisters do you have, Miss Amberley?'

'Ah – two brothers,' Amelie said, momentarily floored by so ordinary a question after all the theorising.

'There, that proves my point entirely. And if I were to ask a similar question of the rest of the guests round this table, no doubt I would elicit a similar answer from each of them. We, the superior people, produce superior offspring. I have not the honour of acquaintance with your brothers, but I have no doubt they are as handsome and intelligent as I might be so bold as to say that you are, Miss Amberley. But there are only three of you. We are dying out, Miss Amberley, dying out. If we don't do something about it soon, the country will be overrun by the degenerate poor and this great nation of ours will fall from its natural position of pre-eminence.'

'Dear me, that sounds rather dramatic,' Amelie said, trying not to laugh.

Orton failed to notice her scepticism. 'The case cannot be overstated. Luckily, a group of us are now aware of the situation and are working to stem the tide. We have recently made a most useful recruit, as fine an example of young British manhood as could be found, a Mr Rutherford. Are you acquainted with him?'

'Er, no, I don't think so.'

'Splendid young man, splendid. Just the type we need. I hope we shall attract many others. And young women as well, of course. Most necessary. Would you be interested in joining our group, Miss Amberley?'

For once, Amelie was glad of her mother's tight restrictions. 'I don't think that would be at all possible, Mr Orton. My mother would never allow it.'

'Pity, great pity,' Orton sighed, and turned back to his partner.

It was almost a relief to listen to Herbert Wyatt again.

She was finally released from the dinner party at just gone eleven, but the evening was not yet over. During the short drive home Amelie was grilled by her mother about Herbert Wyatt and annoyed her by saying roundly how boring he was, and then it was up to her room for another change, for of course however rich and impressive a dinner dress might be, it was not a ballgown. Resplendent now in peach organdie over cream silk, with a fresh corsage of flowers. Amelie set out again for another house and a dance.

The first few dances she had been to, Amelie had looked forward to, for she loved dancing. But the general run of Mayfair houses, however impressive, were simply not big enough. So many guests were always invited that there was hardly any space left on the floor for couples to do anything more than shuffle about together. And then there was always the problem of there being more women than men attending, made worse by the fact that many of the younger men made no effort at all to dance, but just stood and talked and ate and drank while running an eye over the many disgruntled girls sitting down with their chaperons. This dance proved to be no better than any of the rest. Amelie danced just once in three hours and had to wait for ages for a supper that she did not really want. She complained about it to an old schoolfriend over the supper table.

'I do agree with you, but my sister says they're not all like this,' the friend assured her. 'Apparently, if you go to one of the great houses with a real ballroom, it's utterly deevy. A proper orchestra instead of a three-piece band, a sprung floor and lots of space.'

'But do the young men dance?' Amelie asked. Now that really would be divine.

Her friend laughed. 'Well enough not to tread on your feet. What's the matter, Melly, aren't you enjoying your Season?'

'Not a bit. At least – I like going to the theatre, and riding in the park, and I expect I should enjoy a ball in a great house should I be invited to one. But apart from that, it's all so boring, and so pointless.'

'Oh Mel! For someone who was so clever at school, you can be very stupid. Of course it isn't pointless. The point is to meet suitable young men and get married. You do want to get married, don't you?'

'Well, yes –' Amelie conceded, 'but not yet. And not to the sort of men I've met so far. When I do get married, it's got to be to somebody who'll let me carry on with my work at the store.'

'You and your store! I rather think you're asking for the impossible. How is this department of yours going ahead, anyway?'

Amelie told her, leaving out such worrying details as water pipes that burst all over the walls and orders that got mysteriously cancelled.

'It all sounds quite delightful. I must come in and buy a new tennis racquet. Mine is good for nothing and Mama has promised to give a tennis party once the weather improves.'

'Do. I'll show you our range of tennis blouses as well. In fact I'll give you one if you'll promise to invite me to the party.'

'I'm not sure whether I shall accept the bribe, Mel. You're sure to win every match.'

It was the only conversation she found at all amusing during the whole evening. Amelie finally flopped into bed at three o'clock, wishing that instead of setting off on another round of social events the next day she could go to the store and make sure that none of her other orders had been cancelled.

11

'Are you certain there's nobody waiting outside?' Isobel asked.

Daisy stifled an impatient sigh. Isobel really was acting very oddly. Like there was someone about to strangle her or something.

'Look, the store's empty, ain't it? Last customers all went ages ago. There's only us lot left.'

'I know, I know, but would you just make sure, Daisy? Please.'

To keep her quiet, Daisy walked under the archway and took a good look round Ladies' Outerwear. The only people to be seen were Packards' employees hurrying out.

'It's all clear, I promise,' she assured Isobel.

Her friend consented to leave the department, but not without clutching at Daisy's arm. Daisy could feel her trembling.

'What is it?' she asked. 'Who is this bloke? Why are you afraid of him?'

'I can't tell you,' Isobel said.

They fetched their hats and jackets from the staff cloakrooms and joined the flood of shopmen and girls leaving the store. Isobel, usually the one who stayed aloof, pulled Daisy into the centre of a large knot of women. Daisy couldn't understand it.

'You're right funny about blokes, ain't you? You won't give Johnny or Arthur the time of day, and now you're scared of this one. What's he got on you? You owe him money or something?'

'No! No, nothing like that.'

'Here, you're not married to him, are you? Is that it? You run away from him?'

If that was the case, then Isobel did have problems. Married was married, there was no getting away from it. It would explain why she was so standoffish with Johnny and Arthur.

'Married? Oh no, he's –' Isobel stopped short.

'He's what?' Daisy prompted.

'Nothing.'

Daisy looked at her friend. Even now, white and drawn with this fear of hers, she was beautiful. Jealousy squeezed at her heart. It was so unfair. All the men noticed Isobel. Only this afternoon, Miss Packard's brother had been gazing at her. Not that Daisy envied her that, or any other man. It was Johnny. Johnny had taken her breath away the moment she saw him, but he had eyes only for Isobel.

'Wish I had 'em all after me like what you have,' she said.

Isobel shuddered. 'It's horrible. I hate it,' she said, with such depth of feeling that Daisy was silenced. Her friend was the oddest person she had ever met.

At the steps of number twenty-four, Daisy stopped to get out her latchkey. She was just about to insert it in the lock when she heard a gasp and a cry behind her.

'No!'

'Isobel,' a man's voice said. 'So it is you.'

Daisy spun round. Isobel was cowering against the railings, staring like a trapped animal at a man in a homburg hat. He didn't look very frightening. He was of medium height, in his mid-thirties, fresh-complexioned, neither handsome nor ugly. Judging by his clothes and accent, he was a gentleman. And he was speaking very kindly to Isobel.

'My dear girl, you cannot think how relieved I am to have found you. We have both been so worried about you. Your poor sister has been half out of her mind. To leave like that without even a note – but there must be no recriminations. I have found you, that is the only thing that matters. I have found you, and now you can come home to your family.'

Daisy thought he sounded very nice. There seemed to be real concern in his face. But when he put out a hand towards Isobel's arm, she flinched away with a stifled scream.

'Don't touch me!'

He held up both hands as if assuring her he was unarmed.

'All right, all right. You're evidently in a highly nervous state. No wonder, having to fend for yourself in a wicked city like this. But you're safe now, Isobel. I've come to take you home.'

But Isobel only shrunk further from him, her arms wrapped protectively across her chest.

'No,' she whispered. 'No, never.'

A hint of conscious patience crept into his voice. 'Come along now, Isobel, don't be foolish. Your place is with us, with your family. You can't stay here working as a common shopgirl, it's quite unthinkable. If you come now, we could be home before midnight.'

Still Isobel refused, shaking her head. 'Never. I will never go back.'

He changed tack. 'I know you are still suffering from your sad bereavement. Maybe the shock of it has unhinged you a little. But think of your sister. Poor Margery has endured such terrors on your behalf, wondering where you were, not knowing why you left, not even knowing whether you were dead or alive. If you could see the sorry state she is in, Isobel, you would not hesitate. She has not known a night's sleep since you left. She has grown so thin and pale you would hardly recognise her. And all because of you, Isobel. How can you be so cruel as to refuse to come back to her, to your own sister?'

Tears started in Isobel's eyes and spilled down her face. Daisy was compelled to step forward. She put an arm round Isobel's shoulders.

'If they're your family, Izzy – families ought to stick together, you know –'

Isobel started and clutched at her like a wild thing.

'No – I can't – you don't know – please don't make me –'

Nobody could be that scared without a reason. Daisy held her friend as she huddled her head against her, and abandoned her dawning sympathy for the man's cause. She faced him over Isobel's trembling shoulders.

'You heard her – she don't want to know.'

His whole attitude changed instantly. He gave a cold, dismissive look.

'I'll thank you to keep your opinions to yourself, miss.'

Daisy knew just what she was in his eyes. She simply did not count. She was just a working-class girl, there to shut up and do his bidding. Anger boiled inside her.

'I won't do nothing of the sort. Isobel's my mate. If she don't want to go with you, then she ain't going, see?'

Quite a crowd had gathered round them by now. There was a murmuring of agreement.

The man's mouth tightened in impatience. He ignored Daisy.

'It's time to stop playing these foolish games, Isobel. This is getting ridiculous. Come along at once.'

Isobel shook her head and huddled closer to Daisy. The man reached out and gripped her arm.

'I'm not waiting any longer, Isobel. Come now.'

Isobel cried out. Daisy tried to hit his hand aside.

'Get off!'

But he only held on harder, and began to pull Isobel away.

'Come now, Isobel, before I have to use force.'

Daisy held on to her friend with one arm and tried to fend him off with the other.

'Lay off, you great bully!' she screamed. 'Leave her be!'

Voices from the crowd began to join in.

'Yeah, let her be.'

'You got no right.'

Daisy picked this up. 'No, you got no right. You're not her old man. You can't tell her what to do.'

For the first time, he looked at her properly. There was loathing in his eyes.

'On the contrary, I have every right. I am her brother-in-law and responsible for her safety. Which includes taking her from the clutches of little sluts like you. Isobel, you will stop making a public spectacle of yourself and come with me now.'

The sympathy of the crowd swayed. Family was family, it was not for them to interfere. The man gripped Isobel's other arm and wrenched her away. Isobel screamed and Daisy launched herself at him, kicking and punching.

'Let her go! Let her go!'

At that moment, a familiar voice emerged out of the crowd.

'What's going on here?'

'Johnny!' Daisy yelled. 'Johnny, help!'

Two male shapes dived forward. A fist hit the man's face and as he lost his grip his arms were pinioned behind him. Isobel fell back into Daisy's arms, sobbing.

'It's all right,' Daisy said. 'It's all right, you're safe.'

Arthur and Johnny had Isobel's brother-in-law firmly held between them.

'Let me go, you fools. I'll have the law on to you.'

Johnny looked at Daisy. 'What d'you want us to do with him?'

'Get rid of him,' Daisy said. 'Isobel don't want nothing to do with him.'

'Right you are. Leave it to us,' Arthur said.

'You'll regret this!' their prisoner threatened. 'I'll have you both dismissed from your jobs.'

'I'm shaking in my boots,' Johnny said. 'Come on, mate. We're going for a little walk.'

The crowd parted with catcalls and whistles, happy now to see some of their own triumphing over the forces of authority. The man struggled to look back over his shoulder at Daisy and Isobel as they stood on the steps of number twenty-four.

'I won't leave it at this. I know where you are now. I'll be back.'

'You and whose army, mate?' Daisy yelled at him. 'Isobel's got friends now, and don't you forget it.'

To cheers and cries of agreement, she led Isobel into the safety of number twenty-four. It wasn't until the door was closed behind them and the rest of the girls, together with Mrs Drew the housekeeper, were gathered protectively round them that her legs began to shake.

'Blimey,' she said. 'That was a close call.'

The other girls wanted to know what it was all about, but Mrs Drew cut through their questions.

'Leave the poor thing alone. Come along, both of you, upstairs to your room. You'll be needing some peace and quiet.'

Daisy opened her mouth to protest. She was buzzing with excitement now, despite having the shakes. She wanted to go over it all, and hear the cries of horror and admiration. But then she realised that Isobel was near fainting with shock.

'Yeah, come on,' she agreed reluctantly, and helped her friend up the steep flights of stairs to their little attic room.

Still sobbing, Isobel collapsed on the bed and rolled into a defensive ball.

Mrs Drew shook her head. 'Poor thing. I never saw the like of it in my life before. You stay with her, and I'll bring some tea up for the both of you.' She raised her voice a little to carry to Isobel. 'Don't you worry, pet. If he shows his face at this door, I'll soon see him off.'

Isobel gave no sign of having heard. Mrs Drew looked at Daisy.

'Best get her into bed proper. I'll help you.'

Together, they undressed Isobel, unpinned her hair and got her into her nightgown and under the covers. As she promised, Mrs Drew then brought up a tray of bread and butter and tea, but no amount of coaxing from her or Daisy could get Isobel to sit up and take so much as a sip. Daisy, hungry now that the drama was past, wolfed down the lot. She tried to reassure Isobel, to tell her she was safe now and amongst friends, but she could not get a word out of her. Isobel lay with her face to the wall, silent but for the occasional sob.

Daisy could guess what the other girls would all be talking about as they sat round the big table in the basement. Isobel's assailant and the parts she and Johnny and Arthur had played in the affair would be the talk of Trent Street for weeks. Temptation pulled at her. It would be very sweet to go down now and be hailed as the heroine and questioned all about what had really happened, especially as some of the girls had been very snotty to her in the past. But she could not go and leave Isobel all by herself. She might not be talking, but she needed someone to watch over her.

In the quiet of the austere room, Daisy began to wonder just what it was that made Isobel so frightened of her brother-in-law. It didn't take too much deduction. Either he was knocking her about or he was trying to get his leg over. He might have nice clothes and a posh voice, but underneath it all, men were all the same.

'Nasty bit of work, that brother-in-law of yours,' she said, without really expecting a reply. 'Whatever made your sister marry him? I suppose she didn't know what he was really like. Don't get to know people proper do you, your sort, before you go and tie the knot? I bet he was all lovey-dovey until after it was done. No wonder you said you didn't have no family. But ain't there no one else you can go to?'

There was a faint stirring from Isobel's bed. Daisy looked hopefully at her, but she was only pulling the covers more firmly over her head.

'I suppose that means no,' she said. 'Oh well – perhaps you're best off without them. Best off without him, anyway, if he's been trying it on with you.'

There was a faint moan from the bed. So she had been right. That threw light on a lot of things, like the way Isobel was with other men.

'Well, he won't be coming back here in a hurry, that's for sure,' she said.

She talked on for a while, about the shop and the department, Miss Higgs and Miss Packard, anything to let Isobel know there was somebody around. As the excitement died down, she began to feel very tired. A normal day was exhausting enough, today with all its emotional strains had been draining.

'I'm going to bed myself, Iz,' she said, getting to her feet. 'I'm all shot to pieces.'

Suddenly, it was all too much effort to go all the way downstairs for hot water. She stripped off and washed in what was left in the ewer. Washing was something she had learnt from Isobel. At home, it was so crowded that an all-over wash in anything like privacy was almost impossible. They had baths in front of the fire every now and again, but often they went for days without washing properly. Isobel, however, was fastidious about being clean. Daisy, eager to improve herself, followed her example and was amazed to find that she really did feel better for it.

'You want a wash, Iz?' she asked. 'I could go down for some hot water for you.' For Isobel, she would face the stairs. But there was no response. 'You really must be feeling bad,' Daisy said.

She turned off the light and climbed into her narrow bed. Despite her tiredness, she lay awake for a long time while the events of the day ran round in her mind. She was just beginning to drift off when a small voice croaked from the other bed.

'Daisy?'

She was instantly wide awake again. 'Yeah?'

'I – wanted – you were marvellous –'

Daisy brushed off the hesitant compliment. 'Yeah well, couldn't let the sod get away with it, could I?'

'– good friend.'

'You – er – you want to, like, talk about it?'

There was a long pause. Daisy thought she had clammed up again. Then the thread of a voice resumed.

'I couldn't go back – live under – same roof again.'

'No, of course you couldn't,' Daisy agreed. She ventured a question. 'He – er – he was after a bit of the other, was he?'

Another pause, then a 'yes' so faint that Daisy hardly caught it.

'You should of told your sister. That would of put a stop to it,' she said.

'No!' There was real force in Isobel's voice.

'Why ever not?'

'I – because – it was all my fault. I'm wicked, wicked –' The sobs broke out again, wild and desperate.

'Blimey,' Daisy said. Here was a turn-up for the books and no mistake. Had Miss Cold-Shoulder Isobel been giving him the come-on, her own sister's husband? She slid out of her bed and onto Isobel's, stroking the huddled form under the covers.

'Went all the way, did you?'

'No – no – he tried to do – horrible things – said – said – my fault – asking for it –'

'Oh well, they all say that, don't they?' Daisy said.

She had been fourteen when she had lost her virginity. She had been lucky. She had not fallen pregnant.

'– had to get away.'

"Course you did. Once they think they can have it, they won't take no for an answer. You did the best thing, love.'

She could understand now why Isobel didn't want to go back. She couldn't carry on living under the same roof with her sister with him after her like that.

'You – er – you liked him at first, did you?' she asked.

'He – he seemed so nice – kind – I was upset after my parents died – he was – kind –'

And one thing led to another.

'It ain't your fault, love. You wasn't to know, was you? Stop blaming yourself.'

Eventually the weeping subsided. Daisy stroked the damp hair back from Isobel's hot forehead.

'There – that's better. You go to sleep now. You're safe here.'

If there was any more trouble, they had only to call on Johnny and Arthur. And as she climbed back into her own bed once more a new aspect of the affair suddenly struck her with a dazzling light. After this, Isobel couldn't possibly turn down an invitation from Johnny and Arthur. And once they all went out together, who could tell what might happen?

12

Amelie's mother was in her boudoir as usual when Amelie came in from her morning ride. Dressed in a loose muslin négligé adorned with lace and ruffles, she was sitting at her writing desk making lists. She looked up and gave a rare smile of approval.

'Enjoyable ride, my dear?'

'Very. It's such a beautiful day, Mama. It almost feels like summer. The air's warm and the sun is shining through the new leaves. I could have ridden for ever.'

The early morning turn round the park was one of the aspects of the Season that Amelie actually liked. Society – the people her mother was so desperate to be accepted by – were country-dwellers at heart. They left their vast estates when the hunting season was over and returned when the shooting began, and while they were in London they liked to keep in touch with their roots by riding in the park. Amelie had learnt to ride on one of her rare visits to her father's family's estate, and took to it with the relish that she felt for all sports. Winifred herself loathed horses and being out early, but she encouraged Amelie's riding because it was a good way to be noticed by the right people. For once, their interests were in tune.

'And was there anybody in the Row?' By this, Winifred meant anybody who was anybody.

'Oh, dozens,' Amelie said, wilfully misunderstanding her. Of course there had been crowds of equestrians out on such a lovely morning, but many of them were people even less in with Society than Winifred, and even more desperate to be part of it.

'Yes?'

As she was in a good mood, Amelie mentioned a few names that she knew would mollify her mother. Winifred nodded.

'Very well. Now sit down, Amelie. I want you to help me to write names on the cards for our drum on the twenty-third. Your best handwriting, mind. Here is the list.'

Amelie felt her light-heartedness begin to evaporate. Of all forms of evening entertainment, a drum was the worst. It consisted of two hundred or so people crowding through the house, fighting their way to a banquet of refreshments and rushing on to a similar event given by a hostess rather more fashionable than her mother. She could not believe that anyone could take pleasure in being jostled around in overheated rooms, not being able to have a decent conversation, listen properly to the music or even get to see the people they really wanted to meet, but her mother did not measure such things by enjoyment. What mattered was how many people from the right families attended and how many similar invitations she received in return.

As Amelie began to copy names onto the thick cream invitation cards, her mother ran through the programme for the day – a little shopping followed by a dress fitting, a luncheon party, some calls of ceremony, back to the park again, this time for a drive in the victoria, then a dinner party. The usual round.

The telephone on the desk rang and her mother picked it up. At this time of day, it was sure to be for her – some other hostess busy making arrangements.

'Oh – Edward. What a pleasant surprise. Amelie? Yes, if you wish.' She handed the instrument to Amelie. 'Your brother wishes to speak to you.'

Edward had never before telephoned Amelie from the store. Nasty possibilities chased through her mind. There had been a fire in the department, or, much worse, Grandfather had been taken ill. She spoke into the mouthpiece.

'Edward? Is there anything wrong?'

'Nothing that can't be put right, Mel, but I must ask you to take a great deal more care in choosing staff. In fact, in future I think you had better leave that to the staffing department. They know what they are about when they conduct interviews.'

'Why? What's happened?' Amelie asked, and then as the second part of what he said sunk in, 'If there are any problems with my girls, then I'll take responsibility for them. I knew what I was looking for when I took them on.'

An impatient sigh came down the line.

'You may have thought you knew, Mel, but you have

absolutely no experience of handling people. Rightly so. You're a young girl and anyone with an ounce of guile can impose themselves on you. It's not your fault. Just let me guide you in future.'

'But what's happened?'

'It seems there was some fracas outside one of the Trent Street houses yesterday evening. Your Miss Brand is here under an assumed name and somebody claiming to be her brother-in-law came to take her away. There were fisticuffs in the street. It's a wonder the police weren't called. A fine thing it would have been for Packards' good name if some of our staff had been bound over for breach of the peace.'

Amelie stood up. 'I'm coming in right this moment,' she said, and replaced the mouthpiece before Edward could reply.

Winifred was looking at her with her frostiest expression. 'You are not going anywhere, and especially not to the store,' she said, not making the slightest effort to pretend she had not overheard the conversation.

Which was just what Edward was counting on, Amelie realised.

'I shall only be half an hour. Nobody is out at this time of day, so I shan't be seen, if that is what you are concerned about.'

'That is hardly the point, Amelie. I let you have your way about setting up this ridiculous department of yours, much against my better judgement, but I thought I had made it perfectly plain that you were to have nothing further to do with it now that it is in being. Let those who are paid to do so take care of the running of the store. You have more important things to attend to.'

Arguing would get her nowhere, Amelie knew only too well. Instead, she started walking towards the door.

'I shall be back before you've finished answering your correspondence,' she promised, and made for the stairs.

Ten minutes later, she was marching into Packards with a footman hurrying behind her to keep up appearances.

Edward was not in his office. Fuming, Amelie sent his secretary to find him. When he appeared, he was looking surprised.

'Mel! There was no need for you to come round like this.

How well you are looking – have you been for a ride in the park this morning? Can I offer you a cup of tea, or coffee?'

Amelie gave him a fierce look. 'This is not a social call, Edward. I've come to find out what has been happening to my staff.'

Edward settled himself behind his mahogany desk and waved her to a chair. He leant back and laced his fingers together, regarding her with a patronising smile.

'Now, Mel, you really must not take too much upon yourself. Being a debutante is a very exhausting business. When is the date of your Presentation?'

'You know very well when it is, Edward, since Mother has made such a fuss about it. That isn't the reason I have come to see you. What is the problem with my Miss Brand?'

'There is no problem.'

Amelie stared. 'But you said –'

'I merely telephoned you to inform you of what had happened, and to ask you not to take on staff by yourself in future. As far as I am concerned, that is the end of the matter. Naturally, I have dismissed the girl in question.'

'You have done *what*?' Amelie cried.

'I have –'

'Yes, I heard you the first time, thank you. How dare you dismiss her without asking me! Miss Brand is the only shopgirl in my department who knows the slightest thing about sport. And besides, you can't just dismiss her out of hand like that.'

Edward remained irritatingly calm. 'On the contrary, I can and I have. The girl was a liability. She had to go. I shall speak to the staffing department and they will find somebody else for you.'

Amelie jumped up. 'You will do no such thing! I want Miss Brand back. Where is she now?'

'I have no idea. Now just take a deep breath, Mel, and consider for a moment. We really cannot have shopgirls at Packards who bring trouble with them –'

'But what about her?' Amelie interrupted. 'What about Miss Brand?'

Edward looked puzzled. 'I'm sorry, what exactly do you mean?'

'You can't just throw her out on her ear. Where will she go?'

'She can stay at Trent Street until the end of the week, which is very generous of us, considering.'

'Considering what? It's not her fault that someone came making trouble.'

'Giving a false name was entirely her fault. No, I'm sorry, Mel, but we cannot afford sentimentality here. Your feelings do you credit, but we are running a business. That is what you fail to understand. Now, you just leave it with me, and I'll see that you have a suitable replacement in your department.'

'You'll do no such thing! You had no right to go dismissing my staff without consulting me first.'

For the second time that day, Amelie jumped up and walked out. In the corridor outside Edward's office, she hesitated. The obvious thing to do was to go and see her grandfather. Ten minutes' wheedling and she would get what she wanted. But that would be admitting that she could not deal with it herself. Instead, she squared her shoulders, marched along to the staffing department and straight in to the manager's office.

'Good morning, Mr Mason. How are you today?'

The manager was distinctly taken aback. 'Er – very well, thanking you, Miss Packard.'

'I'm so glad to hear it,' Amelie seated herself in front of his desk and leant forward confidingly. 'Now, Mr Mason, I'm afraid there's been a little misunderstanding.'

The man looked anxious. 'A misunderstanding. Miss Packard?'

'Yes. Just a small matter, and I'm sure we can clear it up in no time at all. My Miss Brand should not have been dismissed. She is to be reinstated straight away.'

'I – er – but – Mr Edward Packard said –'

'Mr Edward Packard was misinformed.'

'But Miss Packard, I really cannot countermand his orders. You must understand –'

Amelie understood very well. Edward was a force to be reckoned with within the store. He was heir apparent to the whole organisation, whereas she was just his little sister, who was playing at shops for her own amusement.

'It is not countermanding his orders. I've just been speaking with him, and he agrees with me entirely. I simply offered to come along and inform you, to save him the trouble.'

Mr Mason opened his mouth and shut it again. 'I really feel –'

She felt quite sorry for him. He couldn't call her a liar to her face, but he could not believe that his superior had changed his mind in so short a time. She turned her most brilliant smile on him.

'Don't worry, Mr Mason, everything is sorted out. All you need to do is to make sure that Miss Brand is officially back in the fold again. Mr Edward knows all about it.'

Still the man did not look happy. Amelie was forced to produce her reserve argument. 'And of course Mr Thomas Packard agrees with me.'

The manager knew family politics when he saw it.

'Very well, Miss Packard.'

'Thank you, Mr Mason. I knew we would see eye to eye. Good morning.'

With which she swept out. This time when she reached the corridor she laughed. That had put a stop to Edward. He couldn't change the order again without looking an idiot. And if he did not like it, which he most certainly wouldn't, then that was hard cheese for him. With a skip in her step, she set off for the first floor and Ladies' Sportswear.

As she passed under the archway, she felt the familiar lift of pleasure. Her department. Her creation. And surprisingly busy for this hour of the morning. The three girls were all busy with customers and Daisy Phipps was in the act of wrapping what looked like a large purchase. Miss Higgs hurried forward to greet her. Amelie cut short her effusive welcome.

'You'll be glad to know, Miss Higgs, that I have managed to sort out the difficulty over Miss Brand. She is to be reinstated immediately.'

'Oh – er – that is good news, Miss Packard.'

The woman did not sound overcome with pleasure, but Amelie decided to ignore this.

'Should there be any problems in future, Miss Higgs, you are to inform me immediately. Telephone me at home, if necessary.'

Miss Higgs looked horrified. 'T-Telephone you, Miss Packard?'

'Of course. It's not difficult. Leave a message for me if I'm not at home. Now, I want Miss Brand sent for. She is to come back to work at once.'

'But –'

'Send one of the other girls. I shall take a turn behind the counter until they return.'

'Yes, Miss Packard.'

Over Miss Higgs's shoulder, she could see two of the shopgirls smirking, and guessed that they were as pleased at seeing their superior overridden as she had been in getting Edward's orders reversed. She only just stopped herself from giving them a conspiratorial grin.

When Daisy Phipps returned with Isobel Brand, it was obvious that the dismissed girl had been crying. Her face was still slightly blotchy and her eyelids swollen. Amelie wanted to speak to her in private, and realised not for the first time that she needed an office. Instead, she had to use the changing room.

Miss Brand was haltingly grateful. 'I can't thank you enough, Miss Packard. I – I – don't know what I would have done if I really had been dismissed.'

Amelie waved her thanks away. 'I was very angry when I heard what had happened. It was grossly unfair. Now, Miss Brand, I don't wish to pry into your private life, but is there any danger that this person might come back?'

Isobel bit her lip and looked down at her clasped hands. 'I – I don't know. He knows where I am living.'

'If he does, you are to call the police, and then me.'

She was not at all sure what she would do, but she was certain that she would do something.

'Thank you, Miss Packard. I –' Isobel hesitated.

'Yes?' Amelie asked.

'There is something that this – this – episode has taught me. A silver lining, I suppose.' Isobel gave a shadow of a smile. 'I would never have thought that there could be one, but – it has made me see that I have real friends here at Packards. When I thought I was to be dismissed, it was like – like – well, being cast out into the darkness.'

Amelie looked at her, a young woman only two or three years older than herself, gently reared, although not of the set of people who made up Society, and there she was earning her own living independently of her family and boasting of real friends at Packards. Isobel had a place in the store. She might only be a shopgirl, but she was part of the organisation. Amelie, on the other hand, was merely allowed to play at it, and then only because she had got round her grandfather and it was he who held the family purse strings.

'You know,' she said, 'you're very lucky. I wish I could say the same.'

Isobel stared at her. 'Oh Miss Packard, how can you say that, when you're about to be presented at court? Such an honour –' She stopped suddenly, blushing, and looked down at her hands. 'I do beg your pardon, it was not my place to give an opinion.'

She was quite right. She was merely an employee, and a lowly one at that, while Amelie was the granddaughter of the store's owner. Amelie knew she should put her sharply in her place. Instead she smiled.

'Perhaps we should change places, you and I. But as we can't, I suppose we had better get on with what we are supposed to be doing. Are you sure you feel well enough to work today?'

Isobel took a deep breath and gave a brave little nod. 'Of course.'

There were three customers in the department as she left. She had a last quick word with Miss Higgs and reluctantly left them to it. Now, she supposed, she must go home and face her mother's wrath. As she walked through the store, nodding to floorwalkers and senior salesmen, the remark she had made to Isobel Brand kept floating through her head. Perhaps we should change places. Isobel would enjoy the round of calls and parties and dress fittings, and she would probably be good at it as well, better than she was at being a shopgirl. Her sales were the lowest in the department. Amelie, on the other hand, was always doing and saying the wrong thing at dinners but was good at selling. Not that she wanted to be a shopgirl, she wanted some proper responsibility at the store.

The footman was waiting for her outside the main entrance, and fell in two paces behind her as she walked along Oxford

Street. It was still quite early by Society's standards, but lesser people were out looking at the windows and making purchases. Reluctant to go directly home, she walked along to where Gordon Selfridge's new store was being built. The walls of the building were rising rapidly now, the skeleton of girders showing what the final shape of the building would be. A band, specially hired by Mr Selfridge to help the work along, was playing cheerful marches. Amelie had heard tales of Mr Selfridge's brilliance at retailing when she was in Chicago, and she had seen the wonderful American stores. Her grandfather was going to have a nasty shock when this store opened just along the road from Packards. What they needed to do was to start using some American ideas now, not wait until Selfridges opened and stole half their customers away. If she could only persuade her grandfather to let her try some new methods of display, she was sure it would make people come to Packards. Then she would have some real power to ask for a title and office and real staff of her own.

Then it struck her that she should show him just what she meant. She would write to the family she stayed with in Chicago and ask them to send her some photographs of Marshall Field's windows. That surely would persuade him. With a new spring in her step, she turned for home and the inevitable roasting awaiting her there.

13

Thomas Packard always made a tour of his store from eleven to twelve each day. His staff knew he was coming, but not exactly the time he might appear, since he varied his route and could arrive on any floor at any time during that hour. Sometimes he merely processed through, nodding and passing the odd word of praise or criticism, sometimes he decided to look into a particular department or office in more detail. Either way it was woe betide any person found to be lacking in any way, but similarly, credit was always given where it was due. Thomas was respected as a fair employer.

During the Season, eleven to twelve was also the time when Society did its shopping. Thomas enjoyed seeing members of its gilded circle strolling round his departments. They gave Packards an air of style. The absolute confidence that came with knowing that you belong to the Top Ten Thousand gave them a gloss that could not be bought or imitated. Society people did not have their packages despatched to addresses in the suburbs, they had them taken downstairs to where uniformed footmen almost more lordly-looking than their employers waited to load them into polished carriages or motor cars. Society also brought a lot of business. Many of its purchases were made in the small and exclusive shops in and around Bond Street, but it was perfectly *de rigueur* to have gowns made or cards printed, or to buy any of the myriad small items needed to support fashionable life, at a department store. And where Society led, anyone else with enough money tried to follow. Any mention in the popular newspapers of a Society beauty having bought a hat or gloves or handkerchiefs at Packards always brought a number of requests for the selfsame article.

His last call this morning was to Ladies' Gowns. At this very moment, Thomas knew, his darling Amelie was having a fitting for her court dress. He hoped the session would be done by now, so that he could have the pleasure of her company for a while.

He paused for a moment at the entrance of the department. He loved Ladies' Gowns. To achieve just the right ambience, he had accompanied his wife, his daughter and his succession of mistresses to many top-class dressmaking establishments and spent a great deal of money on dresses for them while he looked around at the décor and amenities and found just what women wanted from such places. Then he had endeavoured to go one better at Packards. The department was decorated in tasteful peach and eau-de-Nil with touches of gold. On the walls were gilt-framed fashion sketches that were changed every week with the latest ideas. There were soft carpets, plenty of looking-glasses and potted palms, and little groups of comfortable chairs to sit on with piles of the latest ladies' journals arranged on tables within easy reach and a selection of light refreshments available so that ladies were encouraged to come and sit around chatting until they were beguiled into ordering another dress. Beyond the velvet curtains there were spacious fitting rooms with further seats for whoever was accompanying the lady being fitted. And to one side, partially screened from the feminine domain, his very best idea, an area fitted up like a gentlemen's club, where long-suffering husbands might smoke, eat, drink and read newspapers until their womenfolk reappeared. He knew for a fact, as Winifred had told him so, that some women could only get husbands to come with them if they bought their dresses at Packards.

Thomas looked contentedly upon it all. Amelie was not the only debutante having her court gown made here. Fifteen others were this Season, two of them girls with the very bluest of blood, so the store was almost sure to be mentioned in the fashionable papers. He ran his eyes over the groups of women arranged so elegantly on peach upholstered chairs, but Amelie was not amongst them. He was about to go when he saw someone coming through from the fitting rooms, but it was not his granddaughter, it was Winifred. With a sinking heart, he realised that she had spotted him. She raised her gloved hand in that imperious way of hers that indicated that she wished to speak to him.

Winifred brushed aside his greeting.

'Father, I was on my way to see you. Might we go somewhere to talk?'

Which meant, he translated, that she did not wish to be seen by her Society friends chatting to her plebeian father, especially if she needed more money, which seemed likely. He escorted her upstairs to his office and sent for coffee.

His daughter came straight to the point.

'I am highly displeased with Amelie.'

This was nothing new.

'Dear me, I am sorry to hear that. How is the child? Does she look beautiful in her court gown? I am so looking forward to seeing her wearing it. I trust my dressmakers are giving satisfaction?'

Winifred did not bother to disguise her irritation with him. 'Yes, yes. It looks very well, or will do when the alterations have been carried out. Amelie looks – well, I think I might almost say magnificent in it. That is the point, Father. Amelie has everything in her favour. She is being launched into Society with far more advantages than I ever enjoyed. Thanks to my pursuit of acquaintances on her behalf, our mantelpiece is crowded with cards. I wear myself to the bone arranging receptions and dances and dinners for her so that all the hospitality might be returned, and I make sure that she is introduced to all the right people. And what do you think her reaction is?'

Thomas was not expecting to be asked a question. He was still amusing himself with the vision of Winifred the Martyr, performing the excruciating task of organising social events all for the benefit of her daughter. He realised that Winifred had paused for an answer.

'I cannot imagine,' he lied. He knew very well that Amelie was not in the least bit grateful. On the contrary, she wanted none of it.

'She says she is bored,' Winifred boomed. 'Bored! When she has amusements arranged for her all day long –'

She continued proving her point for some while. Thomas heard her with only part of his brain. The rest of it was considering the gap between himself and his daughter with sadness. Once he had loved her as he now loved Amelie. When she was little, she used to sit on his knee and play with his pocket watch, or run up to him and put her small trusting hand in his and swing on his arm. Somewhere along the line, it had all gone wrong, and for the life of him he could not remember when. Now they regarded each other with mutual hostility, on his side carefully disguised.

'– sitting on the stair with that dreadful Ellis boy, laughing her head off. And when I asked her why she had not danced with Lord Feiston, she said it was because he was a donkey!'

Coming down completely on Amelie's side was sure to antagonise Winifred. Thomas attempted to smooth things over.

'Well, she is young, and young people like to be amused. I'm sorry she seems to be a disappointment to you –'

'Disappointment! Yes, well you should know how that feels, Father. After all, I was a disappointment to you, was I not?'

The sharp edge of childish pain and resentment shocked Thomas into giving her his full attention.

'Whatever do you mean?' he asked, but even as he did so he knew that she spoke the truth.

'By not being a boy, of course,' she said, confirming it.

'Naturally, I would have liked to have had a son,' he said carefully. 'But a son as well as you, not instead of you.'

Winifred tightened her lips. She patently did not believe him. He despaired of convincing her. How could he, when he was not convinced of it himself?

'Look how you've gone one better. You've given me two grandsons.'

'Then kindly leave me my daughter,' Winifred retorted.

Thomas emanated sweet reason. 'My dear girl, when have I ever tried to take Amelie away from you?'

'All the time! In the past it was not so important. She was still at school. It did not matter if she came here and played about the store. But now it is altogether different. She is a debutante. She should be devoting herself to the matter of making a suitable marriage.'

'To donkeys like Lord Feiston?' Thomas enquired, with a suggestion of a smile.

'To somebody from a good family.'

'Somebody, I hope, whom she likes?'

Winifred flushed. 'But of course. What do you think I am about? I have introduced her to dozens of very likeable young men. Lord Feiston is merely an example. There are plenty of others, but she hardly looks at them. It is her whole attitude that is the problem. She was bad enough without your encouraging her, giving her that ridiculous department. I managed to pass that off when it opened, but she will keep talking about it wherever we go. I certainly cannot see her making a match this Season. In fact, the way she is going, I cannot see it happening at all. And of course my chances with her are very much hampered by not being able to entertain in the country.'

So that was it. Yet another try at persuading him to buy a country estate. The joke of it was, he was really rather attracted to the idea. On beautiful May days like today, the thought of strolling round well-kept grounds or riding a glossy horse – a suitably docile one, since he had never learnt to ride – through woods and fields was very pleasant. He had no doubt that he would soon grasp the workings of landownership. A man who had built Packards from scratch would not find that difficult. It would be a challenge, a complex toy for his old age. If he could only feel sure that Edward would carry on running the store his way, then he might well consider it.

'Now then, Winifred,' he said. 'You know you'll never make a country gentleman of me.'

Winifred contained her annoyance. 'It would be a good investment,' she said with the air of one who has delivered the clinching argument.

'As a stage for a Society hostess, I am sure it would be. In terms of monetary value, I doubt it. Agriculture is in a bad way. The colonies can produce food much cheaper than we can. Why do you think it is that so many estates are up for sale? Because they don't pay their way. The tenants can't make enough out of farming to pay their rents. Those of your friends who don't have nice solid investments or something useful like coal on their land are having to sell up.'

Winifred changed tack. She was sensible enough to know that she could not argue with him on monetary matters.

'It would be so nice for Amelie to have somewhere to invite

her friends once the Season is over. There is nothing so pleasant as a cosy little house party, with some shooting or hunting maybe. You would enjoy shooting, Father. Or fishing. If you bought somewhere with a good trout stream, I am sure you would become quite a sportsman. And Mother would like to be away from the noise and dirt of London.'

There was that as well – the chance that Margaret would really take to country life and stay there when he was in London. It might even make her happy. That was a fairly remote possibility, since nothing he had ever done in all his long years of growing success had ever really satisfied her expectations of him. He wasn't sure if she really knew what those expectations were, simply that he did not measure up to them. Running a big house might at least take her mind off them.

'Nonsense. Your mother would not know what to do with herself in the country,' he said. 'Now, Winifred dear, let us not have an argument. How would you like it if I had a little talk with Amelie, and reminded her of her family obligations?'

'Considering that you are being so stubborn over this matter of a country house, I think that is the very least you could do. I shall send her along to you when her dress fitting is finished,' Winifred said.

She swept out, leaving Thomas with the suspicion that he had been outmanoeuvred. His daughter never had believed she would convince him on the matter of the estate. She simply wanted him to bring Amelie into line.

Five minutes later, Amelie arrived, looking every bit as annoyed as her mother. Thomas asked after the fitting with a sympathetic twinkle.

'Oh the gown is beautiful,' Amelie had to admit. 'It's just Mother –'

Thomas plied her with coffee and listened to Amelie's side of the story. The interminable meals, the boring people, the dance floors that were always too crowded to move properly, the old men who looked down your *décolletage*, the young men with nothing to say for themselves, the grand hostesses who froze you out if you said or did anything the least bit out of line.

'I seem to remember you went to a tennis party only the other day. You liked that, surely?'

Amelie conceded that tennis parties were all right, in fact they were fun. Riding in the park was enjoyable too, and so were boating parties on the Thames.

'I hear your mother's managed to secure a houseboat for Henley. Now that should be a real spectacle. Your grandmother and I are coming to that.'

'I suppose so,' Amelie admitted. 'But that's not what I wanted to talk to you about, Gramps.'

'Oh yes?'

He might have known that Amelie had not come to see him simply to be lectured on being an obedient daughter.

'Yes. It's about Selfridges. Have you seen how well the building's coming along?'

'I have. It all looks very impressive, but I don't think it will outshine Packards. Nothing could be as beautiful as our entrance hall and marble staircase.'

'I know, Grandpa, and I agree. But when it opens, Mr Selfridge is sure to do something really spectacular. He was famous for it in Chicago. People will go to see out of curiosity. Our customers will go there. If we don't do something, he's going to take some of our trade.'

Thomas was touched by her concern. Amelie really cared about the store. It was almost as close to her heart as to his. But in this case she was worrying needlessly.

'Don't bother yourself about Mr Selfridge,' he said. 'It's well known that he's severely underfinanced for this store of his. Look at the way he's going about it, plunging straight into building a complete department store here on Oxford Street. None of us other traders has done that. John Lewis, Peter Robinson, Debenham and Freebody, we've all worked our way up from single shops. That's the way to make a business. I wouldn't be surprised if Selfridges failed even before the building's completed.'

The anxious expression on Amelie's face did not change.

'But supposing it doesn't, Grandpa? Supposing people start going to Selfridges instead of to us?'

'I'm not afraid of competition, my dear. There's plenty of competition now, after all, and a depression in trade, but we're more than holding our own.'

'We might not when Selfridges opens. The Americans do things differently. There's more – more show to it, like – like a parade.'

Thomas was genuinely puzzled. How could a shop be like a parade?

Amelie delved into the bag she had with her and produced some photographs, which she handed to Thomas.

'I asked the Schneiders to send me these and they arrived today. They're pictures of Marshall Field's windows.'

Thomas studied the photographs. He had seen examples of American window dressing in the *Drapers Record*, but these were particularly spectacular. One showed a room, complete to the curtained window and view through to a garden, with a dining table set out as if for a dinner party, and a lady, presumably the hostess, standing gorgeously gowned with one hand resting on a chair back. The second was an outdoor scene, with an open picnic hamper around which a family were grouped amongst what he supposed must be artificial flowers. The third looked like an oriental tent, with drapes and carpets, and a low round table in the centre on which stood an eastern-style coffee set.

'They're very pretty,' he admitted, 'but –'

Amelie interrupted him. 'Yes, that's exactly it. People come especially to see them. They talk about them.'

'But do they come in and buy?' Thomas asked. 'We're not a gallery showing fine art, we're a shop. Our customers want to be able to look in the windows and see exactly what we have on offer. Now, this dining room scene shows just one dinner service, one set of cutlery and one set of linen. When our customers look in the cutlery window, they see an example of every canteen we sell, and its price. That way they know that we have what they want at a price which they can afford. This window tells them nothing.'

'So they go in and find out. The window's so pretty they want to go into the shop and see what else is available.'

Thomas shook his head. 'That's not how it works, my dear. You mark my words, if Selfridge does try these American ways here, people will go and look at his pretty displays, but they'll come here to buy.'

Amelie gave a sigh of frustration. 'Oh Grandpa, won't you

just try it? Let me arrange just two windows this way, and see if it makes a difference to our sales? For me?'

Thomas was torn. It was very hard to resist her when she looked at him like that. He loved to give her what she wanted. But in this case it was bad business, and he had to refuse. Besides, Winifred was right in a way. If Amelie was going to be a debutante and a member of Society, then she had to do it properly.

'I'm sorry, my dear. I know you mean well, and I expect it does work in Chicago, but this is London. And besides, you are far too busy with the Season to be arranging windows.'

Amelie's face crumpled in disappointment. 'Oh Grandpa! I thought you understood. I thought you were on my side. You know I hate the beastly Season. And you let me have my department, didn't you? That's a success, isn't it? I know I could make a success of the window displays if you would only let me try.'

Thomas couldn't bear it.

'Look, my dear, you be a good girl for your mother and do the Season and make her happy. Then next year, I'll see about giving you something else here at the store.'

Amelie jumped up and threw her arms round his neck.

'Really, Gramps? Promise? Oh, I'll be a model debutante, just you see. Then together we'll make Packards even better than ever.'

Thomas hugged her waist and kissed her smooth cheek. Beneath the armour of her corset he could sense the vibrance of her young healthy body. This beautiful creature was his, his flesh and blood. He let her go with reluctance.

'That's my girl.'

The office felt dead and empty after she had gone. Thomas sat staring at the door through which she had departed. He wouldn't change one tiny part of her, and yet – if she had been born a boy, he would have happily left the running of the store to her. Five years teaching her the business from the bottom upwards and he could have gone off to retire in the country knowing that Packards was in safe hands. She would have made mistakes, of course, but she had something that Edward did not. An instinct, a flair which was not definable. As it was, she would only ever be able to play a minor part in the store. By this time next year she might even be married, and even if she wasn't, who had ever heard of a woman running a business as large as Packards?

14

'Do I look all right in this?' Daisy asked, twisting and turning before the small looking-glass.

'You look very pretty,' Isobel assured her.

Daisy still gazed at herself, unsure. The white blouse with the high neck and the ruffled yoke was the first brand-new garment she had ever possessed. She had bought it, from Packards of course, with money saved out of her wages. She loved every stitch, but most of all she loved the sheer newness of it, its virgin whiteness, the crisp feel to the cotton lawn, the very smell of it. Below it, her old green skirt looked drab, but she tried not to look at that. Instead, she completed the outfit by pinning on her newly trimmed straw hat. She had spent hours patiently stitching on pink ribbons and three glorious artificial peonies until it looked like a summer garden blooming on the brim. She smiled, and in the glass her pert little face smiled back. In any other circumstances, she would have been pleased with her appearance. Solid food and much improved grooming had added to her looks no end. Back home, they would think her real posh. The trouble was, she was no longer comparing herself to the girls from back home. She was up against Isobel.

She looked at her friend. Isobel was dressed all in black, with a plain black straw hat. She looked as if she were going to a funeral rather than a music hall, but still she outshone Daisy on all counts. She was taller, her figure was far more voluptuous, her hair was that striking natural blonde and most of all her face was simply lovely. Daisy was consumed with envy.

'It's all right for you. You could wear rags and look beautiful. What've you got all that dull stuff on for, anyway? We're not going to church.'

'I'm still in mourning for my dear mama and papa. I should not be going to a place of public entertainment at all. I'm only doing so because I feel I cannot refuse, in the circumstances.'

'Too true, after what they done – did – for you,' Daisy agreed.

Just as she had guessed they would, Johnny and Arthur had pressed home their advantage and asked the girls out. To make sure it would be an evening to remember, it was not to be simply a walk and perhaps a visit to a teashop, but a trip to the music hall.

The excitement of it welled up in Daisy, overcoming much of the envy. She had built so much on this evening, dreamt so many dreams. Who knew, perhaps Johnny would get fed up with Isobel giving him the cold shoulder all the time and look at her instead. Certainly Isobel showed no sign of pleasure at all. Daisy found she was feeling almost sorry for her.

'Come on, Sourpuss, put a smile on it! We're going to have fun,' she cried.

Isobel said nothing, and followed her reluctantly as she made her way downstairs.

The young men were waiting for them at the door. Both sported rather loud checked jackets in contrast to the dull suits they had to wear all week, and both had bowler hats at jaunty angles on their heads. Daisy was delighted. She had never been out with a man in a bowler hat before. All the lads round her way wore flat caps.

Arthur staggered back in mock amazement as the girls came out.

'Blimey, are these the ladies what we're taking out? I thought they was debutantes or something.'

'We're the lucky ones tonight, all right,' Johnny agreed.

His eyes were only for Isobel. Daisy fought back the pang of disappointment. She might have known it.

Isobel tucked her arm firmly inside that of her friend, and refused to be parted. The arrangement held all the way to the Empire, to the chagrin of the men, but once they were there Isobel was outflanked. As they took their seats in the fourth row of the circle, the girls stayed together, but Arthur sat on Daisy's other side and Johnny on Isobel's.

Daisy was too enchanted by her surroundings at first to let it worry her. She gazed about her at the theatre. It was just about the most exotic place she had ever been to. She was almost used now to the magnificence of Packards, but this was something different. While Packards had restrained splendour, the Empire was a riot of red and gold, with brilliant chandeliers, polished brass rails, plush seats and silk-effect walls, with gilt cherubs and foliage sprouting from every available surface. On top of that, there was the atmosphere. The place seemed to hum with the same happy expectancy that she felt. All around her there was a hubbub of voices as people found their seats, settled themselves in, talked to their neighbours or called across the rows and aisles. Daisy drank it in, along with the smell of cigars and drink and chocolates. A great sigh of pleasure escaped her.

'Like it?'

She realised that Arthur had been watching her, and flushed. She didn't want him thinking she was a little nobody who'd been nowhere.

"S all right. Bit hot. Nice, though,' she conceded.

'They got a good line-up tonight. Little Titch and Clara Deare! You don't often get to see them both on one night.'

'I love Clara Deare,' Daisy said, wanting to sound knowledgeable. It was true enough. She might never have watched her on stage, but she had seen the great star's photographs in shop windows and in the newspapers and had been attracted to her knowing smile. Clara Deare seemed like a woman who was in charge of her own life.

'Yeah, she's a wonder, ain't she? What a performer – gets the audience eating out of her hand, she does. And as for Little Titch – well! Last time I saw him I thought I was going to die, I laughed so much. And the others on the bill, they're all good and all. The Great Khan – you seen him? Now there's an act . . .'

Arthur talked on at length about the entertainment ahead of them. According to him, they were all masters and mistresses of their art. It was almost as if he had personally booked them for Daisy's pleasure. She listened to him with half an ear while continuing to look about her. She especially liked the boxes, which were filled with swells, the men in black and white evening dress and the women in gorgeous gowns, reds and pinks and greens and blues, cut low on the bust and sparkling with jewels. How she wished she had a dress like one of them. Johnny would be sure to notice her then.

The lights dimmed, and with a crash of chords the band began to play a lively selection of popular song tunes. Late arrivals hurried to their places. The audience settled down. The master of ceremonies picked up his gavel and cleared his throat.

'My lords, ladies and gentlemen –'

The show had begun.

Daisy completely forgot she was trying to act worldly wise. She watched each act with total concentration and loved every one. She laughed at the comics, thrilled at the tumblers and the fire-eater, wiped tears away after the sentimental singers and joined in with all the choruses. She hardly noticed Isobel shrinking ever closer to her on one side or Arthur hoping for approval on the other. The first half finished with Clara Deare, and Arthur was absolutely right, she did have the audience eating out of her hand. The curtain came down to deafening applause and roars of 'More!' with Daisy clapping and shouting as loud as any, but Miss Deare did not come back. She was off to top the bill at another Empire across town.

Daisy leant back in her seat, the palms of her hands hot and tingling. When Arthur asked if she was enjoying it, she was still so entranced that she said, 'Oh yes, it's wonderful!' with wholehearted simplicity.

Arthur edged a little nearer. 'I do like a girl who knows how to enjoy herself,' he said. 'You look so pretty when you laugh, do you know that? Knock spots off of any of them lot up on the stage.' And he closed a hand tentatively over hers.

Daisy came to her senses. She snatched her hand away.

'Watch it, mate.'

Arthur just grinned. It was all part of the game.

'Fancy a drink, girls?'

Daisy said, 'All right, then,' at exactly the same moment as Isobel said, 'No thank you.' Daisy laughed.

'Oh come on, Iz. Have a lemonade or something. You must be dry. I know I am, after all that singing.'

When Isobel realised that if she did not come she would be left sitting with just Johnny, she agreed. Their party joined the jostling crowd heading for the bar, Arthur taking the opportunity to steer her round obstacles and allow himself to be pushed up against her. Isobel caught hold of Daisy's arm and put her lips to her ear.

'Daisy,' she whispered urgently, 'I have to go to the er – conveniences. Won't you come with me? Please?'

Daisy was torn. Female loyalty said that she ought to go along with her friend, but with Isobel out of the way in a place where Johnny could not possibly follow her, she might just get some of his attention at last.

'You go,' she said. 'I'll save your drink for you.' And she hardened her heart to Isobel's pleading expression.

When they reached the bar, she found that her strategy did not work. Johnny offered to buy the first round and left her with Arthur. Then when he came back with the full glasses, his first words to her were to ask whether she thought her friend was enjoying the evening.

'Oh – I expect so,' Daisy said.

'I hope so. Only she doesn't seem to be joining in at all. And she doesn't find the comics very funny. In fact I don't think she laughed once.'

'Oh well, she's a bit of the serious type, is Izzy.'

Come to think of it, Daisy didn't think Isobel had much of a sense of humour, but she didn't say so.

'I like a girl who can enjoy herself,' Arthur repeated. 'Daisy's enjoying herself, aren't you?'

'I love the halls,' Daisy agreed. 'Blooming good night out, it makes.'

'I don't think your friend does,' Johnny said. He sounded very worried. 'I mean, she's used to better things, ain't she?'

'Blimey, mate, the Empire's got the best music-hall acts in the country. You can't get better than Clara Deare,' Arthur protested.

'I know, but some of those comics were a bit close to the mark, weren't they? You don't think she's offended, do you?'

'I thought they was good, and so did all of the other girls judging by the laughs,' Daisy said.

'Yeah but, well, we're all like the same, aren't we? She's out of a higher drawer. Maybe we should've gone to a play or something.'

Daisy was getting impatient at all this. 'Rubbish. Look at all that lot in the boxes with their bow ties and evening gowns and everything. They was enjoying it. Don't you worry about Izzy. She's just not the sort to bust her sides at anything. What did you like best? I bet it was that girl with the yellow dress – what's her name, Annie Andrews? She looked just your type. Smashing voice.'

At last she got her way. Johnny stopped talking about Isobel and all three of them had a lively argument over the comparative talents of the artistes. Basking in the attention of both young men, Daisy almost forget about her friend.

After the horrors of the evening so far, Isobel found the queue for the ladies' a welcome respite. One or two women tried to strike up a conversation with her, but when she ignored them they did not persist. She stood patiently in the line, grateful for the peace of her own company. She had known beforehand that she was going to hate it. She had held out for as long as she could, but after the two men had been so quick and effective in dealing with *him* – she could not bring herself to acknowledge her brother-in-law's name – she knew that she was honour bound to give in to their request for an evening out with her and Daisy. And of course, there was Daisy herself. It was obvious that she was desperate for Isobel to accept and Isobel was very well aware of how much she owed to Daisy. But still it was hard. If her dear mama could see here now, at this vulgar place with those two common young men and not a responsible lady anywhere to chaperon her, she would have a fit of the hysterics, and her mama had not been a woman prone to the hysterics. But then, everything about her life now would cause her mama to throw up her hands in horror. It simply did not bear thinking about. Isobel could only hope that she could not see her from wherever heaven might be.

She managed to hang about in the ladies' for almost the entire interval. It was not a pleasant place, crowded as it was with loud-voiced women wearing too much cheap scent in a vain attempt to smother the odours of their bodies, but it was preferable to finding her way to the bar and the company of the two men. As she stood washing her hands and tidying her hair amongst jostling women applying rouge and powder, she did consider walking out and taking a cab back to Trent Street. But the thought of what Daisy might say stopped her. No, she had to stay and endure to the end.

When she finally emerged she found that people were beginning to flood back to their places. Rather than swim against the tide of humanity, Isobel decided it would be best to meet the others in the circle rather than the bar. She was just finding the right set of stairs when she recognised a face in the crowd, a young gentleman in impeccable evening dress. Mr Peregrin Amberley Packard. She was so surprised that she found herself inclining her head towards him as a lady should do if she wishes to acknowledge a gentleman. She regretted it the moment she saw him bow in return and begin to work his way towards her. But the deed was done and she could only stand and wait for him. He was soon at her side.

'Good evening. It's Miss – er – from my sister's department, is it not?'

She supposed she ought to address him as 'sir', but something inside her rebelled against it. She had been born and brought up a lady, whatever her present circumstances. She would behave as if they had been properly introduced by a mutual friend.

'Miss Brand,' she reminded him. 'Good evening, Mr Packard.'

'Of course, yes, Miss Brand. Forgive my forgetfulness.'

She could tell from the expression in his eyes that he was surprised at her manner and her accent, but he rode over it.

'How very pleasant to run into you here, of all places. Are you enjoying the show?'

Isobel was at a loss as to how to answer this. Presumably he enjoyed this sort of thing, or he would not be here, but for the life of her, she could not pretend to like it herself.

'It's – er – very lively.'

Mr Peregrin Packard laughed. 'In other words, you cannot stand it, eh? Am I right?'

Isobel looked down at her hands. 'Er – well –'

'Came with friends, did you? Persuaded you it would be a jolly night out?'

'Something of the sort, yes.' Isobel snatched at the chance to get away. 'I – I must rejoin them now. G-Good evening, Mr Packard.'

'And a very good evening to you, Miss Brand. It has been a pleasure to talk to you.'

He gave a very elegant little bow despite the crowd jostling past. Isobel, blushing, inclined her head in reply and went on her way, hardly knowing where she was going. It was sheer luck that brought her back to the right place for the second half.

The others were standing in the aisle looking anxious. It was Johnny Miller who spotted her first.

'Isobel! There you are. We was getting worried about you. We was about to send out a search party.'

'I – I'm sorry. I was delayed,' Isobel said, while inside she fumed. What made him think he could use her Christian name? Mr Packard had not done so. But then he was a gentleman.

She had hoped that there might be some change in the seating arrangements, but the young men seemed to have agreed amongst themselves that it was to be the same as before, and Isobel found that once more she was sitting with Daisy on one side and Johnny Miller on the other. She sat as far away from him as the cramped space allowed. Daisy leant her head over till it was almost touching Isobel's.

'You all right?' she muttered.

'Yes, yes perfectly, thank you,' Isobel lied.

'Only I wondered, you know, when you was so long.'

Dear Daisy.

'There was a very long queue,' Isobel said.

'Ain't it wonderful? Best night of my life, this is.'

'I'm glad,' Isobel said, and meant it. At least one of them was enjoying it.

The second half was, if anything, worse than the first. There were more women, with crudely made-up faces and skirts right up to their calves, singing sentimental or suggestive songs in corncrake voices. There were dancers who did high kicks and cartwheels which showed all their legs and most of their underwear, to the delight of the males in the audience. There was a strong man in a leopard skin that revealed his hairy chest and arms and even part of his thighs. When he flexed his muscles all the women squealed. But the worst by far were the comics in their loud jackets and baggy trousers and huge bright bow ties who said things that she did not even understand, but such was the tone of voice in which they said them that there was no mistaking their meaning. Certainly the audience understood, for they were in gales of raucous laughter. Beside her, Isobel could hear Daisy gasping for breath and saying, 'Oo, just listen to him! The cheeky devil! Ain't he a one?'

It made Isobel feel queasy with distaste, which in itself was bad enough. But far worse, under the queasiness there was an odd excitement, a stirring that brought back all the most terrible memories of her time at her sister's house. They came to her in flashes, the images she had tried to suppress all these weeks. The first gentle looks of sympathy, the kind words and brotherly holding of her hand and patting of her shoulders, which slid almost imperceptibly into embraces and kisses. She should have stopped it before it began, but she had been so miserable, so bewildered by grief and the sudden reversal of her fortunes that she accepted the comfort. But then, before she knew it was happening, she was more than accepting it. She enjoyed it when he put his arms around her. It was her fault. She was wicked. She was sinful. She only came to her senses when he started to kiss her on the mouth and touch her in places where nobody should touch, with an urgency and passion that horrified her, but at the same time started a hot excitement far inside her. By then it was far too late. When she tried to stop him, he said that she had led him on, that she had encouraged him at every turn. And she believed him. From then on there was no way out. She could not tell her sister, burdened with guilt as she was.

Up on the stage, a girl in a red and black dress was singing a song about a postman, with a great raising of eyebrows and rolling of eyes at each mention of putting letters into pillarboxes. Isobel hardly saw her. Instead she saw the way he had looked at her that last day, when she thought she was alone in the house but for the servants. He came into the morning room as she sat writing letters and said that he could not go on any longer, that she inflamed him beyond bearing, that he must have her then and there.

When she tried to cry out he silenced her with the threat of her sister finding out. Before she knew what was happening she was on her back on the floor with her skirts pulled up and his hand ripping at her drawers. She wept and pleaded and struggled , but it made no difference. He hardly seemed to hear her, and he was far stronger than she. When she tried a feeble kick he hit her savagely across the face. She had been saved only by the absent-minded housemaid coming up to collect cleaning equipment she had left in the room. Isobel used the precious seconds to leap up with more speed and agility than she knew she possessed and rush out of the door and up to her room, locking the door behind her. She packed, watched the street until she saw him go out of the front door, then left the house for good.

'Iz? Isobel? You all right?' Daisy's voice sounded in her ear.

'What? Oh – yes –'

'You're shaking. What's up?'

'I – nothing.'

'You poorly or something? Not the time of the month, is it?'

'No –'

She just felt sick. Sick with shame.

'You want to go home?'

How she longed for the safety of their stark little room in Trent Street, where no men were allowed past the front door. But to get there would mean explanations, lies, fuss. The last thing she wanted was to draw attention to herself. At least here in her theatre seat there was anonymity of a kind.

'No. Really, Daisy, I'm perfectly well.'

And to try to prove it she clapped the postman song girl heartily.

The entertainment finished with a comic who rejoiced in the name of Little Titch. Everyone around her, it seemed, thought he was hilarious. Isobel tried her best to join in, for to do so was better than letting the thoughts back in again. At last it was over. Now she could go back to Trent Street, her obligations repaid.

As she closed her eyes that night in the attic room, the evening's events jangled around in her head, stopping the longed for oblivion of sleep. There was only one small incident that she could rest her mind on. Despite the fact that he knew her only as a shopgirl, Mr Peregrin Amberley Packard had

spoken to her as a gentleman to a lady. It was balm to her
shattered self-respect.

15

Amelie had to admit that the dress was a triumph.

'Not even Monsieur Worth could have done better than our Packards' dressmakers,' she declared.

Winifred was forced to agree. Court etiquette was very strict on what should be worn when one was presented to the King and Queen. A full evening gown with a low-cut corsage and extremely short sleeves was demanded, together with a four-yard train, white gloves and a white veil hanging from three white plumes. Status within Society demanded that this should be the dress that outshone all others. Amelie, Winifred and the entire Packards' Court Dressmaking staff had been in conference over this creation since early March. Now at last the finished result was revealed.

The primrose yellow silk gown with its overskirt of paler yellow silk gauze with a touch of gold was decorated with swathes of delicate pink and gold embroidery. The bronze velvet train fell from the shoulders and was also embroidered round with a wide border of pink and gold. When Amelie finally stood fully attired, with her hair elaborately dressed, plumed and veiled, wearing her elbow-length kid gloves and a superb matching set of earrings, bracelet and necklace from the Packards' jewellery department, and carrying a fan and a huge bouquet, she looked magnificent. Winifred allowed herself a sigh of satisfaction.

'You look very well. Very well indeed,' she said.

Amelie stared at the stranger in the pier glass and wondered if it was worth all the effort and expense just so that it could be known that she had kissed Their Majesties' hands. But it was no use questioning it now. The whole procedure had been set in motion weeks ago with the application to the Lord Chamberlain and there was no backing out. The cards were ready in her mother's bag, the photographer was booked and the 'peacock' party afterwards, so called because it was expressly for the showing off of a debutante's beautiful gown and train, was all arranged. The carriage was this moment at the door. The great event of a debutante's life was about to begin.

The entire household was assembled to see her. The family was waiting in the drawing room. Amelie had expected her father and Perry and Grandfather and Grandmother Packard to be there, but was amazed to find that Edward and even her Amberley grandparents had also arrived. There were exclamations of approval and delight, and each person came forward to kiss her on the cheek, taking great care not to disarrange the smallest detail of this work of art that was Amelie.

'You're a credit to us all, my pet,' Thomas said, smiling into her eyes.

'A credit to Packards,' she replied. 'The diamonds are stunning, Grandpa.'

'Jewels need a beautiful woman to wear them,' he said.

Even Grandmother Amberley gave a smile.

'Very tasteful,' was her verdict, with a hint of surprise in her voice.

Amelie and everyone else in the room was well aware that this was the accolade. It meant that Amelie was deemed worthy to represent the Amberley name that she so carelessly cast aside when trying to be part of the store. Amelie thanked her with dignity.

'I think it is time to leave,' Winifred decided, well satisfied with her in-laws' reaction.

The servants, from the butler right down to the scullery maid, were all crowded into the hall. There was a mighty indrawing of breath as Amelie came slowly down the stairs. They all stood a little taller, thrust out their chests a little further at the pride of being part of a family that produced such a beautiful and gorgeously dressed lady to show at Court.

The rest of the evening, it seemed to Amelie, consisted mostly of waiting. Firstly there was a long queue of carriages and state coaches crawling along the Mall, where a huge crowd of people of all stations of life were gathered to watch the show and pass comments on the great ladies as they went by. When at last she and her mother reached the palace and left their wraps in the cloakroom, a further ordeal of waiting began, together with a good deal of fairly undignified pushing and shoving. Gentlemen-at-arms manning gilt barriers let groups of about thirty debutantes and their chaperons at a time through the Great Hall, up the Grand Staircase and through a series of antichambers. There were plenty of benches on which one could take a rest, but nobody seemed to be using them. Everyone was pressing forward, trying to get ahead in the throng. Amelie saw girls almost in tears because they had become separated from their mamas, mothers practically starting disputes with people whom they thought had jumped the queue, and women of all ages crying out in dismay when a flower got squashed or a train crushed. It was a warm evening and even the spacious rooms of the palace fast became stuffy with human sweat, expensive scent and the perfume of hundreds of roses and lilies.

The sense of expectation was so strong it could almost be tasted. All around, women eyed each other's gowns and jewels and made assessments as to their standing in the pecking order. Amelie, caught up in it all despite herself, decided that her Packards gown was indeed as good as any there, if not better. In fact she saw one or two girls looking at her with something like envy. Winifred noticed them as well.

'Country gentry,' she murmured. 'No style at all.'

Amelie felt a lift in her confidence. It helped to know that she more than passed muster, but it did nothing to soothe her now churning nerves. What if she trod on her train? What if she fell over while curtsying? If she made a mistake, she would die of embarrassment. Worse, her mother would never forgive her.

At last they attained the object of all the waiting and pushing. As they reached the door of the Picture Gallery, Winifred and Amelie let down the trains that they had been carrying over their arms, and the gentlemen-at-arms spread them out on the floor behind them with wands. Amelie removed her right glove and Winifred fussed around, tweaking her veil and smoothing her skirt, then together they crossed the Gallery to the door of the Presence Chamber.

There, seated on carved and gilded thrones, were King Edward and Queen Alexandra, along with various members of the royal family. Amelie felt sick. She gave over her precious card and followed the procession of girls and their mothers across the huge room. There was no unseemly overtaking now, but a stately progress. The surroundings blurred into a kaleidoscope of colour. Amelie kept her eyes on Their Majesties. As each debutante was presented, she watched, and as each one managed the curtsying and the kissing she became more and more determined. If they could do it then so could she.

Then there were no more people between her and the thrones. The Lord Chamberlain had her card in his hand. Her name and her mother's were announced. She stepped forward.

The King was looking slightly bored, but his eyes brightened a little as Amelie approached. The Queen was wearing her gentle, vaguely vacant smile. All the intensive practice that Amelie had been forced to do came into play. She curtsied with grace and control, placed her hand beneath that of the King's and kissed it, stepped back, shuffled sideways, repeated the action before the Queen, backed away without putting her foot on her train, curtsied to the other royals, backed away again.

And it was over. Another girl was approaching the throne and Winifred was squeezing her arm and speaking in her ear.

'Well done, my dear. You managed splendidly. I am proud of you.'

To her amazement, Amelie realised that her mother was speaking with real warmth. There was even a tremble of emotion in her voice. She looked at her and saw tears standing in her eyes.

'Oh Mama –' she whispered. It was so sweet to feel loved. She could not remember the last time her mother had spoken to her like that. She wanted to throw her arms round her and hug her, to be embraced in return.

But the smooth wheels of the ceremony swept them on. They were conducted through to the supper room where the debutantes, light-headed with relief now that the ordeal was over, were shrieking at each other in excitement while their mothers looked on proudly and worked out their chances on the marriage market. Amelie found some girls she knew and joined them to compare notes.

'I nearly died when my name was announced . . .'

'My foot caught in the hem of my dress. I felt it give . . .'

'I thought the waiting was going to go on for ever . . .'

Somehow, a plate of food came to be in her hand. Amelie found she was ravenously hungry. The weariness brought on by the endless queuing disappeared. She laughed and exclaimed with the others and even agreed that though she was glad it was over she wouldn't have missed it for the world. She was really enjoying herself by the time Winifred told her they must be leaving.

There was one more call to be made, to a photographer's in Bond Street, and then, at half-past one in the morning, they made their way home to where the Peacock party awaited them.

Once again the family were all waiting to receive them, soon to be joined by a household of guests. Everyone admired Amelie and asked about how the Presentation had gone and how she had felt, the women reminiscing about their own presentations. Amelie could not help basking in all the attention. It was very pleasant to be the centre of attraction for once in her life.

It turned into quite the jolliest party that Winifred had given that Season, crowded enough to be lively without being an unbearable crush like a formal drum. There was enough space for the older people to sit and talk and for the younger ones to dance to the trio of hired musicians without treading on each others' gowns. The weather was perfect, so windows and doors were thrown open to the cool summer night, and any overheated dancers or young couples wanting to escape from chaperons could wander out into the garden, where Chinese lanterns had been hung from the trees.

The Amberley grandparents departed at about half-past two, followed soon afterwards by the Packards. Thomas put his hands on Amelie's shoulders and kissed her forehead, then held her at arm's length and looked at her.

'My little granddaughter, the most beautiful debutante of the Season,' he said.

Amelie flushed and laughed. 'Oh nonsense, Grandpa.'

'You are to me. Now, don't you bother about returning

those baubles. Keep 'em for all these parties and balls. Little souvenir of today.'

Amelie stared at him. '*Grandfather!* You can't!'

'Oh yes I can. It's an old man's privilege to spoil his favourite girl. Besides, they wouldn't look right on anyone else.'

And with that, he took his leave. Stunned, Amelie looked down at the diamonds glittering on her chest, at the matching ones on her wrist. She knew little about precious stones, but she did not need to be an expert to realise that this set was finer than anything owned by either her mother or her grandmother. She turned her arm and watched the rainbow sparkle as the light caught the facets. She had never even thought that such a luxury would ever be hers.

'I hope you realise what a very fortunate girl you are.'

Amelie looked up. She had forgotten that her mother was standing right behind her. Winifred was looking at the diamonds with a most remarkable expression on her face. She was trying to mask her naked jealousy with a smile, and the two simply did not mix. Amelie just could not resist turning the knife a little.

'Pretty, aren't they?' she said, making the earrings shake, touching the necklace. 'Grandpa is such an old dear to me.' And she bounced past her mother to rejoin the party.

At about three in the morning, Amelie was approached by Perry, trailing one of his many cronies.

'There you are, Melly old thing. Wonder if I could introduce a dear old pal of mine. Don't think you've met before.'

Amelie looked at the young man in question. She wasn't sure whether she knew him or not. Perry's friends all seemed to look very similar. Perry named him as the Honourable Georgy Teignmereton. The name was certainly familiar, being that belonging to one of the more distinguished families of the realm, and pronounced 'Tinton'. The bearer of the name was rather less distinguished, being no taller than Amelie, with a roundish face, brownish hair and greyish eyes, but Amelie was in a tearing good mood and happy to smile on everyone.

'I've seen you several times on the park, Miss Amberley. Been wanting to speak to you for ages. You cut a very dashing figure on a horse, if I might say so.'

'Thank you. Riding in the park is my favourite part of the day.'

They talked about horses for a while, and Perry drifted off with the air of one who has performed a particularly clever task. Amelie was claimed by a dance partner, but when the polka was over she found that Georgy Teignmereton was once again at her side.

'I say, Miss Amberley, it's dashed hot in here. How about a turn around the garden?'

Amelie might well have accepted if he had been at all prepossessing. As it was, she gave him a sharp tap on the shoulder with her fan.

'For shame, Mr Teignmereton, we've only just been introduced! If you want to be of service, you can fetch me a glass of lemonade.'

Far from taking this as a brushoff, he went to do her bidding, finding her the much-needed drink in a remarkably short time. As a reward, she agreed to dance with him again, and as he was a reasonably good dancer and she was in the mood to keep moving, she promised him another one later in the evening. By the time this occurred, it was rapidly getting light. Amelie's wonderful gown was crushed and one of her court plumes broken, but she did not care. It had been the best party she had attended since the round began.

What she did not realise was how her enjoyment enhanced her looks. When she happened to catch sight of herself in a glass she saw only a flushed face and hair that was beginning to escape from its pins. What Georgy Teignmereton saw was a lovely young girl glowing with life. The curve of her lips as she smiled, the energy with which she danced, the outline of her body beneath the layers of silk and whalebone all exuded promise. And on top of that the rumour was going round that her grandfather had just given her as a gesture of affection the impressive set of stones that she wore.

When the musicians finally packed up for the night, Amelie found Georgy at her side once more.

'When shall I see you again, Miss Amberley?'

'Oh, I don't know,' Amelie said carelessly. 'I expect we'll bump into each other somewhere.'

'Shall you be in the park tomorrow – or should I say, later today?'

'I expect so. We go there at some time most fine days.' Amelie was looking over his shoulder to see if a friend of hers was still there.

'Are you going to Lady Cossington's ball tomorrow?'

'I can't remember – Mother does all the arranging – no, I don't think we are.'

'Dash it – well, perhaps I might call on you? What day are you at home?'

'Ah – Thursday. Excuse me, I must go and say goodbye to Maudie. We were at school together, you know. I do hope you enjoyed the party.'

And she swept off, leaving him staring after her.

It was gone five o'clock when she finally stood in her room letting the yawning maid undress her. The excitement of the day caught up with her at last and she was bone weary, though her head was still buzzing with all that had happened. The maid unclipped the wonderful diamonds and laid them in their case.

'Beautiful, ain't they, Miss Amelie? Fit for a princess.'

Amelie agreed, but as she looked at them glowing in their velvet nest, it came to her that they were far more than a very generous present. They were the seal on the day. She was now set on the course of a Society lady, and the business of her life was not to take a part in the running of the store, but to marry somebody with a name and a fortune and then be a proper wife to him. All this she had known, but hoped she would somehow be able to avoid with her grandfather's connivance. But now the truth came home to her. Not only her mother but her grandfather expected her to be a successful debutante. Her grandfather's promise of more responsibility in the store had been hollow. He had just been fobbing her off, believing that it was just a passing fancy, or that she would be married by the time next year came along. She reached out and shut the jewellery case with a snap. They might think she was caught, but she would find a way out yet.

16

'Oh come on, Iz, where's the harm in it?' Daisy begged.

They were in their attic room at the end of another long day. Daisy's blouse was limp and crumpled and stuck to her in places. High summer had come to London and women strolled into the department wearing frothy light dresses in pale colours and talking of garden parties and boating and Ascot. Even now the sun was still bright, though the evening shadows were beginning to lengthen.

'Don't you want to get out? There we are stuck indoors all day, and it's such lovely weather. Just think how pretty it must be out in the country.'

'I'm sure it is,' Isobel agreed.

There was enough of a hint of longing in her voice for Daisy to press the point.

'You must miss it, don't you? I mean, you used to go on picnics and visits and stuff when you was back home, didn't you?'

'Yes,' Isobel sighed.

'Well, there you are then. There's Johnny and Arthur asking us for a nice day out in the country. I want to go, they want to go and you want to really, so why not?'

She knew very well why not, because Isobel didn't like Johnny and Arthur, but Daisy was not going to let a detail like that stand in her way.

'But, Daisy, it will be Sunday. One cannot be gadding about enjoying oneself on a Sunday. It isn't right.'

Now it was Daisy's turn to sigh. 'What other day have we got, Izzy? It's all very well for those as can enjoy themselves any day of the week to sound off about Sunday, but we're working girls. Sunday's our only whole day off. You can always get up a bit early and go to early service if you want.'

Isobel said nothing. Daisy knew she was winning.

'It'll do you good. You're looking ever so pasty these days,' she added. 'Fresh air and all that. I ain't never – I mean, I haven't ever been further than Epping Forest. We used to go there once a year on the Sunday School outing. Lovely it was, all green trees and that. I love trees.'

'I would not want it to be thought that accepting had any sort of – of significance,' Isobel said.

'What?' Daisy said. She was getting good at understanding Isobel, but sometimes she still seemed to be speaking a different language.

'I mean – just because I might agree to go, I don't want the – the young men to think there is any sort of understanding between us, or any sort of special relationship.'

'You'll go then?' Daisy asked, delighted.

'Well, yes, I suppose I might, as your heart is so set upon it.'

'Oh Izzy! You'll enjoy it, I'm sure you will.'

Daisy flung her arms round her friend and kissed her.

The proposed trip filled all of her thoughts for the next few days. Ever since the outing to the music hall, Johnny and Arthur had been trying to persuade the girls to come out with them again, but as Daisy did not want to go out with Arthur alone and Isobel was against any association with them at all, it had been impossible to arrange. Arthur seemed to be cooling off the whole idea, much to Daisy's satisfaction. Isobel wished that Johnny would take the hint as well, but he was as keen as ever. To Daisy, the prospect of any outing with him along was wonderful. A trip to the country was sheer heaven.

On Sunday morning, Isobel got up at the same time as usual and went to early service, as Daisy had suggested. Daisy luxuriated in the extra time in bed, then spent a leisurely half-hour in getting dressed. She had to wear her usual skirt and blouse, since she had nothing else. Once upon a time, when she was still living at home and working in the factory, she would have gone to the second-hand stalls at the market and bought a summer dress. Now she had higher standards to live up to. She could not go out with Isobel and the men wearing second-hand clothes. Instead she spent two and ninepence of her savings on a perky straw boater and secured it to her head with a hatpin with an imitation pearl end. This, together with the bright ribbon at the neck of her blouse and the white cotton crocheted gloves on her work-worn hands gave her quite a holiday air. By the time she had finished, she looked at herself in the glass with satisfaction.

Isobel merely pinned up a couple of stray ends of hair when she returned from church, and the two of them clattered downstairs, picked up their greaseproof-paper-wrapped packets of sandwiches from the kitchen and went to meet the young men, who called for them promptly at ten o'clock. When they got to the door, however, there was only Johnny standing on the top step. He was looking distinctly uncomfortable.

'I – er – I'm sorry about this,' he said, speaking to Daisy. 'Arthur's – er – had to cry off. Got to go and see his family. You know what families are.'

'Oh yeah. Mine get the hump if I don't go and see them regular,' Daisy said, delighted at this development. 'That's all right, ain't – isn't – it, Izzy? Johnny's company enough for us.'

'Oh indeed yes,' Isobel agreed, looking a good deal more cheerful at the prospect of not being paired off.

Only Johnny seemed dissatisfied with the new arrangement, but he made the best of it, offering both arms to the girls, and chatting to them as they walked to the tram stop. He addressed his remarks to both of them, but as Isobel hardly said more than 'Yes' or 'No' to anything, it was Daisy who kept up the conversation, laughing over things that had happened in the shop and remarking on people and places they saw as they went along.

'Where are we going?' she asked, as they joined the queue of people waiting for the tram.

'If we get on this one and ride right until the end of the line, we'll get to Lee Green. Then it's only a short walk to lanes and fields and stuff,' Johnny explained. 'Do you like walking, Isobel?'

'Yes, thank you.'

'Me too. What about cycling? Can you ride a bicycle?'

'No, I never learnt.'

'That's a pity. There's a group of us at the shop thinking of starting a cycling club. You can take your cycle on the train, you know, in the guard's van, so we could ride out to somewhere nice of a Sunday, then cycle round all the lanes and villages. Stop for a nice pint of something, and sandwiches, then back by train again in the evening. Could try somewhere different each time, like.'

'Oh, that sounds wonderful,' Daisy cried, her imagination fired. 'I'd love to learn to ride a bicycle. Is it very difficult?'

'Not when you get the hang of it. It sort of comes to you suddenly. One minute you're wobbling all over the place and the next, you're off. And once you've got it, it's wonderful. Flying along with the wind in your face, you feel like you're king of the road. And the freedom of it, too. No more waiting about for trams or buses, you just peddle off to wherever you want and whenever you want.'

'Oh – I wish I could try.'

Daisy pictured herself cycling along a country lane with Johnny by her side, not with a club but just the two of them, the sun warm on their faces and the birds singing in the trees overhead. It seemed idyllic. Then reality intruded.

'But aren't bicycles very expensive?' she asked. She had seen them down in their basement department at the store. The cheapest ones were over six pounds, the better ones three times that amount.

'Well yes, but you can buy them second-hand.' Johnny turned to Isobel. 'I could always look over a cycle for you, do the brakes and that and make sure it's safe.'

'Thank you,' Isobel said.

'It'd be fun, wouldn't it, Iz? Going cycling?' Daisy said.

They were interrupted by the arrival of the tram. Johnny gallantly handed the girls on board, which gave Isobel the chance to slip into a window seat. Daisy plumped down beside her, so Johnny had to take the seat on the other side of the aisle. It was an arrangement to please everyone but Johnny, since Isobel now completely opted out of the conversation by looking steadfastly out of the window. To Daisy, the whole journey was an adventure. The part of it that went through central London she only knew in sections, and once they were into the new suburbs, it was entirely fresh territory to her.

'Where are we now?' she kept asking Johnny, who was happy to give a commentary on everything they passed.

'What do you think of these places, Isobel? Neat, aren't

they?' he said, trying to draw her in. 'How would you like to live somewhere like that?'

'I think it would be most dreadfully lowering to the spirits. Rows and rows of houses, all looking exactly alike,' Isobel answered.

'I think they're lovely,' Daisy exclaimed.

The new developments were all very alike, it was true, each house built of red or yellow brick with heavy stone pillared bay windows and a front door with stained-glass inserts. But compared with North Millwall they were palaces. They were big and solid and well-built, they had front gardens with coloured tiled paths and back gardens with real grass and flowerbeds, those bays must let in lots of light, and the streets were wide with saplings planted along the edges of the pavements. They were clean and new and had three or even four bedrooms. Daisy could not even think of aspiring to one of them.

'It's so clean out here, and look at them – those – trees. That's one of the things I like about Trent Street, the trees. Back home, we had to go down the Island Gardens if we wanted to see a bit of green.'

'I used to look across to the Island Gardens from Greenwich. Me and my pals went over there sometimes, but it was more for the fun of walking through the tunnel than the gardens themselves. They were a bit tame after Greenwich Park,' Johnny said.

'Did you really? Fancy that! We might of seen each other there. We used to go to Greenwich Park sometimes, but it was a bit of a long haul from where we lived. I used to look across from the gardens at them – those – beautiful big buildings and the green hill behind and it looked like paradise,' Daisy said, smiling at the memory.

'The hill's marvellous for sledging. Ever so steep. We used to take our mum's tin trays and slide down,' Johnny said.

'That must of been good. Did you fall off?'

'Tons of times. It was all part of the fun.'

They chatted easily the length of the journey, comparing experiences and opinions. They had the same sense of humour and similar tastes, although Johnny had travelled and done so much more than Daisy that he seemed quite the man of the world compared with the lads she had known back home.

The tram arrived at the end of the line and they got down. Johnny immediately offered his arms to both girls again and they set off down the little High Street and then along a road similar to any of those past which they had travelled, except that there were many empty plots between the new houses. After a while they came to an unmade road, with just a few houses in various stages of being built beside it, which at length petered out into a country lane.

'There, we've left London behind us at last,' Johnny said. 'Now, isn't this nice? Fresh air, sunshine, flowers – aren't you glad you came, Isobel?'

'It's very pleasant,' Isobel said, evading the question.

'It's beautiful,' Daisy sighed.

She could not get over just how lovely it was. There were wild flowers in the grass verges, dog roses in the hedgerows and poppies blooming amongst the young corn. Birds sang in the trees, animals grazed in the meadows and everywhere flourished with the luxuriant green of summer. High overhead, a lark sang.

'Oh look, sheep!' she cried. 'I ain't never seen sheep before. Ain't they sweet? All fluffy. Can I touch one? Do they bite?'

Johnny laughed. 'Bite? Sheep? Get away! Here, look, see if you can reach this one if you want to touch it.'

Fascinated and slightly apprehensive, Daisy climbed onto the lower rungs of a gate and stretched out towards a grazing ewe. Her fingers met with the wiry, oily outer wool, then sank in to the clean white layer beneath.

'Oh! It's all soft! It's lovely. Oh Izzy, come and feel.'

'No, thank you.'

'You really never seen a sheep before?' Johnny asked.

Daisy blushed, her pleasure abruptly cut short. 'We never went very far in our family,' she had to admit.

It was something of an understatement. Apart from the Sunday School outings to Epping, the only journey she had ever been on was one trip to Southend when she was eight.

Johnny rescued her from her embarrassment.

'You girls hungry yet? If we go down this lane to the left here we get to a village with a nice pub. We could stop there and have a drink and eat our sandwiches.'

'I don't really think I want to go in a public house, thank you,' Isobel said.

Johnny was quick to reassure her. 'You don't have to go in if you don't want to. There are benches outside, and they sell lemonade and ginger beer or even milk if you prefer. And it's a very respectable place. They get a lot of visitors out here as it's so near to London. Lots of ladies walking and bicycling. Just come and see it, and if you don't like it, we needn't stop.'

Isobel couldn't very well argue with this, and when they got to the village, even she had to agree that it was very pretty, with a collection of cottages, some of them thatched, round a little green. The pub was an attractive place with, as Johnny had promised, rough benches placed against the walls. The girls sat down and Johnny went in to get the drinks. Daisy sighed with pleasure, leaning back against the sun-warmed brick of the wall and closing her eyes.

'Isn't it beautiful? I don't think I've ever been anywhere so pretty in all my life. Aren't you glad you came now?'

'It is nice to get away from London, certainly,' Isobel agreed.

Johnny came back with glasses of home-made lemonade for the girls and a pint for himself.

'Mmm, that's the stuff. Better than what you get from the London breweries,' he said. 'Lemonade all right?'

'Delicious,' Daisy enthused.

They opened their now slightly squashed sandwiches and watched children playing on the green and locals and other visitors coming to the pub. As Johnny had said, it was a popular place. A group of cyclists stopped off for a drink, laughing and joking amongst themselves, and two motor cars went by while they were eating.

'Do you want to walk on a bit? There's a pretty stream about a mile down the road,' Johnny asked Isobel.

'Very well,' Isobel agreed.

Daisy could not help feeling hurt that she was not consulted, but was happy enough to go along with the decision. When they got to the stream, Isobel settled down to rest in the shade of a willow tree, closing her eyes and giving every appearance of not wanting to be disturbed. Johnny gazed at her for a while, disappointment written on his face. Daisy took a breath.

'Are there fish in the river?' she asked.

For a moment, Johnny did not answer her. Then he turned to her slowly, as if surfacing from a deep sleep.

'What? Er – yes, there are. Little ones. Minnows, stickle-backs, that sort of thing.'

'Really? Where? Will you show me?'

Once she had managed to distract him, he was a lively companion again, pointing out the fish, picking wild flowers, telling her the names of things. It was worth admitting to her ignorance to hear his pleasure in knowing about the plants and birds and insects around them. Daisy's knowledge of the natural world was limited to drawing pictures of leaves on squeaky slates in school.

'Daisies for Daisy,' he said, presenting her with a handful of meadow marguerites.

Daisy flushed with pleasure. Nobody had ever given her flowers before.

'Thank you,' she whispered, aching inside, wishing that the gesture was as romantic as it seemed.

At three o'clock they had to start back, in order to catch the tram home.

'It's the Sunday service, you see,' Johnny explained.

Isobel was roused from her doze, and Johnny did his best to get her to talk as they walked back through the lanes and then the beginning of the built-up area to the stop. Daisy clutched her bunch of flowers in one hand and held on to Johnny's arm with the other. She could feel the warmth of him through the fabric of his jacket, the brush of his leg against her skirt, and wished with all her being that Isobel were not there, that it was just the two of them, strolling together in a haze of happiness.

Johnny said goodbye to them on the doorstep of number twenty-four.

'I do hope you enjoyed yourself?' he said to Isobel.

'It was very nice,' she replied, coolly polite.

'It's been the loveliest day I've ever had,' Daisy told him, her eyes glowing.

Johnny gave a wry smile. 'Yes, well, I'm glad you liked it, anyway. Perhaps we could do it again sometime?'

He looked at Isobel, but it was Daisy who jumped at the chance.

'That'd be lovely,' she said.

Isobel said nothing. Johnny turned to go.

'Thanks ever so much for taking us,' Daisy called after him as he went down the steps.

Johnny raised a hand in farewell, and set off down the street. The spring had gone out of his step.

Daisy fetched an empty jam jar from the kitchen for her wild flowers.

'They're already looking a bit droopy. Isn't it sad that they don't last?' she said. The thought of their fleeting beauty brought a great lump to her throat. It had been such a wonderful day, but now it was over, and Johnny still only had eyes for Isobel.

'Why don't you press one or two of them?' Isobel suggested.

The idea held back the threatening tears. Daisy chose the most perfect marguerite and put it between the pages of the only book she possessed, her Sunday School prize Bible. She held it to her chest for a while, gazing at the flowers in the vase. Now she had something to keep, something that he had given her.

17

Edward stepped out of the motor with the rest of the family and followed them across the lawns. It felt odd to be out in the sunshine on a weekday, odd to be wearing a striped blazer and a boater. He had not wanted to be part of the family party to Henley, but his grandfather had insisted.

'You know what they say, Edward – all work and no play and all that. The store can look after itself for three days. You come and have a little holiday. You'll be all the better for it.'

And since in the end his grandfather called the tune, here he was, a part of one of the great set pieces of the Season. Now that he was here, he had to admit that it was very impressive. Against a backdrop of trees and green grass a great picnic was assembling, with enclosures and marquees spread out across the lawns, and dazzling houseboats moored along the river bank. In amongst this huge live stage set, hundreds of people were sitting in picturesque groups or strolling about dressed in whites or the brightest of colours, the men in their garish blazers, the women in their prettiest summer dresses, wearing flowered hats and carrying parasols. Society was out in force, along with all its hangers-on.

'There!' his mother exclaimed. 'That is our houseboat.'

Her voice rang with pride. The toy she had hired for the festival was indeed a triumph. A two-decked affair painted in bright blue, it had blue and white awnings fringed with gold shading its decks, and gold and white pennants fluttering from its fragile masts. Flower boxes fixed along its sides overflowed with marigolds and trailing nasturtiums, and at each end of the gangplank there were bay trees in tubs, surrounded by more nasturtiums. The family was duly impressed. They all trooped on board, exclaiming further at the luxuries to be found there. There were Persian rugs, Chinese umbrellas and wicker chairs strewn with embroidered cushions waiting for them, while the servants who had gone on ahead were ready to take any surplus belongings and serve drinks.

'Just the ticket, old girl,' Edward's father, Bertie, said, as he sank into one of the chairs and held out a hand for the day's first glass of champagne.

Edward looked at him with disapproval. Yes, it was just his sort of occasion. He could lounge around all day, eating and drinking and leering at the pretty girls. He would be entertained to his heart's delight without having to lift a finger.

'Very pretty, my dear, and so comfortable,' his grandmother commended, sipping tea.

'Splendid, Winifred my dear. We must have one of the best views of the river here,' Thomas said.

Winifred looked duly gratified, but Edward could see that she was still uneasy. He knew what was worrying her. It was all very well to have a beautiful houseboat in a prime position, but it meant nothing if the right people did not call in to sit on its decks and eat and drink the vast amounts of food and wine she had ordered. It sickened him, this courting of all these people with too much idea of their own worth. Most of them had only their names to be proud of. Maybe in the past their ancestors had done something to gain the titles they held, but the present generation seemed to him to be a talentless lot.

He leant on the deckrail with his glass of champagne and surveyed the scene. Already flotillas of skiffs and punts, bright with awnings and cushions and flowers, were plying the river, powered with varying degrees of skill by men of all ages and a surprising number of young women. The shrieks and cries of the English upper class at play echoed across the water, grating on Edward's nerves.

To his surprise, his grandfather came to join him.

'Splendid sight, eh?' he said, waving with his cigar at the kaleidoscope of people and boats before them.

'Remarkable display of wealth, certainly,' Edward conceded.

'And beauty, my boy. Lots of pretty girls here, too. Look at that little blonde thing. See her driving that punt along! Shows spirit, that does.'

Edward was not interested in girls with spirit, and particularly those with minds of their own.

'Can't abide these New Women,' he said.

'Couldn't agree more,' Thomas said, and rambled on for some time, pointing out what he considered to be beauties, until Edward was drawn in as well, and began making his own comments.

'And they're all on the lookout for a husband, too,' Thomas reminded him. 'You should take the opportunity to look about you a bit. It's time you started to think of marrying. A married man has more of an air of stability, you know. Shows he's serious about life and his future.'

Edward was startled to be given such an obvious hint. Was marriage then the key that would bring him more real power in the store?

'Expensive business, though,' he said, seeking to confirm it.

'I realise that, my boy. None better. You can rest assured that there would be suitable adjustments to your position. I want to see all three of you youngsters well set up. It's Amelie's turn at the moment, of course, but you are not forgotten.'

'I'll certainly bear it in mind,' Edward said.

Thomas was not to be fobbed off with vague assurances.

'File it away and forget it, in other words,' he retorted. 'You have to make an effort in these things, you know. It's not like buying a pair of gloves. Now, these three days will give you a good chance to think about it and maybe make a start. Just look at what's before you! Good as a moving shop window.'

Edward was looking. There certainly were plenty of young girls in the boats and sitting in family parties under the trees on the oppositie bank. Many were not at all pretty, in fact some were remarkably plain, but all of them were beautifully turned out in dainty dresses and flowered hats or perky boaters. All were supremely confident of their position in the Top Ten Thousand.

'Give them a whiff of Trade and they'd be off,' he said.

Thomas snorted. 'Don't you be so sure of it. There are plenty out there with very old handles to their names who wouldn't pass up the chance of an alliance with the Packard fortune. They can't put on all this pretty display without money, you know, and not all of them have been wise with it in the past. They need people like us who can make it, however much they try to look down their noses at us. Take our Amelie, now. It's doing her no harm to be known as my granddaughter. Your father might think she's being launched on the Amberley name, but it wouldn't do her much good without Packards behind her.'

A small glow of satisfaction started. Did this mean his grandfather had no real plans to give Amelie a place in the store after all? It certainly sounded as if he wanted her married off.

'Say what you will about them, they know how to live, these people,' Thomas ruminated. 'Why is it that outsiders like ourselves want to get in? Because it's very pleasant to play all day. I've worked all my life, and the thought of lounging about and eating and visiting and amusing myself at the opera is beginning to look very tempting. And then when this is all over, off they go to Cowes or the grouse moors, and then back to their country estates for a bit of shooting and hunting.'

The glow turned to an excitement so acute that it burnt like a ball of fire inside Edward. Was the old man actually thinking of retirement, or was he just testing him, sounding out the strength of his ambitions?

'I'm sure Mother would agree with you there, sir.'

'But not you, eh?'

'I leave it to Perry to play the man about town. I prefer to do something useful with my time. Look at what you've done in your lifetime, sir. You've built an empire. Most of these Society people only fritter away what others have accumulated.'

'Right enough, my boy, and the empire has to be maintained, or else it collapses like the Roman one. Continuity, that's the thing. Society people understand that all right.'

So there it was. His grandfather was ready to step down, but he wanted to be sure that Edward was going to secure the next generation. All at once the world was a brighter place. The sun shone hotter, the sky was bluer, the trees a more verdant green. The scene before him was no longer an irritating parade of the idle but a happy carnival. Everything he wanted was within reach. Packards was going to be his.

'You're right, sir. Maybe I should think about settling down. There's certainly a feast to choose from here.'

As if timed, a punt went by with a lovely raven-haired girl in a white dress reclining in it. She glanced up at them as she passed, and her dark eyes assessed Edward with a definite glint of interest. Thomas was not slow to notice it. He clapped Edward on the shoulder.

'Handsome young chap like you should have no trouble.'

Edward found himself laughing. 'You've made your point, Grandfather.'

Amelie came up to them, having just toured all over the houseboat. She gave her grandfather a tight smile and turned to Edward.

'Isn't this fun? This boat is like a floating playhouse. Have you seen inside yet, Edward?'

Confident now of his place within the Packard hierarchy, Edward felt something like affection for his sister.

'Never mind the inside, Mel. What do you say to a trip on the river? Mother –' he turned to Winifred, who was sitting beside Bertie in an unusual show of marital harmony '– there is a skiff belonging to this houseboat, is there not?'

'Indeed there is.' Winifred was eager to have her offspring participate in all the rituals of the occasion. 'Have one of the servants show you where it's tied up. Just remember that luncheon is at one. We have the Teignmeretons and the Flynts coming.'

The mention of the Teignmeretons put him, if it were possible, into an even better mood. Though Georgy Teignmereton was just the sort of sprig of the aristocracy that Edward most disliked, he could almost feel warm towards him when he saw the way he was dancing attendance on Amelie. Perry had done a good job there. He did have his uses, even if they cost a fortune. Amelie, not surprisingly, was not giving him any encouragement at all, but there was no need to give up hope. Not when his mother was so obviously keen on promoting the match.

'Don't worry, we'll be back in time,' he assured her. 'Are you coming as well, Perry?'

'Just so long as you and Melly are rowing,' Perry agreed.

'Lazy pig,' Amelie said. 'I'll row both of you, if you like.'

Edward was almost ready to let her try.

It was as crowded as a cattle market on the river, with hundreds of small craft passing up and down and often getting hopelessly stuck in great tangles of oars and poles and paddles. Laughing men and girls waved and called out from one boat to another, admiring each other's outfits and inviting each other to luncheon or tea or supper and a view of the fireworks. Sweating watermen in red coats and brass shield badges cut across the processions, ferrying boatless people from one side to the other. Picnics were being laid out under the trees on one bank, while the other was lined with the bright confections that were the houseboats, green and silver ones with banks of red geraniums, striped ice-cream-coloured ones with hanging baskets of petunias, white and gold ones trailing graceful vines, each perfect in its way as a floating pleasure platform.

Occasionally the river was cleared, and all the cheerful crowd of boats had to pull into the bank, so that a race could be run. People gave a token wave and a cheer as the two teams of young men pulled by in gleaming racing shells, but unless they knew someone in one of the teams, the races were really only an interruption of the main point of the day, which was to see and to be seen. Perry and Amelie were constantly greeting friends as they made their leisurely way up to the bridge and back, and even Edward found there were plenty of people he knew, either from his schooldays or from parties his mother had obliged him to attend. In his present sunny temper, he hailed them all with enthusiasm.

There was a huge crush where the Gaiety Theatre enclosure was situated. Like every other man in the crowd, Edward gazed unashamedly at the luscious beauties under their lace parasols, beside whom the Society misses on the river looked hopelessly plain and undesirable. He had taken up with several actresses and dancers in the short while since he attained manhood, but never had he been able to aspire to a Gaiety girl. He and Perry stood in the boat, in accord for once, discussing the attractions of the various girls, while Amelie chatted to one of her friends in a neighbouring punt.

'See the girl at the side, with the blue dress?' Perry said. 'That's the latest one, Minnie Morgan. Stunner, isn't she? Now, who does she remind you of?'

'I don't know,' Edward said, though staring at the girl's lovely face, he did feel a pull of recognition. He definitely knew someone who looked very similar.

'I'll tell you who I think she looks like –' Perry glanced at Amelie, making sure that she was engrossed in her converation, then lowered his voice conspiratorially. 'Isobel Brand, that's who.'

'Isobel –?' And then it came to him. The shopgirl from Amelie's department whom he had had dismissed, and whom Amelie had managed to get reinstated. Clear and whole in his mind came the brief scene in one of the corridors, when he had happened upon Isobel as she came out of the Staff Manager's office. The fear in her flower face, the tremble of her full lips, the brave way in which she had tried to keep her dignity. Her bluebell eyes had met with his for a second, pleaded, then dropped in submission. As she hurried away, a sob escaped her. It was so vivid that Edward forgot where he was. He was disorientated for a moment when he realised that his brother was speaking to him.

'Prettiest girl in the whole store. More than pretty, a real beauty. Stands out a mile.'

Edward immediately went on the offensive. 'Put her out of your head, Perry. Remember company policy – hands off the staff. Grandfather's absolutely immovable on that one.'

His brother sighed. 'I know, and beastly unfair it is, too. Especially when there's a peach like that there waiting to be picked.'

Edward took in his brother's rapt expression. 'If you lay a finger on her, Grandfather will be stopping your allowance.'

Perry's lower lip took on a distinctive sulk. 'Who's going to tell him, then? I found a swain for Melly, didn't I? Isn't that enough?'

'She's not at all enamoured, and I'm not surprised. Teignmereton's an idiot,' Edward pointed out. 'And in any case, it doesn't need me to spill the beans on your little adventures. The store's a hothouse. A nice piece of gossip like that would be round the place in no time at all.'

'I bet Grandfather doesn't abide by his own rules. We all know he's got a mistress out in St John's Wood somewhere,' Perry said.

'For God's sake, Perry!' It wasn't the sort of thing you discussed with people all around you.

Perry looked mutinous. 'Well, he has.'

They were interrupted by Amelie.

'You two look guilty! What are you talking about, as if I didn't know? Gaiety girls?' There was a note of contempt in her voice.

'They're there to be gazed upon, Sis,' Perry said.

'Well, I hope you've had your fill for the time being. I'm getting bored waiting here.'

Edward sat down, deliberately making the slender boat rock so that Perry had to sit quickly and grab the sides to stop himself from falling overboard. Edward laughed, and used one oar like a punting pole to thrust them out of the crowd.

'Hold tight, old chap. Don't want to get yourself wet, do you?'

Once they were in clearer water, he put all his concentration into powering them along the river, pulling hard for some hundred yards or so before the next log jam of boats held them up. The physical effort released some of the tension that had built so suddenly inside of him. He looked at his brother again, at his soft body and his fair face, reddening in the July sunshine. Perry, who always seemed to get what he wanted without raising a finger. Well, he wasn't going to get Isobel Brand.

18

If all of the Season could be like Henley, then it would be much more fun, Amelie decided. Of course, there were still all the long meals to be got through. The luncheon her mother had put on for the Teignmeretons on the first day had taken two hours to eat through and she had been placed next to Georgy, but even that had been quite bearable when it involved sitting on the top deck of the houseboat with the sun glinting on the water and the trailing branches of the willows tapping the awning above their heads. For the rest of the time, she had been as near to free as it was possible to be in the midst of Society, rowing up and down the river with one of her brothers or, on one occasion, her grandfather to accompany her. In the evening, there were fireworks, and a supper party on the houseboat, and the whole scene turned into a fairyland lit by swinging Chinese lanterns.

That was on the first day. By the afternoon of the second day she felt that she had seen everything several times over. She was trapped in the skiff with Perry and Georgy Teignmereton, who had insisted on taking the oars. He was not very good at handling them. It was only Amelie's steering that kept them out of trouble.

'Oops! Sorry, slight miscalculation,' he called out, as he splashed water all over the boat. 'Oh, I say, have I wetted your pretty dress, Miss Amberley? Most frightfully sorry. Here, let me mop you up –'

He leant forward to dab at her with his pocket handkerchief. Amelie brushed him away.

'It's nothing. I'll do it, thank you. Oh, look out!'

Amelie pulled at the steering rope, but it was too late. With a bump, they ran into the group of punts in front of them. There was a good deal of light-hearted jeering about letting the fair sex take the helm. Amelie fumed beneath a polite smile.

'That was all your fault,' she hissed at Georgy, when they

finally got clear. 'If you hadn't been fooling about, I could have got us round them.'

He grinned happily back at her. 'I say, you're just tremendous when you're cross.'

'Hey, stop squabbling, you two, they're clearing the river again,' Perry called from the bows.

This made Amelie even more irritated. She was not part of 'you two'.

Georgy caught her frown and misinterpreted it. 'Dashed annoying, having to stop for the racing, isn't it? And just when we were enjoying ourselves, too.'

'I thought the racing was what it was all about,' Amelie said.

Both young men gave men-of-the-world laughs.

'Good heavens no,' Perry told her. 'Haven't you found that out yet? The regatta's just an excuse for a three-day party.'

She knew that perfectly well, of course. It was the same as the other sporting events of the Season. Very few people went to Ascot for the racing, or to the Eton versus Harrow match for the cricket. But she liked the thrill of the races, of seeing two teams of young men pulling with all their strength at the oars and the tiny racing shells skimming like rockets over the water. It made her impatient of the amateurish pootling about she was doing, and wish for a bit of clear water, and the chance to see just how fast she could make the skiff move, especially if she could get out of her restricting corsets.

'Would you care for a stroll around the lawns after we get back to your people's houseboat?' Georgy asked.

Amelie was not listening to him.

'Here they come!' she cried.

It was a heat for the Diamond Sculls. One of the competitors was way ahead of the other. Amelie watched as he drew level then shot past, his powerful body bending and pulling, sending his fragile craft flying through the water. His face was set, every nerve fixed on widening the already large gap between himself and the other oarsman, while the sun glanced off his blond curls and lit the line of his muscular back. Amelie felt strangely breathless. There was a man who was striving to be the best, in striking contrast to Perry and Georgy, who never appeared to make an effort over anything.

'Who was that in the leading boat?' she asked her brother. Perry shrugged. 'Sorry, old girl, wasn't looking.'

She looked to Georgy for an answer, but he was no help either, and for once there was nobody in the boats around them whom she knew and could ask. Tired now of the mindless toing and froing of the river party, she suggested they went back to the houseboat.

'Jolly good idea. Time for another glass of bubbly, don't you think?' Perry agreed.

It was not until the dusk was darkening the river that she managed to get an answer to the question of the oarsman's identity. The houseboat was cheerful with a supper party. A trio of musicians was cramped into one corner of the upper deck where they played selections of music from the latest West End productions. Winifred had laid on a spectacular array of refreshments, champagne flowed and everyone was talking and laughing. Amelie spent her time avoiding Georgy Teignmereton. He really was becoming a nuisance, and the more he irritated her, the more the image of the blond-headed oarsman caught at her imagination, until she knew she could not ask outright about him without blushing.

Her grandfather came up to her.

'Enjoying yourself, Amelie? Looking forward to the fireworks, m'self. Always have loved fireworks.'

'It's very nice,' Amelie said dutifully. She had not forgiven him for abandoning her to her mother's schemes.

'Nice? It's splendid! Can't remember having such a good time since I don't know when. And don't tell me you haven't had some fun rowing up and down the river these last couple of days.'

Once upon a time she would not have minded being teased, would have done the same in return. Now she just felt she was being patronised.

'As I said, it's very nice – if you like just playing about all the time. But do you know what my first thought was when I saw all these pretty houseboats? That if we could dress up the store like that, we'd get thousands of people coming to look.'

Thomas laughed and patted her shoulder.

'You and your ideas! They certainly would come to look.

Whether they would buy anything is quite another matter. They wouldn't know it was meant to be a shop.'

'But if they came to look, they'd very likely stay to buy. That's how it works in Chicago,' Amelie said, trying to get a serious discussion going.

Just as she hoped, Thomas could not resist taking up anything to do with the store.

'Ah well, Chicago. Maybe it does work in America, but London's quite another matter. People are different in this country.'

'No they're not, they're just as ready to be tempted to buy. We should try it, Grandfather. A special display. It's too late for a Henley one, but perhaps we could have an autumn theme for September. I can just picture it — sheaves of corn and autumn leaves and fruits, rather like a harvest festival, with all our winter fabrics and clothes and things amongst them. It would look so pretty! A little piece of the country in the middle of London. I'm sure it would work.'

But Thomas just shook his head. 'It would be a lot of expense for no return. In fact, it could cost us money if we got a lot of sightseers getting in the way of the regular customers.'

Amelie fought to keep the frustration from sounding in her voice. 'It wouldn't, Grandfather. I just know it would increase our sales.' She put a hand on his arm and looked at him in the way she always used to, eyes big and pleading. 'Let me do it, Grandfather. Please. Just to try it. If it all goes wrong, it will be my fault.'

Thomas put his hand over hers and gave it a squeeze.

'No, my dear, it's too big a gamble, and besides, you have too many other things to do. You wouldn't be able to oversee something like that.'

'But you said, if I did the Season and kept Mother happy you'd –'

Thomas cut her short. 'The Season's not over yet. Now, shall we find a good seat to watch the fireworks?'

Amelie swallowed down tears of anger. 'I promised someone I'd watch from the skiff,' she lied, and left.

Seething, she made her way to the opposite end of the houseboat. She was as cross with herself as with her grandfather.

It had been stupid of her to try to persuade him here, in the middle of a party. She should have tackled him in his office, when his mind was fully on the store. But if he wouldn't listen to her, she would just have to show him. She would have autumn displays in Ladies' Sportswear, and dress up her window. He would see then that it drew in extra paying customers.

As she stood at the rail, furious at the unfairness of life, she chanced to overhear a conversation between a couple of middle-aged men.

'Young Rutherford walked it this afternoon, didn't he?'

'I should say! I'll lay you anything you care to name he'll take the Sculls again this year.'

Amelie's attention was caught. She eavesdropped unashamedly.

'I'm not taking you up on that one, old boy. Dead cert, barring accidents. Not an Eton man, is he?'

'No, he's from my Alma Mater. You Eton men like to think you have the monopoly of sportsmen, but it's not so. Hugo Rutherford being a case in point. He's not just good with the old oars, y'know. He's an excellent fast bowler *and* a terror on the rugby field. Splendid all-round sportsman, in fact.'

'Ah, but young Rutherford's the only one you can cite, now isn't he? Whereas I can point to any number of Old Etonians . . .'

The conversation ceased to interest Amelie at that point. But she had a name now. Hugo Rutherford. She had a vague feeling that she had heard of him before, but then one spoke to and heard others speaking of so many different people during the Season that it was difficult to place just when it was and in what context he had been mentioned. The important thing was that she now knew who he was. Somehow, the setback over her ideas for the store did not seem quite so important any more.

Winifred sat back after luncheon on the third day and allowed herself a few minutes' respite from her social duties to review the Henley campaign. From several points of view it had been a success. The meals she had offered had been nothing short of a triumph. She would defy any other hostess along the riverbank to have arranged such a lavish amount of food for so many guests. The one that had just been cleared away had consisted of twenty dishes in five courses, accompanied by ten different wines and spirits, including a particularly fine Château Lafite. A number of the gentlemen had complimented her on that.

The quality of guests had been almost what she had hoped for. She had taken the wise step of sending out invitations at the very earliest moment that it could be done without seeming overanxious, and so had prevented those whom she was courting from pleading prior engagements. Consequently, a gratifying number of the titled and the fashionable had graced the blue houseboat during the three days, and return invitations could therefore be expected.

About her family, she had mixed feelings. Bertie had played the host admirably when it was required of him, and had not embarrassed her by paying attention to any vulgar actresses or the like. Her mother had kept quiet, which was all Winifred asked of her. Edward had looked the gentleman, squired Amelie about, been pleasant to important guests' daughters and generally proved himself quite a social asset. Perry could always be relied upon to chat to people and bring along some much-needed unmarried men. Her parents-in-law had been graciously pleased to give the Amberley seal of approval to the events. Which left her father, and Amelie. Her father had been loudly ebullient, almost acting as if the houseboat were his. The fact that it was his money that was paying for the whole junket was something that Winifred preferred to forget. The sound of him laughing and exorting people to enjoy themselves had grated throughout the three days, but she had to admit that nobody had appeared to have been offended by him. In fact several people had remarked on what a character he was, and even seemed to be courting his attention and opinions. Mortified as she was at being the daughter of a shopkeeper, it had not occurred to her before that her father had become enough of a success to be something of a celebrity. If he could just be persuaded to purchase a country estate, she could almost forgive his being the founder of Packards.

But Amelie was quite another matter. Winifred's eyes roved over the guests as they gathered at the sides to watch another race. There was her daughter, leaning eagerly over the rail and straining to see the competitors. Amelie had been a severe disappointment to her over Henley. Everything had seemed set fair. The Teignmeretons had accepted her invitation to luncheon on the first day and supper on the second, the Hon. George had danced attendance morning, noon and night, and what had Amelie made of the opportunity? Nothing. She had treated the Hon. George as if he were a particularly stupid younger brother. Winifred was very angry with her.

'There they are!'

Amelie's cry made Winifred jump. Then as if to confirm her mother's poor opinion, she started to draw attention to herself in a most ridiculous way. While other people were waving hats and handkerchiefs in an elegant fashion and maybe letting out the odd decorous cheer or cry of encouragement, Amelie was jumping up and down and fairly shrieking.

'Come on, come on! Oh yes, yes, he's doing it! Yes! He's pulling ahead . . .'

Winifred arose from her wicker chaise longue and drew her daughter aside. Amelie's face was alight with excitement, making her look so pretty as to be almost beautiful. Winifred could have slapped her. With all her chances, she had been a total failure at attracting a husband.

'For heaven's sake, child,' she hissed, low enough not to be heard by any of her guests, but fierce enough to make her displeasure understood. 'Stop behaving like a hoyden. You are a debutante now, remember, not a schoolgirl. No one looking at you would believe you had been presented at court. You are acting more like a factory girl on a spree. I'm ashamed of you.'

To her chagrin, Amelie laughed.

'Oh Mother! It's the final of the Diamond Sculls!'

And before Winifred could say anything more, she broke away and regained her place at the rails, to begin wheedling an elderly man with a pair of binoculars.

'Who's winning? May I see? Oh thank you, you're so kind! Is it — ? Yes! It's him! He's done it!'

Her father strolled by, and stopped to talk.

'Our little Amelie's enjoying herself.'

Winifred tightened her mouth. 'Yes, you could put it that way.'

Thomas smiled. 'Come now, don't you think it's rather charming to see such enthusiasm? The young should be full of fun. There's time enough to be weary and cynical when you get old.'

'There's fun and there's screaming like an oaf at the football match,' Winifred retorted. 'I am displeased with Amelie. Most displeased.'

Thomas patted her arm. 'I think you've been overdoing it, Winifred. Lot of work involved in organising an affair of this kind, I'm sure. Now come and sit down.'

Winifred found herself sitting back in her chaise longue while her father waved at a passing footman – her footman, that was – to bring her some tea.

'Now then,' he said, settling himself next to her, 'what's my favourite granddaughter been doing to upset her mama so badly?'

'Where do I begin?' Winifred said.

'Let me guess – you're cross because she has not hooked one of these vacuous young men with an undershot chin?'

There were times when Winifred felt murderous towards her father. He had an uncanny way of putting his finger on something then turning it to one's disadvantage.

'Of course not,' she lied.

Her father smiled, patently unconvinced. 'Surely that's the crown of success for a mother and a Society hostess? To get her daughter married off to someone suitable in her first Season? Personally, I think it's barbarous, but who am I to comment? I'm only an old-fashioned merchant, after all.'

It took all Winifred's considerable self-control not to agree out loud with that last remark.

'After all the money that has been spent on her, I do think Amelie might at least play the part,' she said.

'But she has been playing the part! She has been paddling up and down the river looking as pretty as a picture, and decorating all your nice parties and talking to all the young men you've pushed under her nose.'

'She's been abominably rude to the Hon. George Teignmereton, and he's the only one who's shown any real interest.'

And she had had to pay off some of Perry's debts for him in order to get him to bring his friend along to the Peacock Party in the first place.

'Teignmereton!' Thomas laughed. 'The boy's an idiot. You don't really want her hitched to him, do you?'

In agony least his voice should have carried to any of the guests, Winifred hushed him.

'The Teignmeretons are one of the foremost families in Shropshire.'

'That's as maybe. The boy's still an idiot. Our little Amelie can do better than that.'

'It's somewhat late to be saying that now. The Season's nearly over. Everyone will be going off to Cowes or Deauville or to the grouse moors, and where will we be? Still in town! Nobody, but nobody else will be back until next April. Now, if we had a country estate, it would be different. We could invite people to stay and they would invite us back . . .' Winifred poured out at length her thoughts on why they should have a family seat.

It was no use, though. Her father was immovable.

'If you feel so strongly about it, my dear, why don't you get your Bertie's people to invite your friends for you? After all, they're the ones with the respectable name, as you're always so quick to point out. Now, I mustn't keep you any longer from your duties as a hostess. Splendid party. Simply splendid.'

He left her nearly spluttering with rage. The stubborn old man! He could well afford to benefit his family by buying an estate. He was just too selfish to do so.

A black cloud settled over Winifred's Henley party, souring the success it had undoubtedly been. And it was all the fault of her father and her ungrateful daughter.

19

'Bit nippy this morning, ain't – isn't – it?' Daisy said, splashing water rapidly over her body.

'Yes, I think autumn is truly here at last,' Isobel agreed.

'Nice to feel a bit of a snap after all that heat. Like being in a blooming Turkish bath,' Daisy said, though she had never seen one, and had very little idea of what they were like. But everyone had been saying it throughout the heatwave. It had been baking in the attic room during August, even at nighttime, making it difficult for the girls to get to sleep, though the temperature made them tireder than ever and their ankles swelled in the heat.

'But it will mean it will be getting colder up here,' Isobel pointed out.

'Yeah, but we can always sit downstairs of an evening, can't we?'

'I suppose so.'

It was all right while they were talking like this. As long as they kept to light chat, they got on. But as Daisy finished washing and started pulling on her clothes, her eyes strayed to where Isobel was brushing her beautiful honey-blonde hair, and the sick knot of envy tightened once more. Isobel had everything – luscious figure, lovely face, beautiful hair.

'You are lucky,' she blurted out.

'What do you mean?' Isobel asked, her voice guarded.

She did not turn to look at her. Instead she carried on with the complicated task of pinning her heavy tresses into a neat style.

'Having that lovely colour hair,' Daisy said, making do with part of the truth. 'It's so striking, catches your eye, like. Mine's just mouse. Nobody notices it at all.'

'It isn't always an advantage, you know. I often wish I wasn't so noticeable. I don't like it.'

But Daisy couldn't really believe that. Only someone who

had always had good looks could think that. It was different when you were ordinary. Then you longed and longed for something that would make people look at you. Or rather, make one particular person look at you.

'We'd better hurry up. I can smell breakfast,' she said.

It was the usual rush to eat and get out. The girls from number twenty-four grabbed their jackets and hats and hurried out of the door to join the flood of Packards' workers making their way up Trent Street towards the store. As usual, Johnny and Arthur were waiting for them, and as usual, Johnny fell in alongside Isobel, leaving Arthur with Daisy. Also as usual, Isobel made no attempt at conversation, and only answered Johnny's chat with monosyllables. Daisy was forced to acknowledge that Isobel was not just playing hard to get. She genuinely did not want Johnny's attentions. But though it meant she had nothing to accuse Isobel of, it still gave her cause for jealousy. She did not like herself for it, but she could not help it. From the moment she had first spoken to Johnny, seen his ready smile, listened to his cheerful banter, she had loved him. It was as simple as that.

'I wonder if Miss Packard will be in today?' she said, to distract herself.

'You expecting her?' Arthur asked.

'She was in yesterday, all full of ideas for Ladies' Sportswear. We're going to have a special autumn display. All branches and leaves and stuff, with the goods all sort of hung in around it. Kind of like Christmas, only not, so Miss Packard says.'

'Sounds a rum idea to me,' Arthur shrugged.

'It's a wonderful idea! It will make people come and look.'

They debated the issue all the way to the store. It helped Daisy to deal with the sight of Johnny's head leaning towards Isobel's just ahead of her.

Just after nine o'clock, Miss Packard arrived, charmingly dressed in a peach-coloured dress with the new higher waist and kimono sleeves. Trailing behind her were five men carrying great bundles of branches, corn sheaves and artificial autumn leaves.

'I'd rather have real ones, but of course they'd drop in a couple of days and make a mess. Now, we must set all these up, and I've some bunches of chrysanthemums being delivered later, so we must allow for them as well.'

Daisy found herself swept along by Miss Packard's enthusiasm. It was like a fresh wind blowing through the place whenever she turned up.

'Oh, that sounds lovely!' she exclaimed.

Miss Higgs glared at her, but Miss Packard smiled.

'Yes, I think so too. Now, Miss Higgs, if you will be so kind as to allow two of the girls to assist me – Miss Phipps here, do you think, and Miss Brand? – then that will leave you and the other two to the more important job of serving customers. We must do all this without losing any sales.'

Daisy was quick to see the deftness of her approach. She could easily just march in and take over. She had every right. But instead, she gave at least the appearance of deferring to Miss Higgs, and saved the senior saleswoman's face. For herself, she was delighted to be chosen to dress up the department, and she could see that Isobel was pleased to be let off sales duties as well.

It wasn't like work, helping Miss Packard. It was fun. They tied on the artificial leaves, heaved around the branches and put them in place, arranged the wheat sheaves and placed big vases where the chrysanthemums were going to go. Miss Packard changed her mind a lot, stopping often to step back and survey what she had done, then switch it all round another way, but Daisy did not mind. On the contrary, it spun out the pleasure.

'We must remember to leave some things for the window. We'll dress that this afternoon,' Miss Packard said. 'Now, how are we doing?'

'It's already looking pretty. Like an autumn bower,' Isobel said.

Miss Packard considered their efforts. 'Yes, it does, does it not? I think we might give ourselves a pat on the back. But what really matters is that it will bring in the customers. I want to prove that special displays like this can improve sales.'

'I'm sure people will come and look,' Daisy said.

'Exactly, and then you and the other girls must seize the opportunity to sell them something. Not so many women play sports in the winter, so we have to encourage them in.'

Just after midday, they were interrupted by the arrival of Mr

Edward Packard. He strolled in and stood watching them as they arranged the newly arrived flowers, a small smile on his handsome face.

'So this is what you are doing to Ladies' Sportswear, Mel. Very – ah – striking.'

'Thank you,' Miss Packard said, ignoring the edge of sarcasm.

'You only need add a few prize vegetable marrows and it will look like a harvest festival.'

'Yes, and just think how wonderful churches look then.'

Her brother did not answer immediately. His glance had strayed over to where Isobel was sorting tawny and gold chrysanthemums into a big cut-glass vase. Daisy, who had been unashamedly eavesdropping on the exchange, could not fail to notice the interest in his face. It was quickly gone, but unmistakable. He dragged his attention back to the display.

'This is a store, Mel, not a church.'

Miss Packard was unmoved.

'We shall see who's right,' she said.

From just the other side of the archway – now decorated with leaves, wheat sheaves and golf clubs and gloves – came another conversation, conducted in the strident tones of the English upper class.

'Whatever is all this?'

'I cannot think. But how pretty! Do let us go and look.'

A middle-aged lady with what looked like her two unmarried daughters in tow sailed into the department. They gazed about them in surprise, ignoring the Packards and the shopgirls, and making loud appreciative comments. Miss Higgs, primed beforehand by Miss Packard, let them look their fill before moving in. It was easy work then to persuade them to buy hats, scarves and motoring goggles.

Miss Packard said nothing. She didn't need to. Her suppressed smile was enough.

Mr Edward took it well.

'Very impressive, Mel. Keep up the good work.'

'Thank you, Edward. I shall.'

Once he was out of earshot, Miss Packard laughed out loud.

'There! What did I tell you? It does work. I know it does, I saw it being done in Chicago. All we need now is some good advertisements and we shall be all set.'

She sent Isobel and Daisy off for dinner, then when they came back they started disposing goods for sale in an artistic manner amongst the display. Waterproof cycling capes made a backdrop for cornsheaves, golf clubs sprouted amongst the flowers, hats and gloves hung from the branches like strange fruit. And all the while, the curious came to look, and stayed to buy.

'Half-past three already. I shall have to go,' Miss Packard said, her voice sharp with frustration. 'It's all taken much longer than I thought. I had hoped we would get the window dressed as well today, but it will have to wait till tomorrow. It's so provoking! I only have until Thursday week, and then we have to go and stay with the beastly Teignmeretons. I'd far rather stay here.'

Daisy enjoyed the next week or so. It was like the time when they were first setting up the department, with Miss Packard breezing in and out at irregular intervals, stirring them up with her enthusiasm. It helped to dull the hopeless pain of unrequited love, if only during working hours. Keen to help prove that her employer's odd ideas did work, she tried extra hard to make sales. Often when she approached them, women would say that they were only looking at the display.

'Certainly, madam,' Daisy would immediately agree. 'But might I just show you our new range of golfing gloves?' If she seemed unwilling, Daisy tried something else, caps, or stock pins, or warm underwear, depending on the type of woman she judged the potential customer to be. Nine times out of ten, they agreed, and once the goods were out on the counter, most of them bought. A small purchase made, some went on to be led into larger ones. Daisy achieved her highest weekly sales figures since the July Sales.

On the Thursday that Miss Packard was due to go on her visit Daisy felt quite depressed.

'It won't be the same without her coming in,' she said, as she and Isobel got dressed.

'No,' Isobel sighed.

'Yeah, I feel like that and all. Sort of flat, isn't it? Lost the point of it, somehow.'

'Oh, it isn't that. At least, it is Miss Packard, in a way. I cannot understand her. She should be excited at the prospect of going to stay with the Teignmeretons. I expect they have the most beautiful country seat. There will be riding and visiting and dinners and most probably dances as well. And yet she claims she would rather be in the store. It really is very odd.'

'I dunno. Takes all sorts, don't – doesn't – it?' Daisy said. One thing she did know: it wasn't half so much fun in the department when Miss Packard wasn't there.

The day took its usual course. Daisy tried to keep up her sales, but somehow the customers did not seem to be quite so easily persuaded as before. She found she was feeling tired and achy long before she usually did. Perhaps it was just the time of the month. She wished for something exciting to happen. And then, at ten o'clock, a message came. She was to go and see Mr Mason, the Staff Manager. Her stomach gave a lurch of fear that swiftly turned to defiance.

'Why? What've I done? He can't hold nothing against me, I do good work, I do.'

The boy who had brought the message shrugged. 'I dunno. I was just told to tell you. You better come now, he's waiting.'

Daisy shot a suspicious look at Miss Higgs. It must be her doing. She didn't like it that Daisy sold more than she did. Jealous old cow.

'All right, I'm coming,' she said.

She patted her hair, straightened her blouse, and followed the boy, her head held high. She wasn't going to let that bitch think she was frightened. The same applied to Mr Mason.

The boy knocked on the door of his office, waited for the rather absent 'Come in,' and held the door open for her. Daisy marched in and plonked herself down on the chair in front of his desk without being asked. Mr Mason glanced up for half a second, then carried on writing something. Daisy could see that this was set to be a war of nerves. She was not intimidated by the Packards' splendour any more, and what was more, she knew she was a good saleswoman.

'You wanted to see me?' she asked loudly.

Mr Mason finished his sentence, put down his pen, pressed blotting paper carefully over the sheet he had been writing, then looked up.

'Yes. Miss — ah — Phipps, is it not?'

'That's me.'

'I see. Well now, Miss Phipps, you've been with us for — let me see — six months now.'

'Nearer seven,' Daisy corrected.

'Seven. Yes. Well, we've been looking through your records and I see that you have achieved some excellent results in that time.'

'Thanks.'

'So we're transferring you to Baby Linens and Layettes.'

Daisy was dismayed. She loved Ladies' Sportswear, she got on well with the people there, even Miss Higgs most of the time, and she liked the feeling that they were special under Miss Packard's leadership.

'But I —' she began.

'This is, of course, a promotion,' Mr Mason interrupted. 'You will be paid an extra shilling a week.'

Daisy was flabbergasted. Promotion after less than a year was almost unheard of. For several seconds she was speechless, as her loyalty to Miss Packard and the department warred with the thought of what she could do with an extra shilling a week. A shilling was a lot to someone who had known real hunger and cold. After sending money home, there wasn't much left over at the end of each week. A great deal could be done with a shilling all to herself. And then there was Isobel. In a way, it would be a relief not to be with her all the time. But Miss Packard had taken her on, given her the job she had yearned for and the chance to get away from home. If Miss Packard had not been interviewing that day, she might not have got the job, and she liked to feel that she was repaying her by helping to make the department a success.

'I'd rather stay in Ladies' Sportswear,' she said.

Mr Mason looked at her over the tops of his steel-rimmed spectacles. 'You are not being given a choice, Miss Phipps. Packards decides where its staff should be employed. I am merely informing you of your good fortune.'

Say thank you nicely or take your things and sod off, in other words. Daisy knew how matters stood. When it came down to it, the bosses had the power. One shopgirl by herself was nothing, however successful she was at wringing sales from customers.

'Kind of you, I'm sure,' she said.

Mr Mason's face set into rigid lines of disapproval. If she pushed him much further, she was going to get sacked for cheek, and that would be dreadful. She couldn't bear to be expelled from Packards. She might never see Johnny again.

'I mean, thank you very much,' she amended. 'When do I start?'

'Next Monday. You report to Mr Fenton, the buyer. That will be all, Miss Phipps.'

He picked up his pen and returned to the writing. Daisy got up and walked to the door. Just as she was opening it, she couldn't resist one last dig.

'I dunno what Miss Packard's going to say to this.'

She had the satisfaction of seeing a look of apprehension pass briefly over his face.

On the way back to the department, she went over it all in her mind. Something funny was going on here. People weren't usually shuffled around from one department to another. It took time to learn just where everything was and what the prices were and what the selling points were of every item. Some people stayed in the same department from the day they joined Packards till the day they left. Intense loyalties grew up within departments, and rivalries between them. Generally, you were only moved if your department was being closed down or another expanded, and as far as she knew that was not happening in either Ladies' Sportswear or Baby Linens. Promotion certainly would be a reason, but even then you usually got promoted within your department, and then not so soon after joining the store. It was all very odd. Daisy could only think that Miss Higgs was behind it somehow. She didn't like being shown up by Daisy getting better sales figures than hers. Well, she wasn't going to let the old cow know she was sad to be going, that was for sure.

She bounded under the archway to where Isobel and the

other girls were waiting anxiously to see why she had been hauled up before Mr Mason. As luck would have it, there were no customers at all in the department. Daisy looked round at them all, grinning, taking her time.

'You'll never guess,' she declared. 'I been promoted! I'm starting in Baby Linens on Monday.'

Isobel looked horrified. 'Oh Daisy! You're leaving? That's dreadful, how shall I – ? But – but – congratulations. I'm sure you deserve it.'

The other two girls repeated the congratulations, but grudgingly. They were jealous of her success.

'Don't envy you, going to Baby Linens. Funny lot, they are.'

Most surprising was Miss Higgs. She seemed genuinely amazed.

'This is a shock, Miss Phipps. We shall miss you here. You others will have to work extra hard to make up for the sales Miss Phipps achieves, especially if it means we're going to have to train up somebody new.'

As she took her place behind the counter, Daisy found she was close to tears. She was really going to miss Ladies' Sportswear. It was almost like leaving a second family. And she was sure that Baby Linens was going to be dull by comparison, without Miss Packard coming in. It had been an honour, being part of her special department. She touched the tennis racquet brooch on her chest, and envied the girl who would wear it next.

20

Nowhere was really safe, Isobel realised. She had escaped from a nightmare at the huge cost of leaving behind her family and her whole way of life. She thought she had found shelter at Packards, and in a way she had, for she had warmth, food, a roof over her head and the means to support herself. She was protected from her brother-in-law, thanks, she had to admit, to that dreadful Johnny and his friend. But she was not protected from predatory men. They were everywhere. She tried to make herself less conspicuous, dressing her hair in the plainest of styles, wearing severe white shirt blouses without a hint of ruffle or lace. But had she known it, these fashions only served as a piquant contrast to her soft beauty. It certainly did not put off Johnny Miller. Neither did it put off Mr Perry Amberley Packard, who often strolled into the department and exchanged a few words with her. More worrying still, it did not put off his brother. Though he had done nothing overt, she felt the heat behind Mr Edward's eyes, and it frightened her.

The Christmas season was fast approaching. Along with the rest of the store, Ladies' Sportswear was dressed up with trees and ribbons.

'We shall have a display of skis and skates and toboggans,' Miss Packard decided. 'Skiing is becoming very popular with more adventurous women. I have had Ladies' Gowns design a very practical tailor-made with a short skirt – above the ankles – and a neat fitted jacket. Just right for skiing, although trousers of course would be infinitely better. You can recommend that our customers order one of them, and sell the thick golfing knickers and the little Tyrolean hats to go with it, as well as the skis and sticks and gloves, of course. And motoring goggles, too, to protect the eyes from the rush of cold air. Oh, it must be such fun to ski! To go flying down a mountainside . . . But at least we are going to Braisehurst for Christmas, so there will be some riding.'

Braisehurst, Isobel discovered, was the Amberley country seat. Miss Packard departed there a week before Christmas, having left behind copious instructions on promoting practically every item of stock as a suitable Christmas present for the sporting woman. The staff of Ladies' Sportswear was left to cope with the pre-Christmas rush. For the last week before the festival, the store was open until nine o'clock each evening. In departments like stationery, jewellery, toys and the food hall, there was plenty of extra custom to keep the shopgirls and men busy, but for others it was just extra time standing on legs throbbing with fatigue. Isobel hardly knew how she got back to Trent Street each night. Even Daisy, when they met up at the end of the day, was exhausted.

'I dunno about going back to my folks for Christmas day,' she sighed as she dropped into bed. 'It'll be gone ten Christmas Eve before I get home. All I'll want to do is sleep the blooming clock round.'

'You are going home, then?' Isobel asked.

'Oh yeah. Got to, ain't – haven't – I? Never hear the last of it if I don't. Anyway, it'll be nice to see everyone when they're in a good mood.'

'Yes, of course. Families should be together at Christmas,' Isobel said, but a feeling of desolation that had been hovering for weeks finally settled round her heart. She had nowhere to go for Christmas. No family to welcome her.

Daisy's voice, laden with weariness, still managed to contain genuine concern.

'Look, Iz, you must come home along of me. They'll be pleased to see you. It'll be fun, you'll see.'

From what Isobel had gathered from the tales Daisy had told of her family, she was certain that their idea of fun was not hers. She would feel as she had done at the music hall, embarrassed and uncomfortable. She was sure they would all get drunk and sing the sort of songs that would make her ears burn.

'That's very kind of you, Daisy, but I really couldn't impose on your family.'

'Won't be imposing. One more won't make no difference.'

'No, I couldn't really. Thank you.'

Normally, Daisy would have argued, would have worn her down. But now she was too tired.

'Suit y'self,' she mumbled from under the blankets. Seconds later, Isobel heard her breathing steady into sleep.

From the bottom of her heart, Isobel envied her. To go off so sweetly like that must be bliss. She stayed awake, though her body cried out for sleep and her sore spirit craved respite from the constant unanswerable questions. How long could she keep going on like this? What did the future hold? The only defence against them was to focus on the immediate problem of Christmas.

For a while a solution danced before her, warm and tempting. She could go back to her sister's house. The air would be rich with the smells of cooking there. The larder would be full, the house decked with holly and ivy, the tree twinkling with candles. There would be piles of mysterious parcels tied in pretty ribbons. She could take the few shillings she had managed to save from her wages, pack her things, buy a train ticket and be there within hours. She would be welcomed back like the Prodigal Son. Her sister would fall on her and weep and vow not to let her out of her sight again. She would be petted and cosseted, waited on and entertained. She would never more have to stand behind a counter or try to persuade a reluctant customer to buy. Her sister would provide for her, her sister and – her brother-in-law. There the bubble burst. To go back would be to agree to what he wanted her to do. It was just a dream. She had to stay here. Her Christmas would be spent at Trent Street.

The next day was the twenty-third of December, and seemed even longer than the one before. Isobel somehow missed Daisy in the flood of shopmen and girls coming out of Packards at the end of the day, but was too tired to look for her. She plodded towards Trent Street like a dumb animal, hardly noticing anything but the bleak weight inside her.

'Isobel – Miss Brand – excuse me –'

It was Johnny Miller. She did not stop.

'Miss Brand – I was wondering – I know it's very late –'

He sounded unusually hesitant, not his irritatingly perky self at all.

'Yes, it is,' she said.

'Please –'

He put a hand on her arm. She hadn't the strength to resist. She stopped.

'I – I wanted to ask you a big favour. I wondered – would you like to come to my folks' place for Christmas Day? I mean, I know you can't go home, and it won't be much fun at Trent Street, and they'd be very happy to have you. It's not what you're used to, I know, but there'll be a good spread, and we go to church and everything, and my sister will play the piano and there'll be singing and that, and – and I wish you would come.'

Isobel was so low that for a moment she almost considered accepting. The Millers were a good deal more respectable than Daisy's family, from what she had gathered. His father had been a small shopkeeper, his widowed mother now lived with her daughter and her husband, a master carpenter. They would not get drunk and the songs round the piano would not embarrass her. But tired and depressed as she was, she still knew that there was a price. The welcome she would receive would not be just for the day, but potentially for life. Young men, even those as brash as Johnny Miller, did not invite young women to share their family Christmas unless they had serious intentions.

'That's very kind of you, but I can't accept,' she said, trying to put steel into her voice, and failing.

'But why ever not? My sister's got a goose in. I told them all about you and they're dying to meet you. They all really want you to come.'

Isobel could just picture them all looking at her with open curiosity, and Johnny introducing her with a smile of possessive pride.

'I'm sorry, but I have a prior engagement,' she said.

'A prior – ? You mean you're going somewhere else? But where?'

'To Daisy's family,' Isobel lied, avoiding looking him in the face. She wished she was not such a coward. Why couldn't she just tell him she did not want to go?

'Oh – well – but I thought –'

'I'm sorry,' Isobel repeated. Somehow she set herself in

motion again, but she could not get rid of Johnny. He walked along with her.

'Perhaps New Year, then? Would you come for that? We always have a family party. You'd like it, we have First Foot and everything. It's like a tradition. My granddad came from Scotland and they make a big thing of it up there. We all go outside then, and hear the ships hooting on the river, and wish a Happy New Year to all the neighbours. It's ever so friendly, you'd like it, really you would. Say you'll come, do.'

They reached the door of number twenty-four. Isobel took hold of the handrail to haul herself up the steps. She took a deep breath and gathered up the very small reserve of emotional strength she had left.

'I don't think so, thank you,' she said, and went inside before he could say any more.

Christmas Eve was one long rush of last-minute shoppers. Many people seemed to be buying their entire list of presents, and even Isobel found that they were easy to sell to. But by closing time the staff were practically on their knees. Daisy came back to Trent Street, changed, collected her parcels and after one more attempt at persuading Isobel to come with her, went off to join her family.

Isobel crawled into bed. Images chased round her head. Childhood Christmas Eves, bubbling with excitement, and stockings hung ready on the bedpost. More recent years, going to Midnight Mass with her dear parents. Last Christmas, spent quietly grieving their deaths. Outside in the street there was laughter and season's greetings and farewells as other shopmen and girls started home to their families. Isobel had not felt so alone since that first terrifying fortnight in London. She turned onto her face and wept until she finally cried herself to sleep.

She woke to the sound of church bells. Seven o'clock on Christmas morning. Her body ached with weariness and her head was throbbing. At least she did not have to get up and go to work. She could stay in bed all day if she wished. But perversely this made her feel even worse. She almost wished it was another working day, for that would give her a reason for going on. Miss Higgs would be waiting for her, wanting her there exactly on time to polish the counters and tidy the drawers and be ready to serve. Who was waiting for her today? Nobody.

The room was very quiet without Daisy. So quiet that it seemed dead. Even Daisy sulking and snapping at her was better than this oppressive silence. It grieved her that Daisy should be so jealous of Johnny Miller's admiration The last thing she wanted to do was to come between Daisy and the man she wanted. She owed her survival here at Packards to Daisy. She had certainly tried hard enough to shake Johnny off. If she could have switched his attentions to Daisy she would have done, more than willingly. She stared at Daisy's empty bed, still rumpled from her hurried departure last night. Daisy was her only friend in the world, and if she turned away from her because of Johnny, Isobel would have nobody at all.

It was the church bells that saved her from sliding completely into the black abyss. They attacked her as she lay weeping, peeling out their message of joy to the world. It must, she realised, be a sin to feel so totally without hope on the day dedicated to Jesus' birth. She dragged herself out of bed, shivering as the cold air of the unheated room met her warm body. She would go to the next service.

From then on the day did get a little better. She opened the present that Daisy had left for her – a set of handkerchiefs with an italic I in the corner – and hoped that Daisy would like the hairbrush she had given her. The church service gave some solace to her lonely spirit. Then when she got back Mrs Drew the housekeeper made her come and join her and the other girls who either did not have families or lived too far away to get home. There was a very embarrassing moment when Mrs Drew presented her with a parcel, 'From an Admirer, dear,' and insisted that she opened it then and there. It turned out to be a rather gaudy brooch with a blue glass stone, and of course it was from Johnny. Isobel resolved to return it at the earliest possible opportunity. The others teased her about it, but soon lost interest and went on to talk about other things. There was an air of false jollity about the house which they all tried desperately to maintain, Isobel included. She did not want to go back to feeling as she had done when she woke, but it was hard to keep smiling, even when Mrs Drew served up Christmas dinner. It was all such a sham, pretending to be a family when they weren't. She was overwhelmingly glad to be able to plead a headache and go to bed at half-past nine. She knew that they would talk about her the moment she had gone, agreeing about how stuck-up she was, but she did not care. She had survived Christmas, just.

The next hurdle was the January Sales. Miss Packard came bouncing in to decide on the marking-down of the stock, putting a lead offer of much reduced tennis racquets in the window to bring the customers in.

'You're so lucky, being in Ladies' Sportswear still,' Daisy grumbled. 'I just loved it when Miss Packard came in. It's so boring in Baby Linens.'

'The trouble with Miss Packard being back in Town is it means her brother is as well,' Isobel let slip.

'What, Mr Edward? He's hardly been away.'

'No, not him, although –' although he was a worry as well. 'Mr Perry.'

Daisy did not look at all sympathetic. 'Well, it's all right for some, that's all I can say.'

Isobel did not continue with the subject. Daisy did not think that having men pursue her was a problem. Quite the opposite, in fact.

But it was a problem, and a growing one. Every day, Mr Perry would turn up in the department, either with his sister or on his own. When he was on his own, it was always when the department was very busy with bargain hunters. Then he could approach her without attracting the attention of Miss Higgs.

'And how is the most beautiful girl in Packards today?' he would ask, with a twinkling smile.

'Very well, thank you,' she invariably answered, trying not to look directly at him.

'Not working too hard, I hope?'

'Hard enough.'

'Is Packards being fair to you? Are you getting your breaks? Is the food in the dining room still the appalling school stodge it always is?'

The trouble was, she had to try very hard not to smile. The food was appalling stodge.

'It's very sustaining, thank you.'

'How tactful you are. A veritable soul of discretion. You can be honest with me, you know. I shan't tell a single person. How do you like Trent Street?'

'It's very comfortable, thank you.'

'Comfortable! That's rich. Those places are like prisons. Are you hoping that if you're nice about it they'll let you out in ten years for good behaviour?'

Despite herself, her lips twitched. Mr Perry gave a delighted laugh.

'There! You've given yourself away! I can't tell you how relieved I am. It proves you are human after all, not an Ice Princess. I thought you might be something out of a fairy tale, transported here and condemned to work behind the counter by a wicked witch.'

There was just enough of a grain of truth in that to sober her.

'Oh please, don't adopt that stern look again. You're so beautiful when you smile.'

He was always considerate, not getting in her way, not preventing her from serving customers, not embarrassing her beyond the fact of his being there at all. He was the perfect gentleman, amusing and kind. And when she forgot herself and looked at him, his blue eyes were devoid of that hungry look. After three weeks of daily visits, she ceased to feel hunted. In fact she almost caught herself acknowledging that though men were dangerous and frightening, he might be the exception.

It was nearly the end of the Sales when Daisy came storming into their attic room after work and flung open the door so that it banged back against the wall.

'What the bleeding hell do you think you're playing at?'

Isobel gaped at her. 'I – I – what do you mean?'

'Oh, don't give me that little Miss Bleeding Innocent act. You know. You got a Christmas present, didn't you?'

'A Christmas present?' Of course she had. From Daisy. And then it dawned on her. 'Oh – you mean –'

'Yeah, I mean from *him*. You little cow! You never told me, did you? Give you a brooch, didn't he?'

Daisy walked towards her as she spoke, menace in her

movements. Fear churned in Isobel's stomach. She started to retreat. She found herself gabbling.

'I didn't know he was going to give it to me, really I didn't, Daisy. I knew nothing about it. He gave it to Mrs Drew to give to me. If he'd said anything beforehand I would have refused to accept it. And I gave it back the very next time I saw him. The very next time. I didn't want it, Daisy, I didn't keep it –'

'Call y'self a friend? Why didn't you tell me? Why the big secret, eh, eh? Tell me that!' Daisy yelled. Her hand swung back, whipped forward and slapped Isobel hard across the face.

It stung, but worse than that was the look in Daisy's eyes. The rage and the loathing. Isobel cried out.

'No, Daisy, please – I didn't mean to deceive you – but I knew you'd be upset –'

'Too bleeding right I am. Why did you have to interfere, eh? Why did you have to come along? If you hadn't of come here, everything would of been all right. You spoilt everything, you have.'

Isobel could do nothing in the face of this unreason. Sobs rose in her throat.

'Daisy, forgive me. I didn't set out to –'

'That's right, cry,' Daisy sneered. 'Always get your own way, don't you? If smiles don't work then try the tears. Well, it don't work on me no more. I'm never going to speak to you again!'

She slammed out of the room.

Isobel collapsed onto the bed. Her face throbbed where Daisy had hit her, but it was nothing compared with the pain inside, which sliced through her like a physical wound.

Daisy did not return that night. Through the endless cold hours of darkness, Isobel hit bottom. She finally faced up to what her future had in store for her. There was no going back to the old days. She had known it in her head before, but now she accepted it in her heart. Her former life was gone for ever. She now had just two courses open to her. She worked as a shopgirl for the rest of her life, becoming more tired and dull with every passing year, or she married someone like Johnny Miller. Either way there was precious little of comfort or beauty or pleasure. Nothing but poverty and hard work. She did not know how she got through the night.

But somehow the hours did creep round, and Mrs Drew herself came to wake her. Isobel turned her face away.

'Leave me alone, please,' she begged. 'I just want to die.'

The housekeeper clicked her tongue in disapproval. 'Come, come now. That's no way to talk. It's nothing but a silly spat. She'll come round, you'll see. Now get up, there's a good girl, and get yourself off to work.'

It took a good deal more than that to persuade her, but at last she did get out of bed. Like an automaton she went through the motions of the day, hardly hearing what people said to her. Everything was grey, it was like walking through a fog. There was no point to anything, no point to life. Miss Higgs reprimanded her. She nodded slowly, mouthed some words of apology. After a great desert of time, dinner break came round. She took her meal, sat in the noisy dining room, ate nothing, heard nothing. She set out upon the long journey of the afternoon.

Not long after lunch Mr Perry came through the archway. He was speaking to her for a while before any of the words made sense.

'. . . the matter? You look as if the world has fallen in.'

'It has,' Isobel said.

'That bad, is it? Now, take a tip from me. Count to ten and forget about it. Always works. However bad things seem, you put them aside for a while and they're never half so bad when you come back to them. In fact sometimes you wonder why you ever worried at all.'

Isobel hardly heard him. She stood with her hands clasped in front of her as she had been trained to do, and her unfocused gaze directed somewhere slightly to his left.

'Now, I don't believe you've been listening to one word in three of what I've been saying. Looks like a bad case to me. A case for Doctor Perry. And do you know what I prescribe? A little jaunt down to the country, a stroll along a river bank and a nice cosy tea. Earl Grey and toasted crumpets. Now what do you say to that?'

Slowly, as if moving underwater, Isobel turned her head towards him and focused on his face. His blue eyes were brimming with kindness and sincerity.

'How does that sound, do you think? Would tea and crumpets bring a smile back to your face again?'

What did it matter? What did anything matter?

'Why not?' she heard herself say.

21

Rain blurred the winter landscape, turning rolling parkland and majestic trees into a depressing study in grey and black. Amelie sat on the window seat in the massive stone mullioned bay of the drawing room of Mere Castle, the Teignmeretons' seat, and looked out at the enveloping drizzle. The gloom of the day just about matched the gloom of her mood. This stay with the Teignmeretons had at least held the chance to do some riding, and here she was, imprisoned in their ugly pile of a home, which wasn't a castle at all, because she had been stupid enough to sprain her ankle. She turned away from the view to look at the offending joint. Her leg was stretched out in front of her on the window seat. If only it had been her right ankle, she might have still managed to ride, but it was her left, the foot which went in the stirrup.

The one thing that cheered her about the day was that Georgy would be going out. The hunt was due to meet here this morning, on the gravel sweep before the front door, and Georgy, along with practically everybody else in the house, would be following the hounds, at least to the first covert. Half of her uncharitably hoped it would be a bad day's sport, because she couldn't be part of it, the other part hoped just the opposite, so that Georgy would be kept out of her way for as long as possible.

She wondered how the January Sales were going. She had managed to get to the department to decide on the marking down, but that was all. The Teignmeretons did not have a telephone, so she could not call her grandfather and ask him. Perhaps Perry would turn up soon from Town, although it was unlikely that he would have any idea of what was happening at the store. It was odd that Perry should still be in London, come to think of it, when she knew he had been included in the invitation to Mere Castle. Even odder at first was the fact that Edward was here, and on his best behaviour, being charming to everyone. She knew that he despised the world in which their mother moved, and on top of that she would have thought that he wouldn't have left the store at such an important time. But now she was beginning to guess his ulterior motive. He had been paying special attention to a Miss Sylvia Forbes.

The long double doors opened and in came Georgy, smiling cheerfully as usual.

'Oh, it's you,' Amelie said, and looked back out of the window again.

Undeterred by this less than enthusiastic welcome, Georgy picked up a chair and came over to sit beside her.

'Bit of a dismal old morning, isn't it?' he remarked. 'How are you? How's the poor old ankle?'

'Getting better. Shouldn't you be getting changed?'

The meet was in less than an hour, and most of the family and guests were busy pouring themselves into their mirror-shiny hunting boots and tying their stocks.

'Oh – I've decided not to ride this morning. Thought I'd stay and keep you company instead.'

Amelie was horrified. 'What on earth do you want to do that for?'

For a moment, Georgy looked embarrassed. 'Well – I – er – I'd really rather be here with you.'

'Well, I'd really rather you went hunting,' Amelie told him.

Poor Georgy was crestfallen. 'Don't you like me the littlest bit?' he asked.

'No. Now go away, do.'

He looked so pathetic that Amelie relented just a fraction. 'I'm in a really bad temper. I don't want to talk to anyone, so just go off and enjoy yourself and don't give a thought to me.'

Georgy sighed and got up. 'If that's what you want – but I shall give a thought to you. Lots of them. I think about you all the time, don't you know?'

It was the nearest he had got yet to telling her he loved her. It made her even more desperate to get rid of him.

'Oh rubbish,' she said.

He went, only to return five minutes later, carrying a pile of newspapers and magazines.

'I've brought something for you to read. The library's all

incredibly boring old stuff, so I've got you a *Tatler*, the *Strand* —
there's a cracking adventure story in that — and the *Illustrated
London News*, and some others. They might help to pass the
time a bit.'

If it had been anyone else, Amelie would have been touched
by their thoughtfulness. But Georgy just made her feel
emotionally cornered.

'Thanks,' she said ungraciously. 'Now go and change. You'll
be late.'

She had resolved to stay in the drawing room and ignore the
meet, but when it came to the point it was at least some
entertainment, so she hobbled over to the Great Hall where she
could watch what was going on.

The spectacle was one of colour and movement against the
grey backdrop of the weather. A large field had turned out,
despite the rain. Men in hunting pink and women in
immaculately tailored habits sat easily on glossy horses, bay and
brown, chestnut and black, with the occasional showy dappled
grey. Farmers in tweed jackets and bowler hats made another
group, while excited youngsters on ponies were held by stoical
grooms. Whippers-in controlled the milling pack of hounds, all
bright eyes and waving tails and strong black and tan and white
bodies, eager to be off. Amongst the riders went the Mere
Castle servants with silver trays, offering stirrup cup.

Amelie watched it all. There was the Teignmereton family,
moving with assurance amongst the crowd, greeting friends,
acting as hosts. There were two other sons apart from Georgy,
and four unmarried daughters. An inflow of money to the
family coffers would be very welcome. Packard money was not
at all despised, especially as Georgy was not the eldest son. They
were more than ready to have him provided for. Amelie veered
away from this unwelcome fact and searched the crowd for
other familiar faces. Close by were the people who had dined
here at Mere Castle the other day, there was a young man she
had danced with last week before she sprained her ankle, and
the jolly sisters who had been such fun when they all played
charades. There was Edward, looking dashing in his impeccably
tailored hunting pink, and yes, there beside him was Sylvia
Forbes. Amelie knew quite enough now about the ground rules

of society life to realise that Lady Teignmereton must have had designs on her brother for one or other of her daughters. She must be most put out to find Sylvia cutting them out. She smiled to herself, in tune with Edward for once. She disliked Lady Teignmereton intensely. Idly, she shifted her gaze from Edward and saw – Hugo Rutherford.

If anything, he looked even more handsome on a horse than he had done in a boat. Amelie gazed at him. If only, if only she had not sprained her ankle. She would be out there now, beautifully mounted on one of the Teignmeretons' hunters and dressed in her riding habit, in which she always looked her best. Anything could happen on the hunting field. Somehow she could manage to get herself introduced to, or at the very least noticed by him. But as it was, she was stuck here helplessly watching. She hated being a spectator at the best of times. Just at this moment, it was purgatory. She kept her eyes on him, envying everyone he spoke to. When a pretty girl with dark hair laughed up at him, obviously flirting, Amelie clenched her teeth and her fists, digging her nails into her palms without even noticing she was doing it.

'Hussy!' she said out loud. She wished they would go, so that he would be distracted. But then when the horn sounded and they did start to move off, she wished they would stay just a little longer, so that she could still see him.

The colourful parade trotted off down the driveway, first the huntsman and the pack, then the snorting, clattering, chattering field of horses and riders, off for an exciting day's sport, taking Hugo Rutherford with them. Amelie sat back with a great sigh. Now there was nothing to hope for but the remote chance that Hugo might be asked back to dinner afterwards.

He wasn't. Instead she had to sit through a minute-by-minute description of the hunt, with the various participants interrupting each other and disagreeing over the details. The only interest was the frequent mention of Hugo Rutherford's name, how well he had ridden, how magnificently he had taken a certain jump, how he had turned back to catch a horse for a fallen rider.

After dinner the younger people took the gramophone into the morning room and played dance records, so once again

Amelie felt left out. Georgy came up to her as she sat in a sofa watching the others.

'This is all a bit boring for you, isn't it?'

'I simply hate sitting and watching,' Amelie agreed. 'I want to get up and dance.'

'You'll make your poor old ankle even worse if you try. I know – why don't we go to the music room? We could play duets or something.'

At any other time, Amelie would have refused, but she was so tired of sitting and watching other people enjoy themselves that she agreed. Holding Georgy's arm, she hobbled off with him.

Electricity had not yet been installed in Mere Castle. In fact everything about the place had a rather run-down look about it which sat uneasily with the lavish scale on which it was run. The music room was at the end of the building, well away from the noise of the gramophone, and from the older people playing whist and bridge in the drawing room. Georgy lit a candelabra and set it on the grand piano, making a soft glow in the one corner of the room, then drew up an extra stool.

'There,' he said, 'this is cosy, isn't it?'

Amelie said nothing. She was beginning to have her doubts about this. She leafed through the pile of sheet music on top of the piano, looking for something easy to play. Like all young ladies, she had been taught to play and made to practise, but she was a poor musician. She pounced on a familiar piece.

'Ah! Let's try this,' she cried, and proceeded to thump through it loudly and inaccurately.

Georgy clapped. 'You're very good,' he said.

'Rubbish. I'm dreadful. I never wanted to spend time practising, I wanted to be out playing with a ball. I used to wish I was a boy, so that I could do interesting things. Boys had much more fun.'

'I'm glad you're not a boy.'

Amelie was suddenly very aware of his closeness. She could feel the movement of his body just three or four inches away from her on the other stool. She made to take the music off the stand, but he reached out and caught her hand in his.

'I – I liked you from the moment I first saw you in the park. Then when I found out you were Perry's sister I got him to introduce me. At your Peacock Party – do you remember? You danced with me twice.'

'I danced with a lot of people that night.'

Acutely embarrassed, Amelie tried to pull her hand away, he held on with surprising strength.

'Please – what I wanted to say was, I – I've not been able to think of anything else since. Everything about you – you're so – different, exciting –'

If Amelie had been more mobile, she would have got up at this point and run out of the room. But she knew that if she tried it, he would get up and try to help her, so she could only try to stop the limping flow of words instead.

'Oh rubbish, I'm nothing of the sort.'

'But you are. Beside you, the other girls are dull, they – they're all the same. You – you're so daring. I never know what you're going to say next –'

'I'm going to tell you to be quiet.'

'No, I can't, not now. It's taken me so long. You see, what I wanted to say was – to ask – if you'd marry me?'

Amelie stared very hard at the piano keys. She could hear his breathing, and her own heartbeat. A silence stretched for what seemed like a year. A log shifted in the grate. The candles guttered in a draught. Amelie swallowed.

'Well, this is a surprise,' she said, but even as the words came out of her lips, she knew that they were a lie. She had known very well that he would come out with it eventually. Her mother had hoped for it when she accepted the invitation to visit Mere Castle. Lady Teignmereton had probably expected it when she issued the invitation. She felt the weight of both families upon her shoulders. They all wanted the match. It was approved. It was suitable. It would solve a lot of problems.

'You – you don't have to answer now. You can think about it if that's what you want,' Georgy said, desperate to please.

'I don't have to think about it.'

'Then you will – ?'

'No! I mean, I'm sorry, but I really don't think we're suited.'

The trite words trotted out. But they were true. The very idea of marrying someone as stupid and empty as Georgy was laughable. In fact, she could feel laughter building up inside.

'Oh –'

There was such real hurt and disappointment in that one word that she looked at him for the first time, and the laughter died within her.

'Look, I – I'm sorry, Georgy,' she said. 'But I really don't think I'd make you happy.'

She could see from his doglike eyes that he was not going to give up. The only solution was to escape to the safety of other people.

'I'd like to go back to the drawing room now,' she said, and to her horror she heard something of her mother's tone in her voice, that note of command that brooked no disobedience.

The walk back was the longest she had ever taken.

The repercussions were immediate and angry. Of course it was obvious to everyone what had happened from the moment they entered the drawing room. One look at them was enough. Winifred whisked Amelie off to her bedroom for a long lecture which grew more and more acrimonious as Amelie refused to change her mind. In the morning, Lady Teignmereton spoke to her with a politeness so chilling that it was like a slap in the face while the rest of the family and the other guests regarded her with everything from mild amusement to total incomprehension. Amelie knew that for a few days she was going to be the subject of avid gossip. She could almost see the letters that would be departing from the Mere Castle postbox that very day. At least Georgy did not make an appearance. She was spared having everyone watching to see how they behaved together.

After one more long and forceful attempt at making Amelie see reason, Winifred ended the visit. The journey home was one of angry silences punctuated by Winifred's letting her daughter know exactly what she thought of her. Amelie could only be glad that her grandfather had never given into the pressure to buy an estate. If he had, then she would most certainly have been made to go there now. As it was, they were on their way back to London, so she would be able to go to the store.

It was another grey morning as Amelie was driven down Oxford Street, accompanied by the inevitable footman. As usual, she stopped by the new Selfridges store. It appeared to be almost finished on the outside, and there were tremendous sounds of activity from within, where it was being fitted out. She had to admit that it was a most impressive building. In fact, if she had not been so partisan, she would almost have said that it was even more beautiful than Packards. The classical façade in its light grey Portland stone had dignity without heaviness. More worrying, the Selfridge genius for promotion was already in evidence. Hoardings and banners proclaimed the coming opening events. Looking at the reactions of passers-by, Amelie was left in no doubt of the interest the new store was engendering. The emotional strain of the last few days was pushed to the back of her mind. What did Georgy and the Teignmeretons and her mother's anger matter? She had to make her grandfather see the danger approaching.

Packards had the slightly battle-weary look it always took on towards the end of the Sales. The shopmen and girls all looked tired and irritable and the customers, instead of ambling round the store in a leisurely way, barged into each other and picked over the goods as if they were in a street market. Amelie made for Ladies' Sportswear. As always, Miss Higgs had everything in immaculate order.

'We've done very well,' she assured Amelie, in answer to her enquiries after the success of their first Sale.

Amelie hoped so. It was impossible to make comparisons, as they had been functioning for less than a year. Of one thing she was sure, the girl who had been brought in to replace Daisy Phipps was useless. The weekly figures had definitely dipped since Daisy had been moved. Amelie had not forgiven Edward for that. She had nearly gone and got the order reversed, as she had done when he dismissed Isobel Brand, but then she discovered that the change had been dressed up as a promotion. She knew that Daisy Phipps came from somewhere in the East End, and so needed the extra money, and she knew that Edward was playing on her knowing that and feeling unable to have her demoted. She had been outmanoeuvred.

'You're doing a splendid job in the department. Everyone thought we would fail, but we've proved them wrong,' she told Miss Higgs.

The woman coloured faintly.

'Thank you, Miss Packard. It's a pleasure to be working with you personally.' Her face took on an odd look. 'It would take more than an offer from that Mr Selfridge to take me away from Packards.'

Amelie blinked as she took in this information.

'I'm very glad to hear it,' she said.

She limped up to the fifth floor as fast as her injured ankle would carry her and burst into Thomas's office.

'Grandpa,' she cried, 'did you know that Gordon Selfridge is trying to poach our best staff?'

Thomas looked up from the figures he was studying.

'Why Amelie, this is a nice surprise. Come and sit down. What have you done to your leg? And why are you here? I thought you were at the Teignmeretons' place.'

'Oh, we left in a hurry. I'm in disgrace, as usual. But Grandpa, Miss Higgs tells me Selfridges offered her a job. Have they taken many of our staff?'

'One or two. Nothing to worry about. Now tell me, why are you in disgrace? Did the Teignmereton boy pop the question?'

'What? Oh – yes. Yes he did.'

'And you refused him?'

'But of course I did! Mother's furious with me.'

Thomas gave a hearty laugh. 'I can well imagine. She's been angling for that match at least since Henley. I knew I could rely on you to have the good sense not to give in.'

Amelie saw her chance. She came and perched on the arm of his chair.

'She's going to be simply beastly to me now. Won't you let me do something to get me out of her way for a bit? Let me come and work here?'

Thomas patted her knee. 'You can make yourself busy setting up your department for the spring.'

Amelie had thought of this, but somehow it wasn't enough. She loved Ladies' Sportswear. It was her baby, and she had made it work. But Miss Higgs really ran it. She just looked in every once in a while.

'I'm going to do that. But there's something else that I'd like to do, Grandpa. Something to fight back against Gordon Selfridge.'

'Gordon Selfridge! We've nothing to be afraid of from him, my pet. The man's up to his eyes in debt over this new toy of his. The way he's spending money setting it up, he'll be bankrupt within six months.'

'But he could take our custom in the meantime. Let me take charge of advertising. I know I could do it, Gramps! I was right about Ladies' Sportswear, wasn't I? Everybody thought it was just my silly little whim, and it would fail within six months, but it hasn't. People come specially to Packards to go to my department. And I'm sure I'm right about advertising.'

'What exactly are you thinking of doing with the advertising?' Thomas asked.

'We've got to make it more lively. Make new people want to come to Packards, make our old customers want to come back more often. Interest them. Make them wonder what we're up to.' She had been pondering this for some time, and now she was more than ever sure that she could make a real improvement in the number of people coming to the store.

'But they know what we're up to,' Thomas pointed out. 'Exactly what we've always done – the best range of goods at the most favourable prices.'

'So that's what we'll tell them. We'll convince them that they must come here rather than Selfridge's.'

'I don't know. These American ideas of yours stick in my throat. They won't work here, Amelie. The British are different from the Americans.'

Amelie resorted to coaxing. 'Please, Gramps. Just to keep me out of Mother's way. You didn't want me to marry Georgy Teignmereton, now did you?'

'Of course not. The boy's an idiot. You need someone with some substance to him, my pet.'

'So you'll let me take over advertising?'

Thomas smiled and gave in. 'Very well. Until April.'

'April? But that's only a couple of months!'

'Long enough to show me what you can do. Now run along, I've work to do.'

'Thank you, thank you, Gramps! You'll not regret it, I promise you!'

She kissed him on the top of the head and hobbled out, on top of the world. Now she could really show him what she was made of.

Thomas leant back in his chair. If only she had been born a boy. All that flair and enthusiasm harnessed to some solid training, and she would have made a worthy successor. As it was, it wouldn't do any harm to stir young Edward up a bit by giving her a bit of responsibility, at least until the Season started again. And as for Winifred . . . he chuckled to himself at the thought of Winifred's being thwarted of the match she was trying to make. Winifred would be pacified soon enough when she found out what he had been doing these last two or three weeks.

He opened the top drawer of his desk and took out a series of photographs showing views of a gracious mansion with a Palladian portico. Winifred would be sweetness itself once she realised that at last she would have somewhere to play hostess to all those Society friends of hers. The fact that it was her parents' house rather than hers would not stop her. She would have a party of them down there as soon as the ink was dry on the agreement.

22

Daisy tidied a huge pile of frilled and embroidered bibs back into their various drawers, making no secret of her irritation. The last half-hour had been a complete waste of her time.

'You didn't get nowhere with that one, then?' one of the other shopgirls asked, a catty smile on her face.

'Stupid woman never wanted to buy nothing in the first place. Told me she didn't like anything we had to offer, but you won't see nothing better anywhere else in London, that's for sure,' Daisy said, slamming drawers shut.

The floorwalker came over. Daisy fought hard to keep her patience. Now what? Why did everybody have to make a to-do about her not making a sale? She made more than anybody else in the department. The floorwalker sent the other shopgirl about her business.

'Couldn't you find anything to suit the lady?' he asked.

'So she said. I showed her everything we got.'

'She asked a lot of questions, did she? About where the goods came from and what they were made of and how they were made?'

'Well – yes. She did, now you come to mention it,' Daisy agreed. 'I told her all I knew, civil like, but still it didn't suit. She was just a tabby if you ask me.'

'Or spying.'

Daisy stared at him. 'Spying?'

'Just so, Miss Phipps. Either our goods or our staff. Or both. It has happened in other departments, those who consider themselves more important than us, like Ladies' Gowns.' He sniffed, to show what he thought of the pretentions of Ladies' Gowns. 'Certain persons there have been offered positions in Mr Selfridge's new store.'

Daisy had heard of this. Everyone had. Selfridges were taking on staff already, paying them now, before the place was even open.

'I trust you will not succumb to their bribes,' the floorwalker said.

'Oh no, not me. Leave Packards? Never,' Daisy declared.

The floorwalker nodded, satisfied. 'I'm very glad to hear it. Not everyone is so loyal these days.'

Daisy was considering this as she went for her dinner. How could anyone desert Packards? It would be like betraying your own family. She wouldn't even consider it, not for one minute. She stood with her tray, looking for a spare place, but with only half her mind on what she was doing. She did not bother competing for the coveted seats by the barrier any more. She was not interested in flirting. She started towards a place in the middle, but before she could reach it, someone else sat there. Two more became available, rather nearer the barrier, but again they were taken before she could get there. Then she noticed a girl getting up, right next to the barrier, and on the other side, just sitting down – was Johnny. All thought went out of her head. She just had to get near to him. She elbowed another girl out of the way and plumped down, flushed with success.

'Hello, Daisy,' Johnny gave her his nice smile, his eyes crinkling up at the corners. Her heart turned over.

'Hello,' she said. 'How're –'

But already he was looking past her. 'Isobel with you?'

She had to bite her lip and swallow hard to stop the tears from welling in her eyes.

'No,' she managed to say.

'Oh – well –'

'We don't work together no more,' Daisy reminded him.

'No – of course not. I forgot.' Johnny poked at his food for a few seconds, frowning. Daisy ached to put her hand out, to smooth away the anxious look. She knew just how he felt. She was suffering just the same.

He seemed to make his mind up. He leant forward and said in a low, urgent voice, 'Look, Daisy, I got to know, is it true? I mean, that she's walking out with someone else?'

For a moment, she almost considered saying no, just to see him smile. But it was better that he knew the truth. And a small selfish part of her wanted to see Isobel toppled from the pedestal on which he had placed her.

'Yes,' she said.

He stabbed at a potato. 'Well, who the hell is it, then? And what's so flaming wonderful about him?'

Daisy hesitated. There were other conversations going on all round her. Everyone was busy eyeing each other and laughing and flirting, but she could hear them and they could hear her, and any piece of gossip would be round the store in no time. She couldn't do that to Isobel, however much she wanted to open Johnny's eyes.

'I dunno,' she said.

'You must do. You're her friend, aren't you? You share a room with her. She must of told you.'

Daisy rolled her eyes to indicate the people round them. 'I can't say.'

'Oh. Like that, is it?'

'Like what?'

'Big secret.'

'Sort of.'

'Can't you tell me?'

Daisy had a sudden inspiration. 'Not here, I can't.'

'Oh – I see.'

Johnny thought about this for a while. Daisy took a chance and changed the subject, asking him if he had been approached by Selfridges. They talked about what they knew of the new store. The half-hour was soon over. Daisy rose to go.

'Been nice talking to you,' she said, willing him to make some sort of move.

'Yeah – look, Daisy, don't go – how about you and me going out for a drink one evening?'

Joy leapt and bubbled inside her. She held it down, though she felt as if she would burst.

'I dunno – per'aps –'

'How about tomorrow?'

She made a great show of reluctance. 'Oh – well – all right.'

All the way back to the department, she wanted to dance and sing. She was going to go out with Johnny! No Arthur, no Isobel, just the two of them, together. It was what she had been longing for since the moment she first saw him. She held on to the euphoria for the rest of the working day, hugging it to herself, feeling it glow inside, making a barrier of it against the outside world. The most difficult customer could not broach her defences. She smiled brilliantly and ran to fulfil every demand, and at the end of the day instead of being tired, she was still bounding with energy. Everything was wonderful in the world. Anything was possible. Then she met up with Isobel.

Her friend was white-faced with fatigue.

'You look happy,' she remarked.

'I am.'

She was about to spill it all out, when something stopped her. She did not want to tell Isobel. Somehow, it would spoil it. And even as she hesitated, she found that already it was spoilt. For common sense had at last penetrated her heedless mood, telling her what she had known all along, what she had even used to push Johnny in the right direction. He was only asking her out in order to find out about Isobel. The disappointment was so severe that she nearly wept.

By the following evening, she was on the way up again. She had persuaded herself that this was her big chance to speak to Johnny without Isobel there dazzling him. With Isobel out of the way, he might come to see something in her instead. He had to. She couldn't bear it if he didn't.

Isobel watched her as she went through her small wardrobe, trying to decide what to wear.

'Might I – would you be offended if I offered to lend you something?'

They both knew that once Daisy would have jumped at the offer. The few clothes Isobel had brought from her former home were all beautifully made of quality fabrics. But their friendship was now so strained that Daisy looked for hidden reasons behind everything.

Without waiting for an answer, Isobel produced a blouse of the palest shell pink. Daisy was instantly lost. It was so beautiful that she had to reach out and touch it.

'It's silk,' she said, stroking the lustrous fabric, touching the intricate tucks and ruffles.

'Yes.'

There was an uncomfortable silence. They both knew that

this was new, and that Isobel could not possibly have afforded it from her wages.

'Your new beau bought it for you, did he?'

Isobel looked away.

'He must have a bob or two, then,' Daisy commented. And what, she wondered, did Isobel do for him to buy her this? And her always going on about how she didn't like men even looking at her.

'I – I didn't ask him to buy it. I didn't ask for anything,' Isobel said, as if reading her mind. After all, both of them knew that gifts implied favours.

'Oh yeah, I believe you,' Daisy said, but she bit back any further comment. She really wanted the blouse. It was so much nicer than anything she had.

'Look – you have it, to keep. I don't want it. I couldn't ever wear it. It will just lie there going to waste if you don't,' Isobel said. She thrust the blouse into Daisy's arms.

Daisy could not resist it. Shivering in the cold air of the attic room, she undressed. The blouse felt wonderful on. Daisy had never worn silk before. It moved against her skin like a caress. It did not matter that her skirt was old and her jacket, though new, was cheap and ill-cut. The blouse made her feel like a princess.

'Who are you meeting?' Isobel asked, just as she was leaving.

'Johnny,' Daisy admitted.

'Oh Daisy –' Isobel's troubled face lit up. She ran across the room and hugged her. 'Oh, I'm so pleased for you. Have a lovely, lovely evening.'

'Thanks,' Daisy said gruffly. She felt dreadful. That had not been acting. Isobel had meant it.

Johnny met her at the door.

'We won't go to the Horseshoes,' he decided, referring to the nearest pub. 'It's full of Packards' people.'

Daisy was happy to go along with anything he suggested. It was bliss just to be with him. His presence touched everything with magic. The familiar terraces of Trent Street were beautiful, the damp chill of the winter's evening was invigorating, even the buses were imbued with mystery and excitement, bearing their passengers off into the dark. Johnny led the way to a small pub, glowing warm and inviting on the corner of a mews.

'You get all the coachmen here during the Season, but it's quieter this time of year. Nice for talking,' he said.

'It's lovely. Very cosy,' Daisy approved, sipping her port and lemon.

For a while they talked of work.

'You must be doing very well, getting a promotion. I been at Packards three years and I never heard of anyone getting on that quick,' Johnny said.

'Yeah, but they're a funny lot in Baby Linens. We don't have the laughs there what we had in Ladies' Sportswear. All the proud grandmothers cooing over little bonnets and stuff and the nannies wanting best-quality pilches and fine woollen vests. Babies! Blimey, too many of 'em in the world, if you ask me.'

Johnny laughed. 'I thought all women loved babies.'

'Not me, and not a lot of us, if we was honest,' Daisy maintained. 'Nothing but trouble, always crying and smelly. I should know, my mum went on having 'em for years and me and my sisters had to look after 'em.'

'You come from a big family, then?'

'Yeah, ten of us.'

'All I got is one sister. I used to wish I had lots of brothers.'

'Big families are all right if you got the money to feed 'em. Trouble is, it's the poor as always seems to have the biggest families. Funny thing, that.'

'Yeah, you're right there, Daisy.'

'Packards is like a family, don't you think? Like, we all squabble and have jealousies and that, but if anyone from, say, Peter Robinsons was to come in now and say something about anyone from Packards, even that silly cow Ivy in my department, I'd pull 'em to pieces.'

'Oh yes, we look after our own all right. We're all in it together, aren't we? That's why I'm so glad you're sharing a room with Isobel. You're tough, Daisy, you know how to look after yourself. I know you'll look out for her as well.'

A dark cloud settled on Daisy's heart. She had been so enjoying herself up till then.

'Oh yeah, tough as old boots, that's me. Real old warhorse, eh?'

Johnny just laughed. 'You know I didn't mean it like that.

But you been brought up to stick up for yourself. You been working since you were twelve. You know the ropes. Isobel doesn't.'

Daisy was slightly mollified.

'She wouldn't never have survived without me. Didn't have a clue,' she said.

'That's what I mean. She's different to us, ain't she? Delicate. She didn't ought to be here at all, not a lady like her.'

'She's got to earn a living like what the rest of us have,' Daisy pointed out.

'I know. That's what's so sad about her. She shouldn't be slaving behind a counter. She's Quality.'

'And we're not, I suppose?'

Johnny gave a wry smile. 'Oh come on, Daise – we're working people.'

'So what's wrong with that?' Daisy snapped. 'I ain't ashamed of it. I don't owe nobody nothing, I pay my own way and I send what I can back to my family. And I tell you something, not all them Quality people look down on us. Miss Packard don't for a start. She'd much rather roll her sleeves up and get down to work with the rest of us. She said so herself. I heard her with my own ears.'

'You like Miss Packard, don't you?'

'I think she's wonderful,' Daisy said. 'I really miss being in her department.'

'She got Isobel her job back, didn't she?'

They were back to Isobel again.

'Yeah. Went storming off to Mr Mason and made him take her back.'

'She sounds a real card. I'm glad Isobel's in her department. If Miss Packard waded in on her side that time, she might do again, if it was needed.'

Isobel, Isobel, Isobel.

'How's things up in Carpets, then?' Daisy asked.

It distracted him for a while. He told her about the latest tricks the young shopmen had played on each other, and about some of the strange things that customers had asked for.

'You have a good laugh up there, then. Wouldn't never have thought it. I mean, it's a bit slow, ain't – isn't – it? People don't buy carpets every day of the week. I hate it when I'm just hanging about tidying. I like to sell stuff.'

'You're good at it, so I hear.'

'Well, yes. I love it. I love the things we sell, even if they are for babies. They're so pretty and dainty and crisp and new. And I love getting people to buy them. It's like – like I've won if I can persuade a customer to buy something when they've only come in to kill a couple of hours before having dinner.' As she spoke, Daisy leant forward, her eyes glowing with enthusiasm. 'I always wanted to work at Packards, you see. It was like somewhere magic, a palace or something, like in a fairy story. And when I got there, it was more than just a job. I've had other jobs, and they were horrible. Packards is different. I really want to do well there.'

'I know what you mean,' Johnny agreed. 'It's a good place to work. You can learn a lot if you keep your ears and eyes open. I talk to the buyer whenever I can. He's a decent bloke, he likes you if you take an interest. He tells me all about the qualities, and the dyes, and the knotting, and the meaning of the patterns. He thinks I want to learn so as I can be a better salesman, and he's right in a way. I do, and the more you can tell a customer, the better. They trust you if they think you know what you're talking about.'

'You're right. If you can tell 'em what they really want to know, then they'll be happy and they'll come back again,' Daisy agreed.

'That's it exactly! But that isn't all, you see. I want to get on at Packards, but I don't want to stay there for ever. One day, I'd like to set up a shop of my own. I'm saving every penny I can towards it.'

Johnny stopped, flushed. 'There – I never told nobody that before. Well, except for Arthur, and I dunno why I told him. He's a good bloke, Arthur, a good pal, but he doesn't understand. He never looks beyond what we're going to do on Saturday night. But me, I want to get somewhere.'

'I think that's wonderful. And you'd be a success, I know you would,' Daisy said.

She could see it all. A nice shop in a high street somewhere, with carpets hung on the walls and stacked in rolls, and a neat little flat upstairs. When it was busy, Johnny could ring a bell and she would come down and help him. She was a quick learner. She knew she could pick up the ins and outs of carpets easily. They would make a splendid team, the two of them. The shop would flourish.

'Thank you.' Johnny looked embarrassed. He hesitated, then said, 'What I'd really like, what I dream of, is to have Isobel there as well. Not working, of course. She shouldn't be working. I'd look after her and protect and provide for her. I want to take her away from having to slave behind a counter.'

Daisy's happy picture smashed apart. Pain sliced through her, followed by consuming anger. How could he be so blind?

'For God's sake,' she cried, her voice harsh. 'Wake up, will you? She wouldn't marry you if you was the last bloke on earth. She thinks you're common.'

Johnny slammed down his glass. 'That ain't true! You're just saying that because you're jealous she's so much prettier than you.'

Daisy gasped. It was too near the truth to be safe, but she was beyond being sensible.

'It is true. Think what you just said: she's Quality, and we're just working people. What d'you think she'll see in you? And anyway, if it ain't true, why ain't she going out with you, eh? I'll tell you why: because she's going out with Mr Perry.'

She stopped, horrified by Johnny's reaction. The high colour drained from his face. He stared at her in horror.

'*Who?*'

'Mr Perry Amberley Packard,' Daisy elaborated, though they both knew perfectly well whom she meant.

'But –'

She watched a series of emotions chase across his face. Shock, pain, stubborn disbelief.

'She can't be. She wouldn't.'

They were both well aware of the implications. If a shopgirl went out with a young gentleman, especially a real man-about-town like Mr Perry, it meant only one thing. He was out to seduce her, while she wheedled as much as she could out of him in the way of presents. The best outcome, as far as the girl was concerned, was that she became his mistress. Mostly, the man discarded her as soon as someone else caught his eye, or when she became pregnant, whichever came first.

The rage drained out of Daisy, leaving her limp. She lifted the collar of the pink blouse.

'He give her this. Real silk, this is. Feel.'

Dazed, Johnny reached out and touched it, and jumped back as if he had been burnt. His mouth twisted with anger and hatred.

'I'll get him. I don't know how, but I'll get him. I'll make him so he never looks at a woman again.'

'You'll get yourself put inside, and then where'd Isobel be?' Daisy said.

'I don't care.'

The landlord was clearing up round them. There was only one other customer left. They both realised that it was late, that they had another long day's work ahead of them tomorrow. They went out into the bleak night, not talking, each wrapped in a cloud of misery. The cold was no longer invigorating. It shrivelled Daisy's face and penetrated her bones, settling black and heavy on her soul. She could hardly believe that she had walked the same streets earlier in such blind happiness. Now she could hardly contain the tangle of emotions that raged inside her. She still resented Isobel for catching Johnny's heart with such careless ease, but the resentment was mixed with an uneasy sense of guilt at betraying her secret and even a fear of what might become of a girl who knew so little in the hands of a man like Mr Perry. Above all, she still loved Johnny, and it was an agony to see him so faithful to Isobel despite what she had told him.

They stopped at the door of twenty-four Trent Street. Johnny thrust his hands into his pockets.

'Look, Daisy, I'm sorry if I flew off the handle a bit.'

''Sall right,' Daisy lied.

'I'm really beholden to you. You're nice to talk to. I wondered – would you come out again?'

And because she could refuse him nothing, Daisy agreed.

23

'This is the sort of thing we ought to be doing,' Amelie said, spreading out a copy of the *Daily Mail* on the desk.

Two of the members of the Advertising Department, Mr Carpenter and his sidekick, Jerry Mitchell, moved over with deliberate reluctance, scepticism written all over them. The third, the girl typewriter, merely looked up from her machine. She knew that her opinion counted for nothing.

'There,' Amelie said, waving a hand at the journal.

The two men looked at the full-page advertisement. Beautifully laid out and illustrated, it announced the forthcoming opening of the new Selfridges store, along with a statement of policy.

Mr Carpenter was a large cumbersome man, never seen without a cigarette between his lips. He shook his head and gave a short mirthless laugh. Some ash dropped on the paper. He brushed it away with a meaty hand.

'Full page. I heard they were spending a fortune on press advertising.'

'A fortune,' repeated Jerry Mitchell.

'But it's effective, isn't it? There are advertisements like this in all the major newspapers and journals. People will stop and read them, and then they'll go and see what it's all about,' Amelie said.

'They'll run after anything new. As for effective – do you know how much is being spent on these pretty pages?' Mr Carpenter asked.

Amelie didn't, but she was not going to admit as much to this patronising man.

'Money used in good advertising is money well spent,' she said.

'You tell that to Mr Packard then, and while you're about it, ask him to increase our budget tenfold, to bring it up to what Mr Selfridge is laying out.'

'Yes, tenfold,' said Jerry.

Amelie swallowed. She had not realised that Gordon Selfridge had spent that much. It was beyond anything Packards even dreamt of, and they were considered advanced in London store circles for having an advertising department at all. Most stores relied on the buyers to write advertisements for their own departments.

'I've seen the power of advertising in the United States. It works. People take notice of it. We ought to be doing much more exciting things to draw more customers into Packards,' she insisted.

Mr Carpenter gave a smile that showed plainly he was being very patient with the boss's granddaughter. Beside him, Jerry Mitchell grinned, anticipating a put-down. Amelie resisted the urge to hit his nasty spotty face.

'With respect, Miss Packard, how long have you been in this department?'

'A week,' Amelie admitted, 'but –'

Mr Carpenter did not let her go on. 'I've been in the newspaper business for thirty years and with Packards for ten. I think during that time you'll find that more people have come to the store every year.'

'Every year,' said his faithful assistant.

'Except for last year,' Amelie retorted. 'Or if they came in, they did not buy so much. Our sales were down for the first time last year, and it looks as if they will be down even more this year, with Selfridges competing in this way. We have to bring more paying customers in, and the way to do it is with advertisements like this.' She nodded at the one on the desk.

For the past week, she had watched what was being done in the advertising office, asked a lot of questions and made some calculations. Now she was moving into the offensive.

Mr Carpenter sighed. He spoke slowly, as if to a backward child.

'Miss Packard, Selfridges is opening up. They have to tell everyone that they are there. It was not the same for Packards. Our customers know we are here. We merely have to remind them every now and again, and tell them when we have something special we want them to know about.'

Amelie made an effort to remain calm. She knew she was not wanted in the advertising office. She knew that Mr Carpenter and the revolting Jerry resented her and guessed that they thought she was spying for her grandfather. So she had to tread carefully.

'I am aware of that, Mr Carpenter. I am also aware of the fact that what we have to tell our customers at the moment is that however wonderful Selfridges might sound, and whatever offers they might have, Packards is still the best department store in Oxford Street, indeed the best in London.'

'Which is just what we are doing.'

'Yes, we sent out some copy only yesterday,' Jerry agreed.

'And very boring it was, too,' Amelie said, forgetting to be tactful.

Mr Carpenter sat down in his chair and leant back with his arms folded.

'Perhaps you'd like to show us how you would do it.'

It was obvious that he thought this was a knockout blow.

'Since you ask, I have been making some rough layouts,' Amelie said.

She opened her bag and produced a sketchbook. Mr Carpenter looked pained, as if the effort at patience was getting too much for him. Jerry grinned in anticipation of a truly dreadful piece of work. Amelie took a long calming breath. She turned to the first sheet. Across the top was PACKARDS in curly capitals, the P twice the size of the other letters, and underneath it, on an unfurled scroll, 'The Best Range of Goods at the Most Favourable Prices.' Beneath that was a smaller heading, 'A Department for Everyone.' Then there were two columns of lines. The whole thing was enclosed with fashionable Art-Nouveau swirls.

'The motto is my grandfather's idea,' Amelie explained. 'And the lines there represent a list of our departments.'

'I see,' Mr Carpenter said. 'And what exactly is the point of this advertisement?'

'It reminds people that we are more than a match for Selfridges. Then subsequent ones, smaller perhaps, will tell them of particular departments – like this.'

She turned the page and showed the same heading, but this

time with 'Ladies' Sportswear' underneath it, and 'Everything for the active lady,' and a selection of goods from the department with accompanying sketches.

'We could do the same for other departments, and for the restaurant – so,' Amelie said. 'And of course we'd employ a good artist. Selfridges have used the very best black-and-white illustrators, and it shows.'

'So does the price,' said Mr Carpenter. He looked totally unimpressed. 'It's an interesting idea, Miss Packard, and I'm sure it's all the thing in Chicago or New York or whatever, but it's not the way we work in this department.'

Amelie argued her case for a while longer, but she could see that she was getting nowhere.

'I think you're being very short-sighted. Mr Selfridge is bringing American ideas here and we can't ignore them. Better by far to start competing now.'

'So you said before, Miss Packard. Now, we do have work to do today. Jerry, fetch those proofs from the *Ladies Home Journal*. They've got to be corrected and sent off today.'

Amelie fumed. She was being treated like a child. She was tempted simply to walk out. After all, Mr Carpenter was not going to listen to any of her ideas. But if she did that she would be falling in with all the horrible man's expectations of her. He was certainly hoping she would go. And beside that, she really did want to learn more about how the advertisements were put together and costed and sent out and which journals were thought to be the best for addressing their customers.

'Perhaps I can do that,' she offered. 'I can spot a spelling mistake when I see one.'

Mr Carpenter gave her a long-suffering look. 'Very well. But show me before you send them back.'

In the days that followed, Amelie did not give up on her campaign for more exciting advertisements, and Mr Carpenter did not move from his conviction that he knew best. It was a most frustrating time. But she did find out about the workings of the department, and she did keep out of her mother's way. That was a huge blessing, since she was subjected to a lecture over the dinner table every evening.

Then one day her mother came into the dining room looking

positively radiant. It was just a family dinner, but for once they were all there, even Edward. There were the usual enquiries after everyone's day, in reply to which Amelie lied and said she had had a most enjoyable time. That took them through the first course. It was not until the vegetables had been served that Winifred allowed herself the pleasure of announcing her news.

'It seems my father has come to his senses at last,' she said.

Amelie had a sinking feeling of approaching disappointment.

'One thing you can't accuse Grandfather of is lack of sense, Mother,' Edward said, but Amelie could see a sharpening of interest in his eyes.

'I am speaking of social sense, Edward – something which you should spend more time cultivating.'

'What has Grandfather done to earn your approval, then, Mother?' Perry asked.

'He has purchased an estate.' Winifred paused for effect, smiling round at all of them, making sure they all appreciated her triumph. Perry obligingly asked her for the details.

'Tatwell Court, in Hertfordshire. A charming eighteenth-century house with extensive parkland and farms.'

'Oh, the Cunninghams' place, you mean. Yes, very nice,' Perry said.

Between them they canvassed all the advantages of the house and the estate, from the size of the dining room to the number of guns that could be taken out. Amelie listened with a growing sense of betrayal. So her grandfather really was going to retire. Somehow, she had thought he would always be there, a solid pillar holding up the great edifice of Packards, giving her time to prove that she was just as capable of running the store as Edward. She glanced at her brother. Edward was sitting with a small smile of satisfaction on his face, listening politely to what his mother and Perry were saying.

'The decoration was in a sorry state of repair last time I saw it,' Perry said.

'Used to be wonderful in old Sophy Cunningham's day. Now she really did know how to entertain,' his father put in.

'Your grandfather did say that there would need to be some improvements made. Of course, poor Mother cannot be expected to undertake the entire redecoration of a house that size. She will need my help,' Winifred said happily.

The rest of the meal was taken up with Winifred and Perry discussing what could be done, while Bertie reminisced over past parties and Edward put in the odd question to keep them going. Amelie could see just what was going on in his head. He thought he was home and dry. Grandfather was retiring and the house would keep his only possible rival, herself, nicely out of the way for the greater part of the year until such time as she got married and was eliminated from the running. She could have wept with frustration. Just as she was beginning to persuade her grandfather to let her try her hand at more things about the store, he chose to retire.

'– Amelie?'

She realised that her mother was speaking to her.

'You haven't expressed any opinion.'

'Oh – it all sounds very nice,' she said lamely.

'Nice? Is that all you can say? It will be a simply splendid thing for you, child. Now, your grandfather takes possession the day after tomorrow, and we have a dinner to go to the day after that, but then we can all go down there and stay for a few days. Then I can begin to make some real plans.'

'Yes, that's all right,' Amelie said, thinking aloud.

'What do you mean, it's all right?' Winifred asked.

'It's the day after the Selfridges' opening. Amelie thinks Packards will go bankrupt the day the new store opens if she is not here to defend it,' Edward explained.

Winifred frowned over this, but nothing could really dent her pleasure in her new toy. She spent the rest of the evening discussing colour schemes and questioning Edward and even Amelie on whether this or that fabric or carpet or piece of furniture was available at the store. The one advantage Amelie could find in the situation was that not one reference was made to the Teignmeretons.

The much-trumpeted day of the grand opening of Selfridges arrived. Mr Carpenter made no pretence of regret when she announced that she had to go and see what all the fuss was about.

Packards seemed very empty as she walked through the store,

and as soon as she arrived outside, she could see why. The pavements around Selfridges were crowded. Determined to find out the worst, since to know your enemy is to be prepared, she set off to join the throng, her businesslike mood of serious enquiry spiced with the novelty of being out on her own. She hardly ever managed to get out without a member of the family or a servant to accompany her. The simple freedom was intoxicating.

She was soon part of the crush of people gazing at the windows. It was just as she had warned her grandfather. They were spectacular. Gordon Selfridge had hired Mr Goldman, Marshall Field's head windowdresser, to design the displays and he had summoned up a series of set pieces, each one more eye-catching than the last. Londoners had never seen anything like it.

'So artistic,' a woman in front of Amelie was saying.

'They're like stage sets. I could look at them for hours.'

'Oh, but we must go into the shop, dear. If the outside is like this, just think how beautiful the inside must be.'

Amelie wished her grandfather could hear them. It was just the reaction she had had when she first saw Marshall Field's windows. You just had to see what else the store had to offer.

With some difficulty, she made her way inside. What she found held her suspended between admiration and gloom. The store was a wonder. Instead of being tucked away inside drawers and under counters, the goods were displayed like an exhibition of all the very best that modern manufacturing could produce, and it was done with dignity and taste. Gordon Selfridge had not imported an American store, he had brought all the best ideas and made an entirely new British one. Amelie could have wept. It was just what they should have done to Packards. If her grandfather had been convinced, they could have led the way. As it was, Packards and the rest of the London stores would have to stumble after.

The opening had been managed with all the dash of a stage production. An army of shopmen and girls gave out free purse calendars and shopping notebooks. Amelie tested them on their knowledge of the store, asking a succession of them where she might find various obscure goods. They had been very well trained. They all knew just where to direct her. She walked all over the store, in and out of every one of the one hundred and thirty departments. All were well stocked and filled with people gazing and exclaiming. Then there were the other facilities. As well as restaurants and rest rooms for weary shoppers, there was a reading room, a writing room and even a post office. 'Come to Selfridges and stay the day,' shoppers were urged at every opportunity. Amelie could see that they might well do just that. At a leisurely pace it would take a day to see everything properly, especially if there were decisions to be made over purchases, and with so many needs catered for on the premises, there would be no call to venture out. Why walk down the road to Packards when it was all there at Selfridges?

By three o'clock she was tired and dispirited. Her legs ached, she had had no lunch, and all around her were people who should have been in Packards, perhaps buying from her very own department. Even the pleasure of being out on her own had worn off. It would have been very nice to have someone to share her thoughts with. She made her way back to a quiet and very dull-looking Packards. She loved the place dearly, but it looked what it now was – a thing of the past. She went straight up to see her grandfather.

As always, Thomas greeted her with pleasure.

'I suppose you've come to tell me that we're about to be superseded by the amazing Mr Selfridge and his performing circus,' he said. 'Come and sit down and tell me all about it. You look exhausted.'

Amelie drank three cups of tea and ate her way through a plate of dainty sandwiches and two cakes, while describing the extent of the competition they faced. Thomas listened attentively. When she had finished, he put down his own teacup and leant forward.

'Now then, my pet, think. Of all the throngs of people gawping at these wonders, how many of them were buying?'

'Not many,' she had to admit, 'but next time –'

'Next time they'll come back to us. Of course they're all at Selfridges today. It's a novelty, and from what you say, it's a very pretty novelty. But you underestimate people's loyalty. We have hundreds of customers who have been buying from us for years. Women bring their daughters and they become regular customers too. They would not dream of buying anywhere else. It takes years of supplying what people really want to build up that sort of following, and that's what Selfridge hasn't got. Of course people will go and take a look, but they'll come back to us when they want to make a purchase.'

'Some of them won't. They'll go in because it's new and attractive, they'll see something they like and they'll buy it and then they'll buy something else, and then next time they'll say, "Let's go and see what's new at Selfridges," and they'll buy there again, and so it goes on,' Amelie said.

'Over a course of time?'

'Yes.'

'Ah, but time is what Gordon Selfridge hasn't got. That's what comes of starting big instead of working your way up like the rest of us did. Do you know how much money he's sunk in that store?'

'No,' Amelie admitted.

'Nine hundred thousands pounds.'

That did make her think.

'That's nearly a million,' she said.

'Precisely. That includes a great deal of his personal fortune, but it still means he is in hock to the banks for a tremendous amount. He has to make a success of that store quickly, or he's going to be in considerable financial trouble. In the meantime, we may lose a few of our customers, but we can ride it out, we have a sound basis.'

Amelie sighed. It all sounded very reassuring, and of course her grandfather has been in the business ever since he was younger than she was now, but still she was not quite convinced.

'We don't want to lose any customers, surely? Takings were down last year.'

Thomas nodded, impressed. 'You've a good head on your shoulders, my pet. But that's not because we're failing as a business. We are in the grip of a trade depression, you know. All the London stores are feeling the pinch. All of industry is, for that matter.'

'Then shouldn't we try even harder to get more customers in?' Amelie asked.

'Of course we should, but not to the extent of being panicked by this American upstart. Now, your idea of reminding people about why they always did come here is a good one.'

Thomas opened a drawer in his desk and produced a sketchbook. Amelie recognised it as hers.

'Those are my advertisement roughs.'

'Yes. I went and had a look round Carpenter's office last night. This is excellent. "The Best Range of Goods at the Most Favourable Prices." I like that.'

'You said that. I was simply quoting you,' Amelie told him. She felt a glow of pleasure start. She believed in her advertising ideas. It was very sweet to have her grandfather approve them.

'There you are, then. I may be old but I do know what I'm talking about. I shall have Carpenter do these properly and place them. Not,' he added, forestalling her, 'full-page spreads. We don't need them. Just gentle reminders to our many faithful customers.'

Amelie walked out of his office feeling that she had really achieved something. It was not until she had gone down to the sales floors that she realised she had not asked him about Tatwell Court and whether he really was retiring.

24

It was a beautiful place, Edward had to concede. He reined in his horse to take in the view laid out before him. From where he was, on a small hill crowned with beech trees at the north-west extremity of the park, he could see almost the whole of Tatwell and its grounds. The house itself stood on a slight rise, a long building consisting of the main block with its Palladian portico, and two symmetrical wings. Behind one of these were the stables and domestic offices, all built of a pale yellow brick. The weak spring sunshine gleamed on rows of perfectly proportioned windows.

Around the house spread the lawns, the flower gardens and the walled kitchen gardens with their glasshouses. Beyond these was the park, gently undulating grassland studded with mature trees and patches of woodland. Through it ran a stream which had been dammed to form a small lake with a little wooded island in it and a boathouse on its shore. A long drive wound through the grounds from the tall wrought-iron gates to the rectangular gravel sweep before the elegant entrance with its Doric pillars.

It was beyond doubt the best place from which to look at Tatwell, for from this distance one could not see the evidence of neglect, the slipping tiles, the dark stains of rising damp, the creaking floorboards and musty smell of the house, the weedy gardens and empty stables and the exotic fruit trees dying from lack of heat in the glasshouses. Tatwell and its former owners had been in decline for two generations, and now finally they had accepted the inevitable, and bowed out. Edward smiled to himself. The Cunninghams, for all their long history and faultless pedigree, had been forced to sell their family home to a man who came to London at fifteen years old with three shillings in his pocket, the youngest of the six children of a Wiltshire draper. His grandfather, and the forces of commerce and ambition, had defeated the aristocracy. It was a source of fierce pleasure to Edward.

He was stirred into action by the sight of the motor coming out of the stableyard and setting off down the drive. It was going to pick up Sylvia Forbes and her parents from the station.

'Not a regular Friday-to-Monday,' his mother had said. 'The house is all to pieces at the moment, not fit for real entertaining. This will be just a little gathering of friends.' In fact it was a transparent move to throw Edward and Sylvia together, and for herself and Lady Forbes to size each other up. Everybody concerned was perfectly well aware of this, yet Edward knew that none of them would give any hint that this was anything but what his mother claimed: a small informal social event.

He cantered across the park and delivered the horse into the hands of the head groom. In the stableyard there were already signs of improvement. The smell of paint overpowered that of horses as men gave a fresh dark green coat to the flaking stable doors. The once-empty carriage house now contained a smart victoria and a governess cart as well as being home to the motor when it returned, and a couple of undergrooms were busy polishing harnesses outside the tack room. He made his way in through one of the back entrances. Although this was only his second visit to Tatwell, he had made it his business to get to know his way round the many rooms and passages and in and out of the doors so that he would not find himself lost in his own family's home.

In the morning room with its hand-painted Chinese wallpaper, now faded and damp-stained, he found his grandmother stabbing at a piece of needlework.

'Oh, Edward, your mother was looking for you. Something about the visitors arriving.'

'Yes, I saw the motor leaving.'

His grandmother's mouth set in pettish lines of discontent.

'She had the gall to tell me to get ready. I said to her, "Invite people to *my* house if you must, Winifred, but don't expect me to pander to them." That told her. She wasn't happy.'

'I can imagine,' Edward said. Winifred would probably have preferred it if Margaret had stayed in London, safely out of the way. For his own part, he was rather glad that his grandmother was here. She served to remind his mother that she was not in fact mistress of Tatwell, however much she was behaving as if she were.

'And another thing,' his grandmother said. 'She's talking now of turning that nice blue room on the first floor into a boudoir for herself. Well, she shall do no such thing. I want that room for a sitting room for myself. Somewhere to get away from all these snobs she's so set on inviting down here. It's a very pretty room, with a view over the rose garden. I'm putting my foot down.'

Edward suspected that she had not even thought of claiming that particular room until she heard that Winifred wanted it, and was taking pleasure in thwarting her on this issue.

'You do that, Grandmother. It's your house,' he told her.

'And what about these visitors, these Forbeses? Winifred seems to be setting great store by them. Are you going to oblige her by marrying the girl?'

Surprised, Edward gave her a sharp look. He hadn't realised that she knew so much.

'I don't know,' he said.

'Well, you do what you want, not what your mother wants. Like your sister. She stood up for herself and refused to marry that whatshisname.'

'Don't worry, Grandmother,' Edward assured her. 'I think I can make my own mind up over these things.'

He went off to get changed into a tweed suit, running the conversation over in his mind. Did he want to marry Sylvia Forbes? He truly did not know. She was very suitable. She would run his household with admirable efficiency, be a gracious hostess, a careful mother. His grandfather would approve of her as the sort of wife who would be an asset to a man. And yet – he shrugged into the jacket that his valet held ready for him – and yet those very qualities that fitted her for the post of Mrs Edward Amberley Packard faintly repelled him. When he thought of what he wanted in a woman, as opposed to a wife, something quite different slid into his mind. Someone remarkably like Isobel Brand. He stood by the window, knotting his tie, his fingers working automatically while his imagination got Isobel alone in a subtly lit room, saw her full lips tremble, her eyes cloud with dawning fear. She would be reluctant, unwilling even, but she would submit to him, weeping as she offered up all her delicious softness to him. The thought of his power to possess her beauty brought such a surge of desire that he had to dismiss the valet. Isobel Brand. He stared unseeing at the waters of the lake, playing with what was becoming a recurrent fantasy, trying to decide whether to change it to reality. He could have her if he chose. It was just a question of whether he really wanted to take the risk. If his grandfather found out, there would be serious trouble.

A movement in the park caught his eye, waking him to the present. The motor was coming back up the drive. He must go down and greet the Forbeses.

The family, minus his grandfather who had not yet come down from London, had gathered in the red drawing room, a room of splendid proportions with long windows overlooking the lake. A huge fire was burning in the black marble fireplace, dispelling the damp, and two large arrangements of hothouse flowers bought in by Winifred added freshness and exotic luxury, but nothing could disguise the fact that the sparse furniture was very much the worse for wear and the red silk wallcovering was rotting under the windows and had brighter rectangles at intervals where pictures had been sold off.

'This must be the first room to be refurbished,' Winifred declared. 'It really is a disgrace. If only the men would hurry up with the wiring work. I can't think why Father is so keen on having electricity put in. Candles are so much more suitable for these old places. And as for bathrooms, what are servants for, if not to carry hot-water cans?'

It was a source of constant frustration to her that Thomas insisted on having the roof repaired, the damp cured and modern improvements done to the house before any redecoration could start.

'What do you think about this room, Edward?' she asked. 'Do you think I should have this furniture regilded and reupholstered, or should we buy new?'

Edward banished the last shreds of Isobel Brand from his mind and attended to what his mother was saying. She was forever doing this, he had noticed, canvassing his opinion on everything from the horses to the carpets. It was transparently obvious what she was doing: trying to seduce him away from Packards and into playing the country gentleman.

'I think you should ask Grandmother,' he said, to annoy her.

If she thought he was going to fall in with her social ambitions, she had grossly mistaken him. She had Perry to play the young man about town, and she was doing her best to squeeze Amelie into her mould. He had better things to do than to kowtow to Society. He didn't mind coming down here for a weekend every now and again. This weekend was especially useful, since it was going to give him a chance to form a better judgement on Sylvia Forbes, but he was not going to pretend to be anything other than what he was.

At this point the Forbeses were announced. Edward observed them as his parents went forward to greet them. Sir Alfred was square and ruddy-faced, a countryman to his bones, coming to Town only as a great concession to his wife and daughter. Lady Ann was tall and formidable with fixed ideas. Sylvia was tall like her mother, with very English looks, long face, blue eyes, fair hair and lovely complexion. Nobody could call her a beauty, but neither was she plain. When Edward shook her hand, she gave a smile that reminded him why he had lit upon her in the first place, for it lifted her patrician features into something approaching prettiness.

Refreshments were served, the Forbeses' journey down enquired into, amusements for the day suggested. The weekend was under way.

By the evening it looked like shaping into a success for Winifred. The Forbeses appeared to be enjoying themselves, the cook had produced a *tour de force* of a meal, the dining room looked beautiful, its perfect proportions enhanced and its decay softened by kindly candlelight. Bertie chatted amiably to Lady Ann about mutual acquaintances, Winifred and Sir Alfred agreed to disagree over whether carriages would ever be altogether superseded by motors, Amelie and Perry kept their grandmother amused and Edward, seated by Sylvia, was pleasantly surprised to find that she seemed genuinely interested in the store.

'Mother and I have always been attached to Packards,' she

said. 'It was truly remarkable how one can find absolutely anything one might want there. Tell me, how do you manage to anticipate so many hundreds of different needs?'

Edward explained the buying system to her, and she nodded, impressed.

'I never realised there was so much to it. But when one comes to think of it, a store cannot run itself any more than a large house can.'

Edward knew very little about the running of a large house, but his brief introduction to Tatwell had shown him that it needed an army of servants.

'Quite so. They both require a large number of people who all know their own jobs well, and someone to oversee it all. And then there are those who make the large decisions about direction and policy.'

Unspoken between them was the knowledge that this was to be his role. Sylvia asked more questions, Edward explained. She listened and commented, politely interested.

All the time, Edward could feel the covert attention of everyone else around the table. They might appear to be engaged in their own conversations, but he knew that invisible antennae were following the progress of his evening. They might not be aware of exactly what was being said, but they knew whether things were going well or not. Sitting outside of himself and looking on, he wondered whether he was going to fulfil all their expectations.

The next morning Edward was up early, and was surprised to find Amelie already down before him.

'I've been looking at that lawn beyond the cedar trees. I've paced it out and there is definitely room for two tennis courts and a croquet lawn, and we could build a little pavilion by those overgrown rhododendrons.'

'*Two* tennis courts?' Edward questioned.

'Well, why not? Everything else round here seems to be planned on the grand scale. Laying out a couple of tennis courts is nothing to replacing the leading on the roof.'

'Don't you like the house, then?'

'Oh, I like it well enough. But what a white elephant. Edward! What on earth does Grandfather want with it? The money would have been far better invested in expanding Packards. We ought to be opening branches in the provinces. Manchester, Leeds, Birmingham – we should make Packards known throughout the country.'

Behind a mildly amused expression, Edward was distinctly shaken. He had had no inkling before now of just how bold his sister's ideas were. Expanding into the provinces was one of his pet plans, which he was saving until he had control. His grandfather would then be known as the man who had founded Packards, while he was not merely his successor, but the one who took the firm into the twentieth century and made it a countrywide name. But Amelie had been foolish. She had let him know what she was thinking. He had no intention of doing the same.

'You'll never get Grandfather to agree to that,' he said.

Amelie sighed. 'No, more's the pity. It's going to cost a fortune to do this place up the way Mother wants it.'

'He'll keep her under control once he comes to live out here. It is his house, after all. His and Grandmother's.'

'Do you think he will live out here permanently? I don't. I don't believe he has any intention of doing so. Look at this weekend. He's not coming down till late this morning, and he'll be going back this evening. I think he bought this particular estate because it's so near to London. And as for retiring – Grandfather will no more retire than fly.'

'He's more interested in Tatwell than you might think,' Edward said. He paused a moment, then decided to try to squash any ideas she might have. 'If he hadn't bought this place, and committed the vast amount of money it's going to take to put it to rights, he could have bought into Selfridges.'

He had the satisfaction of seeing Amelie look absolutely flabbergasted.

'*What?*'

'Oh, hadn't you heard? Well, I suppose you're too busy with all your social events. Yes, Gordon Selfridge is in serious trouble. You have to hand it to Grandfather, he forecast it all along. Selfridge has sold £350,000 of debentures to Sir John Musker.'

'Of Home and Colonial?'

'The very same. In the old days, Grandfather would have snatched those up.'

He was saying it to convince himself as well. For Amelie had put her finger on a niggling fear of his. Thomas had not so far shown any signs of relinquishing his absolute authority over the store.

Amelie threw him a sharp look. 'So you really think he is about to retire? I wish you luck, Edward, but I think you're on a losing wicket. Packards is Grandfather's life.'

She walked off. Edward let her go, allowing her the pleasure of having had the last word. She wouldn't have taken that tone if she hadn't been sure that he would very soon take over from Grandfather. All the same, she was a good deal shrewder than he had realised and she had Grandfather round her little finger. She needed to be put out of harm's way, and soon. In the meantime, he needed to convince his grandfather that he was more than capable of taking over. He had been given a clear enough hint nearly eight months ago as to one way of doing that. He would wait to see whether the old man approved of Sylvia, and if he did, then he would ask her to marry him.

25

Daisy's new relationship with Johnny had fallen into a pattern. Once a fortnight they would go out for a drink, chew over Packards' gossip for a while, and then discuss Isobel. Every time, Daisy hoped that he might be beginning to get over her. She tried introducing other topics of conversation, news of a juicy murder maybe or some titbit about the lives of those in Society, but though he would answer her and put in an opinion of his own, she never succeeded in deflecting him. She had better success when she asked him about his dream of owning a carpet shop. Then he would open up and confide his latest ideas, listen to her replies and even agree with some of the suggestions she made.

'You're right there, Daise,' he said one evening, when she said that somewhere like Leytonstone might be a good place to set up, because a lot of new building was going on there. 'Yeah, if folk've just moved into a new house, they're going to want new stuff to go in it, ain't they?'

'They will in their front parlours, 'cause they're like for show, aren't they? And that's the only place they're going to have a carpet. Nobody has them anywhere else, not ordinary people, anyway.'

She did not add that where she came from people counted themselves rich if they had a bit of oilcloth on the floor.

'You've got a good business head on your shoulders, y'know,' Johnny said.

Daisy's heart ached. Why couldn't he see that she was just the girl for him? She was an excellent saleswoman, the best in Baby Linens, and she wasn't afraid of hard work. She would be able to keep the flat above the carpet shop as clean as a whistle, cook him all the dinners he liked best and keep the kids in order. Not like Isobel. What good would she be to him? She would never be able to cope. She wouldn't know where to start. She was looking increasingly ill these days, just about getting through each long day on her feet, and going to bed straight after supper. Except, of course, on the evenings when she went out with Mr Perry.

It always came back to Isobel. That was the real reason Johnny wanted to see Daisy. To find out how Isobel was and simply to talk about her. His memory where she was concerned was amazing. Everything she had said to him, and every scrap of information that Daisy had let drop was stored up inside his head. And just as Daisy kept hoping that he would forget Isobel, so he kept hoping that Isobel would drop Mr Perry.

Then one evening when they settled down at their usual table, the pattern changed. Johnny gave Daisy her glass of port and lemon, downed half of his pint at a go and thumped it onto the table.

'I've gone and done something about it,' he announced.

'Done something about what?' Daisy asked stupidly.

'Isobel being taken advantage of by Mr Perry,' he spat out the name as if it were poison.

A feeling of doom wormed in the pit of Daisy's stomach.

'What do you mean?'

'I went and saw Mr Edward.'

Daisy gaped at him. 'You did *what?*'

'I stopped him yesterday when he came round Carpets and I asked him if I could speak to him on a very important private matter.'

'Johnny! Are you mad? You went up to him and asked him? Whatever did he say?'

'He looked at me, you know, that way he has like you're something nasty on his shoe, and he said he didn't think that I could possibly have anything to say that might concern him. But I stood my ground, and I told him it was to do with a certain member of his family and I didn't think he'd want it aired in public. That made him think.'

'Blimey! You are mad. He could've sacked you on the spot.'

'Yeah, but he didn't. He just sort of nodded and said, "My office, ten o'clock tomorrow."'

'That's today?'

'Yeah.'

'Bloody hell, Johnny, I wish you'd of told me before. I'd of talked you out of it.'

Johnny's face was set in lines of determination, just as, Daisy thought, he must have looked when he tackled Mr Edward.

'No, you wouldn't have, Daise. I made my mind up. I've been turning it over and over ever since you first told me, and I decided it was the only thing to do. I got to put a stop to it, you see. It ain't right. Even if she never speaks to me again, I'll have got her away from him. I know she ain't going out with him willingly.'

'No one makes her. It's a free country.'

'He *does* make her. He's got the power, ain't he? She's afraid to refuse.'

Daisy was about to say that if Mr Perry asked her out, she would tell him where to get off, but she realised that Johnny was probably right. Isobel hadn't the courage to refuse.

'So did you go and see Mr Edward? What happened?' she asked instead.

'I did. Our floorwalker, I reckon he thought I was about to get the push, when I said I had to go and see Mr Edward. Actually patted me on the shoulder, he did. Anyway, ten o'clock prompt, there I was at his office. Best not to start off by keeping him waiting, I thought.'

'Right.'

'Mind you, he kept me waiting. His secretary showed me in, and there he was sitting behind his desk reading some paper or other. "Thank you, Miss Whatsit," he says to the secretary, but never a word to me. Just keeps me standing there.'

'They like to do that. They think they're breaking you down,' Daisy said.

'Yeah, well, I sort of coughed and he didn't look up, so I said, "You wanted to see me, sir?" And he still doesn't look at me, but he says, "No, Miller, you wanted to see me, I believe." It's like a war of nerves, see? It really got my goat. I thought, I'm not talking to you while you're reading. I'll make you look at me if it's the last thing I do. So I didn't say nothing. And in the end, he gives a sigh and signs this bit of paper he's been looking at and sort of sits back in his chair and looks at me like I'm a dog what's just thrown up on the carpet.'

Daisy giggled. 'Yeah, he does look at you like that. I seen him.'

'"Very well, Miller, out with it," he says. "But be quick. I haven't got all day." But by then, see, I've got angry. I'm not going to let him push me around. So I explain it bit by bit, slowly.

'"There's a young lady what's working in Ladies' Sportswear. Miss Brand."

'"A shopgirl?" he says.

'"A young lady," I tell him. "A cut above the rest here. Not the sort we usually have working here. Fallen on hard times, she has, and had to get herself a job."

'Well, he didn't say nothing to this. Just looked bored. So I went on, "She's not used to our way of life. She doesn't know what's what. She's been brought up to be a lady, see, and she doesn't know how to look out for herself and she doesn't know how people can take advantage of her. She's always been looked after. Had a chaperon, like, to go about with her. It's not like the other girls in the store." So by now he's getting impatient.

'"You've made your point, Miller," he says, "I take it that this paragon is your sweetheart?"

'I couldn't make my mind up whether it was best to say yes or no. But then I thought that if I said yes he'd go against me just because I was getting on his wick, so I told him no. I said I was a friend of her roommate.'

Daisy glowed with pleasure at being mentioned like this, then almost immediately felt hurt at being referred to as just a friend. Johnny seemed to be waiting for some sort of remark, so she managed a noise of agreement.

'So then I told him that I thought that girls working at Packards was supposed to be protected, and how they wasn't even allowed to eat at the same tables as us men, and how shocked I was to hear that Miss Brand was being pestered by someone she didn't want to have round her.

'By then I could see I was really pushing my luck. He was looking like he was ready to throw me out.

'"Spare me the sermon, Miller. Just tell me what you came here to say. Just who is pestering this Miss Brand?"'

Daisy found she was holding her breath. 'What did you say?'

'I looked him in the eye and I told it to him straight. "Your brother, Mr Perry," I said. "He's been taking advantage of an innocent young lady."'

Daisy gasped. 'What did he say to that?'

'He took it calm as calm. Like I was telling him we needed more Turkey kelims or something.

'"Very well, Miller. Just leave it with me." Cold, like. But I couldn't let it be, I had to make sure he really was going to put a stop to it.

'"You will do something about it, sir, won't you?" I said.'

That had to be it. That had to be the point when Mr Edward gave him the sack. Daisy could hardly bear it.

'What did he do?'

'He glared at me like his eyes was going to bore right through me.

'"Be assured that I will deal with it, Miller, just as I will deal with you if this goes any further than this office. I trust you understand?" I said yes, and I got out while the going was good.'

Daisy let out her breath in a great sigh of relief.

'You got away with it! I can't believe it.'

'Neither could I afterwards,' Johnny admitted.

'You should be out on your ear without a character.'

'I know.'

He knew, and yet still he had done it, gone in there and fought for Isobel against the full power of the Packards.

'I'm so proud of you. That was a very brave thing to do.'

Johnny gave a shrug of depreciation. 'Oh well – I had to, didn't I? No one else was going to stick up for her.'

Not even her so-called best friend, Daisy realised. She could have done the same, but she hadn't. Not because she was afraid of losing her job, though that did come into it, but because she hoped that if Isobel stuck with Mr Perry then it would give her a better chance with Johnny.

'He'll have you marked down now,' she warned.

'I know. But it was worth it. He'll deal with it, like he said.'

'You think he will?'

'Yeah. He wouldn't've said so otherwise, would he? He'd've just slung me out.'

'You're right there. He would've.'

And he had risked that, for Isobel. Tears constricted Daisy's throat and welled behind her eyes. She hadn't a chance against someone like Isobel. He didn't see beyond her beauty and that stuck-up air of hers.

'You're either brave or stupid. I dunno which,' she said. Her voice cracked with the effort of sounding normal. She took a swig of her drink and choked.

Johnny thumped her on her back.

'You all right?'

She nodded, face scarlet and eyes streaming. Everything was so very far from being all right that she could not cope with anything but a lie. It was not until she had recovered and started on a second drink that a momentous thought struck her.

'Of course, you know what he might do.'

'Who?'

'Mr Edward, what he might do to deal with it. He might sack Isobel.'

Johnny stared at her in horror.

'He couldn't do that! It isn't her fault. She's the innocent party.'

'What's that got to do with anything? She nearly got the sack when that brother-in-law of hers came and made all that fuss. It was only Miss Packard sticking up for her that saved her.'

'Oh my God – I never thought of that – what have I done?'

'It might not come to that.'

'But if it did, and she was thrown out, whatever would she do? She's no one to turn to. Unless –' Johnny broke off, and a slow smile spread over his face. 'I could help her.'

Daisy could feel a scream of frustration gathering inside her.

'But she doesn't want you, Johnny. You said it yourself – she's different from us.'

'But if she was in trouble, she'd have to turn to me. She could stay with my family. It'd all be very respectable. I'd make sure of that. I'm not like that bastard Mr Perry.'

'No, you're not, and that's why you ain't got a chance,' Daisy almost shouted at him.

He was not the least like Mr Perry. He was brave, reliable, resourceful – and besotted with Isobel.

236

'We'll just have to see what happens. It's all up to Mr Edward now,' she said.

Isobel awoke reluctantly to face another day at Packards. She could hear Daisy moving around, going to the washstand, splashing water. In a couple of minutes, she would have to get up. She did not know if she could stand it much longer. The physical effort was wearing her down, the long hours standing behind the counter, while the dreary monotony of the days dragged at her spirit. She just wanted to stay beneath the covers for ever. Then she remembered that it was Saturday. Half-day. If the weather was clement, Perry was going to take her for a drive to Richmond for tea. Something approaching pleasure stirred her to get up and get on with the day.

Daisy gave her an odd look. This was nothing new. Daisy blew hot and cold so often that Isobel had come to expect it of her. She just wished she could hand that wretched Johnny Miller to Daisy and tell her to take him away.

'There's something I got to tell you,' Daisy said.

'Is there?' Isobel asked. She was not sure if she could cope with any revelations at this time of the morning.

'Yes. But there isn't enough time now. Not to talk about it properly. How about this afternoon?'

'I – er – I'm going out this afternoon,' Isobel admitted.

'With him?'

'Yes.'

She still could not bring herself to discuss Perry with Daisy. She knew that it was not what Daisy suspected, and that Perry was the perfect gentleman, but she despaired of convincing Daisy of it. Appearances were bad, she knew that. Young ladies did not go about unchaperoned with young gentlemen. But she had no one to accompany her now, and Perry had never given her a moment's unease. Well, not many, anyway. It was so wonderful to be with a man who knew how to behave, who was charming and lively and had impeccable manners. It was all so different from her life at Packards and the people she mixed with there. While she was with Perry, she was back once more in the golden days before the death of her parents. And if he occasionally took her hand, or squeezed her waist, or even, as he

237

had done once or twice lately, kissed her, then it was a small price to be paid.

If she had expressed these thoughts to Daisy, she might have realised how much her attitude had changed over the last few weeks, but as it was, she simply thought she was being sensible.

'This evening, then? It's important, Iz. It's about – well, never mind. You just enjoy your afternoon out.'

'Oh – very well. This evening. And thank you, I expect I shall enjoy myself,' Isobel said, mystified. Daisy had changed again. She had always been disapproving of Perry up till now. She sighed. There was no knowing how Daisy would react to anything.

The thought of going out in the afternoon buoyed her up through the morning. She changed into one of her old but good tailor-mades and put on a crisp new blouse, then hesitated over a hat. Perry had sent her one only a couple of days ago, a darling thing in raspberry pink grosgrain silk with self-coloured ribbons and a froth of tulle. She knew the rules. She could almost hear her mother's voice telling her that young ladies do not accept presents other than flowers or chocolates from young men. But it was so pretty, and Perry was always so well-behaved, that she could not see the harm in it. She put it on, it suited her, it stayed there. She went out to meet Perry at a quiet corner several streets away.

He was there waiting for her in the motor car, and his face lit up when he saw that she was wearing the hat.

'You look even more beautiful than ever in that,' he said, helping her into her seat, handing her a motoring veil.

'You shouldn't buy me things,' she remonstrated.

'I know, but when I saw that hat in the shop window I couldn't resist it. I knew you had to be the woman to wear it.'

'It is lovely,' Isobel admitted.

'It is on you.'

The afternoon followed the course of others they had enjoyed. They drove to Richmond through suburbs where trees were coming into leaf, walked a little on the famous hill and went into a teashop. Here, Isobel was treated to tiny cucumber sandwiches, delicious cakes and finest Assam tea from delicate bone china while waitresses saw to their every need. It was as if she were back in Tillchester with Mama, except that, she had to admit, Perry was a good deal more entertaining than Mama or indeed than any of her relations or friends there. When she was with him, she could almost forget that she had to go back to being a shopgirl at Packards. On the way home, they drove through the park, frightening the deer with the noise of the motor.

'Oh look – poor things – they're running away!' Isobel cried.

Perry promptly stopped the motor.

'There – happy now?'

Isobel gave a shaky laugh. The park seemed to be empty of other people.

'Y-Yes.'

He leant across and took the hands that she held clasped in her lap. She stiffened.

'Oh Isobel, Isobel, you're just like a frightened little fawn. Don't you know now that I would never hurt you?'

His voice was soft in her ear. She looked down at his right hand on hers.

'I – I don't know –'

There was a movement, and his left arm stole round her shoulders. She caught her lower lip between her teeth.

'There's nothing to be afraid of. How could I break something so pretty? It's enough just to look at you.'

His hand touched her face, his finger stroking gently under her jaw and up her cheek. It was strangely soothing. Her tense muscles eased and her breath came out in a sigh.

'Just let me see those lovely eyes of yours.'

Obediently, she turned. He gazed at her.

'So blue. I could drown in them.'

He leant forward and kissed her gently on the lips. Isobel felt no revulsion. It was all right with him. She was safe. It was nice. Nobody else cared for her the way he did. He kissed her again, longer this time.

'That's better, you didn't flinch. Did you like it?'

Honesty compelled her to admit it. 'Yes,' she whispered.

This time as his lips met hers they moved, opened. She pulled back in alarm.

'What –'

'It's all right. You'll like it. I promise.'

He caressed her cheek, smiling into her eyes. Isobel found herself unable to look away. He kissed her again, with such slow insistence that she found her own lips opening to his.

'There – that wasn't so bad, was it?'

'No,' she admitted. She was in such a turmoil that she did not know whether it was bad or good, only that it made her feel strange all over, as if every nerve in her body were tingling.

Perry smiled. She held herself ready, expecting him to do it again, but instead he ran a hand down her arm, then sat back.

'I suppose I had better drive you home.'

'Er – yes,' Isobel agreed. And all the way back, she was conscious of a slight feeling of disappointment.

As always, they parted some way from Trent Street. Perry held her hands in his.

'Till next week, then.'

'Yes.'

She knew that it was going to be a very long week.

'Perhaps – perhaps you could call in at the store.'

'I will – but I don't want to get you into trouble.' So considerate.

'No, I know.'

'I thought perhaps next week we could go for dinner, and the theatre.'

Dinner and the theatre sounded altogether more dangerous than Richmond and a teashop. But she found herself saying yes.

'That would be very nice.'

'*Au revoir*, my little fawn.'

'*Au revoir*.'

He got back into the motor and drove off. This time, instead of walking away directly, she stood on the pavement and watched till he turned the corner. Then she wondered how soon he would come into the store.

26

It was not until he found the bailiffs waiting for him that Perry realised just how bad his debts were getting. The men were lurking in the street outside his parents' house when he returned from his romantic afternoon with Isobel Brand, and accosted him before he could get to the door. The gist of their message was that he should pay up by next week or they would go to his grandfather for settlement. Perry assured them with total sincerity that he would have the money ready, and was left wondering just how they knew that it was his grandfather rather than his father that he was afraid if. He did not realise just how closely the affairs of the rich and their not-so-rich dependants were followed by those whom they carelessly exploited.

The encounter took the pleasurable edge off his afternoon. He was enjoying his pursuit of Isobel. She was something a bit different. He had had affairs with two aristocratic married ladies, several actresses and dancers and an artists' model, but never before with a middle-class virgin. The fact that as a Packards employee she was forbidden fruit only added to the fun.

He made his way into the house, the spring quite gone from his step. This problem had to be solved, and quickly. If his grandfather got to hear of it, there was going to be trouble with a capital T. He might even be required to do something useful to justify his allowance. Money was such a damned nuisance. If only he had some shares in the company. Edward had been given shares on this twenty-first birthday, but Perry had not. It was not fair.

While he changed for dinner he pondered the possible solutions. Ultimately, of course, he intended to marry money, but he was certainly not ready to make even a pretence at settling down yet, and in any case his need was urgent. He had to have something to fob them off with by next week. He shelved the anxiety during the evening at the opera and drank enough to keep sleeplessness at bay, but in the morning it was still there. And of course there was only one solution – to go to his mother.

Winifred was sitting in her boudoir dressed in a loose robe of peach silk, going over her social plans. She looked up with something less than enthusiasm as her younger son came in.

'Perry – you're up early.'

He ignored this and came over to look at the tableplan she was preparing.

'You can't put him next to her any more. They've had a falling-out.'

'Really?' Winifred stared at the two aristocratic names, appalled. 'I didn't know that. When did you hear?'

'Last night at the opera. It was all over the house.'

'Good heavens. But it's happened before and they've made it up. This dinner isn't until a fortnight's time. Do you think they might be back together again by then?'

'Not from what I've heard. He's taken up with *la belle* Roscroft.'

'Well! Poor Christine,' Winifred shook her head over the name on her plan. 'In that case, she hasn't a great deal of chance of getting him back. The Roscroft must be ten years younger than she.'

They were both silent for a moment or two, contemplating the fact that the unfortunate Christine would still attend Winifred's dinner, with her husband, look across the table at her former lover, who would be there with his wife, and all four of them would behave as if nothing had happened. That was the price that had to be paid for straying.

Sensing that he was on the right foot now that he had given his mother such a valuable piece of gossip, Perry went on to consolidate his position by asking her about her plans for the coming Season.

'Well, we shall have to have another ball for Amelie. If I don't get her off my hands this year, she will be an old maid by next Season, and all the time there are new debutantes taking all the attention. I am quite out of patience with her. It's not as if she isn't blessed with looks. She's a very pretty girl. She just doesn't take a proper interest. I swear she deliberately frightens off any young man who does show any signs of being attracted to her. Look at the way she behaved towards your friend! I can tell you, I was very close to hitting her with my own hands.'

'Melly's got a mind of her own. At least she hasn't taken up with the suffragettes. I can just see her putting bricks through windows,' Perry said.

Winifred shuddered. 'Don't!'

'And you have Tatwell now.'

'Precisely. I have a proper house to which I can invite people for Saturday-to-Mondays. I can begin to entertain in the way in which I have been unable to up till now, and I'm saddled with an unmarried daughter. Young girls are such a burden.'

Perry saw his chance. 'I shall have to see what I can do in the way of introducing her to someone suitable.'

Winifred looked sceptical. 'You did that before, and look what happened.'

'Ah yes, but I made a bad choice there, I have to admit it. Nothing wrong with old Georgy, but he isn't the sort for Amelie, now is he? I see that now. What she needs is a sportsman, someone she can admire.'

'Sportsmen have no conversation, in my experience, beyond telling one all about their last match, ball by ball. Amelie's clever, that's her real problem. Not clever in a proper, woman's way. That would not be a problem. But she's quite the opposite of that. She argues with men. I've heard her. Men don't like clever women and especially ones who talk about shopkeeping.'

The last word was spat out as if it were something unpleasant.

'So you need a chap who's a sportsman with brains.' This did tax Perry's powers. He knew plenty of young men who were keen on polo or cricket or rugby, but very few of them had a thought in their heads beyond women and enjoyment. It would not be very useful to admit this to his mother, however. He feigned sudden inspiration.

'Ah-ha! I know just the man!'

'You do? And who might that be?' Winifred sounded suspicious. 'No fortune-hunters, remember.'

Perry looked pained. 'Of course not You can trust me, Mama. There was nothing wrong with Georgy, now was there? Just that Melly didn't like him. Problem with this chap I have in mind, he's not exactly a friend of mine. Not even an acquaintance, really. It's going to take a bit of time to get an introduction. Might take a bit of cash, too. 'Fraid I'm a trifle short at the moment.'

Winifred tightened her mouth.

'Now, Perry, you only had your allowance three weeks ago. I would help you if I could, you know that, but with the Season coming up and your sister to provide for, I really cannot see my way to giving you anything.'

'If you get Mel married off, you won't have to provide for her any more. Grandfather would pay for the wedding and the settlement.'

This was brutally true. Winifred sighed.

'Very well, I can let you have a couple of hundred, but that's all. And I do expect this introduction, remember.'

'Of course!'

Perry tried not to let his disappointment show. Two hundred was not enough to fob off the bailiffs, let alone throw something at his other debts and carry on with his usual way of life. And now he was saddled with the problem of finding some man who measured up to the tale he had spun and getting his sister introduced to him. He left the room with a burdened mind.

The weather outside did nothing to raise his spirits. A chill wind blew down the street, flinging cold raindrops in his face. It felt more like winter than spring. Perry bowed his head and walked into it, not entirely sure where he was going. He felt a pressing need for somebody to cosset him and tell him that his problems would soon go away. If only he had got a little further with Isobel – well, a great deal further in fact. How pleasant it would be now to go and surprise her in the cosy little love nest he envisaged for her, to find her still warm and loose in her peignoir and rest his head on her wonderful breasts and tell her all his troubles. How sweetly she would sooth them all away. It did not occur to him that Isobel with her middle-class upbringing and the terrible example of what her father's debts had done to the family would be very shocked to hear of his.

The daydream lasted until he found himself in Park Lane. A particularly heavy shower lashed him, making him both cold and wet. It was no use, he realised, going for a walk in the park, as it would be almost empty of company. And since he could not go and console himself with Isobel, there was still the problem of the money to solve. As earning any, or even making some economies in his spending, did not even cross his mind, then borrowing was the only solution. His mother had not been much use there, his father was likely to be as pushed for cash as he was himself and going to his grandfather was out of the question. That left his brother. He did not relish going cap in hand to Edward, but there did not seem to be any alternative.

He was just about to set off for Marble Arch and Oxford Street when his attention was caught by a horseman trotting past, probably returning from a gallop in the park. He was not sure what made him look up, except perhaps that there were few riders about that day and most of the traffic was composed of closed carriages and motor cars. But having noticed the man, he vaguely recognised the features. They set off a train of connections in his mind that ended in the image of his sister watching the Diamond Sculls final at Henley, waving and yelling when most people were only giving the race half their attention at the most. And then it came to him. Hugo Rutherford. He looked after the tall figure on the dark bay horse, sitting with easy grace and apparently oblivious to the rain. Hugo Rutherford. Now he answered all the criteria needed for Mel. If Perry could get an introduction and it appeared to be working, he could touch his mother for a far bigger loan.

Feeling much more cheerful, Perry turned into Oxford Street. All he had to do was to get enough out of Edward to tide him over. Everything was going to be all right. He marched past the impressive façade of the new store that his grandfather and Edward and Mel seemed to be making such a fuss about, and wondered whether he could use Selfridges to his advantage in his interview with Edward. Off hand, he could not think of any way to do so. There must be something he could do, though, some lever he could lean on to move his brother. He breezed through the main doors of Packards and up the marble stairs to the gentlemen's rest rooms to shake his wet clothing and run a comb through his hair. Then he looked in at Ladies' Sportswear, teased Miss Higgs and the girls a little and had the pleasure of seeing Isobel blush at the very sight of him. Not long now with that one. Once they fell in love with you, it was easy.

He was just about to leave when Amelie came in under the archway, dressed in a dark green tailor-made with a stiff collar and little silk tie, and carrying a sheaf of papers, very much the businesswoman.

'Oh, Perry,' she said, 'what are you doing here? I hope you're not distracting my staff. What do you think of my spring display?'

'Very pretty. Very tasteful,' Perry said. And now that his attention had been drawn to it, he noticed that the department did look most attractive, done up in green drapes with branches of apple blossom, bunches of daffodils and displays of white sportswear. 'As good as anything in Selfridges' windows,' he told her.

Amelie glowed. 'That's what I think. And what's more, I've nearly persuaded Grandfather. I was right about the advertising, and now he's beginning to see that I'm right about display as well. What we need to do is to employ one of the top Americans to arrange our windows, but failing that, I think we should take on a theatrical designer. Somebody young and full of ideas. That will make Edward sit up and think, when I have everyone talking about it and coming to Packards just to see what all the fuss was about.'

Perry could feel the stirrings of an idea in his head. He couldn't quite get hold of it, but he knew it was there.

'Edward wouldn't like that,' he said.

Amelie grinned. 'He hasn't got it all his own way. He might think he's going to take over the store when Grandfather retires, but I'm sure Grandfather has no intention of retiring yet, and I've only just begun to show him what I can do. I've managed to get him to let me carry on doing the advertising. He did say I could have a try at it until April, but now I've persuaded him to let me continue. That means I can go into all the departments and see what's happening in them while I'm working out their advertisements. You'd be amazed how much I'm learning. And of course Edward does not like it one little bit.'

Perry clapped her on the shoulder. 'Keep up the good work, Sis. Edward needs taking down a peg or two.'

The idea was definitely taking form now. Perry parted from his sister and walked more slowly through the store, letting it grow. By the time he reached the office floor, he thought he knew what approach he was going to take.

He was given more time by the fact that Edward was not in his office when he arrived. His secretary, a plain young woman with a severe manner of dress and even more severe hairstyle, requested him to wait. Perry was vaguely irritated. Now that he was here, he wanted to get it over with. There were more important things to be done today, like looking up an old pal who had just come up from the country.

When Edward finally came marching into the office, he looked at Perry with some surprise.

'Oh – you received my message, then? They said you weren't at home.'

Perry just stopped himself from saying 'What message?' and adopted his most insouciant air.

'Don't know a thing about a message, old boy. Just thought I'd call in and see how things were going in the family store, don't y'know.'

Edward sat down behind his wide mahogany desk.

'You care about the family store, then, do you?'

'But of course I do. Where would we all be without it?' He realised that he might be taking the wrong tack here and qualified his statement. 'Not that I know anything about the running of it, of course. Don't need to, do I? Not with you to see to it. You and Melly.'

The effect was not as dramatic as he had hoped, but the light of suspicion did flare briefly in Edward's eyes.

'What do you mean, Melly? She has nothing to do with it.'

Perry shrugged. 'She looked very much part of the place just now when I ran into her.'

'She's playing at it, that's all. It pleases the old man to let her have her head a bit.'

Perry was about to say something about the way in which Amelie always got her way where their grandfather was concerned, when Edward changed the subject.

'That's not what I wanted to see you about. Something has come to my attention that I am not at all happy about.'

His tone of voice sent a shiver of apprehension through Perry. His little plan suddenly seemed very flimsy when measured against his brother's formidable strength of purpose. Edward always played to win.

'Whatever do you mean?' he asked, all innocence, and even as he said it, he knew. Somehow, Edward had found out about Isobel.

'You know exactly what I mean,' Edward said, confirming his fear. 'You're a fool, Perry. I warned you last summer. What on earth made you think you'd get away with it? You know how Grandfather expects our shopgirls to be a cut above the general run. This store is not the place for a cheap pick-up, and you as a family member must absolutely not be seen to treat it as such.'

Perry tried to talk his way out of it.

'It wasn't like that at all. I don't know where you got your information, but it's all gossip, I can tell you. I was sorry for the girl. All I did was to take her out for the occasional run in the country and a nice tea. All very respectable.'

Edward was impatient. 'I can't think that you really expect me to believe that.'

'But it's true! That girl's as unbroken now as she was the day she was born.'

When Edward looked incredulous he found himself struggling to explain.

'I was softening her up. She was worth it. She's certainly not been with anyone else. It makes a change to be with a girl who doesn't know every trick in the book.' But he could see that Edward was not convinced.

'It's a good story, Perry. I'm almost tempted to believe it. But nobody else is going to, least of all Grandfather.'

The threat dropped into Perry's understanding like a lead weight. If his grandfather got to know about this, it could mean the end of his allowance. He swallowed.

'He – he needn't find out.'

'No, not if I stop the gossip at its source.'

Perry broke out in a sweat. The end of his allowance would mean the end of his whole way of life. Having the bailiffs after him suddenly seemed like a mere nothing. He had to convince

Edward that it was worth his while to keep quiet. His strategy for extracting a loan had to be turned into a weapon to save his skin.

'I could be useful to you,' he offered. 'I could get Melly out of your way. I know just the man to distract her.'

Edward appeared unimpressed.

'I seem to remember you saying something of the sort last year and all you could come up with was that fool Georgy Teignmereton.'

'Well, he did propose to her, didn't he? I can't help it if Melly turned him down,' Perry protested, in a brave attempt to give some substance to his offer.

'Anyone could see that he was a nonrunner from the start.'

'Well this one's different. He's a sportsman and – and a scholar and a jolly decent chap. Just the sort for Melly.'

'Indeed? Who is this paragon, then?'

'Hugo Rutherford. You remember – chap who won the Diamond Sculls.'

'Oh yes. And you know him, do you?'

'He's an acquaintance – friend of a friend.' He prayed that he sounded convincing. 'Once the Season gets going it shouldn't be too difficult to get them together. Nice little jaunt down to Hurlingham when he's playing. Tea in the interval, treading the old divots, that sort of thing.'

'And what makes you think that he will like Melly?'

Perry opened his mouth and shut it again. How on earth could he guarantee that? However confident he managed to sound, Edward would not believe him. He resorted to honesty.

'Can't vouch for that, now can I, old boy? No knowing what two people are going to think of each other. All I can do is get them together. But Melly's a pretty girl and Lord knows she can talk about sport with the best of them. Must be an attraction to a chap who's an all-rounder like Rutherford. You have to admit, it does sound like a runner, now doesn't it? And I could get them to the starting line, so to speak.'

Edward sat frowning at him. Perry felt as if he were back at school. He resisted with difficulty the urge to fidget.

'Very well,' Edward decided. 'I'll give you a month. Of course, you'll have to give up the girl.'

This gave Perry a strong pang of regret.

'Oh but –' he started. But he could see that it was no use. Holding on to his comfortable existence of idle pleasure was more important than a passing love affair. 'Of course,' he agreed.

'I don't mean next month or next week or even tomorrow. I mean now. You are not to communicate with her again.'

'Oh I say, that does seem a bit tough –' Perry's protest trailed off under Edward's hard eyes.

'I think I'm being very generous. I'm keeping this from Grandfather, and I ought to dismiss the girl. As it is, you're both getting away with it. I hardly think you're in a position to argue over terms.'

'No,' Perry agreed.

'Then I don't think there is anything further we need to discuss. I'll wish you good day.'

Perry found himself dismissed, with no loan, no romantic entanglement and a threat hanging over his head. He slouched out of the store in the grip of the first really strong and sincere emotion to strike him since attaining adulthood. Hatred for his brother.

27

'Amelie, I have accepted this invitation on behalf of both of us and therefore you are going. It would be extremely impolite of you to stay away, and very embarrassing for me to have to explain your absence.'

'Oh rubbish, Mama. Who is going to notice whether I am there or not? These garden parties are always huge. There will be a couple of hundred people there, spread out over the grounds and in and out of all the tents and marquees.'

'Our hostess will certainly notice whether you are there or not, and she will think it a gross insult.'

'She will be glad that I have not come. It will be one less awkward unmarried girl for her daughters to compete with.'

Amelie stood in the hall of the Amberleys' house, wearing a jade-green day dress and jacket in the new slim cut and holding a portfolio. It was perfectly obvious where she was heading for, and Winifred was having none of it.

'Nonsense. Your status is immaterial. You are a guest. You were invited together with me, the invitation was accepted and you will go together with me. That is my last word.'

Amelie looked her mother in the eye. 'You accepted the invitation, not I. It's none of my doing. I have to see the people in China and Glassware and agree on the lines which are to be featured in their advertisement. It has to be done today so that the details can go to the artist in time for him to meet the deadline for next Saturday's papers.'

Winifred went quite red with anger.

'You have to do no such thing. Your grandfather employs people to do menial jobs like that.'

That did it. Amelie had meant to keep her temper, to use reason, to make her stand in an adult but firm manner. But a remark like that was too much for her to bear.

'It is not a menial job! Advertising is essential for success and if I don't go in today to do it that stupid Carpenter man will and he'll send in one of his boring old-fashioned things that nobody will bother to look at. But of course you wouldn't understand that, would you, because all you care about is position. As if it mattered! You're as stupid as Carpenter.'

She knew she had gone too far as soon as the words had left her mouth. Winifred's expression became glacial. She took a long breath in through her nose. Then she spoke.

'You will go to your room now. Luncheon will be served to you there on a tray. You will change into a suitable dress and be ready at two o'clock to accompany me to the garden party.'

There was no arguing with that tone of voice. The time for compromise had come and gone. Amelie could only submit. She did so wordlessly, walking past her mother and up the stairs with exaggerated dignity.

In her room she gave vent to her feelings, flinging down the portfolio, stamping her foot and screaming her loathing of her mother and all the restrictions placed on her. Then she set about retrieving some order out of the mess by sending a note and a list of tasks to be done to Mr Carpenter. He was going to be delighted by her absence. She just hoped he would do what she had asked him to, but had her doubts. If she knew him, he would seize on the chance to revert to his own way of doing things. She ground her teeth in frustration. All this trouble over a silly garden party. It was not even as if it was very nice weather. They would probably spend half their time huddled in tents waiting for the rain to clear, and to what end? It was just one more pointless Society gathering.

At two o'clock Amelie was ready, decked out in an afternoon gown of yellow and white silk trimmed with lace and self-coloured embroidery and topped by a large hat with the oversized crown that was all the rage this year. Winifred looked her over and gave a nod of cool approval.

'Do you have your tennis racquet with you?'

Amelie was astonished. 'My tennis racquet?'

'Yes. There is to be tennis.'

All the frustrations of the morning resurfaced.

'Mother! I cannot possibly play in this outfit. This corset is difficult to sit in, let alone hit a ball. It nearly comes down to my knees. Why didn't you tell me earlier?'

Winifred was still wearing her frostiest face.

'Had you been at all civil, I would have been able to do so. As it is, you had better go and change. You have twenty minutes.'

Not quite believing her ears, Amelie went. Twenty minutes was an almost impossibly short time to get out of all the layers of the intricate outfit and into another, even with the help of a maid. But the fact that her mother had allowed, even told her to do so was unprecedented. The journey time to the garden party must have been calculated down to the last minute and punctuality was one of Winifred's gods. Yet in sanctioning the change she was almost guaranteeing their arriving late. Amelie could not understand what was going on. What was obvious, though, was that the afternoon promised to be a good deal more entertaining than she had first thought. Instead of just standing around saying the same old things to the same old people, looking and being looked at, she was being offered the chance of a game of tennis. She began to feel a good deal more cheerful.

The party was being held in the grounds of a pretty old house just beyond the tide of new brick terraces that were spreading out from the metropolis. Sloping lawns of manicured emerald grass alternated with informal beds of flowering shrubs and tangles of spectacular azaleas, rhododendrons and magnolias. The effect was embellished by pretty striped tents and marquees set with refreshments and a plentiful supply of wrought-iron chairs and tables set in picturesque groups beneath the trees. Somewhere, a band was playing a selection of melodies from *The Merry Widow*. Against this pretty background the ladies fluttered like so many butterflies in dainty gowns of every colour of the rainbow, while the gentlemen in their sober grey suits provided a foil for them.

Winifred explained away their late arrival with a smooth lie about trouble with the motor, enquired as to the location of the tennis and swept Amelie off to the courts. A couple of dozen young men and women were already gathered there and two games of mixed doubles were in progress. To Amelie's surprise, Perry was there.

'Ah, here you are, Mother! Come and sit at this table. I'll fetch you some tea. Hello, Mel, ready for a game?'

'You're playing tennis, Perry?' Amelie teased. 'Whatever has come over you? Are you feeling unwell?'

Perry laughed it off. 'I can hit a ball, you know. You and Edward aren't the only sportsmen in the family. Jolly afternoon, isn't it?'

They were interrupted by some friends of Amelie's coming to greet her, so she only half heard the exchange that went on behind her back between her mother and Perry.

'Where is he, then? You said he was going to be here.'

'Don't fuss, Mother. I know he was invited. Perhaps he's been held up. You've only just arrived yourselves.'

Then he joined in with the general conversation, and before long Amelie found herself agreeing to partnering Perry in a match against a pair of mutual friends whom she knew to be good players.

'Righty-oh, I'll go and sign up for the next available court, shall I?' said Perry.

Winifred beckoned him over. Amelie could see that she was not happy about something. Perry's reassuring words floated over to her.

'Don't worry, I know what I'm doing, Mother. You'll see.'

The last thing Amelie wanted was her mother sitting there watching everything. Just to know she was there annoyed her.

'Perry's here to chaperon me, Mother. You could join your friends, if you wish. I know you find tennis boring.'

Winifred was repressive in the extreme. 'Thank you. I intend to remain here.'

And watch her every move, no doubt. Amelie pointedly went off to join a group of young people gathering by the touchline, but however closely she followed the game in progress, and however much she commented on it to the people around her, she still could not rid herself of the sensation of her mother's eyes boring into her back.

She did not really take much notice when she heard Perry cry, 'Ah, just the chap I wanted to see!'

Then the next moment the world seemed to tip slightly around her. For there was her brother by her side, holding Hugo Rutherford by the arm. He was speaking in his most cheerfully persuasive voice.

'Now then, Rutherford old chap, I need you to save my neck for me. I've simply got to tear off elsewhere, not a moment to lose, and it means leaving my sister here in the lurch. You do know my sister, don't you? No? Ah well, Melly, allow me to introduce Hugo Rutherford. Splendid fellow, can play any sport you care to name. And, Rutherford, this is my sister, Amelie. Terrific eye for a ball.'

Automatically, Amelie held out her hand. Her mouth had gone dry. She stretched her lips into a smile that she knew looked silly.

'How do you do?' she managed to say.

Hugo Rutherford's grip was warm and firm. Close to, his height, the breadth of his shoulders, his sheer air of physical power was overwhelming.

Amelie's knees felt weak.

'How do you do, Miss Amberley?'

'Now, you'll partner Melly for me, won't you, Rutherford? Poor girl's dying for a game and I know you never turn down the chance.'

Amelie could not believe this was happening.

'Mr Rutherford might not want to play pat-ball with us. I'm sure he'd rather be in a singles match,' she heard herself say, and immediately regretted it. Supposing he agreed? What an idiot she was!

But he gave a pleasant smile. 'On the contrary. It will be a pleasure to partner you.'

'That's settled then. Splendid! Must be away. Have a jolly time!'

Perry left, but Amelie hardly noticed him go. She felt suddenly tongue-tied, standing here at last next to the man she had admired from a distance for nearly a year. Fortunately, he was not suffering from the same problem. He asked her if she enjoyed playing tennis and where she had learnt, and all Amelie had to do was answer, though she was sure she sounded stupid as she did so. The chance that she hardly dreamt she might ever have was being ruined by her own inability to act naturally. She felt an utter failure. She was almost relieved when their opponents appeared, and exclaimed over Perry's disappearance.

'What a beastly trick to play! We had a good chance of

beating you when your brother was partnering you, but Mr Rutherford is quite another matter,' the girl declared, flashing him a smile. 'Ah well, at least I am wearing one of your patent tennis blouses, Amelie, so I shall not come apart in the middle. If one must lose, at least one can do so elegantly.'

'I'm very glad to hear it, Maude. No sporting lady should be without one, or better still, two,' Amelie said.

'You would never guess that Amelie here was a shopkeeper, would you?' Maude said to Hugo Rutherford.

If she meant to nip any dawning friendship in the bud, she failed. Hugo turned to Amelie with real interest in his eyes and a quite different tone of voice from when he was merely making well-bred small talk.

'Of course, your grandfather is Thomas Packard, is he not? He must be a remarkable man. I admire excellence, whatever form it takes.'

'He is a remarkable man. He came to London when he was fifteen with three shillings in his pocket, and now he owns the biggest and best department store in London.' Amelie's pride was evident to everyone.

'And you are following in his footsteps, are you?' Hugo asked.

Amelie caught Maude's fleeting look of malicious glee. So she thought Amelie was digging a grave for herself socially by talking about her Packard connections, did she? Well, so be it. Even for Hugo Rutherford, she was not going to deny they existed.

'I hope to,' she told him. 'I opened a Ladies' Sportswear department within the store last year, and now I'm responsible for the advertising as well. I'm hoping to persuade my grandfather to let me take over display next.'

'All that and you're doing the Season?' Hugo sounded impressed.

Amelie pulled a face. 'I'd much rather be working at the store than going to silly parties. I'm only here this afternoon because my mother insisted.'

They were interrupted by a rather petulant Maude.

'Come along, you two, the court's free.'

Amelie spun her racquet and caught it.

'I'm ready if you are.'

The usual way of playing mixed doubles was for the gentleman to run around taking the difficult shots while the lady just patted any balls that came right up to her racquet. This was not Amelie's method. Under normal circumstances, she always put her all into a game. Today, with Maude across the net mocking her every move and the best all-round amateur sportsman of the day playing beside her, she was truly on her mettle. She drew first serve, and stood at the back line, nerves mixed with excitement surging through her until she felt quite sick. She took a steadying breath, threw the ball in the air and smashed it right between Maude and her partner to land neatly six inches inside the court before either of them moved to return it.

'Splendid shot!' Hugo commented.

The scene was set. Their opponents fought back valiantly, but they did not stand a chance. Amelie and Hugo annihilated them. At the end of the game they all shook hands over the net, Maude and her partner conceding defeat graciously as befitted good sports. Then Hugo turned to Amelie.

'Congratulations. I cannot remember ever having had a better partner.'

Amelie felt a breathlessness that had nothing at all to do with the strenuous game. She found herself burbling in reply, 'You weren't so bad yourself. I might even play with you again some day.'

Hugo laughed. 'I'll hold you to that, so be warned! Now – I think some tea might be in order, don't you?'

The rest of the afternoon passed in a roller coaster of emotions. While Hugo was beside her, she was both exhilarated at the attention he paid her and terrified that he would find her wanting. But at half-past four he had to leave, pleading another engagement. Amelie was plummeted into despair that she hid with a smile.

'But of course you must go if someone is expecting you,' she insisted, hating whoever it was with a deadly loathing.

'Perhaps I might call on you. When are you at home?' Hugo asked.

Despair turned to dancing joy. 'Th-Thursdays,' she told him.

'Till Thursday, then.'

And he was gone, leaving a huge aching gap. From then on Amelie hardly noticed what was going on around her. Wrapped in her own thoughts, she was blown between exalting at the kind fate that had brought them together, longing for Thursday and doubting whether he would indeed call. She certainly did not notice the look of satisfaction on her mother's face.

The next morning brought a dilemma. Normally, if she had been forced to leave a task at Packards in order to attend some society function, she would have been there at the store as the sales staff arrived, ready to make up for lost time. Today, everything was different. Today was only Tuesday, which meant that there were still fifty-six hours at the very least before she could hope to see Hugo Rutherford again. But if she went for an early morning ride in the park, there must be a good chance that he would be there. She couldn't remember ever having seen him at the more formal midday parade in the park, but it was possible that he might join the nine o'clock ride with those who actually rode for exercise and enjoyment rather than to see and be seen. In the end, there was no contest. She could not possibly wait till Thursday. She told the maid to lay out her riding habit.

By ten o'clock she was back again. She had been up and down the Row till she could have taken an examination on who was there and what horses they were riding. By the time she left, there was nobody of fashion there at all. Hugo Rutherford had not put in an appearance. Disappointment robbed her of all her usual energy. She could hardly stand up for the maid to help her out of her riding habit. As for going to the store, it seemed to require an effort too great even to contemplate. So when her mother told her that she was to go to a dress fitting, she first pleaded exhaustion, then changed her mind, for she had remembered just which outfits had been ordered.

'Do you think that pretty afternoon gown might be finished by Thursday? The blue and grey one?'

'Most certainly, if I ask that it should be.'

That decided it. It was absolutely essential that she had that dress to wear for their At Home afternoon. As an afterthought, she decided that once the fittings were over she would slip along to see what Mr Carpenter had done with that glassware advertisement.

It was almost the longest two days Amelie had ever spent. Every hour was an age, and fraught with the worry that at the end of it, he might not after all appear. On Wednesday afternoon, Amelie was required to take part in the ritual of card-leaving and calling that every Society lady had to keep up throughout the Season. Amelie never did enjoy these rounds. But then, enjoyment was not the point of them. They were designed to keep the wheels of Society well oiled, and in Winifred's case, to ease herself more and more into the set of people with whom she longed to be associated. Consequently, they set off in the victoria at half-past three to leave cards with three titled ladies whom Winifred was attempting to cultivate, then paid strict quarter-hour calls on two families with whom they were fairly well acquainted but not yet on dinner-party terms, and ended up at a tea party at a close friend of Winifred's whose daughters Amelie found overwhelmingly boring. Altogether it was a pretty dreadful afternoon as far as Amelie was concerned, and seemed to go on for ever. When they arrived home, there was the usual charade of looking over other people's cards to be gone through. The cards that had been left while they had been out were to be found on the hall table, where the footman left them. Winifred always picked them up with an air of unconcern, but she could never quite sustain it. She just had to comment, either disparagingly or with pleasure. Today there were just three. Two were from people lower down the ladder than herself and therefore not to be regarded except as bodies to fill the space of a large evening reception or ball, but the third called forth an arch smile.

'Dear me, who is this? Hugo Rutherford? Now where have I heard that name before?'

A blush spread right over Amelie from her head to her toes.

'I – he was my partner at tennis at the garden party on Monday. I introduced him to you, if you remember.'

'Ye-es, I believe I do. Tall young man. Rather handsome. Well, it seems he wishes to be known to us. Rutherford – do I know the family? Is he related to the Hampshire Rutherfords?'

That was all her mother cared about. The fact that he was a brilliant all-round sportsman would not mean a thing to her. The fact that he had complimented Amelie on her tennis and was actually interested in the part she played in the running of Packards, instead of being contemptuous of it, meant even less. It could even count against him.

'He may be. I believe his close family are from Hereford-shire,' Amelie told her, in as off-hand a manner as she could manage. Of course, she knew exactly who his family were since she had looked it up.

'Oh *those* Rutherfords. Oh yes. Very acceptable. If he calls again, I shall be in to him.'

Amelie sometimes wondered whether her mother knew the entire *Burkes Peerage and Baronetage* off by heart. But at least that was one hurdle jumped. Hugo was judged to be worthy by her mother's standards. But would he call again? She had definitely told him Thursday, so he would have known that they would not be at home today. Did his leaving his card today mean that he had deliberately missed her, and would not be coming tomorrow, or that he was making an extra effort at courtesy and would call tomorrow as well? She hoped for the second but feared the first. In the meantime, there were still twenty-one hours to get through until she could hope to find out.

Even the longest wait does end eventually, and the next afternoon saw Amelie and Winifred in their prettiest gowns – the blue and grey frock had arrived in time and was a credit to Packards' dressmakers – and sitting in the drawing room to receive calls from all those whom they had called upon during the last couple of weeks. The usual pattern prevailed. First there were the formal callers, either patronising them or hoping to ingratiate themselves with them, depending on whether they were higher or lower socially, then the people with whom they were on easier terms. Amelie kept glancing at the clock. The hands that had crept so slowly now seemed to dash round. Half-past four chimed. Amelie despaired. By five, only informal calls were paid, between people who knew each other well. However much she wanted to be on that footing with Hugo, she certainly was not yet. Around her, conversations were going on, mostly about parties past and future. Amelie answered when spoken to, but had no idea what she was saying.

Then the door opened once more. Amelie's head jerked round and her stomach twisted up inside. It was him. She sat rigid, unable to do anything but watch his progress across the room.

A frisson of excitement went through the females in the room. Any male visiting was a pleasant change, since they tended to leave such niceties to the womenfolk of their families. One who was young, handsome, becoming rather well known and a bachelor was a definite catch. Each woman, young or old, sat a little straighter, made a little adjustment to her dress, became that much more animated in her talk. Those who had been on the point of leaving, having sat for the regulation fifteen minutes, put off their departure.

Amelie noticed nothing of this. Her whole being was focused on Hugo. He looked different in a formal dark jacket and grey trousers, different, but just as impressive as the cut set off his broad shoulders and the easy confidence with which he held himself. Beside him, the other men in the room looked poor specimens. He shook hands with Winifred and stood speaking to her for a minute or two. Amelie unashamedly strained to listen, but was prevented by the girl next to her, who chose to remark about him.

'I didn't know you knew Hugo Rutherford,' she said, envy mixing with surprise in her lowered voice.

'He's a friend of my brother's,' Amelie said, keeping her eyes on him and her mother. Winifred seemed to be acting in a particularly gracious fashion.

'Lucky you. I think he's utterly deevy, don't you?'

'Oh yes,' Amelie breathed, too engrossed to even think of hiding her feelings. He was divine. There was no other word for it.

The other girl smirked at having found her out so easily.

Her mother finished speaking to him, looked round the room, saw the seat available on Amelie's other side and waved him towards it before turning to bid farewell to some visitors who really could not sit it out any longer.

Amelie was in heaven. He was here, he was sitting right next to her on the sofa, he was smiling and talking. The only problem was that the need to appear natural robbed her of all her usual ease. She laughed and chattered, and all the while she felt as if she were acting like an overwound toy.

Visitors came and went. Before she knew it, Hugo was standing, picking up his hat and stick, taking his leave. Winifred sailed over.

'We are just about to take tea, Mr Rutherford. Won't you stay and join us?'

Amelie could have hugged her. At that moment, she truly adored her mother.

Hugo smiled, thanked her, but declined. Amelie's spirits plummeted.

'So kind of you, but I have to be elsewhere. I don't know whether you ever watch polo, Mrs Amberley, but if you cared to drive down to Hurlingham tomorrow, my team will be playing. You might find it diverting for a while.'

Amelie held her breath. Winifred said that they might possibly find time to make an appearance. Amelie could not stop a smile from spreading over her face. As he turned to leave, he paused by Amelie.

'Don't forget, Miss Amberley, we must make a team at tennis again one day soon.'

'I shan't forget,' Amelie promised.

And then he was gone, leaving her floating in a world of enchantment.

28

The world was a bleak and comfortless place. Worse, the people in it were not to be trusted. Or so it seemed to Isobel. She got out of bed each morning because she had to, walked to work along streets that mocked her with their green leafy trees and colour-filled gardens, and spent the day in a haze of exhaustion doing a job which she disliked and was only just competent at.

Her only confidante was Daisy, who listened endlessly and supported her through the dreadful time.

'I can't understand it,' Isobel repeated time and again. 'I just can't understand it. Why did he drop me like that, without a word, without a sign?'

'I dunno, lovey, honest I don't. He's a bastard. They all are.'

Isobel was so low that she was not even very shocked by her friend's language. It only confirmed the opinion she had held of men before Perry came along to make a large enough chink in her defences to find a way to her heart.

'Yes I know, I know, but – I thought he was different. He seemed so kind, so thoughtful –'

'They can all be thoughtful when they're after you. Knights in blooming shining armour, they are, till they got what they want.'

'But he didn't – I didn't –'

Daisy sighed. 'P'raps you held out too long, love. Comes a time when they get fed up of waiting.'

'But to go off like that without saying anything –'

That was what hurt most of all. She had thought that as a gentleman, he had been treating her like a lady. It seemed that he had not. He did not regard her as a lady, simply as one more shopgirl to take up or put down as he wished.

'Well, it's easier for them that way, isn't it? If there's one thing they don't like, it's scenes.'

'But it's so discourteous –'

Daisy hooted. 'Discourteous! I like that. Discourteous is the least of my worries when it comes to men.'

Which only went to show up the huge gap between the world Isobel had once inhabited and the one she lived in now. Courtesy, her mother had always insisted, was the rock upon which society was built. Thank goodness that in this brutal place she now found herself, she had one friend. Daisy was wonderful. There were no sudden changes of attitude now, she was a well of sympathy and understanding. But some things she could not even reveal to Daisy, for she was too ashamed. Daisy did not know what a bad person she was. She must be for men to pursue her the way they did, not with respectable intentions, not even with love, but just wanting to defile her body. Worse than that, she knew she was a wicked woman by the way in which her body was reacting. Since she had started her outings with Perry, she had experienced the renewal of the strange longings that her brother-in-law had kindled, the odd visions of heat and flesh that she knew could only be the promptings of lust. With nobody to tell her that this was quite normal for a young woman, especially one who was in love for the first time, she could only believe that she deserved to be outcast from respectable society. She was lost for ever.

'I don't know why you bother with me. I'm no use for anything,' she said to Daisy.

Her friend told her not to be so daft.

'Come out for a night on the town. Let your hair down a bit, forget about the sod,' she suggested.

But Isobel recoiled. 'No, no – I'm too tired. I'd spoil it for you.'

''Course you wouldn't. Come on, it'd do you good. You don't never enjoy y'self, you don't.'

It was true. But she didn't want Daisy's rough brand of enjoyment. She yearned for the visiting and provincial parties of her past life, even more for the genteel outings and pretty teas with Perry, and most of all, for Perry himself. Despite everything, if he had come back with anything like a plausible excuse, she would have believed him. But he did not, and now she wanted only to burrow into the safety of her hard little bed. If she could have done, she would have stayed there for good.

She went in to work each day fit for nothing. With the

coming of summer, Ladies' Sportswear was busy and a larger proportion of the customers were genuine buyers rather than time-wasters, which was fortunate for Isobel as it meant she did have some sales to her name by the end of each day. But she had never been a good saleswoman and now the apathy brought on by depression made her even less effective. Where Daisy could persuade a willing customer to buy twice as much as she had come in for, and even get a sightseer to purchase a small item, Isobel sold only what was asked for. The effort it cost her to smile was enormous. The muscles of her face felt heavy and dead. Her politeness did not desert her, for that had been drummed into her so successfully in childhood that she was unable to be otherwise, and it kept her plodding onward. She would look at girls her own age shopping with their mothers, and know that she would never return to that golden way of life. She was one of the poor now, and everyone knew that poverty was the fault of the poor themselves. They were either idle, or drunken, or – worse. She knew she was neither idle nor drunken, so she must be that other, unspoken, wicked thing. That was why she had had to run away in the first place, for her brother-in-law had seen that thing in her. All her troubles stemmed from it.

Miss Higgs was a further trial.

'You should have shown her the calf gloves as well,' she would say, when a customer went away empty-handed.

'She asked for knitted, Miss Higgs, green knitted. I showed her what we have, but they didn't suit,' Isobel would explain, knowing all along that she was in the wrong again.

An exaggerated sigh from Miss Higgs, and a casting of the eyes to the ceiling.

'For pity's sake, girl, how many times do I have to tell you? You always show them something else. Nine times out of ten it's what they want anyway and if it isn't they'll soon think it is if you tell them how much better it is than what they first asked for.'

'Yes, Miss Higgs.'

'"Yes Miss Higgs",' the head saleswoman mimicked savagely. 'That's all you can say, isn't it? But you never seem to learn.'

'No, Miss Higgs. I'll try harder, Miss Higgs.'

'You had better. You let down my sales figures, you do. You'd've been out on your ear months ago if you weren't Miss Packard's little favourite.'

And even Miss Packard was a doubtful ally now. They only saw her briefly once a week or so in Ladies' Sportswear, and she wasn't doing half so much in Advertising either. Rumour about the store had it that she had an admirer. Bets were being laid as to whether or not she would marry him.

When a messenger came into the department one morning, Isobel did not take any special notice. Orders from on high were Miss Higgs's responsibility. But then the head saleswoman beckoned her over. The expression on her face was enough to give Isobel a sinking sensation.

'You're wanted in Mr Edward's office,' she announced.

For a moment Isobel felt something close to relief. If it had been dismissal, it would have been Mr Mason asking to see her. The next second, relief was replaced by fear. What did Mr Edward want with her? It could not be anything good. Her mind leapt from him to his brother. Was it Perry? Was he ill? Had he had an accident and was asking for her? Was he dead? A small moan escaped her.

Miss Higgs's lips stretched into a malicious smile. 'Yes – Mr Edward. You'd best hurry, hadn't you?'

Wordlessly, Isobel nodded and followed the boy mesenger, the questions churning round her distressed head.

She was shown into a large office by a secretary who was told to go and take her tea break. The door closed behind her. And there was Mr Edward, sitting back in his big chair, regarding her with an appraising look that ran slowly from her face down the length of her body. Fear congealed in her. She stared down at the mahogany desk, at the military precision of the papers stacked in their baskets, the pens in their tray.

'Miss Brand – or should I say Miss Norton? The time has come for us to have a little talk.'

Isobel gasped. Her eyes flicked up to his face to find that he was smiling. It was not a pleasant smile.

'Oh yes – I know. I only had to look at your file. But it is not your past that I wish to discuss. It is your future.'

So it was dismissal. Isobel's legs felt weak. She longed to sit down, but there was no chair on her side of the desk. She stood as she had been taught, with her hands clasped in front of her. She studied the desk again. There was a faint rustle of paper as a page in a book of figures in front of him turned.

'You cannot be described as our most successful shopgirl, can you? Rather the opposite, in fact.'

Isobel said nothing. There was nothing she could say. It was true.

'I cannot think why you have been kept on. Anyone else would have been dismissed long since.' He paused a second, then went on. 'I would imagine that you are not qualified for any other form of employment?'

Isobel shook her head.

'No, I thought not.'

He paused again, and in the gap Isobel saw regular meals, her wage packet and worst of all, the attic room disappearing into the abyss. Standing all day in Ladies' Sportswear, failing to sell enough to satisfy Miss Higgs, seemed the most desirable fate in the world now that it was being taken from her.

'However –'

The word brought a painful surge of hope. She looked up from the desk to find that he was still watching her with that speculative expression. This time she found she could not look away.

'I have heard that you do have talents in a far more interesting direction.'

She could not pretend to misunderstand him. Through a black whirl of confusion she tried to think how he had found out. Not Daisy. Surely not Daisy. But who else had known? Who else would have told? Betrayed. She was betrayed on all sides.

'Yes –' Her tormentor was following the expressions that crossed her face. 'My brother speaks very highly of you '

'Perry?'

Shock tore his name from her. Perry had not only deserted her, he had discussed her with his brother. She felt sick.

'The same. Whatever his failings might be, he does have an interesting taste in women. You realise, of course, that I could also have you dismissed for that.' This was pointed out in a matter-of-fact tone that almost but not quite masked the implicit threat.

'Come here.'

Isobel started at the unexpected order. She stared at him, hardly able to take it in.

'I said, come here,' he repeated, quite quietly, but with a deadly insistence.

Isobel could only obey.

'That's better. Come closer.'

Mr Edward was still leaning back in his chair, elbows resting on the arms, fingers laced. Trembling, Isobel took a tiny step nearer. Her skirt touched his leg. An inarticulate sob of fear gathered in her throat, threatening to break out with each shallow breath.

He reached out and ran his hand over her hip, into her waist, up to her breast. She shuddered, cried out, shrunk way, but he caught her arm and pulled her back.

'Oh come now, don't tell me you don't like it. That's not what Perry told me.'

'I don't − I didn't − we − he −' The words spattered helplessly.

'I'm not sure that I understand you. What are you saying?'

'He didn't − t-touch −'

'Not at all? I do find that rather difficult to believe.'

'Not − not like −' Not like her brother-in-law had tried to do.

'Not like this?'

He cupped her breast again, running his thumb over the soft, vulnerable part above the armour of her corset. Her fragile control snapped. It was happening all over again. There was no escape.

'Please, please don't,' she sobbed, looking desperately towards the door. 'Please, let me go −'

'Don't worry, we shan't be interrupted. My secretary will be away for some time yet. Now stop crying and listen.'

Isobel shook her head. 'I can't −'

'You can. I am not dismissing you.'

The words broke through her panic, calming her a little. She listened.

'Rather, I am offering you the possibility of something far better. You will go back to Trent Street now. At half-past seven this evening I shall send a cab for you. Do you understand?'

Helplessly, Isobel nodded. Anything, just to get out of this room.

'And of course, you will not tell anyone about this interview.'

'No, no –'

As if she could even begin to speak of it. And then, unbelievably, it was over. She was outside in the corridor, and footsteps – the secretary's? – could be heard approaching. Swallowing tears, she started walking.

Somehow, she got herself to Trent Street. Her first instinct was to pack her belongings and go. She even started to take things out of drawers. But when she thought about what she would do when she went out of the door, she stopped. It would be worse than last time. She had come to London knowing nothing, and had met with stupendous luck. Now she had learnt something of the ways of the world, she knew that no other shop would employ her. She would get no reference from Packards and she could not hope for another Miss Packard to take her on on the strength of her knowledge of tennis. Once her money ran out, she would be destitute. She sank onto the bed and curled into a ball of despair, unable to think of anything beyond the horror of her situation.

When Daisy came in, Isobel pleaded illness. She managed to convince her that she did not need sitting with and that Daisy should go and meet Johnny for their regular evening out. The moment Daisy had gone she regretted not telling her, though she could not think how her friend could have helped. The nearby church clock chimed the quarter. She had to make her mind up. She got up and looked at her bag. She could still leave. But in the end she did what she knew all along she was going to do. She splashed some cold water over her face, tried to get her hair into some kind of order, and went down to meet the cab exactly as it arrived at half-past.

She sat right in the corner of the seat, rigid with dread, noticing nothing of the streets through which she was taken. All too soon, the cab stopped and the driver opened the door. She found herself at the foot of a flight of steps leading up to an impressive pillared porch and the green front door of what looked like a standard Mayfair house. She looked at the cabby for reassurance.

'That's it, miss. Just knock on the door.'

On legs that had lost all their strength, she tottered up the steps and did as she was told. Immediately, she was let into a gilded and carpeted hall by a footman in full livery and wig. If she had not been so utterly miserable already, she would have been embarrassed by her rather dishevelled appearance in such opulent surroundings.

'Miss Brand?' he enquired.

She nodded. She was led up the stairs to a first-floor room and shown in. The rococo elegance of its decoration was lost on her, for all she could see was Mr Edward, in full evening dress, seated in a chair by the tall windows. The door closed behind her.

'Ah, Isobel the Innocent – or is it the not-so-innocent? We shall soon see. Come here. Let me look at you properly.'

With the sick feeling of dread mounting by the moment, she went forward. The windows were open to the sweet summer air. Through them she vaguely comprehended a pretty garden, as remote and unattainable as the sky outside a prison. Mr Edward slowly surveyed her, his eyes lazily travelling over her body until Isobel felt as horribly exposed as if he could see through her crumpled working clothes. Instinctively, she folded her arms across herself, a feeble protection. He smiled.

'If you're not genuine, you're certainly a consummate actress. I think this is going to be a very enjoyable evening. So much better in a place like this, don't you think? Now we have all the time we could wish for with absolutely no danger of unwanted interruptions. But first we shall dine. You must be hungry after your day's work. I know I am. Ring the bell, will you, and then sit down.'

Almost relieved by the straightforward orders after the rest of what he had said, Isobel located the bellpull and sat at the round table, elegantly set for two. Mr Edward sauntered over to sit opposite her just as the door opened to the footman with a trolley of food. There followed a dinner the like of which her dearest mama had often aspired to but never achieved. It ran the full eight courses expected for such a meal; soup, fish, entrées, removes, game, sweets, ices and fruit, and all cooked to a perfection such as could only be reached by a French chef of the first order. Ordered to by Mr Edward, Isobel tried to eat the salmon, the sweetbreads and mushrooms, the iced asparagus, the quail, but every morsel she swallowed threatened to come straight up again.

Worse, he expected her to talk.

'I'm sure there is a fascinating little tale behind your change of name. Tell me who Miss Norton is, or rather was. Why did she have to leave Tillchester?'

Isobel shook her head in horror. 'I couldn't – really –'

'Oh but you could. Come along. Who were Mr and Mrs Norton? You did have parents, I take it?'

'Oh yes, of course.'

The words were torn from her. How could he think otherwise?

'Then tell me. What line of business does your father follow?'

It hurt so much to speak of her parents. To do so to him was a hundred times worse.

'He was a solicitor,' she admitted in a hoarse whisper.

'A solicitor! How perfect. But no longer with us, I presume, since you use the past tense?'

Bit by bit, like pulling teeth, he dragged the story from her. But only part of it. She did manage to avoid admitting to a sister or to the reason for leaving her old life, thanks to the lie she first made up for his sister and now repeated. It was like keeping a last piece of clothing about her to cover her nakedness.

The light was beginning to fade from the sky as they sat over dishes of early strawberries, Isobel tense and upright, her back not touching that of the chair, Mr Edward leaning back, relaxed, savouring the perfect lushness of each fruit, watching her every move with eyes that were a dark glitter in the shadows of his handsome face. It was then that Isobel realised that terrible though it had been to have to expose her family to him, it had at least postponed the horror beyond. As the last strawberry disappeared she began to talk, chattering about Packards, the department, the people, the dining room, Trent Street, anything and everything, desperately hoping that the torrent of words would keep the inevitable at bay. It did not.

'I don't think I want to hear about Packards now. I like to leave it behind me in the evenings,' he told her. 'Draw the curtains and light the lamps. It's getting too dark to see in here.'

She did as she was bid, blinking as the electric lights sprang into life.

'Those curtains as well. Draw them back.'

She had not noticed the curtains where usually the double doors through to the adjoining room would be found. When she drew them back she revealed a large alcove containing a huge double bed, the corner of the frilled covers turned down to reveal satin sheets. Gasping, she turned to face him and found that he had taken off his jacket and undone his bow tie and stiff collar.

'Now – come here.'

She shrunk away from him with an inarticulate cry, but he caught her arm and pulled her close, forcing her mouth open with his, running one hand down her back to clamp on her buttocks, pushing her hips towards his. Suffocating under the attack of his tongue, she then became aware of something hard and demanding through the layers of clothing that still separated them. Memories of her brother-in-law came flooding back. She tried to twist free, choking sobs rising in her throat. He released her mouth, only to press her more closely against him.

'Please –' she sobbed. 'Please don't.'

He laughed quietly, his mouth close to her ear.

'I wanted you this afternoon, right there on my desk. But this is going to be better.'

He let go of her, took her by the wrist and pulled her through to the inner alcove. Then to her confusion, he let go of her and sprawled back on the bed.

'Take my shoes off.'

She stared at him.

He repeated the order. With shaking fingers, she obeyed.

'Now undo your blouse.'

The tears were running uncontrolled down her face now.

She fumbled at the buttons. They slid out of her grasp, refused to go through the holes.

'Hurry up.'

His impatience only made it worse, but somehow she managed it, and the hooks of her skirt. Shaking with humiliation, she stood before him in her corset and cheap cotton underclothes.

'Come here.'

He was sitting on the edge of the high bed. He pulled her between his thighs and undid the laces of her corset, threw it aside and fondled her breasts, commenting greedily on their shape and size and colour. Isobel closed her eyes against the avid expression in his, but she could not avoid the sound of his voice.

'Look at me.'

She kept her eyes firmly shut. He slapped her cheek, just hard enough to shock her.

'I said look at me.'

He stood up and took off his trousers and underpants. The panic that had been steadily mounting in her erupted at the sight of his erect member. She screamed and backed away, sobbing and pleading, to find the controlled tormentor transformed. He caught her arms, forced her to the floor and held her down, pulling and ripping at what was left of her clothing. His hands were at her bare flesh, kneading, probing, penetrating her most private places until she cried out in humiliation, but it served only to increase his harsh breathing, his disjointed remarks. And then her legs were forced apart and his body was heavy on hers. Something hot and hard was poking at her, was inside her, tearing her apart with a piercing pain that drew a scream from her. It went on and on, thrusting and jarring until she was nothing but a nightmare pulp of terror. And then there were hoarse shouts of triumph, thrusts that she knew must surely kill her – and unbelievably, the worst was over. He was laughing and gasping, slumped on her with all his considerable weight. He was still moving spasmodically, and every time was an agony, but finally he stopped, and was still, and seemed even to sleep. Isobel wept uncontrollably.

He rolled off and sat, looking at her.

'Christ, that was good. You're so tight, like a vice. You've bruised me.'

Released, Isobel curled into a defensive ball, but still she could not shut out his voice.

'You weren't acting, then. It really was the first time. Perry must be even more of a fool than I took him for.'

She sensed rather than saw him get up and move away. There was the pop of a cork. Then he was back again.

'Come on, get up, it isn't the end of the world.'

She stayed silent and still. He reached down and pulled her to her feet.

'Lie on the bed. Champagne?'

She shook her head and crawled into the slippery womb of the bed, every movement making her whimper with pain. Her whole body felt bruised and torn. He sat up beside her, leaning against the pillows and drinking champagne, while she lay still as a stone, just hoping and hoping that it was all over and now she could die. But it was not all over, for now he put down his glass and turned his attention to her again, exploring every crevice of her violated body, probing and sucking and biting, and finally entering her again in a slicing agony.

Some time in the first grey glimmer before dawn, she became aware of him leaving the bed and moving into the main part of the room. A door opened and there were voices, his and another man's. The door closed. For a long time she lay with every nerve strained, listening, expecting him to return and the nightmare to start all over again, but there was silence. He was gone. She should have felt relief, but she did not. For there was hardly anything of her left. She was nothing, nobody. She was worthless, just a torn and broken body on a satin-covered bed.

29

The line of guests stretched ahead of them up the elegant curve of the staircase. Amelie felt as if she were going to burst with impatience.

'Oh come *on*,' she muttered under her breath.

Through the open double doors she could hear the band playing a merry polka. Inside her satin shoes, her toes danced.

'This is the second time this evening we've had to wait just to be received. Why on earth did we have to go to that boring old drum when we could have been here all the while?'

'Nobody refuses an invitation to one of the Duchess's drums,' her mother replied, with great satisfaction in her voice.

Amelie knew just why. It had been the first time they had been invited, and a coup for her mother, who had wanted to get inside the doors of that particular house for years. She suspected that the invitation had something to do with the rumours that her grandfather was about to get a knighthood.

'It was one of the most tedious things I've ever been to,' she complained.

'Ah well, it's only natural that young people should want to dance,' her mother replied, in such an indulgent tone that Amelie sent a sharp look at her. Winifred was smiling. 'And shall a certain person be here?'

To her chagrin, Amelie felt a blush sweep over her.

'I'm sure I don't know what you're talking about,' she snapped.

'It does no harm to have them wait for you,' her mother told her. If anything, she sounded even more satisfied than when talking of the Duchess's reception.

At last they got to the head of the queue and were greeted by their hosts. This was no run-of-the-mill ball cramped into the inadequate rooms of an ordinary Mayfair house, but a grand affair in one of the great houses on Berkeley Square with a proper ballroom. A rush of heat and music enveloped them as they entered, spiced with perfume, the scent of flowers and sweating bodies. Amelie searched the dancers, her eyes raking methodically over the pairs as they revolved round the floor. Anticipation collapsed into sick disappointment. He wasn't there. Blindly she followed her mother as she steered through the crowds to a couple of empty seats.

A young man, one of Perry's many friends, appeared and asked her to dance. She drew breath to refuse, but her mother answered for her.

'How kind. Yes, she would be pleased to.'

Amelie glared at her and got up. She knew very well that she was lucky to find a partner so quickly. There always seemed to be more girls than men at dances, and the men that were there seemed to spend their time drinking, gossiping and watching rather than taking part. Plenty of girls around her would be envious. She was just annoyed that she would now be distracted from her anxious scanning of each new arrival. She went through the motions of the dance automatically, answering her partner's remarks at random. Over his shoulder she kept looking at the crowds of people round the edge of the floor in case she had missed seeing him there.

The music came to an end. There was a spatter of polite gloved applause. Amelie's partner started to escort her back to her seat. They passed one of the pairs of French windows that stood open to the lantern-hung garden, through which couples were drifting back in from sitting out the dance in the inviting darkness, some of the girls surreptitiously patting hair and gowns back into place.

'. . . seen the new dancer at the Palace?' her partner was saying.

Amelie opened her mouth to answer, but instead uttered a small cry. There, coming in from the garden was Hugo, his beautiful blond head inclined to listen to the lovely girl who was holding on his arm and talking to him with great animation. Amelie stood, paralysed with pain, envy and anger, just containing the urge to confront the pair of them.

'. . . unwell?'

A persistent voice penetrated the poisonous surge.

'Yes – no – I mean –'

Unsuspecting, Hugo and the girl passed into the jumble of people crossing the dance floor. Amelie tried to pull herself together. Never show anything, that was the greatest and most sacred rule of Society. Put on a face, keep the glittering surface intact. To let anyone guess that things were less than perfect was bad form in the extreme, and bad form led to exclusion. She let herself be steered back to her mother, who nodded pleasantly to her and carried on the conversation she was having with a friend. She sat with the approved expression of light interest on her face while inside battle raged. What was he doing out there with That Woman? It was obvious what he was doing, everyone knew what sitting out was for. How dare he? But then again why shouldn't he? There was no understanding between them, nothing but a handful of meetings in company and some snatches of conversation. He was Hugo Rutherford, feted and admired. He could sit out with whom he chose. No he couldn't, not with That Woman, not with anyone. He had specifically asked her if she was going to be at this ball, had said he would see her here. She hated That Woman, she hated him.

Another dance, another partner. Still she kept watch. She couldn't stop herself. There he was, there, at the back of the room. She could hardly breathe. He wasn't with Her, he was talking to a middle-aged man. As she gazed at him, their eyes met. Instantly she looked away, a hot flush racing over her. He knew she was here. She deliberately avoided looking at that part of the room, started to chatter to her partner. The music seemed to go on for ever.

Then at last it was over and there he was again, this time chatting to her mother, laughing, at ease, as if nothing untoward had happened. He smiled as she approached.

'Ah, and here she is. Good evening, Miss Amberley. I was just remarking to your mother that you dance as well as you play tennis. I hope you have left one free for me?'

'I'm not sure that I have.'

Wouldn't you rather be out in the garden with Her?

Her mother gave her a little tap on the arm with her fan.

'Now then, Amelie, don't be naughty. I'm sure you are not engaged for the supper dance.'

Between them, Hugo and Winifred kept the conversation

going, often addressing remarks to Amelie, which she answered as shortly as possible. She could hear herself sounding like a spoilt child, but somehow could not stop it. The long interval between dances limped by and Hugo excused himself. Amelie watched him cross the room ready to hate whomever it was he was engaged to dance with. If only she had not been so short with him. Now he would think she was cross and rude and had nothing to say for herself.

Amelie pasted on a smile and trudged through the desert of time until supper. Of all the long evenings she had suffered, sitting next to boring dinner partners or making meaningless small talk at overcrowded receptions, this seemed infinitely the worst. Everybody else was enjoying themselves immensely. Talk and laughter swirled with the lilting notes of the music. Edward danced by with Sylvia Forbes, the pair of them totally absorbed in each other.

'That seems to be progressing very satisfactorily,' Winifred commented. 'Such a nice girl. Very suitable. Your grandfather will be pleased.'

'Grandfather?' Amelie repeated, jolted for the first time that evening from under her jealous cloud.

'Oh yes, your grandfather wants to see all of you well married.'

So Edward was going to get in first as usual, with efficient, well-bred Sylvia Forbes, who would make an excellent wife for the future head of Packards. But for once Amelie was not thinking only of her rivalry with Edward over the store, but more that it was all right for him, for he was a man, so he could take the initiative. All she could do was to wait.

At last one o'clock came round and Hugo appeared to claim his dance. Amelie put her hand in his and the evening was transformed. She moved into his arms and her whole body came alive.

'I was quite right, you do dance as well as you play tennis,' Hugo said.

Amelie flushed. 'Thank you.'

'It's a pleasure to watch you, but a much greater pleasure to dance with you.'

Amelie did not know quite what to say to that. Had he said the same to That Woman?

'At least one can dance properly here,' she answered.

'Yes, it is a treat to have space to move,' Hugo agreed. Then his voice changed, became softer and more teasing. 'Now, are you going to tell me what I have done to upset you, or do I have to endure your freezing me out for the rest of the evening?'

Amelie's insides churned. 'I'm sure I don't know what you mean,' she said.

'Oh come now, you could hardly bring yourself to speak a word to me earlier, and it's obviously a great effort to do so now.'

She hadn't realised quite how bad she was at covering her feelings.

'Nonsense. Of course it isn't,' she lied.

'You wouldn't even dance with me until your mother made you. And you know I only came here to see you.'

'Really?' Amelie was stung into saying what she meant. 'It did not look like that to me.'

'And what is that supposed to mean?'

'Nothing.'

'It must mean something.'

'If you don't know then there's no point in my telling you.'

There was a silence between them while they circled half the floor, bodies moving in unison, hearts at war.

'We can't talk here with half of Society looking on. Will you come out to the garden with me? It's much quieter there,' Hugo asked.

'You know that already from experience, of course,' Amelie said, unable to keep the sharp edge from her voice. Immediately, she regretted it. How she had really ruined everything. He would never want to have anything to do with her again.

To her utter bewilderment, he laughed.

'Oh, so that's it. No wonder. I can explain everything, if you'll let me.'

Limp with relief, she could only agree.

Outside in the velvet night, the air was perfumed with the scent of roses and night-scented stocks. Chinese lanterns hung from the trees, turning the English garden into a scene from a fairy tale. Hugo tucked Amelie's arm under his and led her down a brick-paved pathway past a trickling fountain. This way and that they walked, round clipped yew hedges and under trees, and on every bench couples were seated. Those under the coloured lamps were talking together, maybe with hands joined, but in the darker corners the glimmer of pale ball gowns in the warm June night gave away couples locked in breathless embraces. With every step, Amelie could feel painful excitement building inside her.

'I think there are more people out here than in the ballroom,' Hugo said. 'Here – a vacant seat at last. Would you care to sit down?'

He indicated a wrought-iron bench under a cherry tree. Amelie hardly knew whether she was relieved or disappointed that it was hung with red and pink and orange lights. She sat, her hands clasped in her lap, while Hugo sat slightly sideways on the bench, so that he was looking at her. Their knees touched.

'Now then, let me guess. You saw me coming in from the garden earlier this evening with a young lady?'

'I'm sure it's no business of mine,' Amelie said.

'We won't argue about that for the moment. Let me just tell you that Evie Markham and I are cousins. We practically grew up together. We're like brother and sister. Evie's been away for three months and we were catching up with each other's news.'

She wanted to believe him. It was certainly true that this Evie Markham was his cousin, for she had read the Rutherford entry in *Burkes* so many times that she knew every member of his family off by heart. But cousins could be sweethearts, even ones who grew up together.

'I see,' she said.

'I'm closer to Evie than to my real sisters. We can confide in each other. This evening she was especially eager to speak to me, as she had a very important piece of news and she wanted me to be the first to hear it. It will be officially announced tomorrow. She is engaged to be married.'

'Oh – ' Amelie could hardly stop herself from laughing. She felt quite dizzy. 'I see,' she said, but this time she meant it.

'I would like to introduce you to Evie. I think you would like each other.'

'Thank you, I'm sure I would.' In her relief she spoke without thinking. 'How lucky you are to have someone to share secrets with. My brother Edward and I have always fought. I can't remember a time when I wasn't trying to be better than him. I don't like my Amberley cousins at all and Perry –'

She stopped, suddenly realising that she was about to say that she could not altogether trust Perry. It threw her off-balance.

'Perry's an Amberley,' she said, trying to explain it to herself. 'But I'm a Packard, and so's Edward. That's why we fight. At the store, I'm called Miss Packard. It's as if the Amberleys did not exist.'

'Which do you prefer to be, an Amberley or a Packard?'

'Oh, a Packard.'

Except that it was as an Amberley that she had met him.

'The Amberleys are such a boring lot. They never *do* anything,' she said by way of explanation.

Her mother, of course, would maintain that they did not need to do anything. They were an ancient family. They did not need to justify themselves by being anything else.

'They're an old family,' Hugo said, as if reading her thoughts. The Rutherfords, she remembered, were very similar. Hugo would see things from her mother's point of view. 'Like many old families they've become weak and degenerate. One can see it all around. It comes of too much inbreeding, it enfeebles the line. I know all about the Amberleys. Tell me some more about the Packards. They interest me far more.'

Amelie recounted some of the most dramatic details from the story of how her grandfather had built the store from nothing.

'And now your brother Edward is set to take over the reins?'

'Yes.'

'But you are still fighting him? You run the Ladies' Sportswear and undertake the advertising?'

'Yes.' Except that since she had met him, things had changed. Little by little, the store had ceased to be the centre of her ambitions. 'Ladies' Sportswear was my idea. I persuaded Grandfather to let me set it up, and it's been a great success.'

'You set it up yourself?'

'Oh yes, I interviewed the staff and chose the merchandise and arranged the department and designed the advertising. Edward was just waiting to see it all go wrong, but it didn't. It's flourishing, so he tries to treat it as if it's a little toy that I'm playing with.'

'I should very much like to see this department of yours.'

Amelie felt as if the breath were being squeezed out of her chest.

'It's a shop. You're very welcome to go in any time you choose,' she said.

'I know, but it would be far more enjoyable if you were to show me round.' He reached out and placed his hand over hers. 'Would you do that?'

'I – I'd be pleased to,' Amelie stammered.

'When are you likely to be there next?'

'T-tomorrow, or the next day,' she hazarded. It all depended on him.

'It's already tomorrow,' Hugo smiled.

He put an arm round her shoulders and drew her closer. Music from the ballroom stole over the garden, and around them the air was alive with sighs and whispers. Under the coloured glow of the lamps, Hugo's face was very close to hers. She could feel his breath on her cheek. She closed her eyes and felt his lips meet hers, kissing her once, then repeatedly. The evening that had threatened to be a disaster was lifted into the realms of magic.

30

It seemed to Daisy that she lay awake all night. Guilt gnawed at her. If she hadn't told Johnny about Mr Perry and Isobel, he would not have told Mr Edward, Mr Perry would be taking Isobel out still and she would not be so desperately unhappy. And after all, where was the harm in it? Isobel was in love with him, or thought she was, and he had treated her well. If she had played her cards right, she might have got him to set her up in a nice little house somewhere with a maid and everything. Since she wasn't much good as a shopgirl and wouldn't look twice at nice blokes like Johnny who would marry her, it seemed like a good idea. Except of course that Isobel wouldn't consider being set up anywhere, her being brought up the way she was with no idea about how life really was. Round and round went Daisy's thoughts, but they always came back to the same question – where was Isobel now?

According to Mrs Drew she had gone out in a cab at half-past seven that evening, without a word of explanation to anyone. Again, Daisy blamed herself. She should have realised that her friend was not really ill, though heaven knew she had looked it. But in that case Daisy should have given up her evening with Johnny and stayed in with her. She was sure that she could have stopped Isobel from whatever she was doing.

When first she heard the story she hoped that Mr Perry had relented and come for her and everything was now all right between them, but as the night went on and faded into morning, this seemed less and less likely. Isobel would never willingly stay the night with a man.

She tried to persuade Mrs Drew of this.

'Willing or not, you know the rules, and so does she. In by half-past ten. And those as doesn't obey the rules can pack their bags.'

'There must have been an emergency. Family or something,' Daisy said.

Mrs Drew gave her a sceptical look.

'You know as well as I do that she ain't got no family. Spent Christmas here, didn't she, when nearly everyone else went home?'

Daisy knew that was so, but she also knew that Isobel was not in fact totally without family. There was the sister and that sod of a brother-in-law. Surely she could not have gone back to them? A look at Isobel's drawers in the shared chest told her that wherever Isobel was, she had not intended to stay away, not even for the night, for both her nightdresses were still there.

For the first time since coming to Packards, Daisy did not want to go to work. Her first thought on arriving at Baby Linens was as to how soon she might have dinner and a chance to ask about Isobel. She set to polishing the mahogany counters and tidying the already meticulously tidy banks of glass-fronted drawers, but her heart was not in it. Even a choice sale did not rouse her to her usual degree of enthusiasm. A lady came in enquiring after American monthly gowns, Daisy's favourite item amongst the huge range of merchandise the department held. She got out a selection of the dainty baby dresses, ones trimmed with embroidery and insertion work, ones trimmed with Valenciennes lace, the most expensive one of all, at an incredible sixteen shillings and sixpence, the one trimmed with embroidery and real torchon lace. Any other day, she would have prided herself on selling the expensive one. Today she let the customer get away with a mere embroidery-trimmed gown at a measly four and elevenpence, and not even a cap or a muslin bib to go with it. She just could not bring herself to be persuasive when all the while she was worrying about exactly where Isobel might be at that very moment.

Dinner time found her hurrying not to the dining room, but up to Ladies' Sportswear. One glance told her that Isobel had not reappeared, as she had dared to hope might happen. So she waited, practically dancing with impatience, for Miss Higgs to be free. The senior saleswoman pounced on her the moment she had got rid of her customer.

'Ah, Miss Phipps, just the person. Perhaps you can tell me what has happened to Miss Brand?'

Daisy's heart sank. She had been depending on Miss Higgs

having had some sort of message. It was no use lying about illness, since it was Mrs Drew's responsibility to notify the store if any of her residents were sick.

'I – er – I think there's been some sort of emergency, Miss Higgs. Isobel wouldn't never just stay away. It ain't – isn't – like her at all. Ever so conscientious she is, you know that.'

Miss Higgs sniffed. 'All I know is, I need her here. She may not be the best shopgirl I have, but I need someone to do the tidying away. We're rushed off our feet in here, and I've not seen hide nor hair of her since she was sent for yesterday afternoon.'

'Sent for?' Daisy echoed. 'Who sent for her?'

'Mr Edward. She went off to see him and never came back.'

'Mr Edward?'

Daisy's head went round the track of thoughts again – herself, Johnny, Mr Edward, Mr Perry, Isobel. And Mr Edward said to leave it with him. Certainly he had put a stop to Mr Perry taking an interest in her, but what had he done now? The only conclusion she could come to was that he had given her the sack. There was no other possible explanation.

Daisy went off to the dining room more worried than ever. picked at her meal and returned to Baby Linens for the longest afternoon she had ever spent at the store. When she finally left at the end of the day, she found Johnny waiting for her at the door they always used. For once, her heart did not give a skip when she saw him. Here was more trouble, for just how much should she tell him? Supposing he went off and tackled Mr Edward again? This time he would surely get the sack.

'Daisy! Am I glad to see you.'

Through all her anxiety for her friend, it still hurt, for she knew he only wanted to hear about Isobel.

'Hello, Johnny.'

There was none of her usual cheerfulness in her voice. Johnny noticed it immediately.

'Poor old Daise. You must be out of your head with worry. I only heard late this afternoon. How much do you know? Why did he want to see her?'

'I don't know,' Daisy told him, more dejected than ever, for it seemed that there was to be no keeping anything from him. The Packards' bush telegraph had been its usual busy self.

'What do you mean, you don't know? She must've said something to you.'

'She never said nothing, otherwise I'd of told you last night, wouldn't I? All she said was, she was ill. She never said nothing about being called to see Mr Edward.'

'I know that, but what about when she come in? Or this morning? She must've said something.'

'But I never saw her last night, or this morning. She never come back, did she?' Daisy snapped, before she realised that this was something she could have kept covered up for a while.

Johnny's kind face went quite white.

'She never came back?' he repeated.

While the flood of Packards' workers broke and passed round them, chatting and calling out to each other as they headed for home, Daisy told him as much as she knew. By the time she had finished, there was a dangerous light of anger in his eyes.

'There's only one thing to do, and that's to see Mr Edward. First thing tomorrow, I'm going to speak to him.'

Anguish caught at Daisy. She took hold of his arms with both hands.

'Oh no, please, don't do that! It won't do no good. Promise me you won't.'

'I got to, Daisy. He's the only person who knows the truth of it.'

'But he won't know where she is now. Oh please, Johnny, don't do it. He'd give you the sack and all and I couldn't bear it!'

Awkwardly, Johnny patted her shoulder. 'You're a good pal, Daisy.'

'Promise me you won't. Not yet. Please. She might be back right now.'

Eventually, reluctantly, he agreed.

'Not yet, then, but I still might have to if she don't turn up.'

Isobel did not turn up. The official story, as issued by Mr Mason at the staffing department, was that Miss Brand had been sent back to Trent Street because she was ill and had not been heard of since. Under the strange circumstances, her job was still open. Two days passed, and a third. The police and the hospitals were contacted, but no persons answering to Isobel's description had been found. By Saturday both Daisy and Johnny were beside themselves with worry. Johnny was convinced she had met with an accident. Daisy was not so sure. It was the fact of her going off in a cab that complicated things. She did not know what to think, except that it must be bad.

'Look, we got to do something. How about asking at all the cab ranks if they picked up a special fare from Trent Street that evening?' Johnny suggested.

Daisy was doubtful. 'There's so many. And they might not remember.'

'But it's a start. And it's the only thing we got to go on. We could do it, Daisy. I'll get a map, and we'll mark out who's going to go where. I'll get Arthur to help. If all three of us do it, we could cover all the ranks in central London. Somebody must know something. People don't just disappear.'

So the next morning, Daisy found herself armed with a list, a sketchmap and a ten-shilling note.

'To oil the wheels, if it's needed,' Johnny told her.

She was very impressed with his organisation, and he was right, doing something was better than just waiting around wondering, even though she did not hold out any hopes of success.

At midday they met up at a pub to exchange information. None of them had come up with anything, but Johnny was still sure that they would, and there were plenty more cabbies yet to speak to. They split up again for the afternoon.

It was about four o'clock and she was getting tired from all the tramping about when Daisy came to the last but one rank on her list. She approached the most fatherly-looking of a group of cabbies who were exchanging cigarettes and gossip. He claimed not to have been working on Monday evening, but found her someone who was.

'Sent round to Trent Street? Nah, would of remembered that. Sorry love.'

Daisy thanked them and turned away, when one of the men called her back.

'Here, miss – hold on. Something just rang a bell, like. I got a feeling old Smithy said something about a fare on Monday evening. You hang on here a bit till he comes back.'

'Yeah, come and have a cuppa char and keep us company a bit.'

Half suspicious that they only wanted a chance to while away the time between fares by chatting to her, Daisy agreed. She had to follow any possibility of finding something out, and anyway her feet were killing her and a cup of tea was very tempting. She gratefully sipped stewed sweet drink strong enough to tan leather and parried the men's remarks, while one or other of their number came and went on fares. She was beginning to think that there was no such person as Smithy, when one more cab pulled up and the others called out to him.

'Here, Smithy, you got a young lady waiting to see you.'

'What you been up to, you dirty old man? I'll tell your missus of you.'

Daisy repeated her question. To her surprise and delight, Smithy nodded.

'Yeah, I remember that one. Trent Street. Yeah. All paid up beforehand, like.'

'You do? That's wonderful! I been asking all day. Where did you take her?'

The man gave her a considering look. 'Friend o' yours, is she?'

Daisy sighed and took her purse out of her pocket. She opened it and pulled the ten-shilling note out far enough to be seen.

'Yes, she is, and I'm blooming worried about her.'

But Smithy did not put his hand out for the money. Instead he looked resigned.

'I wouldn't of thought you was the type, nor her neither. Specially not her. Looked bloody terrified, she did. Shopgirl, are you?'

'Yes,' Daisy said. 'What of it?'

'Well, they do say nine out of ten tarts was once shopgirls.'

Furious, Daisy rounded on him, hands on hips. 'Just what are you saying, mister? I ain't no tart and neither's my friend. We're both respectable working girls, so just you blooming well take that back.'

The man shrugged. 'Maybe you are, duck. I'll take your word for it. But your pal ain't. Respectable girls don't go where I took her.'

'Where did you take her, then? That's what I'm trying to find out.'

He mentioned a Mayfair address. The other cabbies sucked breath in through their teeth and shook their heads.

'He's right, love,' said the one who bought her the tea. 'High-class knocking shop, that is.'

Daisy found she was shaking. 'I don't believe you!' she cried, shouting to keep the truth at bay.

'Believe what you like, girl, but it's a fact. Not for professional tarts. It's where the toffs like to take actresses and such like.'

'Or the wives of other toffs,' added someone else.

'Yeah, that and all. Hire a room for however long they like, meal cooked by a French chef, clean sheets, no questions asked and all not a sixpenny fare from home. Very nice and cosy.'

Daisy felt sick. 'You're having me on,' she said.

'I wish I was, girl. But I remember that friend of yours. Like I said, she looked bloody terrified.'

'You might of warned her!' Daisy cried.

Smithy looked truculent. 'Now look here, I was just doing my job. I ain't her keeper, am I?'

'You still could of asked if she knew what she was doing.'

'Look, girl, in this job you don't ask questions. I didn't have to tell you nothing, did I? I told you what you wanted and all I get is an earful.'

It went against the grain, but Daisy had to admit that she had found out just what she had set out to discover. It wasn't his fault that she didn't like it.

'Thanks,' she said stiffly. 'You been a big help.'

She took out the note and offered it to him, but Smithy waved it away with a great show of injured pride. 'I don't take blood money,' he said.

'Suit y'self,' Daisy told him. She shoved money and purse back into her pocket and marched off.

For the length of a street she walked without even knowing where she was going while her newly acquired knowledge slotted uncomfortably with what she knew already. Mr Edward sends for Isobel. She goes back to Trent Street, supposedly ill. She gets in a cab that has been already paid for and it takes her to a place where rich men have it off with their mistresses. It was only too obvious what had happened. The only real question was, where was Isobel now? Daisy knew what she had to do to find out. She stopped the next policeman she saw and asked for directions.

Twenty minutes later and she was at the end of the street. She looked down the row of white- and cream-painted stucco fronts and impressive pillared entrances. No use going down there. She found her way into the mews at the back, went through the pretty garden, heady with the scent of June roses, and knocked at the kitchen door.

'I got a message for one of the chambermaids,' she told the girl who answered.

'Who, Betty or Ethel?'

Daisy took a breath and plumped for Betty.

A girl of about her own age appeared, and leant against the door jamb, her arms folded across her aproned front and an unhelpful expression on her face. Daisy described Isobel, and gradually the expression changed. Betty almost looked sympathetic.

'Yeah, poor little cow. Gawd, was she in a state. Never seen nothing like it, I ain't. 'Course,' she added, 'we ain't supposed to say nothing about who comes here, on account of this place is supposed to be the best kept secret in town. More'n our job's worth, it is, to say anything.'

She paused significantly. Daisy was very glad she had not forced the ten-shilling note on Smithy. She passed it to Betty, who whipped it into her pocket with the skill of a conjurer. She settled herself more comfortably and lowered her voice.

'Yeah, few days ago, weren't it? Monday or Tuesday? 'Course, we ain't supposed to see who comes in and out of here, it's the footmen what answers the door and sees to the customers. We just do the cleaning. But Jim, he says to me, "For Gawd's sake go and do something about the bint in the first-floor back. We got to get her out of here and the place put to rights or before we know where we are the afternoon lot'll be here." So in I goes and there she is, all huddled up in the bed like someone's given her a right doing over. Won't say nothing to me, just sobs and says to go away and let her die. Well, I can't do that, can I? So I gets some water and cleans her up. Blooming mess there was and all. Blood on the carpet, blood on the sheets. I said to her, "You shouldn't be doing it when it's your monthlies, you'll get something nasty, you will," but she says it wasn't that, so I suppose it must of been her first time, poor cow. Didn't look like she enjoyed it much, but then who does, first off?'

Daisy murmured agreement through the sick feeling of horror that gripped here. She could feel Isobel's pain and terror. She wanted desperately to take her in her arms and comfort her.

'What happened to her?' she asked.

'Motor come for her, didn't it? I got her dressed and tidied up a bit and took her out round the back here. Someone's looking out for her, anyway. Not that she wanted to go, mind you, but as I said to her, it's better'n being chucked out on the street, ain't it?'

No amount of questioning or the promise of a bigger bribe would get a description of the motor out of Betty, and in the end Daisy gave up. Exhausted now, but filled with fury at the way Isobel had been treated, she made her way back to the pub where they had arranged to meet.

Johnny and Arthur were already there, sitting at a corner table with pints in front of them. Both had a despondent slump to their shoulders. Arthur spotted her first and alerted Johnny, who looked up with hope in his eyes. The sensible lie on her lips nearly died. She ached to run across the room and see his face light up as she told him that she knew that Isobel was still alive. It would be worth almost anything to have him hug her and tell her how clever she was. Almost anything. Just in time she checked herself. It wasn't worth having him tackle Mr Edward again and get chucked out, which was certain to happen. She couldn't bear that.

So she walked across to them, shaking her head.

'No luck,' she told Johnny.

He thumped the table in frustration, making the beer slop over.

'Us neither,' Arthur explained, unnecessarily.

'I was sure it was going to work. It was our only hope,' Johnny said. 'I thought it was a good idea.'

Daisy put her hand on his arm. 'It was a good idea,' she said, and longed to tell him just how well it had worked.

'Not good enough. I failed.'

'You tried. You didn't just sit there and give up,' Daisy pointed out.

Johnny took a long breath and let it out again. 'Yes. Well. Sorry, Daisy, what do you want to drink? Port and lemon? How about a brandy? You look like you could do with it.'

They sat gloomily over their drinks, going over the day's fruitless search.

'I'm sure she's still alive,' Daisy said, in an effort to spread some brightness. 'I just know she is. I feel it.'

Johnny squeezed her knee, sending a rush of pleasure through her.

'You're a brick, Daise. You've been a real pal. There's not many girls'd spend their Sunday tramping round London talking to a lot of cabbies. If there's ever anything I can do for you –'

Pleasure turned to pain. A brick. A pal. Tears burnt in her eyes. All she wanted him to do was to stop thinking of her like that. Fat chance there was of that.

''S all right,' she said gruffly. 'She's my friend and all, y'know.'

Isobel's disappearance was the talk of the store. For the next couple of days Daisy found herself accosted by all and sundry hoping for some fresh news on the story, but she could only tell them that she knew nothing. Then on Wednesday, one of the typists actually stopped her outside the staff lavatories. Daisy was surprised. The typists did not usually deign to speak to the shopgirls.

'I hear your little friend has resigned.'

Daisy was so shocked that she could only gape at the girl and say, 'What?'

'You mean you don't know? Oh yes, they got a letter from her in Staffing. Addressed from some hotel, saying she had found alternative employment. I think we can all guess what that means. Sorry to have to be the bearer of bad news.'

'Oh piss off,' Daisy told her.

She spent the rest of the day wondering just how soon Johnny would find out.

When she arrived back at Trent Street, there was a letter waiting for her. Recognising Isobel's writing, she snatched it up and rushed upstairs.

The address inside was not a hotel, but a road in Camberwell. She read:

Dearest Daisy,

Please do not tell anyone about this letter. Nobody else must know where I am. This is very, very important, Daisy. Once you have read it, please destroy it. You must not tell anyone. I should not be writing to you at all, but my dear friend, I would like to see you so very much. Is it possible that you might call on me? Wednesday evening should be all right, but if there is a motor car outside, please do not knock, but try again the next week. Also, would you please not mention anything to the maid about your being at Packards.

I know this must all sound very strange, but I cannot tell you how much it would mean to me to see you again.

Your affectionate friend,
Isobel.

For a long time, Daisy sat staring at the letter trying to make out the significance of the dos and don'ts. Then she did what Isobel had asked. She memorised the address and tore the letter into tiny pieces and went to flush it down the toilet. It seemed a melodramatic thing to do, but until she had seen Isobel face to face and found out what was going on, she was not going to take any chances.

31

'No, I don't like those. Try the peach.'

Isobel cringed inside. Another undressing. How much longer was this going to go on? An array of tea gowns, camisoles and underskirts had already been tried on, each one paraded up and down the fitting room for Mr Edward to make his judgement. Now they were on to the knickers. Hot with embarrassment, Isobel stood as the assistant took off the pair that he didn't like and held out the peach-coloured ones for her to step into. She still hated being naked in front of him in private. To be dressed and undressed before him like this, with the dressmaker and her assistant looking on, was one long humiliation. Both women were well aware of her position. The dressmaker did not once ask Isobel whether she liked whichever undergarment she happened to be trying. Every remark on shape, colour and attractiveness was addressed to Mr Edward. Isobel might just as well be a doll with no senses or feelings. That was all she could expect, now that she was a kept woman.

'Now, those are very pretty. Sir has excellent taste. What is more, you won't find coloured silk knickers like those in any other establishment in London,' the dressmaker boasted.

'Turn round. Slowly,' Edward ordered. Isobel obeyed. Sprawled on a little gilt and velvet sofa, his long legs stretched out in front of him, Edward considered her. 'Yes, very alluring. I'll take those, and probably the pink ones as well. Try them on.'

He was enjoying it, she knew that. Not just enjoying seeing her in a series of exotic undergarments, but enjoying her sense of shame. Even if she had been capable of putting on a show of not caring, he would have seen through it, for he knew just how much she was hating it. That had been the whole point of the expedition. He could easily have ordered a selection of garments to be delivered to the house, for they did not need to be fitted like dresses.

At last it was over, and she was allowed to get dressed. At his insistence she was still wearing her Packards outfit, right down to the silver racquet brooch.

'My little shopgirl, always ready to serve,' he frequently said. 'What would my sister say if she knew just what services you are now providing?'

She should have enjoyed the ride home in the cab. It was not often that she saw the outside world now, and Mayfair in high summer was buzzing with life. The elegant squares were bright with leafy trees and summer flowers, the Season was at its height. Shining carriages and motor cars went by, carrying ladies resplendent in the latest fashions. Brighter colours had taken over from the dreamy pastels that had been so popular, and the women looked like exotic birds in flame and chrome and magenta, their fair complexions protected from the sun by pretty parasols and hats piled high with ribbons and flowers. Once, Isobel would have gazed at them with fascination, but not any more. The ride was spoilt by Edward speculating out loud on what they should do when they got back. Isobel felt sick. It was horrible enough to have to do it. Talking about it was repulsive.

'What's the matter?' Edward asked. 'Don't you like it? There are so many things you don't like, you're a veritable mine of prudery.'

He reached down and pulled up her skirt, then ran his hand up her leg and over her thigh. Isobel went rigid. Her eyes went to where the driver sat on the other side of the glass screen, the back of his head and his thick red neck only feet away. Edward grinned.

'Do you think he knows what I'm doing? He must be wishing he was sitting here in my place instead of in the driver's seat. He'd love to have his hand where I've got mine, even if you are still wearing these schoolgirl drawers. When your new things arrive, I want you to wear them under this ugly skirt. The contrast will be most exciting.'

His fingers moved expertly between her layers of petticoats and found the way into her drawers. Her flesh shrunk from his touch.

'All afternoon I've been looking at this lovely creamy body. It feels even better than it looks.'

Greedily he moved over her belly and between her legs. Isobel winced and tried to bite back a cry. She was continually sore and bruised there. Instinctively she tried to move away from the probing and rubbing, but that only made him rail at her, his breath harsh and ragged in her ear. 'Come now, that's no way to behave. You should be very grateful to me, I've just spent a fortune on pretty things for you. Show me how grateful you are. Come on.'

He took her hand and placed it over the bulge in his trousers, making her work on him. Isobel looked again at the cabby's head. She was sure his neck was even redder. He did know what was going on. If they could just get back to the house, she did not care what was done to her or what she had to do, just as long as there was nobody else there.

'Oh yes, that's good, isn't it? The motion makes it even better. We'll do it right here, in the cab.'

Isobel gasped with horror. That was all he needed. He made her kneel astride him and, grasping her buttocks, pulled her down onto him. Her head hard against the leather upholstery, Isobel tried to muffle her sobs as he drove into her resisting body. Acutely aware of the driver, of the vehicles going by, of people crossing the road, she felt as exposed as if she had been doing it in the middle of a park. Every eye must surely be upon them, condemning her for what she was, a fallen woman. She knelt, her hands fisted, waiting for it to be over. After what seemed like for ever, he shouted in time with the last, punishing strokes, and was still. Isobel stole a look at his face. He seemed happy and relaxed, all the cruelty drained away. Carefully, she eased off him.

They were turning the corner into Elmer Road, the street where Isobel now lived. Edward stirred and grinned at her as she attempted to straighten her clothes.

'Well, what a brazen little hussy you are. Doing it in a hired cab in broad daylight. You should be ashamed of yourself.'

Scalding tears gathered in Isobel's eyes. She concentrated on untangling her petticoats and tucking in her blouse. The cab pulled up at the door of number forty-eight.

'I don't think I'll bother coming in. I have an important call to make this afternoon,' Edward told her. Perversely, Isobel felt rejected. He reached over and opened the cab door, patting her bottom as she climbed awkwardly out.

'Remember, I shall want to see you in your new things when I next call.'

Isobel nodded, unable to answer.

'Aren't you going to thank me for them?'

'Thank you,' she whispered.

'Thank you, sir,' he reminded her.

'Thank you, sir.'

'That's better. Now off you go, and be ready for me whenever I should come again.'

Released at last, Isobel crossed the pavement and knocked at the green-painted door of the neat terraced house. The maid let her in and at last she was safe from inquisitive eyes.

The place to which she had been sent the day after her dreadful initiation was a flat-fronted three-bedroomed house with a basement and railed area and pretty rounded-topped windows. Looking through the lace curtains, Isobel could see an identical terrace on the opposite side of the road, each house with its polished knocker and its scrubbed steps, some with geraniums on the windowsill, others with roses growing up trellises on the wall, but all very much the same. Their inhabitants were all a similar type of people as well. Isobel spent many a vacant hour watching their comings and goings. First the menfolk would leave, all in their pressed suits and clean white collars, to catch their trams and trains into the City. Isobel knew just what they were like, for the clerks in her father's office looked just the same. Next the children would set off for school, skipping ropes and balls at the ready, satchels on their backs, laughing and calling out to each other, playing chase up the road. Later the wives would emerge, respectably gloved and hatted, baskets over their arms, to do the day's marketing. Sometimes they would stop and chat with each other, nodding and smiling, and Isobel would feel an ache of envy. How lucky they were, to live such simple and normal lives.

For though her house looked just like all of theirs on the outside, inside was a different story. It shrieked 'Love nest'. The predominant colours were scarlet and gold. There were drapes and mirrors and comfortable couches. There was a fur rug in front of the parlour fireplace. On the walls were paintings of women in various states of undress. Worst of all, upstairs in the main bedroom there was a huge bed with diaphanous hangings and a mirror set into the ceiling. It was not to this room that Isobel hurried, but to the smaller one behind it that was meant merely to be a dressing room, furnished with three large wardrobes, a washstand, dressing table and couch. It was here that Isobel chose to sleep, or rather try to sleep, when her lord and master was not there to command otherwise.

At seven in the evening, there was a tap on her door.

'Dinner's on the table, miss. I'm going now.'

Isobel roused herself to say thank you, but did not get up. She did not want any dinner. She listened to the maid's footsteps thudding down the stairs, to the slam of the front door, and at once felt both relieved and bereft. She disliked the maid, a dour middle-aged woman who appeared to come with the house. She was obsequious towards Edward and just short of insolent to Isobel, who felt totally unable to assert herself or issue a reprimand. Sunday afternoons and Wednesday evenings were her hours off, and Isobel looked forward to her not being there, but now that she was gone the house was still as a grave. Since Edward was unlikely to come again that evening, Isobel would not speak to another living being until the morning.

Desperately lonely, she made her way downstairs to her favourite station by the parlour window. At least there was some life to look at out in the street. A group of girls in white pinafores had a long rope stretched across the road and were playing skipping games, chanting a rhyme and running in to perform complicated steps and jumps. The men were coming home from their days sitting at high desks and scratching away with their pens. They looked tired and worn, their shoulders bowed, each one walking eagerly through his front door, ready for a welcome and a hot meal. Isobel imagined the cheerful family groups inside each house, the day's news exchanged, and knew herself to be an outcast.

And then, miraculously, a familiar figure came into view. A

young woman in a dark skirt and jacket and a white blouse, a plain straw hat on her head.

'Daisy!'

Isobel jumped up and flew to the door, opening it before her friend even reached for the knocker. She flung her arms round her.

'Oh Daisy, it's so good to see you!'

Daisy returned her hug.

'Well, there's a welcome and a half,' she said. 'You going to ask me in, then?'

'Yes, of course. Oh, I'm so glad you're here.'

Isobel led the way into the parlour and plied Daisy with tea and the blancmange that had been left for her dessert.

'How are you? What have you been doing?'

'I'm all right. You know me, strong as an ox. This stuff is lovely. Can I have some more?'

Tears pricked at Isobel's eyes. She had forgotten Daisy's bottomless appetite.

'Have it all,' she said, placing great spoonfuls on her plate.

'Mm, thanks.' Daisy eyed the rest of the meal as it sat cold and congealed on the plate. 'You get fed well here, at any rate. Why didn't you eat that? Looks like it was good.'

'I wasn't feeling hungry.'

Isobel did not want to be drawn into discussing herself yet.

'What have you been doing?' she repeated.

'Oh – same old things, you know. That Vi in my department's really got it in for me still. She had the best sales before I came, and now she's second to me every week. Really put her nose out of joint, that has. Mind you, the week you disappeared she beat me. You should of heard her! Couldn't stop crowing, she couldn't. But I soon put her in her place again.'

Isobel listened to the store gossip, who was courting, who was feuding, which couples had had a row, what stupid new demand the floorwalker had made. How easy, how straightforward it all seemed now.

'And what – what is happening at Trent Street?' she asked.

'I got a new roommate.'

Isobel felt a shaft of pure jealousy.

'Indeed? What is she like?'

Daisy made a face. 'All right, I suppose. I had to get her trained, like keeping her stuff on her side of the room and who was going to wash first in the mornings and fetching the water and all that. I mean, she don't smell or snore or nothing, but it's not like having you there. We don't sit and talk like you and me used to. She's not my pal, she's just someone I share the room with.'

Isobel could not even pretend to be sorry. It meant that she still had Daisy for herself.

'What's her name?'

'Gertie More. Tell you something, though, I'm going to introduce her to Arthur. I think they'd get on like a house on fire.'

'That sounds like a good idea,' Isobel said. She wasn't exactly sure if she meant it. What a perfect foursome they would make, Johnny, Daisy, Arthur and Gertie. She did not want anything to happen that might take Daisy away from her.

'How – ah – how is Johnny?' she asked.

Daisy's face closed. 'He's trying to find you.'

'Oh no.'

Isobel was horrified. 'What do you mean, trying to find me?'

Daisy explained, and as she did so, Isobel felt like a hunted creature. She reached out and caught Daisy's hands.

'This is dreadful. Nobody must find me. Daisy, you must stop him.'

'I can't stop him, Iz. I can only put him off. I been telling lies left, right and centre for you. He won't give up. When we didn't get nowhere with the cabs, or at least, when he thought we didn't get nowhere, he got us going round all the hotels and all the employment offices. He says we got to ask for you by name and say what you look like in case you changed your name, and he's got maps and lists so we don't miss any place. All planned out, it is. I said to him, you ought to be in the police, you did.'

Isobel couldn't help a stirring of admiration, and of something like gratitude. It was warming to know that somebody cared enough about her to go to all that trouble.

'But you won't tell him, will you Daisy?'

Daisy sighed. 'Oh don't worry, I won't let on. But that's what I mean, Iz, about telling lies. Each time he has a new plan, I know it won't work, and I know he's going to be so disappointed. It cuts me to the quick, it does. And I have to go along with it. I have to pretend I'm going to all these places on the lists, and come back and make up stuff about what people have said to me.'

'He'll have to give up sometime,' Isobel said.

'Yeah, but he'll still wonder, won't he? He'll never know what happened to you.'

Yet another layer of guilt settled round Isobel like a fog.

'And then there's Miss Packard.'

'Miss Packard!' A great jolt of fear went through Isobel. 'Has she been asking after me? What did she say? What did you say?'

'She hasn't yet. She hasn't been in much at all lately, from what I hear. Not that I see her so much anyway up in Baby Linens. The word is that she's got an admirer, so that accounts for it. She's busy with him. Lucky her, that's what I say. But she'll find out that you're gone sometime, won't she? So what do I say if she does? Just keep pretending I don't know nothing – anything?'

'Yes – no – I don't know –'

'I could say as you've got a living-in job,' Daisy suggested.

Isobel was about to reject this out of hand when the sense of it got through to her. It sounded respectable. How she longed for respectability.

'Yes. Yes, that's a very good idea. Say that, if she asks, but don't give her my address, will you?'

'No, I suppose not,' Daisy agreed. 'It doesn't matter so much about the others, but Johnny and Miss Packard are different. I hate lying to them, Iz. If you'd only let me tell Miss Packard the truth, I'm sure she could do something for you.'

'No!' Isobel cried, the queasy feeling of danger returning. 'Look, Daisy, you have to stick to that story. She mustn't find out about me, she absolutely mustn't.'

Daisy looked obstinate. 'I don't see why not.'

'She's his sister!' Isobel almost shouted. 'She would go to him, speak to him. There would be the most terrible trouble –'

Daisy did not look convinced. 'But she could help you, I

know she could. Why don't you let me say, Iz? After all, you're not happy here, are you?'

This was so overwhelmingly true that the tears which were never far from the surface welled up and spilled down her cheeks. Isobel could fight it no longer. She let herself be gathered into Daisy's strong arms and wept on her shoulder.

'Oh Daisy,' she sobbed. 'It's horrible, horrible –'

She could never explain to her friend just how dreadful. It was not just having to do That Thing with him, it was the constant fear of knowing that he could turn up at any time and make her do something she hated. The humiliation of it made her crawl inside with hatred of herself and what she had turned into.

'Then why do you stay here?' Daisy asked.

'I have to. There's nothing else for me, nothing –'

For she was nothing.

Daisy let her cry herself out. Then she found her way into the kitchen and made a pot of tea.

'Now,' she said, 'you listen to me. It's just daft to say you got to stay here. This is a free country, isn't it? And you're not a prisoner or anything. You could walk out of here with me right now this minute.'

Isobel shook her head. 'No.'

If only it were that easy. She had walked out of her sister's house, bruised and shaken and soiled, but still able to hold on to a scrap of pride. But not this time. Now she was sunk in a mire so deep there was no washing it away ever again.

'You can, Izzy. We could find you lodgings somewhere, and then look for a job.'

'No, no, I couldn't.'

The thought of even trying to go out into the world appalled her. She could not do it.

'If only you'd let me ask Miss Packard –'

'No!'

'Then – then let me get Johnny to help. You could – you could go to his family. They'd look after you until you got on your feet again.'

Isobel shook her head. She could not even begin to try to

make Daisy understand. They were respectable people. She was something contemptible. It was impossible.

Daisy thumped the table in frustration.

'You must let me help you!'

'You can't,' Isobel told her. 'Just – just tell me some more about Packards. I like to hear about it.'

How she had dreaded the days when she was there. Now it seemed like a golden age which would never return.

At half-past nine, Daisy said she had to get back to Trent Street. Isobel clung to her at the door, loath to let her go.

'Promise me you'll come again,' she begged.

''Course I will. You're my pal, aren't you?'

'I'm so grateful, I can't tell you. If it wasn't for you, I'd just die,' Isobel told her, and realised that it was the truth.

Daisy wagged a finger at her. 'Now then, I don't want to hear none of that talk, d'you understand?'

Isobel nodded. It was easy for Daisy to say. She was strong and whole.

'You're so good, Daisy. I don't know why you still bother.'

'Rubbish. Like I said, you're my pal. Now you think about what I said, eh?'

Isobel nodded obediently, but knew that though she would indeed think about it, she would never be able to change now. She stood at the door, waving goodbye until Daisy turned the corner. Then she went into the gaudy, empty house, to await whatever might be done to her next.

32

Amelie could not make up her mind just where to stand. She did not want Hugo to find her waiting for him, but on the other hand, she did not want him to have to wait around for her in the main entrance. Well, not for too long, anyway. In the end she decided to get down to the entrance five minutes before he was due and lurk behind one of the counters just inside the glass doors through to Stationery and watch for his arrival. As it happened, she had only just got herself into place when in he came through the main doors. Her heart turned over as she caught sight of him, so tall, so handsome in the formal grey and black of his morning suit. For a few moments she allowed herself the pleasure of just looking at him, then she went to greet him and had the further pleasure of seeing his smile as he saw her.

'Now then, I have the whole morning free, so I hope you are going to show me all over your store,' he said.

'I shall be delighted to, but I do hope that it's not the first time you've been here,' Amelie said.

'Of course not. I often shop here, and so do my sisters. But I am sure I shall see things quite differently with you as my guide.'

It was a morning of unalloyed happiness for Amelie. Like her grandfather, she never tired of touring the store, of keeping her fingers on the pulse of the great living organism that was Packards. To have an attentive companion was an extra delight, and when that companion was the man she had fallen in love with it was sheer heaven. She took Hugo behind the scenes to the stores, maintenance and packing departments in the basements, round all the sales floors and up to the offices. Hugo took a lively interest in all of it, asking questions and making comments.

'I never realised just how much was involved in the running of a store,' he said. 'That is, I had never really given any thought to it. And you seem to understand all of it so clearly.'

'I was brought up with it. I understand the running of the

store in the same way that you understand the running of an estate. Though my grandfather appears to be getting to grips with Tatwell as well.'

'Am I to meet your grandfather this morning? I should very much like to.'

Amelie longed at that moment to have her mother overhear the conversation. Here was a member of the Top Ten Thousand actually wanting to meet the founder of Packards. She saved it up to flourish before her at the very earliest opportunity.

'I'm sure he'd be very pleased to see you,' she said.

But long before they went to see Thomas, they ran into Edward. He was talking to the Staff Manager, but broke off to greet his sister and her guest. Amelie felt a qualm of unease. She never quite knew how Edward was going to react. But she need not have worried. He was charming and friendly, shaking Hugo warmly by the hand.

'Very glad to see you here at Packards. Are you in training at the moment? I take it you're defending the Diamond Sculls this year?'

'I am indeed. I don't intend to let that slip from my grasp.'

'Most exciting final last year. You even managed to draw some of the spectators from their champagne teas.'

They all laughed at the expense of those who went to Henley only for the social scene.

'I know most people regard the races as an interruption to the party. One can't really regard Henley as a serious sporting event. The river there is far too narrow to allow a fair race. But it's certainly a very pretty setting,' Hugo said.

'We shall be there to cheer you on,' Edward said. 'I hope you're enjoying your tour of Packards. My little sister isn't being too much of a bore, I trust?'

'Not at all. Quite the contrary, in fact. Your sister has opened up a whole new world to me.'

'I'm very glad to hear it. You will have seen the famous Ladies' Sportswear department, I take it?'

'No, I have not yet had that pleasure.'

'I'm saving it up till last,' Amelie explained.

'Well, when you have had enough of tramping round the

sales floors, do come and have a drink in my office,' Edward invited.

'Pleasant chap, your brother,' Hugo commented, as they made their way back down to the first floor. 'Very useful fly half too, I believe.'

'Yes, and he was captain of the First Eleven at school,' Amelie said, glad to be able to say something nice about Edward for once. She did not want to be always parading the family differences in front of Hugo.

They walked through Ladies' Outerwear.

'There,' Amelie said, pride suffusing her voice. 'There it is. My very own brainchild.'

She pointed to the archway, which was decorated with tennis racquets, cricket bats and summer greenery.

'Most attractive, and very original, too,' Hugo commented. 'It's as if it's a small shop within the big store.'

'You have it exactly! That's just the effect I want to achieve,' Amelie cried, delighted.

She showed him round the department, pointing out all her favourite innovations, but her mind was only partly on the task. For Isobel Brand was no longer behind the counter. There was another girl in her place. Hugo insisted on buying some gloves for his sisters. Miss Higgs came forward to serve this obviously very important customer, but Amelie stopped her, calling for one of the shopgirls to attend Hugo and drawing Miss Higgs aside.

'Oh, her,' Miss Higgs sniffed, when asked about Isobel. 'She's gone and left us all in the lurch, she has.'

'Whatever do you mean?' Amelie asked.

'Just upped and left, she did. Went back to Trent Street in the middle of the day ill, then went out for the evening and never came back. Not a word to anyone.'

Amelie could not believe it.

'Are you saying that you don't know where she is? Have no enquiries been made? She might be ill. Something dreadful might have happened to her.'

'Just what everyone said, Miss Packard. Plenty of enquiries was made, I can assure you. Police and everything.'

'But Miss Phipps? Does she not know?'

'Never even told her. Worried out of her mind, she was. Then a

306

week ago, what do we get but a note saying as she's found other employment. Just like that. Never heard anything like it in my life, I haven't. Nobody walks out on Packards like that. Disloyal, that's what I call it. And after all we've done for her.'

Amelie was shocked. Isobel Brand was the last person she would have thought would have left like this. She had been gently brought up and knew that one did not abandon one's obligations. And beside that there was the personal angle. She had been so grateful to get the job in the first place, and even more grateful to be restored to it when Edward sacked her. But in spite of that she had gone without a word of explanation. It was indeed disloyal.

'Why was I not informed of this before?' Amelie asked.

Miss Higgs looked uncomfortable. 'You've – er – not been in for a while, Miss Packard,' she pointed out.

With a jolt of guilt Amelie realised that this was true. She had rushed in to the advertising department a couple of times recently, but she had not been here to Ladies' Sportswear for well over a fortnight.

'You should have sent a message,' she said.

'I'm sorry, Miss Packard. I wasn't sure that you wanted to be bothered with it. I've made sure the department hasn't suffered. Staffing sent us a new girl and she's shaping very nicely. Better than Miss Brand ever did, if I might say so.'

'Oh – good. Yes, thank you, Miss Higgs.'

She asked after the various lines and how they were selling, nodded her satisfaction and made a note to make sure some overdue deliveries were pursued. But the mystery of Isobel Brand nagged at her. She was frowning over it as she left the department.

'Is there something wrong?' Hugo asked.

'Yes – that is, there is nothing seriously wrong with the department, just the odd problem, but that's easily dealt with. It's one of my shopgirls I'm concerned about. There's something that just doesn't ring true. Do you mind if we go to Baby Linens? I'm afraid there will be nothing much to interest you there, but I need to speak to someone.'

'I am entirely at your command.'

Daisy Phipps was free when they reached Baby Linens.

Amelie beckoned her over and asked what she knew about Isobel's whereabouts. A wary expression came over Daisy's face. Her eyes flicked from Amelie to Hugo, standing discreetly to one side, and back again.

'She – er – she's found another place, Miss Packard.'

'I know that, Miss Phipps. The question is, whatever made her leave Packards suddenly? She can't have had a character reference, we wouldn't have given one to somebody who walked out like that. What sort of a place is it that she's gone to?'

'It's a – a very good one, Miss Packard, and it come up sudden, like.'

'But doing what, precisely? Miss Brand was living at Trent Street, wasn't she? That was one of the reasons she wanted to work here, because she had nowhere to live.'

Daisy Phipps avoided her eyes.

'It's a living-in job, Miss Packard. A – er – companion, like.'

'So she just left, without a word? I thought better of her, Miss Phipps. I have to say, I feel rather disappointed in her.'

Amelie couldn't understand it at all. Being a companion, presumably to a crotchety old lady, was a horrible job, very badly paid, and probably with hardly any free time.

'I'm sorry, Miss Packard.'

'You cannot be held responsible for her,' Amelie said. But there was something very odd about Daisy Phipps's attitude. 'Are you sure there isn't anything that you haven't told me?'

'She – she wasn't very happy here,' Daisy Phipps said.

'Not happy?'

'No, she wasn't really cut out to be a shopgirl.'

'Are you happy here?'

Immediately, Daisy's face lit up, losing whatever defences she had been putting up before.

'Oh yes, Miss Packard, I love it. Only I'd rather be back at Ladies' Sportswear.'

Amelie smiled. It was nice to know that Daisy was still loyal.

'I would rather you were there as well, Miss Phipps. You were my best shopgirl. I hope I shall be able to do something about it in the future.'

Daisy was delighted. Amelie left, still feeling troubled. There was something there that was not right. She had the distinct impression that she was being lied to all round.

'Have you managed to find out what you wanted to know?' Hugo asked.

'Not entirely,' Amelie admitted.

'Is it important?'

'I suppose not.'

After all, she was not responsible for Isobel Brand. But despite knowing this, she still had the nagging suspicion that somehow she should be involved.

'Have we seen all of Packards now?'

Amelie looked at him, tall and handsome, waiting just for her, and immediately shelved the problem of Isobel Brand.

'I believe we have, but it's taken rather longer than I imagined. It's nearly half-past one.'

Hugo seemed genuinely surprised. 'Is it really? I had no idea.'

'Do you have time to come and meet my grandfather?' Amelie asked anxiously. 'Or have you a luncheon to go to?'

Unattached young men, she well knew, were very much in demand for luncheon parties, which tended to be overloaded with females. Many hostesses issued open invitations to them to call in for the midday meal whenever they cared to.

'My time is entirely yours. I should be honoured to meet Mr Packard.'

Glowing, Amelie led the way up to the top floor and along the corridor to her grandfather's offices. His secretary, as always, was unwilling to let them through.

'Mr Packard is extremely busy today, Miss Packard.'

Amelie turned on her most winning smile. 'Oh come along, Archer, you know that Grandfather is always pleased to see me.'

Amelie was on the point of simply walking past him and into the inner office when Thomas himself emerged.

'Amelie!' He placed his hands on her shoulders and kissed her cheek. 'I was thinking only this morning that it was too long since I last saw my favourite grandchild.'

Amelie could not resist a brief glance at Archer, who was looking deliberately bland.

'You're quite right, Grandfather, it is too long. But now you see I'm trying to make up for it. I've not only come myself, but

I've brought a friend with me. May I introduce Mr Hugo Rutherford?'

The men shook hands, Thomas giving Hugo one of his appraising looks.

'I have just spent a most enjoyable morning touring your store, sir,' Hugo said. 'Your granddaughter appears to have a remarkable grasp of affairs here.'

'She does indeed. Very clever girl, my Amelie. Very sharp. And what did you think of Packards?'

'That it lives up to its claim to provide the best range of goods at the most favourable prices.'

Thomas laughed. 'Very good, young man. You've done your homework, I see.'

'One thing did strike me, sir. There do seem to be a fair number of foreign-made goods on your shelves. Could not all your needs be supplied by British or Empire companies?'

Thomas looked at him with new respect. 'That was well observed. Yes, it concerns me that we have to stock foreign goods. Once upon a time practically every manufactured item in the store was British. That was when we were the workshop of the world.'

Hugo looked surprised. 'Can we no longer lay claim to that title?'

'Not exclusively. The United States and even the Continental countries are beginning to catch up with us now. I regret to say that some of their products are both better and cheaper than ours, and as I aim to stock the best at this store, we are forced to import.'

'Why do you think this is, sir? A lack of ability or enterprise on our part, or laziness, maybe?'

'It's certainly not a lack of ability. Complacency comes into it, though. I think possibly we're so used to leading the world that we cannot believe that anyone else can come anywhere near challenging us. But these are heavy matters to discuss standing in my outer office. I was about to go down to the restaurant for luncheon. Would you both care to join me?'

They sat at the table in the restaurant that Thomas always used, at the top end, where he could observe all that was going on and, when eating alone, eavesdrop on the conversations around him and find out what his customers were saying about his store. The discussion that had started in the office was revived, and the decline of the British workman and the threatened rise of socialism deplored. Amelie had not had her mind so stretched since she had left school. It made a very welcome change from the inane small talk that passed for conversation at most Society events.

'There seems to be an alarming decline in the British race,' Hugo said. 'We rule over the greatest empire the world has ever known and yet there is something wanting at its heart. Your generation, sir, produced great soldiers and explorers and statesmen and men of enterprise like yourself. My own seems somewhat lacking in comparison. I think you were right when you said that complacency has crept in. We are all far too pleased with ourselves, and we don't see that something needs to be done, or we shall no longer be the pre-eminent nation.'

'Perhaps we've had things too easy for too long. There are some people who say that we need a war to shake us all up,' Thomas said. 'Personally, I don't agree. Bad for trade and disastrous for all you young men.'

'It would be the ultimate test, though.'

'What, to get killed?' Amelie cried.

'No, to pit oneself against an armed enemy.'

'Better to stick to sport. You're a sportsman, aren't you?' Thomas asked.

'I aim to be, sir.'

'There you are, then. Test yourself against all those foreigners in that. Far better way to prove who's the superior race.'

When Thomas stood up to leave, he held out his hand to Hugo.

'It's been most interesting talking to you, young man. You must come and visit us at Tatwell. I'll ask my wife to send you an invitation.'

'Thank you, sir. I should be honoured.'

Amelie was walking on air. The two people she loved most in the world liked each other. Things could hardly be better.

33

'I have to tell you, Mother, that it was most embarrassing to send an invitation to the young man only to find that he had already been invited by you.'

'How was I to know that you were set on inviting him? It was your father who asked me to send the invitation.'

'You should have told me. It made me look as if I don't know who is coming to my own house parties.'

'May I remind you that this is not your house yet. Your father has many more years in front of him, God willing, and in the meantime this is my house and my house party.'

Thomas hurried by the open door. The last thing he wanted was to be drawn into yet another disagreement between his wife and his daughter. The whole point of buying Tatwell had been to provide a peaceful retreat from the pressures of business. Instead, it seemed to have provided extra cause for dissention within the family. He trod carefully across the square entrance hall, trying not to make a noise on the rose-veined marble tiles. One thing at least was certain: the place was so big that it was easy to get away from the warring factions. He paused at the front door, which stood open to the warm summer air. He had been on his way to the library, but the sunshine beckoned him. He stepped outside and leant over the balustrade.

Nothing moved under the clear blue sky. The gardeners were all at work out of sight, the houseguests amusing themselves elsewhere. Even the waterfowl on the lake were motionless. Beyond it, the grass of the park was beginning to yellow from the long dry spell, making the foliage of the trees stand out more distinctively green. The peace of the scene wrapped itself around Thomas. All this was his, as far as the eye could see. The boy who had once been chased off the local landowner's grounds by a gamekeeper with a shotgun was now a landowner himself, with gamekeepers jealously guarding deer and pheasant for him night and day. He smiled to himself, acknowledging as he never would to her face that Winifred had been right. Land, that was the key to acceptance. Since he had been master of Tatwell, there had been approaches from both political parties – Thomas did not count Labour as a proper party – and rumours of a knighthood on the next honours list.

The idea of going into politics appealed to him. The lot that were in power at the moment were a lumpen crowd, lacking in imagination. There were exceptions, like Lloyd George and that Churchill fellow, but on the whole Thomas felt that either side would benefit from someone like himself who knew from the inside how to run things efficiently. But even he had to admit that the moment for real greatness had passed. By his age, he should be an elder statesman, not a new boy. If he had been able to leave the shop under the care of sons, it would have been different. He could have entered political life maybe twenty years ago. As it was, he had had to keep his hands firmly on the reins and British politics had had to do without him.

He pushed any regrets away. Pining over what might have been had never been one of his faults. He had this splendid toy to play with and he was enjoying seeing it improve under his care and huge investment. The gardens were emerging from wilderness, the house was now sound and dry, and modern plumbing was being installed. Electricity from their own generator was planned. After that, the redecorating could go ahead. It had afforded him a great deal of amusement to watch Winifred's reaction to his decree that all new furnishings must come from Packards. There was still plenty more to be done, enough to give him an absorbing hobby for his dotage. All he really needed to do was to settle the future control of Packards. He frowned, knowing that never before in his life had he dithered so much over taking a decision. He delayed it once more, by descending the sweep of stone steps and crunching across the gravel.

To the west of the house the ground dropped a little to where the new tennis courts had been laid out in the shade of two magnificent cedars. Here the stillness gave way to life and noise.

'Out!'

'I beg your pardon, but it was not. It hit the line, I saw the chalk!'

'She's right. It did.'

'Oh very well. Fifteen all.'

Two games of mixed doubles were being played, offering a complete contrast in style. On one court Perry and three of the house party guests patted the ball about and laughed a lot. On the other, Edward and Sylvia Forbes faced Amelie and Hugo Rutherford in a match of intense effort and concentration. Four very competitive young people battled for every point, with the added edge for Edward and Amelie of a lifelong rivalry. The veneer of good manners and good sportsmanship expected of them only served to hone the needle-sharp atmosphere.

Thomas sat in a deck chair and helped himself to a glass of lemonade. He knew little about the subtleties of tennis, but even so it did not take him long to realise that Hugo and Amelie were outplaying the others, and that Edward in particular did not like it, however well he was managing to hide the fact. Thomas diplomatically applauded points gained by each side while mentally approving both his grandchildren's choice of partner. If they succeeded in making them partners for life, he would be well pleased. Sylvia Forbes was a reserved sort of girl, certainly. Thomas had never succeeded in getting more than polite conversation out of her. But then Edward was a cold fish as well, and she would make him an ideal wife, managing his home and hostessing his social life with frightening efficiency. Thomas had watched her the evening before as she chatted to the business friends he had invited down for the weekend. She was just as gracious to them as she was to Winifred's Society folk. Yes, she would do very well.

He turned his attention to Hugo Rutherford. Now there was an interesting young man, clever as well as a splendid physical specimen. Thomas watched as he ran to slam a difficult ball back across the net. They made a fine pair, he and Amelie, both of them tall and fair with a glow of good health about them. Hugo seemed genuinely interested in the store, in contrast to Sylvia Forbes, who simply accepted it as the source of family wealth. Thomas wondered if he was interested in politics. Some of the questions he asked and opinions he expressed showed a belief in the need for the nation's improvement. That would be good for Amelie, who needed something to get her teeth into. He wondered how serious the young man was, for it was obvious to him that his granddaughter was head over heels in love.

It was not until tea time that he had the chance to speak to her. Tea was carried down to the lakeside and laid out under a copper beech. Servants dispensed dainty sandwiches, scones and jam and three kinds of cake with either Indian or China tea to house guests, who sprawled elegantly on rugs, deck chairs, chaises longues and hammocks. Thomas chose an upright folding chair and Indian tea. Amelie came to sit beside him on a tartan rug.

'Enjoying the party?' he asked her, though the answer was written clearly on her face.

'Oh yes! This is such a lovely place, isn't it? I have to admit it, Mother was right. It is nice to be able to get out of Town.'

She took a smoked salmon, an egg and a cucumber sandwich from the plates offered to her.

'Mmm, delicious. I'm as hungry as a hunter. We've been playing tennis all afternoon.'

'Did you win?'

'Mostly. But, Grandpa, that wasn't what I wanted to talk to you about. It's about Monsieur Blériot's aeroplane.'

Thomas had been wondering when she was going to bring that up.

'Yes, bit of a blow, that, wasn't it? A Frenchman the first to fly the Channel! I should imagine young Rutherford had a thing or two to say about it,' he said, deliberately sidestepping what he knew to be the real issue.

'Yes, yes, he did. But, Grandfather, that was not what I meant and you know it. Mr Selfridge really stole a march on us. Hundreds, no, thousands of people have been to see the aeroplane at his store. There was a queue there the other day when I went by! That is just what we ought to be doing to attract people into Packards.'

'Perhaps you're right,' Thomas said.

'I know what you're going to say, that they only go to see the aeroplane and don't stay to shop, but –' Amelie broke off as she realised just what he said. 'You mean – you agree with me?'

'To a certain extent, yes.'

Sales had in fact been slightly up in smaller, cheaper goods during the time in which Louis Blériot's famous machine had been on display at Selfridges, but his overhearings in the restaurant had told him why – it had been so crowded in the store that people desperate for a meal or just for a cup of tea had stepped along the road to Packards instead. Once refreshed, they had probably been tempted to make the odd purchase of stationery or stockings or handkerchiefs.

'I think possibly your theory of getting them inside the store on any pretext and trusting to them buying something once they're there might well work with the smaller items,' he admitted. 'It's different with larger or more expensive purchases. People don't buy them on the off chance, but the ground-floor goods they do pick up on impulse.'

'Oh Grandpa! I'm sure you're right. Now what do you think we could do? What do people want to see? It's not every day that someone flies the Channel for the first time. How about some*body* they want to see? Like – like – oh yes! Gaiety girls. Look at the crowd they had round them all the time at Henley. People were pushing and shoving to get a peep at them.'

The thought of a Gaiety girl in his store was a breathtaking idea. They did sometimes come and shop there, and twice he had managed to be on hand when one of the exotic creatures was purchasing gloves or hairpins. They had certainly turned heads and caused excitement once it became known who they were. But to have one on display? Reluctantly, he shook his head.

'No, my dear, it would be too much like a slave market, or a zoo, even supposing I could come to some agreement with the theatre, which I doubt.'

'Oh – well – I suppose so,' Amelie agreed. 'But I'll think of something, don't you worry. It has to be something in the news, so when it comes up, we must move to get in first before Mr Selfridge. And in the meantime –'

She broke off, completely distracted from the conversation that just half a second ago had absorbed her. Thomas followed her gaze. Hugo Rutherford was standing by a hammock in which reclined a lovely dark girl with a languorous smile, the daughter, Thomas recalled, of one of his business friends who had married a South American beauty. They were deep in conversation. Thomas looked at his granddaughter's face. It was blazing with such naked jealousy that he was quite shocked with the force of emotion. He had to protect her.

'In the meantime, how about the windows?' he said.

It took several moments for Amelie to answer.

'The windows?' she repeated stupidly.

'Yes, you've been talking about them ever since you got back from Chicago. Perhaps you'd like to take them on,' Thomas said.

It was, after all, a plan with possibilities. It would annoy Winifred, it would give Amelie something she wanted, it would make the Rutherford boy try harder if she was less available, and it might even work as a commercial move.

'But – you – I –' Amelie floundered, caught between the intensity of her need to break up any connection whatsoever between Hugo and that girl, and her amazement at her grandfather's capitulation. 'You always said –'

'I know what I always said. I've admitted that I might have been wrong in one instance so while I'm about it I'm willing to see whether I might have been wrong in another. So what do you say, my dear? Would you like to be in charge of window decoration?'

'Would I? You know I would! Oh Gramps, I'll make our windows the talk of the town, I promise I will. I've so many ideas I want to try out. I shall need, let me see, probably a couple of assistants, and I shall have to employ a designer. It would be wonderful if we could get someone who's already done window dressing in America, but maybe I could find a stage set designer, in fact that might even be better because they might have more original ideas. How big a budget shall I have to use?'

Thomas had not been thinking in terms of any budget at all. At present, the shop men and girls arranged the windows as part of their everyday duties.

'I haven't done any costings yet,' he said. 'I'll tell you when I have. I think we'll start with just the windows on Oxford Street, for a six-month period, to see how it works.'

'Splendid, that will include Christmas. I'm sure I can produce something really breathtaking for that. And, Grandpa, while you're working out my budget, you won't forget my salary, will you?'

'Your salary?'

'Yes of course. Dressing the windows will be a proper job, so I should be paid a proper salary, just like Edward.'

Thomas laughed so much that he almost spilt his tea.

'My word – you're a chip off the old block and no mistake,' he said, when he could speak. 'Very well, I shall put you on a Scale Five, but it will be pro rata, mind. You must keep a strict note of the hours you work and give it in at the end of each week.'

'Gramps, you're wonderful!' Amelie jumped up and hugged him. 'Oh, I'm so pleased, I must go and tell Hugo.'

Thomas watched her as she hurried over to interrupt the tête-à-tête between her young man and the dark beauty. It was worth it, just to see her happy.

Edward was far from happy when he heard about it. But he had more sense than to complain to Thomas. Instead he congratulated Amelie and told her to let him know if she needed any help. He was just about to go upstairs to dress for dinner when he was accosted by Perry.

'Mel looks happy,' he said.

'Yes,' Edward agreed, knowing just what was coming next. 'But she's not engaged to him yet.'

'I hear she's been given the job of arranging the display windows at the store,' Perry said. 'It's a good thing she's got Rutherford around to distract her, isn't it? Or she might end up getting Grandfather to give her a real job in the store.'

'It's only a toy for her to play with,' Edward said, with more conviction than he felt.

'All the same, if she makes as good a job of it as she has the advertisements and Ladies' Sportswear, you'll have to look out.'

Edward gave his brother a look of contempt. He was so transparent. Why didn't he just come out with it and say what he was offering to do for the money he so obviously needed?

'So what is it that you're going to do to guarantee a ring on her finger?'

318

'I could distract that girl who's making eyes at Rutherford.'

Edward laughed. 'That will be a real trial for you, I'm sure! She's so repulsively plain, isn't she? No, Perry, you'll have to do better than that. She's no real danger, she's on the lookout for an earl at the very least. When Mel and Rutherford become engaged, I might just be soft enough to be touched for a loan, but until then just be glad that I've said nothing to Grandfather about your little adventure with Isobel Brand. You're very lucky I didn't mention it when the girl went missing.'

He left his brother fuming.

If only other members of the family were so easily routed. Amelie he was feeling far less worried about now, despite the latest development. As long as Rutherford came up to scratch, Amelie would be neutralised. Rutherford did not strike him as the sort of man who would want his wife working in a shop. Perry had done a good job there, though Edward had no intention of telling him so. The major problem was still his grandfather. Despite the fact that he was spending quite a lot of time and a vast amount of money on Tatwell, he was showing no signs whatsoever of relinquishing any control over the store. Edward knew what it was he had to do. He had been given a large enough hint, after all. Not so much a hint as a royal command. Between tying his tie and putting on his black jacket, he came to a decision: he would do it this evening.

It was difficult to concentrate on anything else. Throughout dinner, his eyes and his thoughts kept straying back to Sylvia. The doubts that had held him back kept recurring, to be countered by the same well-tried answers. She was too poised, too confident, too utterly English upperclass. But she was excellent wife material. She was not beautiful, not even pretty. But she was pleasant-looking, perfectly groomed and knew exactly how to behave on every occasion. She was totally unlike Isobel, the very thought of whom excited him. But he did not have to give up Isobel. He could have them both.

Several times his dinner partner had to repeat remarks to him, until, seeing who was engrossing his thoughts, she said, 'Sylvia's so clever, isn't she? She always knows just what to say to everyone. Just see how she's charming that boring old banker.'

The perfect hostess.

'Yes, she is,' he agreed.

'And such an attractive girl too. So very English.'

'Absolutely,' Edward said.

'The Forbeses are such pleasant people, too.'

'Yes, they are.'

And poor enough, comparatively, to be glad of their daughter marrying into the wealthy Packard family.

The conversation gave him just the extra impetus he needed. When the gentlemen rejoined the ladies after dinner, he went directly to Sylvia.

'It's a beautiful evening, much too nice to stay indoors. Would you care for a stroll down to the lake?'

She gave him a quick, assessing look.

'Yes, I think that would be very pleasant.'

They slipped out quietly before anyone else could decide that they wanted to join them and make it a general expedition. Outside, it was still light, with a glow lingering in the sky though the trees were beginning to look black, as if the evening had already gathered beneath them. They walked slowly down the slope to where the lake glimmered grey.

'I hope you're enjoying your stay?' Edward asked.

'Oh yes, very much so.'

'The place is more comfortable than the last time you came, I think.'

'It is. Your grandfather seems to have had a vast amount of improvements done in so short a time. The grounds especially are beginning to look cared for now.'

'I'm glad you like it. I especially asked my mother to invite you and your parents.'

'Did you? Thank you, that was most kind.' Sylvia took this calmly.

'I did so because I hoped there would be an opportunity to speak to you alone.'

This time even Sylvia's composure was shaken.

'Oh – really?'

He launched into the speech he had worked out beforehand.

'I know we have not known each other for very long, but it has been quite long enough for me to come to admire and love you greatly, and for some weeks now I have been convinced that you are the one woman who could make me happy in life. Sylvia –' he stood still and took one of her hands in both of his, a gesture he had once seen in a play '– I very much hope that you feel that I could make you happy too, enough to consent to be my wife.'

He had no idea what she felt for him, but he was reasonably sure that she had been hoping for this proposal. She certainly hadn't discouraged him at all. As she stood before him, cool and self-possessed in an ice-blue evening gown, he found himself thinking of Isobel. If he could bring her here . . . the prospect threw up a vision of her running away from him towards the lake, dressed only in a shift.

'Edward –'

With difficulty he dragged himself back to reality.

'I am very honoured and flattered by what you have said –'

For a moment he thought she was going to refuse him, and felt a surge of resentment. After all the time and effort he had put into pursuing her.

'And I would be very happy to be your wife.'

The relief brought a genuine smile to his face.

'My dear Sylvia.' He bent his head to kiss her lips. Now he had done what had been asked of him. His grandfather had better start letting go of the reins.

34

'So what do you think of the news, then?' Daisy asked.

Isobel looked blankly at her. 'What news?' she said.

They were sitting, as usual, in the dining room of the house in Camberwell. Isobel never suggested they sat in the vulgar parlour, and even though it was a pleasant summer's evening with a breath of warmth still in the air, she had vetoed going into the garden. She seemed afraid even to put her nose out of doors.

'Why, about Mr Edward,' Daisy said. 'Surely he's told you?'

Isobel went even paler than she was already. 'Told me what?'

'You mean he hasn't? It's all round the store. It was in the papers. Gertie went and bought *The Times* just so as to see it for herself, and there it was. Engaged to be married, to some society lady. Miss Sylvia Forbes.'

Daisy had expected a reaction, but nothing as dramatic as the one it drew from Isobel. She gave a gasp of horror. Her hands flew to her face. Her terrified eyes gazed into Daisy's.

'Oh my God, what am I going to do? What will happen to me?'

Daisy could not understand her, but then she understood very little about her friend these days.

'What do you mean, happen to you?'

'He'll turn me out, I'll have nowhere to go. Whatever shall I do?'

She began rocking backwards and forwards. Daisy went and put a comforting arm around her.

'Of course he won't. Why ever would he do that?'

'But he's to be married! He won't come here any more.'

'You mean you want him to? I thought you hated him, and what he does to you?' Daisy was mystified.

'Yes, yes, but what else is there? I've nothing –'

That was true, Daisy realised. If Mr Edward were to drop Isobel, she had nowhere to go, and no way of making a living, except to get herself another rich gentleman to look after her, and Daisy could not see Isobel actually setting out to do that. She wouldn't have the faintest idea where to go or what to do in order to find a protector.

'Well, he hasn't turned you out yet, has he?' she pointed out. 'When was he last here?'

'Yesterday, and the day before and – oh this is the first day for a week he hasn't –'

'There you are, then. Sounds like he's more keen than ever, doesn't it?'

'Yes, I suppose so, but once he's actually married he'll have to stop coming.'

'Says who?'

'But –'

'Listen, mate, it's the married ones that go to – er – er – other women the most, believe me,' Daisy told her. She could not quite believe she was having this conversation. Time and time again she had comforted Isobel when she was weeping over the horror of her situation, and now she was reassuring her that it was going to carry on. Eventually, she managed to calm Isobel down with reassurances that if she were to be turned out, Daisy would fix something. Privately, Daisy decided that that would be the point at which she went to Miss Packard for help. It was nearly time for Daisy to go before Isobel asked what else was happening at Packards.

'All much the same as usual,' she said. 'Johnny still hasn't given up hope of finding you.'

'Oh dear,' Isobel sighed. 'Hasn't he?'

'No, and I'm seeing him again Sunday. We're supposed to be going round places over Paddington way. He's very determined, you know, and the longer it goes on, the worse it is lying to him.'

'I know. I do see that. I'm so sorry, Daisy. I don't want you to have to lie for me. But if he were to go to Mr Edward –'

'He'd lose his job,' Daisy concluded for her. This was the only thing that kept her mouth shut on the issue. It cut her to the quick to see him carrying doggedly on with his fruitless search. 'One day soon he'll come to Camberwell. Not that he'll be knocking on front doors, so he won't find you, but it'll be even worse for me, knowing you're only streets away.'

'I know, I'm sorry. I don't know why you keep coming to see me, I'm nothing but a burden to you.'

'Oh rubbish. Just stop talking like that. We been through this before, and you know what the answer is – you're my pal and I love you. Now, I really better go. I'll be late back.'

Isobel went with her to the street door.

'I'll do something to repay you, Daisy, I promise.'

'Just you take care of yourself, that's all I ask.'

Daisy waved goodbye, and worried about her all the way back to Trent Street. The promise she simply dismissed.

But on Saturday when she got back from work, there was a letter waiting for her. Recognising Isobel's writing, she flew to the lavatory and locked herself in. It was the only way to be sure of some privacy. She ripped open the envelope and drew out a single sheet.

My dear Daisy,

I have been thinking long and hard about you and how much you have done for me and have decided that I cannot allow you to go on telling lies on my behalf. So I have written to Mr Miller telling him something of my situation. He will not want to continue searching for me when he knows what I am. I also told him that I saw you for the first time on Wednesday and that you don't know where I live.

I hope this will help both you and Mr Miller.

With all my love,

Your friend,

Isobel.

For a long time, Daisy sat staring at this, reading and rereading it, trying to take in all its implications. At first she could feel nothing but astonishment that Isobel should have taken such a decisive step. Once she had come to terms with that, she was overwhelmed with relief. The secret had been taken away from her. It was like a great weight rolling off her shoulders. Then she wondered just what difference it would make to her friendship with Johnny, and realised that he must even now be reeling from receiving a letter from Isobel. Without further thought, she shoved her own letter into her pocket, unbolted the door and hurried out of the house and down to number fifty-eight, where Johnny lived.

The lad who opened the door grinned when he saw her on the step.

'Well, here's a nice surprise! What can I do for you, darling?'

Daisy told him that she wasn't his darling and that she wanted to see Johnny. The lad winked and went off to fetch him, leaving her standing at the open door. It would be all up and down the street in no time that she had gone running after one of the men, but she did not care. Some things were more important than staying on the right side of the Packards' gossip. Right now, Johnny needed a friend.

But when the messenger came back he was shaking his head.

'Sorry, love, he said he ain't seeing no one. Seemed a bit upset, he did. You two had a spat, have you? Why don't you come out with me tonight? I'll give you a good time.'

'Oh get stuffed!' Daisy told him, and marched off up the street fighting back tears of rejection.

It was a long, long Saturday night. Daisy's new roommate, Gertie, went out, as did most of the other girls, and Daisy was left wondering what effect Isobel's letter was having on Johnny, whether he would turn up tomorrow morning now that he no longer had to search for Isobel, indeed whether he would want to see her at all now that they had no common purpose. If only fate had never sent Isobel to Packards. If she had not come to share her room, everything would have been different. Or so it seemed to Daisy.

She slept very little and woke early and unrefreshed. Gertie was still snoring softly in the other bed. Daisy got dressed quietly and crept downstairs. The kitchen was deserted, as everyone got up late on a Sunday, and as the girls were not allowed to touch the tea or make themselves toast without permission, she went out again, unbolted the front door and let herself out of the house. All was quiet in Trent Street. The milkman had already done his round and filled the two quart cans on the top of the steps leading down to the basement, and now nothing seemed to be stirring except the sparrows chirping in the plane trees.

Daisy stood for a while, breathing in the fresh morning air and wondering just what to do, when a movement further down the road caught her eye. Someone came out of one of the other houses and sat down on the steps. With a great leap of the heart, Daisy knew just who it was. She ran down the street.

At the area railings to number fifty-eight, she stopped, not quite sure what to say. Johnny glanced up. He looked tired and haggard, and he had not shaved. A lump formed in Daisy's throat.

'Hello,' she said, and her voice came out as a croak.

Johnny held out a hand to her. Daisy took it and sat down beside him. Johnny's fingers gripped hers tightly.

'So,' he said. 'You know.'

'Yes,' Daisy said, wondering exactly what Isobel had told him.

'How could she do it, Daisy? How could she? A lovely girl like that!'

'I don't know.'

'You saw her, didn't you? How was she? What did she say?'

'She – she seemed very well. She – er – she never liked it at Packards, you know.'

'I know, I know. She was too good for Packards. I could have taken her away from Packards. I would have married her if she'd've had me. To go and do this, to go and live with some – some bastard for his money. How could she do it?'

'I – er – I'm not sure just what she's told you,' Daisy said.

Johnny fished in his pocket and pulled out a crumpled letter. 'Here,' he said.

Daisy unfolded it.

Dear Mr Miller,

It has come to my notice that you have taken it upon yourself to discover where I am living. I would ask that you cease doing this. I am currently residing with a gentleman of means and have no intention of changing my situation in the foreseeable future, so I do not wish to be sought out by you or anyone else from Packards. I met with Miss Phipps on Wednesday in order to acquaint her with my circumstances. She does not know my address, so I would beg that you do not inconvenience her with requests to reveal it.

Yours faithfully,

I. Brand.

Daisy stumbled a little over the formal language, but the gist of it was clear enough. No wonder he was so bitter. It was a particularly cold letter.

'I see,' she said. 'Oh Johnny, I am sorry –'

'You saw her Wednesday, didn't you? Why didn't you tell me before?'

'I – I didn't know what to say to you. I knew you wouldn't be happy about it –'

'Happy! Bloody hell, Daisy! But how did she contact you? Where did you meet her?'

Daisy had to think fast. If only Isobel had given her the odd clue beforehand, she thought, she could have had her story straight.

'She – she wrote to me, and we met at a tea shop, after work. I – I didn't like to say anything to you till I'd seen her, and anyway she told me not to, and then after – well, like I said, it was difficult to know what to say –'

'Who is this bastard she's living with? What did she say about him?'

'Not – not much. He doesn't actually live with her. He – er – visits. He's very rich, she says.'

'Old bloke, is he?'

'No – er – not very.'

Johnny groaned. 'So he's young and rich. Got bloody everything, and now he's got her. I only hope he appreciates her. Is he good to her, did she say?'

Daisy hesitated, then decided that one more lie was necessary. 'Yes.'

Johnny put his elbows on his knees and rested his head in his hands.

'She never said where she was living? Where he's got her set up?'

At least she was ready for this one.

'No. She doesn't want anyone to know. Not you, and not

327

even me. She wants – she wants to make a new start, away from Packards.'

'A new start! As a – a –'

Daisy could see him mentally surveying all the terms that could describe Isobel's present state. He settled on the least offensive.

'– kept woman?'

'Yes.'

'And is she happy? Does she like it?'

'She doesn't want to leave.'

That was the truth, after a fashion.

'So that's it, then. The end.'

Daisy put a hand on his arm. 'I'm so sorry, Johnny.'

For a while he was silent. Then he said, 'Do you know, when I first got that letter, and I saw who it was from, I thought – well, I thought this was my big chance, you know? That she wanted my help, that I could do something for her. And then I read it, and I just couldn't believe it. Not from her. She was always so – I thought it couldn't be true. But then I saw that she'd told you as well, and now from what you say, I've got to believe it.'

'It is true, Johnny. I wish there was something I could say, but there isn't.'

He put his hand over hers.

'You're a good pal, Daisy. You must be upset as well.'

'Yes.'

They sat side by side on the cold stone step, close, but with the closeness of friends, not lovers. She wanted desperately to lean her head against his shoulder, but knew that it was not the moment. Ahead of them stretched an empty day.

'Well –' Johnny began.

Daisy jumped in to prevent his leaving. 'How about us going out somewhere? Now that –' She broke off, realising how tactless she was being.

'Now that we don't have to search for her, you mean? I'm sorry, Daisy, but I'm not what you might call cheerful company at the moment.'

'That doesn't matter. I understand. And it'd do you good. No use moping about here all day, now is it? You'll only go and get yourself drunk or something.'

'Did that last night,' Johnny admitted. 'Stupid thing to do. Feel like death warmed up this morning.'

'You don't look much better.'

'Thanks.'

'All the more reason to come out. We could go somewhere we've never been. Hampstead Heath. Everyone says as how Hampstead Heath is lovely, and I've never been there. Come on. Say you will.' She held her breath, convinced that if he backed down now, that would be the end.

He hesitated, then agreed. 'All right. I expect you're right. No point hanging round here. I'll go and smarten myself up and I'll come and call for you about ten. That suit you?'

Few things would have suited her better. Daisy scampered back to number twenty-four with wings on her feet.

It was not the jolliest day out Daisy had ever spent. Johnny tried his best not to lapse into gloomy silence, but when he wasn't being quiet, he couldn't help going over the whole business of Isobel several times. Daisy let him talk it out.

When they returned to Trent Street, he walked her up to the door of number twenty-four.

'It's not been much of a day for you,' he said.

'Oh rubbish,' Daisy said, though she had despaired several times of his ever thinking of her as anything other than Isobel's friend.

'No, I've done nothing but go on and on to you. Most girls would've walked off. I – er – well, thanks. It was a good idea.'

Daisy shrugged. ''S all right.'

'No, you were right to make me go out, and I did nothing but bore you. I'll make it up to you. How about – how about a trip to the music hall? How'd you like that?'

All at once the world was full of wonderful possibilities. Daisy turned a glowing face to him.

'Oh yes! That'd be lovely.'

35

The little parish church of St Peter's, Mayfield, Northampton-
shire, was full to the doors. Separated by the central aisle, the
bride's and the groom's families discreetly eyed each other. The
Forbes side represented the backbone of the English gentry. For
centuries they had lived on their own modest estates, passed the
land on in good order from father to eldest son, furnished
younger sons to man the army, the navy and the established
Church and married off their daughters to men just like
themselves. They regarded the Packard side with thinly veiled
distrust. Times were hard indeed when one of their young
women had to marry into Trade. Trade at its most lofty, to be
sure. The Packards to a man and woman were more richly and
fashionably dressed by far than the barons, squires and clergy-
men and their ladies of the Forbes clan, but who were they?
When it came down to it, they were nothing but shopkeepers.
The Amberleys were acceptable. They were the right sort of
people and the groom did bear their name, but that did little to
take away from the fact that these upstarts had pushed
themselves right into the heart of English society. The old order
was changing, and the Forbeses did not like it.

On her side of the church, Winifred was very pleased.
Edward had done well, better than she had expected, given his
prickly attitude. He looked very handsome, sitting in the front
pew with Perry. The Forbes girl was lucky to get him. When
Edward inherited Tatwell Court, Sylvia would be mistress of a
house three times the size of Mayfield Hall, her parents' home.
On top of this, Winifred was happily aware that her own outfit
outshone that of the mother of the bride, that her daughter,
when she walked down the aisle behind Sylvia, would look
much prettier than the rest of the bridesmaids, who were all
Forbes sisters and cousins, and that she would have organised the
whole event in a much more lavish and fashionable manner. If
she could just be certain that Amelie would soon be making as

suitable a match, she would be completely contented with her lot.

In front of her, Perry was already bored with the whole affair. The Forbeses struck him as the very worst type of the stuffy old school, the wedding breakfast promised to be tedious in the extreme and worst of all, Edward did not seem to be at all inclined to be grateful for all the trouble he had gone to playing groomsman. In fact, he had refused point-blank to go to the party Perry had organised.

'But it's all arranged – food, champagne, girls. You should see the girls, Edward! Real high-class stuff, actresses, not common tarts. You'll have the time of your life. Got to have your last fling before you put on the chains, now haven't you? Get in a bit of practice for the wedding night, eh?'

'I don't need you to organise that for me,' Edward had told him.

So Perry invited some of his friends instead and a very good time was had by all, but it had made his precarious finances even worse than they were before, with as little prospect as ever of a loan from Edward. He was going to have to get himself an invitation to a country house as far away from London as possible and lie low for a bit. In fact, if things didn't improve fairly soon, he was going to have to seriously look about for a rich girl and get married himself. Perhaps an American girl. They were all dripping with money. He suddenly sat up straighter. That was it. He would get Amelie to write him a letter of introduction to those friends of hers that she stayed with in Chicago, borrow the fare from someone and try his luck in the States.

There was a stir at the back of the church. The organist, who had been playing a selection from Bach, sounded the first chords of the 'Bridal March'. The congregation rose. Edward and Perry stepped forward. Sylvia walked up the aisle on her father's arm dressed in white satin and swansdown with a full-length veil and long train, followed by six bridesmaids of various sizes wearing pink silk and organdie and carrying posies of hothouse rosebuds. As she reached the front of the church, Sylvia gave Edward a small smile. The Rector stood, holding his prayer book.

'Dearly beloved –'

Edward took his bride's hand from Sir Alfred with a sense of triumph. He had been accepted on his own terms by Society. The boys who had taunted him at school had been vanquished. He was marrying just the sort of girl they would aspire to, and in doing so, he was getting closer to achieving what he wanted.

He went through the form of the service, his mind detached from the solemn words that rolled round him. He did not need to be told why God had ordained marriage, for he had his own reasons. He spoke the vows in a clear and firm voice, not quite meeting Sylvia's eyes, a feat more easily achieved because of the veil clouding her face. During the prayers his mind began seriously to wander, and doubts crept in. After the wedding, they were to honeymoon for three weeks in Switzerland, stopping en route for a few days in Paris. Three weeks of Sylvia's exclusive company. Three weeks away from Isobel and the intoxicating absolute power he held over her. On the night that Perry had arranged his bachelor party, Edward had taken Isobel to the store. It was a treat he had been promising himself for a long time, and now seemed just the occasion to fulfil it. She stood by his side as he unlocked one of the side doors, almost whimpering with fear.

'Oh please don't – not here – what if someone should find us?'

It was that element of risk that appealed to him, taking the pleasure to a new and delicious height. The night watchmen would be patrolling the store. He would have to avoid and outwit them. By the light of a camping lamp, they passed through the ground-floor departments. Edward kept his arm round Isobel's waist. He could feel her shaking with the terror of discovery. In the main lobby he hesitated, looking up at the moonlight flooding through the great dome. The store was a beautiful and mysterious place at night. The lifts with their bronze fretted doors beckoned him. He considered for a minute or so the prospect of taking her while riding up and down in a lift, but though the thought of it roused him almost unbearably, that was taking risk to foolhardy proportions. Besides, he had an even more exciting plan. He guided her up the stairs, prolonging the pleasure of anticipation by touring round each of the floors. New settings tempted him at every turn – the fitting rooms in Ladies' Gowns, the restaurant, his sister's cursed sportswear department, the piles of oriental carpets. He resisted each one of them, using them only to tease Isobel. The threat of having to do it in her old department particularly upset her, very nearly deflecting him from his object, but he rejected it. Another time, perhaps. He had something better in mind.

They were passing through Furniture when he heard the tread of heavy footsteps. Beside him, Isobel gasped. He blew out the lamp and pulled her into the gap between two bookcases, his hand over her mouth. She was shaking so much that she could hardly stand. He had to hold her up, pressing her tightly to him as he did so, so that she could feel how much he wanted her. The night watchman walked slowly by, swinging his lamp from side to side as he went. The light glanced off the glass front of one of the bookcases, then passed on. Isobel went limp in his arms.

'That was a close one, wasn't it?' he said in her ear. 'Don't you find this exciting? It's as good as a *Boy's Own* adventure.'

He waited until the man was out of earshot, then headed for the stairs again. On the fifth floor he walked with confidence along the dark corridors. There was nothing to bump into here and he knew every inch of the way.

'Can you guess where we're going?' he asked Isobel, as they approached his office.

'Yes,' she whispered.

'Well, you're wrong. We're aiming higher than that.'

He walked right to the end of the corridor, took out his pass key and let himself into his grandfather's office. Enjoying Isobel's renewed expressions of horror, he went through Archer's domain and into the inner sanctum. There across the thick carpet, bathed in moonlight, was his grandfather's desk.

It was quite simply the best ever. They did it on the desk, in his grandfather's chair, then on the desk again. He felt like a god. Nothing now was beyond his reach . . .

He came back to the present to find his participation was required in the ceremony. He went through it all with a decorum that was noted and approved by both his own and his bride's family, and finally emerged from the vestry with Sylvia on his arm, a married man. He caught his grandfather's eye as they walked down the aisle, saw him nod and smile his approbation, and knew that he would now achieve his every ambition. It had all been worth while.

As she followed her brother and her new sister-in-law down the aisle, Amelie had eyes for only one person in the church: Hugo. They exchanged smiles. Amelie tried to contain her impatience. This was Sylvia's day. She still had her duties as a bridesmaid to perform. They all emerged into the damp November day. Photographs were taken, kisses and congratulations were given, rice and flowers were thrown, and the bridal couple stepped into the Packard Rolls-Royce for the short journey to Mayfield Hall. Then there were countless new relations-by-marriage to be introduced to and to be nice to. This was particularly hard work since those who wanted to speak to her all seemed to be either leering old men or stupid young ones. She was relieved when the wedding breakfast was announced. The bridesmaids were all seated together, a clump of pink organdie interspaced with suitable young men, which meant that she had a Forbes cousin on each side. Amelie looked down the long tables to try to locate Hugo, and saw the back of his head. He appeared to be in animated conversation with his neighbour, of whom Amelie could only see an elaborate hairstyle. It made her quite sick with jealousy. The meal seemed to go on for ever, course following course and all washed down with champagne that she did not dare drink too much of. For any lady to be tipsy was very bad form, for an unmarried girl to be so was disastrous. There were toasts and speeches – mostly too long, but Edward's was short and witty – and then the cake was cut, and at last they were all allowed to get up.

'Would you care for a turn around the garden?' one of the Forbes cousins asked Amelie.

'Thank you, but there's someone I have to speak to,' she said, oblivious of his hopeful expression and too eager to escape to think up any more tactful excuse.

She had hardly got halfway across the room, though, when she was waylaid by her mother.

'Where are you running off to, Amelie? Come and talk to your grandmother and grandfather Amberley.'

Fuming, Amelie did as she was told.

'You're looking very pretty today,' her grandfather said.

'Yes, quite the best of the bridesmaids. In fact I think I may safely say that our side is definitely blessed with the handsomest looks. The bride's a nice little thing, though,' her grandmother conceded. 'Now, when are we going to see you married? Two seasons now and still not engaged. I can't think what you're about.' Grandmother Amberley was nothing if not forthright.

'I'm waiting for the right man,' Amelie told her, looking over her shoulder to find just where he had got to. She couldn't see him anywhere.

'Quite right too,' her grandfather agreed. 'No need to be in too much of a hurry.'

'If she leaves it much longer she'll be on the shelf. Look what happened to the Gregson girls. Still single, all four of them. Their mother's at her wits' end, poor woman. She's trailed them through seven seasons. Seven! Your mother won't be wanting to do that, Amelie.'

Miraculously, Hugo appeared at her side. A big joyful smile spread itself irresistibly across Amelie's face. She ached to hold onto his arm with both hands, to reach up and kiss his cheek. Instead, she introduced him, noting the quick assessing look he got from both grandparents.

'I'm delighted to make your acquaintance. I have had the pleasure of meeting Miss Amberley's Packard relations, and now I hope I shall get to know the other half of her family. Charming wedding, don't you think?'

Hugo stayed chatting with them long enough for their expressions to turn from suspicion to approval. Then he got Amelie away from them by saying that he had promised some people that he would introduce her to them.

'The trouble with weddings is that they're full of relations,' he said. 'Is there anyone else I ought to meet?'

'There are some Amberley aunts and cousins, but they're amazingly boring,' Amelie said. Then as she spotted some of them looking her way, 'Quick! Let's go in here and avoid them.'

They escaped into the next room. Guests were spreading all over the house now, busily discussing the food, the wedding

335

service, the new relations-by-marriage and most of all, though indirectly, whether the bride or the groom had got the better of the deal. Opinion on this, naturally, divided sharply according to which of them the speaker was related to. Hugo ran an eye over them all.

'Do you especially want to talk to anyone?' he asked.

'Not at all,' Amelie said.

The only person she wanted to talk to was him.

'Good. Would you like to come and walk round the garden?'

There was nothing Amelie would rather do. They found a side door and let themselves out.

Amelie drew in a large breath of damp air and let it out in a sigh of relief.

'Thank goodness! If I have to be polite to one more person, I think I shall scream.'

'And if I have to share you with one more person, I might do the same,' Hugo said. He drew her hand through his arm and set off along a gravelled path. 'It was very distracting having to look at your back all through the wedding service. I wonder you didn't feel my eyes on you. I was trying to make you turn round.'

A hot thrill of pleasure ran through Amelie. She tried to keep her voice light and teasing.

'You're supposed to look at the bride, not the bridesmaids. Sylvia did look pretty, didn't she?'

'Not as pretty as you.'

Amelie had had enough of being told how pretty she looked from everyone else she had spoken to. Now that she had Hugo to herself, she wanted to be able to talk on a different level.

'Strange to think she's my sister now. Edward's wife. I hope they'll be happy.'

'You sound as if you're not too certain about it.'

'Well – I think they're very well suited, so I suppose they will be, in their own way.'

'Then surely that is a good basis for marriage?'

Amelie felt oddly breathless. She had wanted a deeper conversation, she had chosen the subject herself, and found it pitted with possible hidden implications.

'I – suppose it is, on the surface. But that wasn't the only reason for their marrying.'

'Money, you mean?' Hugo said.

'Yes.'

Now that he had been so open about it, she could be.

'Money and breeding. Edward has the one, or will do, and Sylvia has the other. It's a trade. It's horrible.'

All that she had disliked about her two Seasons welled up and overflowed.

'That's what it's all about, isn't it? All this business of presentations and balls and dinners and so on. It's so hypocritical. All those strict rules about calling and invitations and exactly what to wear and where to go, who to be seen with, all so terribly formal and correct, when what the mothers are doing is parading their daughters like – like a slave market. I wonder they don't put out notices. "Nice-looking girl, related to two baronets and a viscount, thirty thousand pounds dowry, only eldest sons need apply." I hate it.'

'So what do you think should replace it?'

'I don't know. I just hate all this business about money and families. I think people should get married because they love each other.'

'Even though they might be totally unsuited to each other? An attraction of opposites?'

'At least that would be better than all this cold-blooded trading,' Amelie said. Then, wakening to the fact that this was a very one-sided exchange, 'What do you think? You haven't said anything yet. Do you think I should have married Georgy Teignmereton, because he belongs to an ancient and titled family?'

They had reached a small shrubbery with gravel paths winding between dripping bushes. Hugo stopped by a stone bench beneath a glossy camellia.

'I think,' he said, turning to face her, 'I think you ought to marry me, because I love you.'

For a long moment, Amelie could only gaze at him, not quite believing her ears.

'Well?' he prompted.

A glow of joy started somewhere inside her and spread through her whole body.

'Yes,' she said. 'I think you're right.'

36

Sometimes, when it was all over, he became quite pleasant. It was as if whatever he had done to her had drained the cruelty out of him. He would talk, then, about the store or about his family, and not expect anything but noises of agreement from her. She was able to lie still and set her mind on the fact that it was finished for the time being and soon he would be gone.

It was not so easy when they were in the huge draped bed, because of the mirrors. Isobel hated the mirrors. They made it impossible to distance herself from what was going on, for how could she believe that it was not happening to her when she could see herself doing all these vile things? Closing her eyes was no use, for he knew how much she loathed it and made her look. They were lying in the bed now. She tried to unfocus her eyes, to look through or past the naked bodies on the crumpled sheets, or failing that to look just at her feet. But her eyes were continually drawn to the movement of his hand as it ran lazily over her. It made her fearful when he started to do that, for sometimes it meant that he would start all over again, or worse still, demand that she do things to him. Then a name jumped out from what he was saying and her mind was mercifully distracted from watching her own shame to listening to him.

'– Perry's latest idea. He really is a lazy little toad. Wants it all handed to him on a plate without ever lifting a finger to help himself. He always has been like that. Never made an effort in his life. When he was a child he would just charm Mother rather than do anything like learning his lessons to please her. It's the same now. He expects to live off Packards' money without doing a thing to earn it. Not that I want him in the store. He'd be nothing but a nuisance. That is something one can say for him, at least he doesn't try to muscle in on my territory. It was bad enough having Mel pushing her nose in there. Now she really was a danger. She's got brains, one has to admit, and a good business sense. That idea for Ladies'

Sportswear was a damned good one, I saw that from the start. That's why I had to move quickly to try to stop it before it took hold. I encouraged Mother to forbid it, but Grandfather overrode her. I could see she was really keen on it. I could see that it was going to be a success. If Mel gets her teeth into something, she doesn't let go. So I arranged for a nice little water leak. Christ! You should have seen her on that first morning. But she got round it, damn her. When I tried cancelling her orders, she went traipsing off to the darkest East End to see to it herself. And when I tried sacking her staff or transferring them to other departments she just had them reinstated or trained others up – but of course, you know that, don't you?'

Edward broke off, turning over and propping himself up on one elbow so that he could look into her face.

'It was sacking you that first brought you to my notice. How very foolish of me to have wanted to get rid of you. That is one contest I'm glad that Mel won. Won temporarily, that is, because I got you out of the store in the end. But do you know who really made me appreciate your possibilities? Perry.'

She could not prevent a slight gasp. His boasting about trying to sabotage his sister's department hardly touched her, for she felt totally divorced from that old life now, but Perry's name still had the power to wound.

'Yes, he spoke about you at Henley, the summer before last. But you see, once I wanted you, he didn't have a chance. I always get what I want, eventually. I wanted Mel out of the way, and now she's being taken on very competently by this Rutherford chap. She thinks she's still going to keep an interest in the store, but that's hardly likely once she's got a household of her own to run and starts producing little Rutherfords. So that's her disposed of. Then I wanted a suitable wife, and I got her. And most of all I want the store, and now it looks as if I'm going to get that at last. Grandfather's got his knighthood and he's being approached by no end of bodies to sit on their boards. He won't be able to resist it. He knows I can do the job. He'll move over now, and especially since I'm going to give him an heir. You never know with the old boy, but I think I shall be behind his desk by summer. Remember that desk? We christened it well and truly, didn't we? I think we'll repeat the experience when it belongs to me.'

Isobel remembered that evening all right, it stood out as a particularly bad memory amongst all the other horrors and humiliations.

'An heir?' she said, to distract him.

'Yes. My wife's expecting. It's made her very difficult, but it's worth it to see the old man's reaction. He was delighted. You mind you don't get pregnant. I don't like difficult women. I like women who do exactly as they're told. You know that, don't you?'

'Yes,' Isobel whispered.

'Good.'

He gave her breast a squeeze, making her wince with pain.

'Just remember that, and I'll have no cause for complaint.'

Edward rolled over, got out of bed and started dressing. Isobel felt sick with relief. He was going. As he was tying his tie he stopped and looked down at her, an expression on his face that filled her with alarm.

'I shall have to find a way of getting you into the house one day. It would make my nights with her immeasurably more interesting knowing I'd had you in the same bed.'

She was quite unable to hide the utter revulsion she felt. He smiled.

'Yes, imaginative idea, isn't it? That will give you something to think about till I come again. No, don't get up. I shall picture you lying there just as you are, waiting for me to return. *Au revoir.*'

Isobel listened for the front door closing after him, then waited another five minutes just to be sure. When she was certain she was safe, she crawled out of bed, put on one of the flimsy négligée Edward had bought for her and went downstairs. Her fingers shaking, she poured herself a small brandy from the decanter. She dared not take too much, in case he noticed. Just a little, to help her to sleep. Then she went and curled up on the couch in the dressing room, trying not to dwell on all that he had said and done that evening. There was very little she could rest her mind on amongst the miseries of her existence, but she did have the prospect of a visit from Daisy to

341

look forward to. At least he had never found out about those. Without Daisy, she could not have gone on.

When Daisy did arrive, she was in a combative mood.

'You ought to start making a few demands,' she said. 'You must have some power over him. Getting married hasn't changed him, has it? He still comes just as often. It's been months now and he hasn't cooled off. He must be really stuck on you. You could get anything you wanted off of him if you went about it the right way.'

The very idea turned Isobel's insides to water.

'Oh, I couldn't,' she said.

'Why ever not? Mistresses are supposed to do that. You got to look after your own interests, Iz. Get him to give you some things. Jewellery and that. You want to line your nest a bit.'

'I couldn't,' Isobel repeated. 'He wouldn't like it. He doesn't like difficult women.'

'Well at least get him to take you out a bit. You never see the outside of these walls, you don't. It's like you're in one of those harem places.' She pronounced it 'hairum'.

Isobel thought of the times he had taken her out, and shuddered.

'Oh no. At least I'm safe in here. Nobody sees.'

'Yeah, and you don't see nobody. It can't be good for you. It's so lonely.'

Tears gathered in Isobel's eyes. 'Yes,' she agreed.

'There you are, then. Get him to take you to the theatre or something, or just for a drive round in that motor of his.'

'I'll see,' Isobel said.

Daisy snorted. 'Yeah, we all know what that means, it means you won't do nothing about it.'

'How is life in Baby Linens?' Isobel asked.

Daisy allowed herself to be sidetracked for the time being.

'Very busy. Everybody seems to be having babies.'

Unwanted, Edward's words of the previous day came back to Isobel. *My wife's expecting.* His wife must think she was safe and loved, with her new husband and now a baby on the way, and yet all the time she was being deceived. What was rightfully hers was being tarnished. Isobel was swamped with guilt.

'Yes,' she managed to say.

Fortunately, Daisy was well away talking about the latest Packards' news. She went into details about the new lines they had to sell to all those proud expectant parents, then about the latest tensions amongst the staff.

'. . . she does her damnedest to beat me, but she never does. She's too eager, you see. It's one thing persuading them to buy, it's quite another trying to make them. She, like, hits 'em over the head. They don't like it. But it doesn't do her any good, 'cause my figures are still better than hers. Sir Thomas himself congratulated me the other day.'

Daisy paused, obviously expecting an answer.

'Really?' Isobel said. 'Sir Thomas?'

'Yes. He stopped on his round and he spoke to me personal, in front of everyone. Said as I was a credit to the store. That Vi was so jealous she didn't know what to do with herself. Been making nasty remarks ever since, she has, but I don't care. She can go boil her head. Sir Thomas. Sounds ever so important, doesn't it? We're all ever so proud of him. That lot down at Selfridges, they haven't got a Sir for a boss. That Mr Selfridge is nothing but a jumped-up American for all he gives all those big parties you read about in the papers. Anyway, we'll be reading about our Miss Packard soon, with her getting married. The dressmakers up in Ladies' Gowns are trying to make a big secret out of what the wedding gown is going to be, but you know what the store is like. We already know it's wild silk with pearls. She'll look so beautiful, I know she will, and that Mr Rutherford is ever so handsome. He's been round the store, you know. I saw him. They make a lovely couple.'

'Yes,' Isobel said.

How easy things were for some people. Miss Packard just sailed through life. She had a loving family, she was presented at court and did the Season, she got her own way about working in the store, and now she was to marry the man she loved. But then all the Packards seemed to be touched with the ability to get just what they wanted. They were a charmed race. Isobel did not want to talk about them any more. The contrast with her own situation was too painful.

'How is Johnny?' she asked.

'Oh, he's very well, thanks.'

'You're still walking out together?'

'Yes.'

This was one of the few satisfactions of Isobel's life. Daisy deserved to be happy. She was a good and stalwart friend. If Daisy was happy, Isobel felt the reflection of it. She looked at her now, and noticed a self-conscious flush about her cheeks.

'What is it? What's happened? Something nice?' she asked.

'Well –' a big smile spread itself over Daisy's face. 'He's taking me to meet his family. I'm going to Sunday dinner with them.'

'Oh Daisy!' For the first time in weeks Isobel felt something near to pleasure.

'I'm ever so nervous, Iz. What do you think I ought to wear? I bought this nice new blouse, with a high neck and ruffles and I'm going to tie a bit of velvet ribbon round the neck to make a bow. And I was wondering if I should buy a new hat and all. They got lovely ones down in Millinery. Felt, you know, but I could buy some of those bunches of artificial cherries to put on it. Do you think that'd look nice?'

'I think it would look very – bright and cheerful. Like you,' Isobel said.

'Do you? I'll get one then. Oh Iz, do you think they'll like me? What if they think I'm common?'

She was common, if you counted things like taste and manners and accent and family. Dearest Mama would have disliked everything about her, most especially her forthright views and chirpy confidence. And dearest Mama, Isobel realised with a jolt, would have been totally wrong. Daisy was not in the least common. She was a rare and precious person. Isobel reached out and took both of her hands in hers.

'Don't ever change, Daisy. Not for them, not for anyone.'

Daisy looked bewildered. 'But I have changed. Packards has changed me, and so have you. When I first came to Packards I didn't know n– anything. I was just an ignorant little girl from the East End. Now I can do all sorts of things, and I been to different places – that's because of Johnny – and I know what to do and how to talk properly and all that sort of thing. If you hadn't told me about eating nice and so on, I wouldn't never have dared go to Johnny's place.' She paused, frowning. 'Wouldn't never isn't right, is it?'

Isobel's throat was very tight. Praise so rarely came her way. To think that she had actually been useful to someone, had done some good, was overwhelming.

'It doesn't matter,' she said.

'But it does matter. The moment you open your mouth, people judge you. I tell you, Iz, I don't ever want to go back to the East End. I don't want to live like my mum and my sisters do. And talking right is one of the ways to get on.'

'Oh, you'll get on, Daisy, I'm sure you will,' Isobel said.

But in her heart she wondered. It was the big people who controlled the world, the Packards, not the Daisys and the Johnnys.

'Oh thanks, Iz. But look, can you just remind me a bit, like? Go over it, so as I'm sure?'

So Isobel coached her for a while on shaking hands, sitting down gracefully, using the right cutlery and asking for embarrassing things the polite way.

'Try not to worry about it,' she advised. 'Bear it in mind, but don't let it make you a different person. I'm sure they'll like you.'

After all, they were only small shopkeepers and craftsmen. And if they didn't like Daisy, they didn't deserve her.

'I do hope so. It's so important to me, Izzy. I feel worse than when I went for the job at Packards. But I've been leading on all about me. What about you? You don't look well. You ought to go out, like I said earlier. If you won't get Him to take you, then just go for a walk. It's lovely in the parks, all daffodils and that everywhere, and blossom on the trees. You ought to go for a walk every day. Do you good.'

And because she could not possibly explain just how unattainable that simple pleasure was, Isobel just agreed. She could not express her horror of going out of the front door and walking down the street, of passing the people she saw each day outside the window and seeing their eyes slide away from her in disgust. For they knew, all of them, what she was. Sometimes she saw them when they were talking together, their shopping baskets over their arms, saw them glance towards her house and incline their heads a little closer together, lowering their voices no doubt as they condemned her and the way she lived. At home, in the golden days that now seemed so far away as to have happened to someone else, she had enjoyed going for a daily walk. Now, like everything else that was innocent and uncomplicated, it was quite beyond her reach.

'I'll say something, though. You have put on weight. Shows round your face,' Daisy was saying. 'You eating a bit better now? I was afraid you were going to fade away.'

The thought glowed in front of Isobel for a moment or two. To fade away. That must surely be the answer.

'No,' she said. 'I'm hardly eating at all, really. Especially in the mornings. I feel so sick that I cannot even look at food.'

It was just one more problem, and she had not thought much about it. But Daisy was staring at her, her mouth slightly open and her eyes round with horror.

'You got morning sickness? Every morning, not just once in a while?'

'Yes,' Isobel said, puzzled.

'What else? You feel faint at all?'

'Well – yes,' Isobel admitted. But who would not feel faint, having to do all the things she was required to do?

'And how about your – your –' Daisy was casting about for a delicate way to put it '– bust? Does it feel tender?'

'Yes, very, but –'

'Oh my God!' Daisy clenched her fists and made an anguished face.

Isobel looked at her in bewilderment, a faint but clear presentiment of doom starting deep inside her.

'What –' she started.

Daisy interrupted her. 'When did you last have your monthlies?'

'Well –' Isobel cast her mind back. It was difficult to remember, as there were few landmarks in her life to hook events on to. She'd not had one in the last two or three weeks. She'd had one at Christmas. She remembered that because it made her even more miserable than she would have been anyway. And yes, she had had one in January. Her mind veered away from what He had done to her at that time. But not since then.

'Oh my God!' Daisy repeated. 'Izzy, you do know what this means, don't you?'

'No,' Isobel admitted. But the feeling of doom was getting very strong.

'Izzy, didn't no one ever tell you about your own insides? Your mum, or your sister?'

Isobel shook her head. Daisy cast her eyes up to the ceiling.

'Iz, your're pregnant. You're having a baby.'

Isobel could not believe her. It was too far-fetched for words.

'But – I'm not married,' she said.

'Married! Married's got nothing to do with it. It's what you and Mr flaming Edward have been doing what's done it.'

There was a ringing in her ears. Daisy seemed to be a long way away. She was speaking, but Isobel did not hear what she said. The realisation of disaster came at her with all the force and speed of an express train. It was far worse than when she learnt he was getting married. He had specifically told her not to get pregnant. This time she really would be thrown out on the streets.

'Oh no,' she whispered. 'What am I going to do? What am I going to do?'

She hugged herself, rocking backwards and forwards in her seat. This was the end.

From somewhere, from a different life, a voice came through to her. A familiar voice. Daisy's.

'– money. And it's not nice. But it can be done.'

Isobel clutched at her friend, holding her fiercely round the waist.

'Daisy, I'll be turned out –'

'No, no, you won't. That's what I'm saying. There are ways to get rid of it, but you'll have to get hold of some money.'

She heard the words but they made no sense.

'Get rid of what?'

'The baby. There are people who will do it for you.'

It was some time before she could begin to grasp what Daisy was saying.

'You mean – there are people who will kill babies?'

'Well –' Daisy sounded uncomfortable. 'If you put it like that – yes.'

'What, take little babies and murder them?'

'No, not like that. Before they're born. While they're still inside you. Like now. You go to one of these people and – and – it's like you have a miscarriage.'

'A miscarriage?'

'Yes, like when you lose the baby before it's born. When it comes out before it's due and dies. Don't you know about that? It happens all the time. My mum's always having them.'

Isobel was groping through a fog of ignorance and fear. Babies were happy events that happened to married ladies. Pregnancy, miscarriages and the working of the female body were not things spoken about in front of unmarried girls. If it did happen all the time, then she had never known about it.

Daisy tried to explain. Isobel listened with growing horror. In the end she put her hands over her ears and begged her to stop. The time for Daisy to go was fast approaching.

'Look, Izzy, think about it, and try to think of a way to get some money. I'll come back as soon as I can, and if you want me to I'll try and get you fixed up.'

For once, Isobel wanted her out of the house.

When she had gone, she stood in the hall, looking down at her stomach. Then she put her hands on it. It didn't feel any different. Yet inside there, if what Daisy said was true, a baby was growing. But it couldn't be true. Of course it wasn't. It couldn't happen. She absolutely refused to believe it.

37

It all went like a fairy tale. Even the weather smiled on them. After a week of March gales and driving rain the sun came out, the wind dropped and the temperature rose to a pleasant warmth. Amelie was brimming with happiness as she was driven to the Tatwell parish church with her father at her side. Her only care was to prevent the delicate silk of her dress from being crushed. No doubts or fears troubled her. She was going to marry the man she loved. Seeing him waiting for her at the chancel steps only confirmed it. He was the most wonderful man in the world, and soon he would be her husband. He smiled at her reassuringly as they took their place together, but she needed no boost to her confidence. She knew she was doing the right thing.

The solemn vows affected her deeply. She had often been to weddings before, but attending, or even being a bridesmaid, was quite different from being married herself. Each promise she felt in her heart, and made with total commitment.

And then all too soon it was over, and she was walking down the aisle holding Hugo's arm with her veil thrown back, smiling at all the happy faces of well-wishers. Outside, the bells were ringing and local people were gathered to watch the free show. The wedding guests flooded out to offer congratulations. They posed for the photographer – especially brought down from London by Winifred – and passed through a snowstorm of petals and rice to step into the Packard Rolls which was decorated for the occasion with ribbons and flowers. The door was closed, everyone waved, the motor pulled away, and for the first time that day they were alone together. They turned to look at each other.

'Hello, Mrs Rutherford,' Hugo said.

'Mrs Rutherford,' Amelie repeated, smiling. 'It sounds very well. I think I'm going to like it.'

'No second thoughts, then?'

'None at all.'

Of one accord, they moved together, their lips meeting, their arms sliding round each other. Amelie drowned in the slow passion of his kiss, melting to the demand of his lips and tongue, responding with fervour. Breathless, they drew apart just a little, to look into each other's eyes.

'I wish we didn't have to go back to the house. I want to go away with you right now,' Amelie said.

'So do I, but you'd look a little silly on the train in that beautiful dress.'

Amelie giggled. 'It would make people's heads turn.'

They drove in at the gates, the lodge keeper and his wife bowing as they passed, their children cheering and waving.

'Kiss me one more time before we have to face the hordes,' Hugo said.

Amelie readily complied.

They just managed to straighten themselves up before the motor drew up on the gravel forecourt. All the servants were lined up to greet them under the strict eyes of the butler and housekeeper. Proper and correct now, Hugo got out and helped Amelie, and the two of them ascended the steps arm in arm past bowing footmen and curtsying maids, and went in to the great entrance hall. Winifred's personal maid fussed about repairing the damage to Amelie's hair and dress and veil caused by the brief journey from the church, and then before they had time to draw breath the servants had scuttled back inside to take their places, both sets of parents and the bridesmaids arrived and the receiving of guests began.

Amelie went through her public duties in a dream. Fortunately, her role was not a very demanding one. The bride was only required to look radiant, speak to as many people as possible and keep smiling. She managed all three with ease. Around her, guests enjoyed criticising the food, the display of wedding gifts, the newly decorated rooms and each other, but all agreed that the bride looked beautiful and that she and the groom made an extremely handsome couple, a fact made more touching by their being so clearly in love.

Towards the end of the afternoon, Winifred suggested that Amelie should now go upstairs and change. Rarely had she obeyed her mother so willingly. The bridesmaids — Amberley cousins and Hugo's three sisters — came with her and sat about in their layers of apricot silk and chiffon gossiping about the guests and giving Amelie advice while Winifred's maid got her out of the wedding dress and into a *Directoire*-style tailor-made of finest dark green wool and fancy braiding with a cutaway jacket and lace jabot.

'How do I look? Will Hugo like it, do you think?' Amelie asked, turning round for their benefit.

'It's simply deevy, Melly. Hugo will adore you in it.'

'Hugo adores her anyway. He talks about her almost as much as he talks about rugger.'

'Or even cricket.'

'He's certainly one of the catches of the year,' one of the Amberley cousins said. 'How did you do it, Mel?'

'What our brother, a catch? We Rutherfords have hardly a penny to bless ourselves with.'

'Oh come now, stop exaggerating!'

'Well, we're certainly hoping to benefit from his marrying into you Packards. Now, Amelie, promise us that you and Hugo will give lots of parties and invite us and plenty of eligible young men.'

'I'll do my best,' Amelie agreed.

The maid opened a huge hatbox and took out a large-crowned creation of green and russet watered silk trimmed with self-coloured rosettes. She settled it on top of Amelie's piled-up hair and fixed it into place with two foot-long hatpins. The assembled young women declared their approval.

'It's utterly darling. So elegant!'

'Will I pass, do you think?'

'With full marks.'

Amelie pulled on the matching kid gloves, pausing to look at her shining new ring. The bridesmaids all kissed her and wished her luck.

'I'm sure you'll both be very happy,' one of Hugo's sisters said.

'Yes. Don't take any notice of his funny ideas,' another told her. 'It's just his way.'

'Ideas?' Amelie echoed.

'Yes, all this nonsense about eugenics. It's not really important.'

Before she could find out more, Winifred came in.

'Are you ready, my dear? Oh yes – you look charming, quite charming.' She advanced across the room, her arms outstretched, took Amelie by the shoulders. For just a moment, there was a real mother's concern in her face. 'Take care, my dear. I hope everything goes well for you.'

She kissed Amelie on the cheek, looked for a moment into her eyes, then snapped back into her usual role.

'Well, come along. Your luggage has all been loaded and everyone is waiting to see you,' she said, and went off, with the bridesmaids, to join Bertie in the hall.

Hugo was waiting for Amelie on the landing.

'You look wonderful,' he said.

'So do you,' Amelie couldn't resist answering.

She took Hugo's arm and descended the stairs to where a sea of upturned faces was gathered in the entrance hall. Cheeks were kissed, hands were shaken, wishes for luck and happiness expressed, and finally they were able to leave the carnival behind them.

'At last,' Hugo said, sinking back in the leather upholstery of the motor. 'You don't know what torture it was to sit beside you all that time and do no more than hold your hand.'

'Mother didn't like even that. She gave us both some very frosty looks,' Amelie giggled. 'Well, she can't stop us now.'

'Did she choose that hat?'

'Er – yes, I think she did.'

'I thought so. It's the perfect chaperon. I can't get near you.'

'That's easily remedied.'

Amelie drew out the hatpins and carelessly tossed hours of skilled millinery work onto the floor.

'There,' she said, and fell into his arms.

They travelled by train up to London and thence to Claridge's. It was as the porter shut the door behind him that Amelie experienced her first attack of nerves. Now they really were alone, for the very first time.

'It – it's a beautiful room,' she said, wandering round,

touching things. 'Such lovely flowers! And so tastefully decorated. I wonder what the view is like.'

Hugo came up behind her as she stared unseeing out of the window. He put his arms round her and ducked underneath the restored hat.

'It's a much nicer view from the room next door.'

'Next – ?' Amelie began, then realised that he meant the bedroom. 'I – er – I have to – you know –'

'I believe the bathroom's next door again,' Hugo told her, interpreting.

'Ah.'

She made her way past a vast double bed draped in peach satin and locked herself safely into a bathroom that made even the new ones being put in at Tatwell look Spartan. She ran the taps and stood staring at herself in the looking-glass. All the hints and whispered information that helpful married friends had given her over the last few weeks flooded through her mind. Try as she might, she could not quite relate it all to Hugo and herself. Kissing was one thing, and very nice, but what they were supposed to do now, if her information was correct, was quite different.

She found she really did need to use the lavatory, and sat there for a long time, chewing her lip and worrying. Supposing she couldn't do it? Supposing he was disappointed in her? Was it going to happen now, as soon as she unlocked that door, or would they have dinner first? After all, it was supposed to take place in bed, and no one went to bed at six o'clock in the evening. Taking courage from this thought, she emerged from the bathroom to find the bed turned back and a maid unpacking her overnight trunk.

'Will you be wanting some help changing, ma'am?'

'Er – yes,' Amelie said. She could not, after all, wear her travelling outfit all evening.

The maid helped her undress, ran an experienced eye over the contents of the trunk and held out a rose silk négligée.

'Very pretty, if I may say so, ma'am. And your hair?'

Obediently, Amelie sat at the dressing table while the woman undid all the elaborate pinning and brushed out her hair.

'Will that be all, ma'am?'

Amelie got up. 'Yes – thank you.'

She was left standing in the middle of the bedroom, feeling very exposed and wondering just what to do next. She did not have to wonder for long, for Hugo came in, wearing a dressing gown. Embarrassed, Amelie looked down at his feet, and realised that they were bare. She had never seen his bare feet before.

'My darling –'

He took her in his arms and began kissing her. Amelie responded happily. This she could do. His hands moved over her, caressing a body unconstrained by corsets and layers of clothing. The strange pleasure of it was frightening. Amelie knew she was rushing towards something she could not control, and yet she did not want to stop. She pressed against him, wanting to be closer still, and found something hard there that excited her even more.

Hugo's lips pulled apart from hers. His breathing was ragged. 'My lovely girl. I've dreamed of this moment. Come –'

He picked her up and carried her over to the bed. Amelie was swept up in a hot tide of delight as he caressed her breasts, her belly, her thighs. She was no longer thinking, just reacting to the new sensations. There was something that she wanted, something empty and aching inside her. She opened up to him, caught her breath as he entered her and cried out as a sharp pain went through her. Her eyes flew open. She was being torn apart. She wanted to stop. Then Hugo gave a rising shout that turned into a cry of triumph. A few more movements and it was over. He was cradling her head against his chest and kissing her hair and telling her that he loved her.

Shaken and bewildered, Amelie lay still as he fell asleep and slipped out of her. So that was it. That was what husbands and wives did.

Hugo stirred, opened his eyes and smiled into hers. He took her face in his hands and kissed her.

'That was wonderful, darling. Truly wonderful. I hope I didn't hurt you?'

'Not much,' Amelie lied.

'It's always difficult at first. But you'll come to like it, I promise you.'

354

'Oh. Good.'

Did all wives like it? Did Sylvia? She could not imagine her sister-in-law enjoying anything so uncontrolled.

'You will, I promise,' Hugo repeated, kissing her doubting face. 'But now, I'm ravenously hungry, so I am going to run a bath for you, and order dinner for an hour's time. How does that suit you?'

Amelie thought it would suit her very well. Through dinner they gossiped about the wedding, laughing at their relatives and guests, and talked about the coming honeymoon in Tuscany. When they went back to bed again, Amelie found that Hugo was right, and that she did enjoy it much more than last time. So much so that she was left with a faint sense of dissatisfaction. There was more to it, something that she had not reached. But by then she was so tired that she fell asleep and slept soundly through the night.

She woke, warm and relaxed, to find Hugo propped up on one elbow looking down at her.

'Good morning, Mrs Rutherford. How are you?'

'Very well, thank you.'

'Good.'

He ran a hand over her body, caressing her breast, then bent to kiss her nipple. The rush of pleasure made her gasp.

'Did I hurt you?'

'No, no – please –'

'More?'

'Yes –'

This time she was fully roused, striving towards something that seemed beyond her until it burst inside her, leaving her dazed with pleasure. She lay with her arms and legs entwined with his, soft and slippery and replete, wondering just what had happened, while he laughed softly and gave her little kisses.

'Oh Amelie, Amelie, you are the most amazing girl. I was right, I knew I was. You have the most beautiful body. Strong and perfect. We shall make such beautiful babies.'

'Babies?' Amelie repeated.

'Lots and lots of beautiful babies. And not just beautiful, but strong and intelligent. Olympians.'

355

Through the golden sea of utter contentment, a sharp black rock appeared. Amelie steered round it.

'Yes, but not yet, I hope.'

'Oh but we must, straight away. We have to lead the way, to set an example. We must prove how important it is to choose one's partner in life properly so that all that is best can be passed on.'

'But –' Bewildered, still drugged from their lovemaking, she did not quite follow him.'

'You agree with me, my darling, I know you do. Do you remember at your brother's wedding, when you said you were sick of people marrying for money and family names?'

'Yes.' She remembered that very clearly, for just after she had said that, he asked her to marry him.

'So many people have the wrong ideas. You see it all the time. Rich men marry beautiful women and everyone says that their children will have their mother's looks and their father's brains. It's so unscientific. They don't seem to see that it's just as likely to be the other way round, and that they'll produce children that are ugly and stupid. There's no danger of that with us. Whichever one of us our children take after, they will still be both beautiful and clever, and if the traits are combined, they'll be exceptional.'

Through this speech, Amelie felt a growing sense of dismay. She stared at him, the man who had said she should marry him because he loved her. The man who had just shown her the ecstacy of making love.

'Is that why you married me, then? To – to breed?'

He laughed at her horrified expression and kissed her.

'I married you because I love you, my darling. But children are the natural product of marriage, and ours will be perfect.'

She remembered his interest in the Packards, his admiration of her grandfather, his remarks about the degeneration of the old families.

'So you took care to fall in love with somebody suitable, did you?'

'But of course. There's nothing wrong in that, surely?'

There was so much wrong with it that Amelie did not know where to start. But before she could collect her thoughts, there was a tap on the door to the sitting room and a rumble of trolley wheels. A waiter had arrived with their breakfast.

'Good heavens, I had nearly forgotten – we have the boat train to catch,' Hugo said. 'Do you want breakfast here or in the sitting room?'

'I don't mind,' Amelie said.

She no longer cared about the romantic trip to Tuscany. What did Italy in the spring matter when Hugo had chosen her not for herself, but for her breeding qualities?

38

Daisy jumped off the bus and ran through a heavy April shower down Isobel's road, hoping against hope that this time her friend would listen to reason. She rapped on the door and stood pressed against it for shelter.

'About time too, I'm drowning out here,' she said, when Isobel finally opened it.

'Oh.' Isobel stared at the weather with a vaguely uncomprehending expression. 'Is it raining?'

Daisy's heart sank. She was not going to get much sense out of her today.

'Yes it is,' she said, stepping past Isobel, taking off her jacket and shaking it. 'But how are you? How are you keeping?'

'I'm very well, thank you,' Isobel responded. She switched into her hostess role and took Daisy's jacket and hat. 'Dear me, you're wet. Do come in and sit down while I make us some tea.'

Daisy sighed and followed her into the kitchen.

'Day like this you could do with a nice coal range to dry things out,' she commented, as Isobel placed the kettle on the shiny new gas stove. 'Don't trust those things myself. They can blow up, they can.'

'Really? How extraordinary,' Isobel said, and reached for the teapot.

Daisy waited till they had drunk their tea and she had imparted all the latest Packards' gossip. Then she started on her campaign.

'Now then, tell me how you really are. You still got the morning sickness?'

'No, no, that was just a passing trouble. I'm very well.'

'You don't look well. He been knocking you about again?'

'No, no. Not at all. He's very happy at the moment.'

'I should think he flaming well is. He's got a nice wife with a baby on the way, he's got you for his fun, and there's all this talk round the store about Sir Thomas retiring, and we all know who'll be in charge then. Everything's just hunky-dory for him, isn't it?'

'Yes, he's very pleased about Sir Thomas retiring. He's been waiting for that to happen for a long time.'

'He tells you about it, does he?'

Try as she might, Daisy could not at all imagine the formidable Mr Edward lying in bed chatting about the store.

'Sometimes. He was very excited yesterday. Something about the company being re – re – reconstituted, I think it was. I don't remember. But it is going to be very good for him.'

'Well, perhaps that'll keep him so busy that he won't be round here so often.'

'I don't think so.'

Daisy could tell by her expression that she was not going to say any more. It was what Isobel did not say about her life that worried Daisy the most. She was sure there were a lot of things went on that her friend just could not bring herself to talk about.

'You're going to have to tell him sometime, Izzy,' she said gently.

'Tell him?' Isobel repeated.

'About the baby.'

'No! No, I can't. Not after – he'd be so angry, I can't tell you.'

'But he'll see it for himself. He's not stupid, and his wife's expecting, so he knows what's what.'

'No he doesn't. It's all right, Daisy. His – his wife doesn't – she's – she has her own room.'

Daisy hesitated. It was at times like this that she wondered if her friend was quite right in the head. It was as if she had managed to convince herself that if she did not admit to there being a baby, then it would just go away.

'So she's not letting him have it while she's carrying, eh? Very nice too. Must be wonderful to be rich and have things all your own way. But Izzy, that's not going to stop him from finding out. Another few weeks and it's going to show. You're already bigger round the bust. Soon you're going to get a belly on you.'

But Isobel just shook her head. Daisy sighed and changed tack.

'He might like pregnant women. Some men do, you know. I mean – he's got you and his wife in the family way both at the same time. It shows he's got it in him doesn't it?'

'He doesn't. He – he said so, several times, that I wasn't to.'

'Then you got to think ahead, Iz, about what you're going to do. Leave now, before he suspects.'

Isobel stared at her, her lovely blue eyes widening with fear. 'I can't!'

'You can. I been thinking about it, Izzy, and it's the best way.' Daisy leant forward and held Isobel's hands. She looked into her face, trying to impress her with the seriousness of what she was saying. 'I can come back next week with a carrier. It's no good taking a cab 'cause they can be traced. You get all your clothes packed up ready, then when I get here we'll take everything we can carry.'

Isobel gasped, horrified.

'Daisy! That's stealing!'

'Rubbish. It's your wages. You been giving him what he'd have to pay for and no danger of him catching something nasty and he ain't given you nothing except a kid. What are you going to live on, else? It's only fair. He's rich. He ought to support his child, didn't he?'

Isobel's soft mouth set into a stubborn line. She shook her head and looked away, refusing to meet Daisy's eyes. Daisy held on to her temper with difficulty. Shouting at Isobel never did any good.

'What we'll do is, I'll find you a room, and we'll say you're a widow. We'll say your husband just got killed in an accident. Then you can sell off the stuff from here bit by bit, and that'll make enough for you to live on until the baby's born, and then afterwards you can get it minded while you get a job or something.'

Privately, Daisy did not think it would come to that. Knowing Isobel, some man would come along and want her. With a bit of luck, he might even believe the story and fall in love with her and marry her. All that was necessary was to get her out of the house and away from Mr Edward. While he had this hold over her, there was no getting her to see sense.

'It'd work, Iz, I know it would. I'd help you. Say you'll do it.'

But Isobel bit her lip and said nothing. Daisy wanted to shake her.

'For God's sake, Izzy, listen to me. I'm right, you know I am. There's nothing to be afraid of. Just trust me.'

'And why should she do that, pray?' asked a male voice behind her.

Daisy gasped, fear and shock slicing through her. She jerked round. There, standing in the dining room doorway, was Mr Edward.

Beside her, she heard Isobel moan, but she could not drag her gaze from the man who stood looking at them both with a small unpleasant smile on his face. He stepped into the room. Isobel's fingers dug into her arm as she huddled closer to her.

'You can stop that,' he said, addressing Isobel. 'Leave go of her and go and sit on the other side of the table. I'll deal with you later.'

A sob broke from Isobel's lips, but she released her hold on her friend. Daisy looked at her. Her face drained of colour and her eyes dilated with terror. Anger began to overcome Daisy's fear. She caught at Isobel's wrist.

'No, you stay here. You don't have to do what he says. He don't own you,' she said.

But Isobel was already standing up, shaking in every limb. She pulled away from Daisy and, holding on to the table for support, she did as she had been bid and moved away. Daisy stared back at Mr Edward. How much had he heard? Had he been listening when she told Isobel to take what she could and run? Even if he hadn't, this was the end of all her ambitions. It was the sack for her now.

'I know you, don't I?' Mr Edward was saying. 'You're another of the Ladies' Sportswear sluts, aren't you? The one I had to move. Phipps. That's right. Phipps. And what, might I ask, are you doing here, Phipps?'

Daisy swallowed. 'I'm visiting my friend,' she said.

'Visiting your friend,' he repeated. 'And what makes you think you can do a thing like that?'

Very clearly, Daisy foresaw what would happen. She would

361

have to leave Trent Street. She would have no references. She would have to go back home and have her family crow over her failed dreams. No more Packards, no more warmth and cleanliness and beautiful things. No more Johnny. She looked at Mr Edward, and she hated him.

'Why not?' she said. 'It's a free country, ain't it? She's not your prisoner. And even prisoners get visitors. You can visit the Scrubs, so I'm visiting here.'

'Not any longer. I don't care to have anyone interfering with my private life, least of all sly little shopgirls.'

'You can't stop me,' Daisy said.

'I think you will find that I can. I shall simply tell Isobel not to let you in. Isobel always does as she is told.'

'You can't –' she began.

Edward ignored her. 'So you can go back to Trent Street now – you are at Trent Street, aren't you? – and pack your things. You will leave in the morning, and I shall let it be known that you have been dismissed for insubordination.'

In the morning. By this time tomorrow she would be back in North Millwall, sharing a room with her sisters.

'I – I'll tell Miss Packard,' Daisy threatened. 'She'll stick up for me. She won't like it when she hears what you been doing to Isobel. She won't like it a bit.'

Edward's mouth twisted into another unpleasant smile. 'I don't think she's going to find out, do you? You forget, you will not be at Packards any longer.'

'I'll find out where she lives. I'll go and tell her,' Daisy said, not knowing how she was going to do it, but utterly determined to succeed. Johnny. Yes, that was it. She would get Johnny to help her.

'Even if she were to listen to you, which is most unlikely, I'm afraid Mrs Rutherford no longer has any influence over what happens at the store. Now that she is married she has other interests.'

There had to be something, someone he wouldn't want knowing about what he was getting up to.

'She could tell your wife.'

For just a moment, she thought she saw a flicker of a reaction to that, but it was instantly gone.

'I think not. And besides, if you were so unwise as to try to spread rumours, just think what might happen to your little friend.'

It was spoken so lightly that she did not immediately catch the meaning. Then it sunk in. To underline it, Edward walked round the table to where Isobel was sitting. Before he even reached her, she whimpered and shrunk away from him. He raised an eyebrow at Daisy.

'See?'

Daisy saw.

Edward placed his hands on Isobel's shoulders and ran them along until they met in a collar round her neck. Daisy felt sick.

'You leave her alone!' she cried, jumping up.

The chair toppled over. She lunged towards Edward, but a scream from Isobel stopped her in her tracks.

'No – Daisy – don't!'

Daisy hesitated. Isobel's eyes pleaded with her.

Edward smiled. He ran his fingers up and down the front of Isobel's throat.

'I think your friend wants you to go now. Don't you, Isobel?'

'Yes,' Isobel sobbed. 'Please go, Daisy. Just go.'

Edward took two quick strides across the room. He caught hold of Daisy's arm and twisted up behind her back until she thought it was going to come out of the socket. She gasped and bit back a cry of pain.

'You've been told to go,' he said, his voice horribly near her ear.

He began to march her towards the door. Unable to resist, Daisy was borne along, out of the room and along the hallway. At the front door, he stopped.

'Remember,' he said, 'you leave Trent Street first thing in the morning, and if I find that you have said one word about this, one word, then your precious little friend will suffer for it. Understand?'

He jerked her arm further up her back. Daisy yelped. Tears of pain stood in her eyes.

'Yes,' she gasped.

'Good. And be assured that I mean every word.'

Daisy believed it.

He opened the door, pushed her outside, slammed it shut. Daisy found herself on the street in the pouring rain, shaking in every limb, churning with rage and a sense of failure.

For several minutes she just stood there, unable to take it all in. It had all happened so quickly. She stared at the outside of the house, so ordinary-looking, just like all the others in the road. She groaned out loud at the thought of what might be going on inside there right at that moment. She had been useless. Instead of helping Isobel she had made everything ten times worse. She cast desperately about for a solution. The police. But her childhood experience told her that they would be no use. A man had to practically kill his wife before they would intervene in a domestic dispute. A mistress had even less protection. And even if they did investigate, Isobel would admit to nothing. Tell Miss Packard? She was concerned about her girls. She had wanted to know what had happened to Isobel when she left. She would wonder at Daisy's being dismissed. But she was still away with her new husband and nobody knew when she would be back in London. Sir Thomas? Even as she thought it, Daisy knew it was useless to approach him. If by some remote chance she actually got to see him, he was not going to believe the accusations of a mere junior shopgirl. It was hopeless.

And as she came to that conclusion, Daisy became aware of her own situation. She was wet and cold. Her hair was clinging to her face. Then she realised that her hat, her only jacket and her purse with her fare back to Trent Street were all on the other side of the closed door.

'Oh God, no!' she wailed.

She sat down in the doorstep, utterly defeated. She had no power at all against the likes of Mr Edward. She was soaking, jobless and penniless. For a long time, she sat with her head on her hands, unable to move, until the cold bit into her bones. Then at last it occurred to her that if she did not get going, she would not get back to Trent Street by ten o'clock and she would be shut out for the night, her very last night in her beloved attic room. Stiffly, she got to her feet, and began the long trek across town.

As she plodded along, she revolved the whole episode over

and over in her mind, burning with impotent anger, trying to think of a way in which she could have made it turn out differently. As she did so, anxiety as to what was happening to Isobel gnawed at her, made worse by the fact that she could think of no way to help her. When she looked ahead to what was going to happen to herself, it was even worse. It was just as she had pictured it from that very first moment that Mr Edward found her there with Isobel. Without a reference there would be no chance of another job in a big store. There was nothing she could do but to go back to her family, to the overcrowded house and a job in a factory. Most of all, there was Johnny. She tried not to think about him at all, but it was impossible. She longed to see him, to tell him of what had happened, to feel his sympathy and ask for his help, but she did not dare in case someone saw them and his job was put in jeopardy. She could not do that to him. It was bad enough that she had been sacked. She could not let him be ruined as well.

She walked automatically, one weary foot after the other, her mind unable to find any hope at all. In a life that had known plenty of hardship, she had never been so utterly miserable.

39

'Now this morning I really do have to go and put in some practice at the nets,' Hugo said. 'Shall you mind terribly if I leave you to amuse yourself?'

'Of course not. I shall be perfectly all right,' Amelie said, swallowing down the sense of rejection.

'You are very good. Not every wife would be so forebearing on her first day back from her honeymoon.'

'I know how much it means to you.'

His foremost sporting ambition for that summer was to be picked for the MCC team. Amelie knew that if that was what he wanted, then that was very probably what he would achieve. Hugo might be every inch the gentleman amateur, but he worked at sporting prowess with all the dedication of a professional. She had no quarrel with him over that. She admired him for it. It was one of the things that singled him out from the generality of young men, people like Perry and his friends who did not put any effort into anything except amusing themselves. It was when he took the same attitude to his personal life that it hurt beyond bearing.

Amelie looked across the breakfast table at him, tall and strong and handsome, the spring sunshine glancing on his blond head, and her heart contracted with love.

'I shall come and watch you when you play. I want to see you score your first century for MCC,' she said.

Hugo frowned. 'Don't tempt fate,' he warned.

'Sorry,' Amelie said. She kept forgetting how superstitious he could be about some things.

'I'll make it up to you this evening,' Hugo said, returning to the day's plans. 'We could go to the theatre, if you wish.'

'Yes, I'd like that,' Amelie agreed.

'And then tomorrow evening, I would very much like it if you were to come to a meeting with me.'

Something in his voice roused her suspicions. 'What sort of meeting?'

He avoided her eyes. 'The Eugenics Society.'

'No!'

'My dear, it would mean so much to me to be able to introduce my wife to the other members.'

'Your brood mare, you mean.'

She hated the Eugenics Society. It was because of them that Hugo had sought her out not for love, but because she would make a fitting mate, physically and mentally. It was because of them that every time they made love it was shadowed by the knowledge that he was eager to father the first of the super race he was set on procreating.

'Darling, it's not like that.' Hugo leant forward, his blue eyes earnest. 'I'm proud of you. I want to show you off to my friends. There is nothing wrong in that, surely?'

He sounded so sincere. He was sincere. He was proud of her, she was sure of that. But – but it was the reasons for his pride that distressed her. She was a splendid specimen, one to match his perfection.

'I will not meet those people and that's an end to it,' she stated.

'Don't you think that you're being unreasonable to condemn them before you've even met them?' Hugo asked.

'I don't need to meet them. I know what they stand for. That's enough,' Amelie insisted.

'You're condemning them out of hand on the basis of the little I have told you. I think that if you were to study their ideas rather more closely you would come to see, as I have, that what they say is extremely important. They hold the future in their hands.'

'Not mine,' Amelie said, and even as the words came out of her mouth she knew that it was not true. Through Hugo they did have a hold on her future and there was nothing she could do about it. It made her feel physically sick.

Hugo stood up.

'I have to go now. But I would ask you to reconsider your decision. It means a great deal to me.'

Amelie kissed him goodbye, and was left feeling that she was being disloyal. The other members of the society would be sure to ask about his new wife, would wonder why he had not brought her along. He would be made to look weak and foolish if he had to admit that his bride of one month was refusing to accompany him. But she could not bring herself to do it. She could not associate with people who seemed to want to breed babies in the way that farmers produced prize beef.

She stood at the window of the dining room of the house they had rented for the Season, and looked out over a garden bright with spring bulbs. She passed a hand over her stomach. She was two weeks' late. Perhaps she was expecting already. She should be happy. Hugo would certainly be deliriously happy. But what if it turned out not to be the perfect child he wanted? What if, heaven forbid, it was lame or deaf, or worse still, weak in the head? These things did happen. Would he reject it? His friends at the Eugenics Society would. From what she could gather, such a child would be regarded as being somewhat less than human.

She shied away from a prospect too painful to dwell on. She had the rest of the day to herself. Apart from giving her orders to the cook, there were no constraints on her time, no mother to arrange what she should do. She was a married woman now, and able to go where she liked without a chaperon. With a lift of the spirits, she realised that she could go to the store.

On the pavements outside Packards, people were looking at her spring displays. Amelie got out of the cab and lingered amongst them, unashamedly eavesdropping.

'Just look, how pretty!'

'Like a tableau. Very tasteful. I do like that hat on the left there.'

'The green one? That wouldn't suit you at all.'

'I know, but they will have other colours inside. Shall we go and see?'

Amelie's sore heart was soothed a little. She was right, and she would tell her grandfather so. People were attracted in by the windows despite there being much less in them now. What she must work on next was having far more goods out on display inside the shop, instead of all tucked away in drawers. She went through the main doors and stood for a moment in the marble entrance lobby, looking up at the great glass dome. She took a deep breath in. Packards. She was home. Her marriage may have turned out not to be the fairy tale she expected, but the store was still here.

She progressed through the departments, looking at changes, speaking to staff, noting where goods could be set out to tempt customers. She was eager to get to her beloved Ladies' Sportswear and see how well it was doing now that the sun was shining and women would be turning their thoughts to tennis and croquet and archery. Miss Higgs welcomed her as she passed under the archway.

'Mrs Rutherford! What a surprise. We're very pleased to see you, I'm sure.'

'I'm pleased to be back, Miss Higgs. How are you?'

She asked about the girls, then turned to general sales turnover, the popularity of her favourite lines and, most importantly, what the customers were asking for. As she talked and listened and wrote down points she wanted to remember, she watched the shopgirls serving. One customer went away empty-handed. Another just bought a tie.

'We must see about getting Daisy Phipps back here. She was by far our most successful girl. She could sell to people without their feeling that they were being forced into buying what they didn't want,' she said.

Miss Higgs pursed her thin mouth.

'Phipps has been dismissed, Mrs Rutherford.'

'Daisy? Dismissed?' Amelie was stunned. 'When, and whatever for?'

'Last week, Mrs Rutherford. For cheeking one of the seniors, I believe. Can't say as I'm that surprised She always was a bit above herself.'

'How ri–' Amelie began, then checked herself. She was about to say that it was ridiculous to sack such an able salesgirl, and one who was so loyal to Packards. If she had been cheeky, then a reprimand or maybe a fine would have been sufficient. Somebody had exercised very bad judgement, but she could not criticise the management in front of Higgs. 'Well, I must say I'm very disappointed. I always found her to be very willing,' she said, and resolved to find out more.

When they had covered all that had been going on while she had been away, and Amelie had noted any problems that needed sorting out and orders that should be chased, she took her leave of Miss Higgs and the girls and made her way up to Baby Linens.

Neither the floorwalker nor the buyer had much to tell her.

'The first we knew of it was when she didn't turn up on Thursday morning. Very inconvenient it was, too, with two of the girls already off with the influenza.'

'So it was not one of you whom she upset?'

'Oh no. She was a very useful girl. Very biddable. No, it was someone down on the ground floor.'

'That's not what I heard. I heard it was one of the managers.'

Amelie thanked them and left. She would go to Mr Mason at Staffing and find out.

Up on the fifth floor, the Staff Manger received her with badly disguised apprehension.

'Miss Phipps, Mrs Rutherford? Er – yes. I did have to dismiss her. Apparently she was extremely offensive towards Mr Edward. Practically attacked him, she did. Had to be restrained. Terrible business. Naturally she could not be kept on after that.'

'Naturally,' Amelie said, but she was not satisfied. The whole thing sounded odd. 'Were there any witnesses to this, Mr Mason?'

'Ah – well, I couldn't say, Mrs Rutherford. It did not occur to me to question Mr Edward on the matter.'

'Of course.'

He would not dare suggest to Edward that there might be any doubt as to the truth of his allegations. Amelie went off, more mystified than ever. What had Daisy Phipps been up to, arguing with Edward? The girl had enough sense to know that it would cost her her job, and she had always seemed so enthusiastic about working at Packards. One thing was certain, she was not going to rest until she found out the truth of it. She marched along the corridor to Edward's office, past his secretary and through the inner door. Edward jumped up with every appearance of delight.

'Mel! How very good to see you. Most unexpected, but a

pleasure none the less. I did not realise that you were back in Town.'

'We returned yesterday,' Amelie explained. 'Edward –'

'And how was Italy? Did you enjoy it?'

'Oh, yes, it was beautiful. Far more than I ever imagined.'

'And then you went to stay with Hugo's parents, I hear. Are they well?'

Amelie found herself obliged to be polite about Hugo's family, then to ask after Sylvia, whom Edward reported to be feeling a great deal better and busily choosing nursery equipment and decoration.

'If you've come to visit Grandfather I'm afraid you're going to be disappointed. He's down at Tatwell,' Edward told her.

'At Tatwell? During the week?' Amelie asked, astonished.

'Oh yes. He spends the better part of his time there now. It's all part of his plan to reconstitute the management of the store. Oh, but of course you won't have heard of that.'

'No, I haven't,' Amelie said. She had the distinct feeling that she was not going to like what he was about to say.

She was right. Edward sat back in his chair and assumed a suitably serious expression.

'Grandfather has decided to retire from running the store. There is to be a meeting next week at which he will announce his detailed plans. Nobody knows what they are to be, of course, but –' Edward gave a slow smile. He did not need to say any more.

It required all of Amelie's limited acting ability for her to smile back.

'Congratulations,' she managed to say, as she saw all her hopes of further responsibility at the store fade away.

'Thank you. Was there anything in particular you wanted to speak to me about?'

'Er – no, no, I just dropped in, you know, to let you know I was back.'

It was no use confronting Edward over the case of Daisy Phipps, she realised. She had no power to help her. She would talk to Daisy first and hear her side of the story.

'It's been a pleasure to see you, Mel. Do call on Sylvia, won't you? I know she'd be delighted.'

'I shall,' Amelie promised, and made her escape.

Out in the corridor again she stopped, eyes and fists squeezed tight as she fought back tears of anger and frustration. How could Grandfather do this to her? How could he bow out at this very moment? Once Edward was in control, he would not only stop her from taking on any new role in the store, but she was very sure that he would try to take away what she was already doing. For the life of her, she could not see a way of stopping him.

A door opened and someone came out. Amelie took a shaky breath and started to walk back the way she had come. She paused at Mr Mason's door. Daisy Phipps. She experienced a distinct fellow feeling with Daisy Phipps. They had both been outmanoeuvred by Edward. She went into Mr Mason's outer office and asked his secretary for Daisy's home address. The young man was away for several minutes, and came back looking apologetic.

'I'm very sorry, Mrs Rutherford, but her records don't seem to be there.'

'We do keep the records of former employees, do we not?' she asked.

'Oh yes, Mrs Rutherford. We keep them in case we are applied to for a reference. I looked in both the current and the past files, but they weren't in either. It's very odd.'

'Very odd,' Amelie agreed.

And very suspicious, too. Now she was determined to find out what had happened. Trent Street seemed to be the best place to try next. The housekeeper might know Daisy's home address. She walked down the nearest service stairs and out into Carpets on her way to the main staircase, nodding to the floorwalker as she passed him.

'Excuse me, Mrs Rutherford, if you please –'

Amelie stopped. One of the young shopmen had stepped in front of her.

'Yes?'

'I – beg pardon, Mrs Rutherford ma'am, but I had to speak to you. It's very important, like. It's about a friend of mine. Daisy Phipps.'

372

'Daisy?' Amelie brought all her attention to bear on him. 'You know her?'

'Yes, ma'am.'

'And do you know why she was dismissed?'

The young man raised his chin a little.

'I know what was said, ma'am, and I don't believe it. That's what I wanted to speak to you about.'

Amelie studied him. He had an open, honest look.

'I don't believe it either,' she agreed. 'Tell me, what's your name?'

'Miller, ma'am.'

'And what has Daisy told you about it, Miller?'

'Nothing, ma'am. She'd gone before I could talk to her. She had to leave Trent Street the morning after she was dismissed. I didn't know what to think. But then I got a letter from her, and she wants to meet me tomorrow, so perhaps I'll find out. I just — well, I just saw you and I thought I must speak to you. She always admired you, like. I thought you might be able to help.'

'I do want to help,' Amelie said warmly. 'I want to hear her side of the story, for a start. Would you give me her address?'

'Well — er — it's a bit of a rough area, ma'am. Not the place for a lady to be visiting,' Miller said.

'I have been to the East End before,' Amelie told him.

'If you're sure, ma'am? Then it's 17 Dock Street, North Millwall. That's on the Isle of Dogs.'

'Thank you, Miller. You've been extremely helpful. I'm very glad you stopped me.'

'Thank you, ma'am.'

Amelie made her way downstairs and hailed a cab. One she had silenced the driver's doubts about her destination, she sat back and thought over all that she had found out that morning. Everything was coming apart in her hands. Her marriage was not the love match she had thought it to be, and now Edward was taking over the store and soon her part there would be reduced to next to nothing. Her hopes and ambitions were crumbling. But at least she could try to save someone else's, and if it meant giving Edward a poke in the eye into the bargain, then so much the better.

The cab drove through the shopping streets of the West End

and into the city with its imposing office buildings. They passed the Tower and then abruptly entered the docklands, with the high wall of St Katharine's Dock on the one side and warehouses on the other. The bowler-hatted clerks of the city were replaced by working men, street traders, sailors from every outpost of the Empire, drunks and beggars. Amelie stared out, fascinated, distracted from her troubles for a while by this world so alien to her own.

The drab streets with their teeming population of poorly dressed people seemed to go on for ever. At midday hordes of children streamed out from the schools, dirty children with pinched faces, straggling hair and ragged clothes, larger ones dragging younger brothers and sisters by the hand. Amelie was struck by the lack of colour. Everything, people, buildings, traffic, seemed to be a shade of grey or brown.

At length they passed over a bridge from which great ships could be seen tied up at the quaysides and into a street of small, ill-stocked shops and tenement buildings. The driver turned down a side-street, past another prison-like school and pulled up outside a row of tiny terraced houses with front doors letting straight on to the pavement.

'Here you are, ma'am. D'you want me to wait?' the cabbie asked.

Amelie looked at the crowd of interested spectators that had immediately gathered round the cab. She was not easily going to find another one in this part of the world.

'Yes, wait.'

She stepped out to a swelling murmur of comment and speculation and knocked on the door of number seventeen.

'Door's open, missus. You can go right in,' somebody told her.

At the same moment, a small dirty child dodged in front of her.

'What you want at our house?' she demanded, and without waiting for an answer, pushed open the door and yelled, 'Mum! There's a posh lady.' A smell of frying fat wafted out.

To Amelie's relief, it was not the mother, but Daisy who came hurrying to meet her. Her face registered utter amazement.

'Miss P – Mrs Rutherford! What on – But please to come in.'

She stepped back to let Amelie into the tiny parlour, then addressed the crowd at the door. 'What are all you lot staring at? You got nothing better to do?' before shutting them out. Most of them gathered by the window instead and peered in.

Amelie found herself in a little room furnished with a battered sofa and four wooden chairs, all occupied by children of various ages munching sausage and mash. They stared at her, their jaws busily working. All of them looked pinched and undernourished, with eyes too big for their faces. None of their boots seemed to be the right size for their feet. They did not smell pleasant.

'We can't get 'em all round the table in the kitchen,' Daisy explained. She shooed them away, invited Amelie to sit down and asked if she would like a cup of tea. Amelie refused.

'Daisy, I was very distressed to hear that you had been dismissed from Packards,' she said, coming straight to the point.

'So was I, Mrs Rutherford,' Daisy said, with a mutinous set to her mouth.

'I always thought you to be such a sensible girl. I found it very difficult to believe that you had been so foolish as to cross Mr Edward.'

'Yes, Mrs Rutherford.'

'So I came to find out exactly what happened. I want to hear your side of the story, Daisy.'

Daisy did not quite meet her eyes. 'Yes, well – I had a row with him, didn't I?'

So it was true. But still Amelie felt there was something more to it.

'You had a row with him?' she repeated. 'Over what, precisely?'

'He – he didn't like something I said, and – and I give him what for,' Daisy said.

'But, Daisy, surely you knew that was a stupid thing to do? You must have known you would never get away with it.'

'Yes, well – I lost my head, didn't I?'

This was not the bright, enthusiastic Miss Phipps she had known. Perhaps she had misjudged her. Another failure.

'But I thought you liked working at Packards,' Amelie said.

The transformation was amazing. The dull truculence vanished.

'I did!' Daisy cried. 'I loved it there. It was like wonderland, all them lovely things and all the posh customers. And now I'm back in this place again and I suppose I'm stuck here for good now.'

'Then why –' Amelie began. And then it came it her, what should have been obvious from the start. 'Daisy, are you hiding something?'

'No, Mrs Rutherford.'

'I think you are. Something to do with Mr Edward.'

He did pick on certain members of staff, she had seen him do it. If they wanted to keep their jobs, the only thing they could do was to submit to it. So what had he done that had provoked Daisy into rebelling, despite the fact that she knew she would lose the job she loved?

'Did he – ah – make an improper suggestion to you?'

'What?' It took a moment for Daisy to fathom just what she meant. 'No – no, he didn't.'

It was like talking to a brick wall. She had been just like this when she had questioned her about Isobel Brand's disappearance.

'How is Miss Brand?' she asked, on impulse.

Daisy's face froze. For a long moment, she looked at her. Then she spoke.

'She's expecting. And he's the one what done it. Mr Edward.'

'*What?*'

Daisy sighed. 'You don't believe me, do you? I knew you wouldn't. Dunno why I told you. Wish I hadn't, now.'

'I – I –' Amelie's mind was racing. Isobel Brand, the gently brought up girl in fallen circumstances, who did not even want the people in her home town to know she was working in a shop? She was the mistress of her brother? And yet it all fitted neatly into place. Slowly, she said, 'I think I do believe you, Daisy. But – but why wait till now? Why didn't you tell me earlier?'

It could have been a very good weapon to use against Edward, for a start.

376

'Isobel didn't want me to. She doesn't want me to now. She'd have forty fits if she knew. But he's going to chuck her out anyway, once he finds out she's breeding, or so she thinks, so what does it matter? Except that she'd hate it. She's ashamed, you see.'

'Ashamed?' Amelie was finding it very hard to follow.

'Yes, well, she never wanted to, did she? He made her. She's terrified of him. Scared to set foot outside the house in case he finds out. She's like a blooming prisoner.'

'This is terrible.' Amelie was shocked. 'I'm so glad you told me. I'll have it out with Edward straight away.'

'No!' Daisy shouted. 'No, you mustn't do that. Not till I've got her out. I'm going round there tomorrow when it's the maid's afternoon off and I'm getting her out if I have to carry her, before he goes and does for her. After that, you can do what you like. What does it matter? I got no job to lose and Isobel'll be on the streets if I can't find nothing else for her but at least she'll be out of his way. If you can make things nasty for him, more power to your elbow, but let me get Isobel away first.'

There was a movement in the doorway through to the back of the house. A large moonfaced girl stood there, her slightly Chinese-looking eyes fixed on Amelie, her tongue protruding from her open mouth.

'Pretty,' she said.

Daisy jumped up. 'Ivy! Get back in the kitchen. Mum! Keep Ivy out of my way.'

A haggard woman appeared, wispy grey hair escaping from her scragged-back bun. She shot a searching look at Amelie, then grabbed the girl and dragged her away. The thought went briefly through Amelie's mind that maybe Hugo was right, and the poor should not be allowed to breed uncontrolled. Not if their children had to grow up in conditions like this. And it occurred to her that however heartbreaking her own situation was, Daisy and Isobel were far worse off. She was going to do something to help them if it was the last thing she did.

'All right, I'll see to Edward later. But let me assist you now,' she said, pulling out her purse and selecting a five-pound note. 'You take this and get lodgings for yourself and Isobel.'

A shutter came down on Daisy's face.

'I don't want no charity,' she said.

Amelie cursed herself. Now she had offended her.

'It's not charity, it's recompense for what my brother's done to you. If you like, you can call it a loan. Then when you're settled, I want you to let me know where you are, and I'll see you get a good reference so that you can apply for another job.'

Daisy fairly glowed with delight.

'Oh Mrs Rutherford, would you? That'd be wonderful!'

So small a thing, and it made such a difference to Daisy's life. Amelie felt ashamed. She gave Daisy her card, wished her luck, and went back to the waiting cab. At least she had done something useful today.

40

The key turned in the lock. Isobel gasped, fear clutching at her, paralysing her with its icy fingers. Below, she heard Edward's voice, the maid's heavy step. He was asking if there had been any visitors, she was assuring him that there had not.

'Very well. Remember that nobody is to be allowed in. You may go out now.'

'Out, sir? But my hours are from seven –'

'Today they are from this minute.'

'Until the usual time, sir?'

'Yes. Now go.'

'Certainly, sir. Thank you, sir. Most generous of you.'

More footsteps, the street door opening and closing. Isobel sat huddled on the couch in the dressing room, shaking uncontrollably. She knew that if she could just walk next door to the hated bedroom, could lie on the satin sheets and smile and look welcoming, she might deflect something of the horrors that were approaching. But she could not. She was incapable of moving.

He was coming up the stairs. Isobel retreated tighter into a defensive ball. He reached the landing. A few seconds' grace as he looked into the bedroom and found that she was not there, and then he was by the couch, towering over her. She squeezed her eyes shut.

'So here you. What are you doing skulking in here? You're supposed to be ready for me.'

Isobel said nothing. Whatever she did was going to be wrong.

His hand fastened on her arm, making her wince. The bruises from last week were still tender.

'Get up.'

She was hauled to her feet. Her legs shook.

'Look at me.'

Unable to disobey, she raised her eyes to find a new expression on his face. Impatience.

He gave her a shake. 'For God's sake. You're useless. What sort of welcome is this? You're like a limp rag.'

'I'm sorry,' Isobel whispered. She tried to stand up straighter. It was difficult when every instinct told her to protect herself from the blows he might rain on her.

But he did not hit her. He gave her another shake and let go of her.

'Tidy yourself up. You look like something that's been blown in off the street. I want you without a hair out of place. Then put this on. I shall be waiting for you in the other room.'

He thrust a briefcase into her arms and walked out.

Isobel collapsed onto the couch. For fully half a minute she sat looking at the door, grateful just to have been let off. Then she looked at the briefcase. Slowly, with trembling fingers, she opened it and looked inside. It contained a folded white garment. With grave misgivings, Isobel drew it out.

It was a nightgown of the finest quality lawn, trimmed with embroidered flowers and torchon lace. But it was not brand-new, in fact it was not even newly laundered. It was creased as if it had been slept in the previous night. As she held it up by the shoulders, a faint scent came off it, of a flower perfume, and of a woman's body. Isobel's arms dropped. She stared at the thing as it lay crumpled in her lap while it dawned on her that here was a new horror. It belonged to his wife.

She realised then why he had been so impatient with her. He did not want her cowering from him today. She was required to play a part. She began to undress. It did not occur to her to refuse. If that was what he wanted, then that was what she must do, though it made her insides crawl with sick apprehension.

With nerveless fingers, she struggled out of her clothes and pulled the nightdress over her head, her flesh shrinking as the scent filled her nostrils. She fumbled with the fiddly buttons and ribbon ties. She must hurry. She must not keep him waiting. She remembered his order to tidy up, and nerved herself to look in the glass. A white face with dark shadowed eyes gazed back at her, hair straggling and unkempt. She poured water into the basin on the washstand, spilling a little as she did so, splashed it onto her face, pinched her cheeks, looked in the glass again. Now she had a little more colour. She brushed her hair. The tangles were smoothed out, but the shine had gone out of it weeks ago. It was dull and lifeless.

On leaden feet, she walked out of the room. On the landing she hesitated, trying to nerve herself for the ordeal. Then she pushed open the bedroom door and went in.

He was lounging on the bed, still fully dressed.

'Stay right there,' he said.

Isobel stood as he looked her over, waiting for his reaction. A slow smile pulled at the corners of his mouth. Isobel felt something close to relief. It was all right. She had done what he wanted so far.

'Yes – very effective. Stand up straight. That's better. The hair's wrong, though. Make it into a plait.'

She gathered her hair up and pulled it to one side, divided it into three parts. Once, she could have plaited it in no time at all with deft fingers. Now she seemed unable to make it go right. She dropped strands or they ended up going the wrong side. It was always the way, these days. She could not do the simplest of tasks properly. At last she managed it and looked about for something to stop the thing from unravelling. The only thing she could find was a hairpin from the dish on the dressing table. She slipped it over the end and stood looking down at the rose pattern on the carpet.

'That will do nicely. Come here.'

The bed creaked as he moved. Isobel shuffled over. He was sitting on the edge, his feet on the floor.

'Kneel down.'

She knew what was coming, what she had to do. Swallowing down the revulsion, she knelt, and began to undo the buttons of his trousers.

It was late afternoon by the time he went, taking the nightgown with him. Isobel was left naked on the floor of the bedroom. For a long time she just lay there, her face pressed into the carpet, broken and humiliated. She wanted only to stay there for ever, to dissolve and become part of the floor.

Afternoon slid into evening. Outside in the street, the children played. Their clear voices floated in at the window, chanting a skipping rhyme. Isobel felt a fresh wave of self-loathing. She had been like that once, innocent and untouched.

Now she was soiled, despicable. Children should not even look at her, in case they became contaminated. Cold and stiff, she reached out and dragged one of the satin sheets from the bed, convinced that someone might see her, ashamed of her naked body. She struggled to her feet, wrapping the sheet round her, and then realised that she was after all alone. Completely alone. He had gone, the maid was out, Daisy would not come. Daisy. The one friend she had in all the world had lost everything she had worked for and taken pride in. She had been turned out of the attic room and sacked from her job, and all because of Isobel. It was all her fault. Everything was her fault. She was bad.

She caught sight of herself in one of the gilt-framed looking-glasses, naked shoulders rising from the soiled satin sheet, hair unravelled and falling about her face. A wicked woman. A woman with nothing at all to live for. She turned away and walked slowly out of the room, the sheet trailing behind her. Everywhere she went, she caught glimpses of herself. There was no escape.

She arrived at the kitchen. Beyond the back door, evening sunlight slanted into the small garden. Normal life, the real world, where ordinary people went about their ordinary lives. A world she had left behind the day she was brought to this house, a world she could never again rejoin. Her gaze flickered round the kitchen, lighting on the everyday objects. Larder, sink, plate rack, gas stove, table . . . gas stove. She stepped forward, stopped in front of it. It was very clean, its blue and white surface polished to a shine, its row of knobs gleaming. Isobel looked at the one in the middle. There was a way to escape. She watched her hand as it reached out. It seemed to have nothing to do with her. It turned the knob, opened the oven door. She knelt down.

Daisy stood outside Selfridges, watching their shopmen and girls flood out. Perhaps she would apply here for a job. They paid the best wages in Oxford Street. So much had happened in the past twenty-four hours that she could hardly take it all in. Before Mrs Rutherford's visit she had despaired of ever again aspiring to a better life. That beautiful white five-pound note and the promise of a reference had transformed everything. This morning she had paid a week's rent in advance for a room just off the Tottenham Court Road for herself and Isobel. It was not as clean as the one they had shared at Trent Street, and the kitchen that they had to share with the dozen or so occupants of the house was cramped and smelly, but it was a hundred times better than being at home in Dock Street. Tomorrow she would write to Mrs Rutherford, telling her where she was living, and then she would start looking for a job. It was not going to be easy, supporting Isobel and herself on a shopgirl's wages, but they would manage. The remainder of Mrs Rutherford's five pounds would cover doctor's fees and baby clothes when Isobel's time came. The difficult bit was going to be persuading Isobel to come with her. That was why she needed Johnny's help.

She looked along the street towards Packards. Their people would be coming out as well. Any minute now she would see him. Her heart raced, joy mixing queasily with trepidation. She wanted so much to see him again, but she was afraid of what his reaction was going to be when she confessed that she had known all along where Isobel was. He was sure to be angry. What if he was really still in love with Isobel? He had not talked about her except in passing for a long time now, but that might be because he had given up all hope of her. Once he saw her again he might still want to marry her. Daisy wasn't sure if she could bear that, but she had to risk it, for she couldn't leave Isobel where she was. The look on Mr Edward's face as he had told her that he would deal with her later had been frightening.

Groups of weary shopworkers were plodding along Oxford Street. Between two large detachments was a lone male figure. Daisy waved and called.

'Johnny!'

'Daisy!'

He broke into a run, dodged round the intervening people, swept her into his arms.

'Daisy, I've been so worried about you. What happened? What's going on?'

Daisy wished that the moment could never end. He was holding her as if he never wanted to let go. He was worried about her. But they had to get to Camberwell.

'I'll tell you as we go along,' she said. 'We got to catch a bus.'

'A bus? Where are we going? What's it all about, Daisy?'

They walked together along the street, Daisy holding tight to Johnny's arm.

'I'm so glad you came,' she said.

'Of course I came. Like I said, I was dead worried about you. It was like you'd just disappeared off of the face of the earth. No one seemed to know where you came from, so I didn't know where to start looking. I was so glad when I got your letter, I can't tell you. I –' he hesitated, then went on, 'I really missed you, Daise. Sunday wasn't the same without you.'

Daisy wanted to sing and dance.

'That so?' she said.

'It is. I even stopped Miss P – Mrs Rutherford and asked if she knew what was going on. Did she come and see you? She said she would, but you never know.'

'It was you told her where I lived?'

'Yes,' Johnny sounded worried. 'Was that all right?'

'Oh yes! Oh thank you. It changed everything. She's going to give me a reference so as I can get another job.'

'Well thank God for that. After she'd gone I wondered if I'd done the right thing. But, Daisy, you still haven't told me what happened, why you got slung out.'

They came to the bus stop and joined the queue of homegoing workers. Daisy took a steadying breath.

'Promise me you won't do nothing stupid at work when I tell you. Only that's why I didn't tell you before, because I didn't want you going and having it out with Mr Edward and losing your job.'

'Mr Edward? I might've known he'd got something to do with it.'

'Promise me,' Daisy insisted.

Reluctantly, Johnny promised. Daisy began to explain. As she told the tale, Johnny's expression grew increasingly grim.

'– and so we got to go and make her leave,' she concluded.

At that moment, the bus arrived. They climbed on board and managed to get seats together.

'Are you angry?' Daisy asked.

'Yes, I bloody well am, Daise. You should've told me.'

Misery swamped her, all the more poignant for her having been so happy only minutes ago.

'Isobel begged me not to. She didn't want anyone to know. And like I said, I was afraid you'd go and say something to Mr Edward. You was so upset at the time.'

'So instead you go and do the same yourself.'

'But he found me there, Johnny. I was done for anyway. He wasn't going to let me stay on and spread gossip like that all over the store, was he?'

'I suppose not.'

'I done it for the best.'

'That letter she sent me. Was that your idea and all?'

'No! She done that off of her own bat.'

'I see.'

For what seemed like a long time, he sat looking out of the window, not speaking. Then he reached over and clasped Daisy's hand.

'I suppose you did what you thought was best at the time. I just don't like being treated like I'm a kid, Daisy. You shouldn't have to protect me like that. I should be looking after you.'

Daisy breathed a sigh of relief. The world was suddenly a brighter place again.

'That's why I asked you to come along today. I need your help. I might not be able to manage her without you.'

'I'll do whatever I can,' he promised.

They got off at Camberwell, and as they rounded the corner into Isobel's street, Daisy peered anxiously along it, half expecting to see Mr Edward's motor car parked outside the house. It was not.

'It's all right,' she said. 'She's on her own.'

They knocked at the door, but there was no answer, knocked again louder but still no reply.

'That's funny. She never goes out,' Daisy said, a small thread of fear starting within her.

She bent down and opened the letterbox and called through.

'Izzy? Isobel, it's me, Daisy. Come and open the door.'

She listened. The house was as still as the grave. She shouted again.

'I don't understand it,' she said. 'She usually runs to the door before I even knock. There's a funny smell in there,' she added.

Johnny bent down and sniffed.

'Bloody hell, that's gas. We better go round the back.'

'Oh God –'

They ran up the street, counting houses as they went, raced down the passageway at the end of the terrace and along the weedy alleyway at the back, counting again.

'This one.'

They were confronted with a six-foot-high fence. Johnny tried the gate. It was bolted on the inside.

'Give me a bunk up,' he said.

Daisy caught his foot and heaved. He got his waist over the top of the gate and swung over, there was a rattle and a thud, then he was letting Daisy in. They ran down the garden and wrenched at the back door. It was locked.

'Stand clear.'

Johnny picked up a stone from the edge of a flowerbed and smashed the glass in the door. The sickly smell of gas oozed out. He put his hand through the gap and turned the key. The door swung open. The smell was overwhelming. And there on the floor by the open oven door, was a prone figure draped in white.

'Izzy!'

Daisy stared at her, frozen with shock.

'Stay there.'

Johnny took a deep breath and ran in. He grabbed Isobel under her arms and dragged her out. Her head fell back, the sheet slid down her naked body, her bare heels bumped across the flags of the floor. Daisy snapped into action, snatching at the sheet then taking hold of her feet. Choking and gasping from the effect of the gas, they carried her into the fresh air at the end of the garden and laid her on the lawn.

'I'll get a doctor. We must get her to a hospital,' Daisy cried, making for the gate.

'No.'

Johnny caught her arm. Together they stared down at Isobel. Her jaw sagged open, her limp arms lay with the hands turned palm up on the grass. Her utter vulnerability contrasted horribly

386

with the seductive folds of satin. Johnny bent down, and pulled the sheet over her face.

41

When the news reached Sir Thomas Packard, he was first shocked, then angry. He sent for Edward, and while awaiting his arrival, stood frowning at the floor plans of the store as they hung on the wall opposite his desk. Isobel Brand. One of Amelie's girls. The one who had mysteriously disappeared. A mystery no longer. The implications of his successor's deeds multiplied in his mind.

Archer tapped at the door and announced Edward. Thomas swung round to face him, his head thrust forward, his hands still clasped behind his back. His grandson stepped into the room.

'You wanted to see me, sir?'

Edward's expression was bland, his tone neutral. All the cumulative strain of the last few months, Thomas's misgivings about him, the anguish of finally relinquishing his control of his beloved store, came rushing to a head.

'Yes, I damn well do! What the devil have you been playing at?'

Edward gave nothing away, but he hesitated, fuelling Thomas's rage.

'And don't pretend you don't know what I'm talking about. I won't be played with. I want an explanation, if there is one.'

'Ah –' Edward had the wit to look uncomfortable. 'You've heard about the – ah – I'm sorry you had it from someone else. I should have told you myself.'

'Yes, you damn well should. That would have been honest of you, at least, though it hardly takes away from what you've done. You know perfectly well what my rules are – no meddling with the staff. I will not have my store treated as a venue for a cheap pick-up. I have decent respectable folk coming to do their shopping here, and I employ decent respectable girls to serve them. They are not tarts and are not to be treated as such. Any man in my employ caught taking advantage of one of Packards' shopgirls is out on their ear.'

Apprehension flickered in Edward's eyes, to Thomas's satisfaction.

'I am aware of that, sir. However –'

'However nothing! You more than anyone else should abide by the rules. You should be setting an example. And instead, just what manner of message is being signalled to the rest of the staff, eh? "Do as I say, not as I do?" How do you think that is going to look?'

Edward reddened slightly, but not with shame. There was controlled anger in his voice now.

'Sir, I don't think I am the only man in this family to keep a mistress.'

Thomas exploded. 'Are you presuming to criticise me?'

He stalked up to Edward and poked at his chest, emphasising each point with a stab of the finger.

'Now you just listen to me – I had none of your advantages. I wasn't brought up to be a gentleman and sent to the best schools. But I did know not to soil my own doorstep. I kept my women away from the shop and away from my home. The girls who worked for me were in no danger from me and your grandmother was never given a moment's unease. Which is a damn sight more than can be said for you. How do you think your wife's going to take this? And her in a delicate state at the moment?'

Edward's eyes dropped.

'She's – not happy, sir,' he admitted. 'But if I might point out, sir, she would never have known anything about it if the girl hadn't –'

'Hadn't taken her own life?' Thomas finished for him. He prowled about the room. 'How very remiss of her to give the game away! For God's sake, boy, what were you doing to her to drive her to suicide?'

Edward became totally wooden-faced. He looked at a point somewhere over Thomas's shoulder.

'I realise that it is going to lead to some awkward questions, sir. I apologise for that. It might have some unfortunate consequences for the store.'

'Unfortunate! That's hardly the word I would use. I've spent my life building the good name of Packards –' Thomas realised he had been sidetracked and broke off.

'Now I don't pretend to be a saint,' he said, moderating his voice with some difficulty, glaring up at Edward from under his thick eyebrows. 'But at least I kept my women happy, and when it came to a parting, I made sure they were well provided for. None of them was ever so desperate that they killed themselves.'

'The girl was unstable, sir. I cannot be held responsible for that. I regret it, naturally –'

'Regret! Aye, regret that she's exposed you, no doubt.'

At that moment, what Thomas most regretted was not being able to do what he most wanted to do – tell Edward that the store was going to go to somebody else. He toyed with the idea briefly, but even in his anger he knew that it was no use. There was nobody else. So instead, he said nothing, and waited for Edward to fill the silence.

When Edward did speak it was stiffly and with difficulty, as if the words hurt him.

'I – should not have acted as I did. It was – ill-judged of me.'

Thomas still kept silent. Edward flushed under his gaze.

'And – I can assure you that nothing of the kind will ever happen again. It was – an aberration. I am very concerned that the good name of Packards should not be in any way compromised.'

Thomas ground his teeth in frustration. The boy had him there and he knew it. Far from publicly showing his displeasure, he was going to have to make moves to cover up what Edward had done. His own pride in what he and his business stood for demanded it.

'I'm glad we understand each other on that point at least,' he growled, 'and should you ever come to forget it, bear this in mind: I am not dead yet, and even when I am, I shall leave a will behind me.'

He gained the scant satisfaction of seeing Edward seethe under this threat.

'I am aware of that, sir.'

'Good. And I have your word that nothing of this disgraceful nature will ever happen again?'

'I said as much, sir.'

'And you will of course act honourably by the girl's family, if she has any, or if she has not, see to her having a dignified funeral?'

Edward looked genuinely startled at this. It did not seem to have crossed his mind that his responsibilities extended that far. But a stony look from Thomas brought the proper response.

'Of course.'

A great weariness rolled over Thomas. He turned away and looked blindly out of the window.

'Go,' he said.

Edward began to say something, but Thomas cut him short. 'Just go,' he repeated.

Only when he heard the door shut did he move. He walked slowly over to the Pembroke table at one side of the room and poured himself a stiff whisky. Archer poked his head round the door.

'Is there anything I can do, sir?'

'No. Thank you.'

The secretary withdrew. Thomas sat down at his desk with a sigh. He had done all he could to keep Edward in line. Now he had to consider what was to be done to keep talk about this dreadful business to a minimum. It would come down to money, of course. Everyone had their price. He did not look forward to it, but if there was dirty work to be done, then he would do it himself. That had always been his way.

The inquest into the death of Isobel Jane Norton, also known as Isobel Brand, pronounced a verdict of death by suicide. Edward, Johnny and Daisy were all called as witnesses. Johnny and Daisy described how they had found her, Daisy said that Isobel had been terrified of what might happen when Edward found out she was pregnant, Edward maintained that she had nothing at all to be afraid of and that the last time he had seen her she had been quite normal. The fact that she was pregnant was explanation enough as far as the coroner was concerned. Pregnant women were known to be unstable. The case was closed.

'He killed her, as sure as if he put a knife into her,' Daisy declared loudly as they went out of the courtroom.

Several heads turned her way.

'Yes, but proving it's impossible,' Johnny said. 'The bastard's got off scot-free.'

'It's so unfair!' Daisy was close to tears. 'She was terrified of him. She never wanted to live in that place. He made her. But they wouldn't listen to me. I tried. You heard me, didn't you? I tried, and they wouldn't listen.'

'It was your word against his, that's why.'

'Yeah, and they believed him. They thought as I was lying. I tell you something, I'm a hundred times more honest than what he is, any day.'

'I know you are, Daise. But you're never going to get that lot to think so. Come on. You're doing no good here.'

He took her arm and began to lead her down the steps of the courthouse.

'I tell you one thing we can do, and that's make sure everyone at the store knows about it. Until I get the push, that is,' he said. 'It's the talk of the place already –'

He stopped short. There in front of them was Sir Thomas Packard himself.

'I'd like to have a word with both of you. Would you kindly come this way?' he said, and without waiting for a reply turned and led the way towards the Rolls-Royce motor car that was waiting at the kerbside, the chauffeur standing to attention by the open door.

Daisy and Johnny looked at each other.

'You got nothing to lose and my job's sure to go anyway, so we might as well,' Johnny said.

Daisy nodded. There were one or two things she wanted to say to Sir Thomas. She would rather have said them to Mr Edward, but his grandfather would do.

If she had not been so distressed, she might have enjoyed the ride. It was the first time she had ever been in a motor car, and this was a particularly luxurious one. But as it was, she had so much grief and anger boiling inside her that she hardly noticed where she was.

'It's a crying shame, that's what it is,' she cried. 'Isobel's dead,

I lost my job and now I suppose you're going to give Johnny the push and all, and all because of Mr Edward. It ain't right!'

'Daisy.' Johnny put a restraining hand on her arm. 'She's upset,' he explained to Sir Thomas.

'I realise that. You have every reason to be upset, Miss Phipps. I believe Miss Brand was a friend of yours?'

'Yes she was. A very dear friend. And I was the only friend she had in the world. Those men back in that court, they was talking like she was a tart. She wasn't. She didn't know nothing about life. Before she came to London, she never worked or nothing, she was a lady, she just done calls and that, and went everywhere with her mother. She was taken advantage of, that's what, and now she's dead.'

Once more she saw Isobel's lifeless body lying on the grass. Scalding tears spilled down her cheeks. Johnny put his arms round her. It was a while before she heard what Sir Thomas was saying.

'– back to life, but I can ensure that injustice is not done to you.'

He was holding something in his hand. Daisy realised that it was an open wallet.

'I don't want no blood money,' she declared.

'This is no such thing, Miss Phipps.'

'Mrs Rutherford gave me five pounds and promised me a reference. I don't want nothing else.'

If she had been calm enough to see it, she might have noticed that Sir Thomas looked impressed by this. But he still drew five white notes out of his wallet and placed them in her hand.

'Nevertheless, I would like you to take this. It will make a nice dowry for you when the time comes.'

Daisy stared at the pieces of paper. She had handled sums like this in the store, but never in her wildest dreams had she thought of possessing so much herself. She was speechless.

'And you, young man,' Sir Thomas turned to Johnny. 'You realise of course, that this unfortunate business means that you cannot be kept on at Packards. I am sorry, because I understand you have the makings of a good salesman. Indeed, both of you were loyal Packards people. But your staying on is out of the question, so I would like to make sure that you have something to tide you over until you can obtain new employment.'

Another twenty-five pounds was handed over. Sir Thomas picked up the speaking tube and told the chauffeur to stop.

'I'll let you out here,' he said. 'I hope you will both be able to put this affair behind you.'

Still stunned, Daisy and Johnny climbed out. Before they closed the door, Sir Thomas leant forward.

'Of course, you will not speak to any members of the press about what you have seen, will you?' he said.

The motor glided off. Daisy and Johnny were left standing on the pavement staring after it.

'We've been bought off,' Johnny said.

'Yes.' Indignation burned in Daisy's heart. 'As if I'd talk to the press. Poor Isobel would have hated having her name in the papers.'

'Still –' Slowly, Johnny folded the notes and tucked them into his inside pocket. 'Put that stuff away safe, Daise, or someone'll nick it.'

He took her arm. Daisy found herself being walked along, though she had no idea where she was or what direction she was going. They went over and over everything that had happened until they both realised that they were exhausted and went into a teashop. Daisy sat and looked at the sugar bun she could not eat.

'Daisy –' Johnny began. He stopped, then went on in a rush. 'Look, I know this ain't the time or the place, but when you're feeling up to it, like, will you come and help me look for a place to open a carpet shop?'

For the second time that day, Daisy could hardly believe what she was hearing. She gazed into his anxious eyes. The first smile since they found Isobel spread slowly across her face.

'I'd love to, Johnny,' she said.

42

'I have to say, I am disappointed in Sylvia,' Winifred said. 'Hers is not at all the right attitude to take. Every married woman has to accept that her husband may have other interests, especially when she is in a certain condition.'

'I think she's quite right to be disgusted in him. So am I. Isobel Brand committed suicide because she was frightened of him,' Amelie cried.

Winifred brushed this aside. 'Oh, the girl. She must have been hysterical. That sort often are.'

'She wasn't "that sort", Mother. She wasn't a street girl.'

'She was a shopgirl. They're practically as bad.'

'She was the daughter of a provincial solicitor. We know that now. She had an extremely respectable upbringing before she fell on hard times.'

'My dear, the bourgeoisie are the worst of all. It's common knowledge. Beneath that middle-class respectability it's all hypocrisy.'

'Mother!' Amelie was shocked. 'Don't you care at all about what happened to her?'

'My dear girl, nothing happened to her. She killed herself. Self-murder. That is a heinous crime. I really don't think she deserves any sympathy at all. Far from it. It was a very wicked thing to do and it has not done our name any good, though fortunately most of Society is sensible enough to see it as the storm in a teacup that it is. Which brings me back to Sylvia. She should be supporting Edward, not condemning him.'

'Well I'm very glad she's condemning him. She seems to be the only one who is. He's behaved appallingly and everyone seems to be sympathetic to him because he was found out. I think it's shocking,' Amelie declared.

'Then you are being as silly and naïve as Sylvia. I think both of you have a good deal to learn,' Winifred told her.

Amelia got up. She could not bear to be in the same room as her mother any longer. 'I shall see you at the meeting,' she said.

'Oh, the meeting. Another of your grandfather's strange ideas. As if I have any interest in how the store is administered. But I suppose I shall have to go,' Winifred sighed.

'You know very well that you will go, since it will be in your interest to do so.' Amelie said.

For once she had the satisfaction of seeing her mother look put out. That was the only pleasure she could extract from the prospect of the coming meeting. Everything else about it filled her with dismay. It was obvious that her grandfather was going to announce his retirement and Edward's taking over the running of the store. It was also obvious that she was not going to have any significant part to play. Her grandfather had gone along with her ever since she had come back from America, but she had to face the fact that he had only thought she was playing at shopkeepers until she got married. A few weeks ago, when she was still happily ignorant of Hugo's real motive in marrying her, she would not have minded so much. All she had wanted was to be married to him. Now it was different. Now she was bound for life to a man who wanted her to breed a race of supermen, and all her old ambitions for a place of real responsibility in the store were rekindled. But with Edward in charge, she had no chance at all.

The family assembled the next day in Thomas' office for the meeting. The big mahogany desk had been pushed back and a table and chairs put in the middle of the room, set with pens, ink and notepads. All of them were early, even Perry, who had put off his trip to America yet again when he was informed that his presence was required. Their spouses were not invited. This was for blood relatives only, so Winifred and her three offspring stood about like guests at a particularly stiff party. Amelie, boiling at the thought of what was about to be revealed, could not resist an attempt at pricking Edward's air of complacency.

'You must be glad that I managed to find poor Isobel Brand's relatives. It was lucky that I kept that card of hers, wasn't it? Especially since her records disappeared from the staffing office files.'

'Most fortunate,' Edward agreed, his smooth confidence seemingly undented.

'Really, Amelie, I hardly think that this is the time or the place to discuss such matters,' Winifred interposed.

'Don't you? I do. What else should one discuss at Packards but Packards' business? Yes, it was most fortunate, as you put it, Edward. If they had not come forward, you would have had to arrange the burial, and I'm sure Sylvia would not have liked that.'

'We all have to do things we don't like sometimes, Mel.' he said, but his annoyance showed in his eyes.

'I wonder how long this meeting's going to take? Does anyone know? Only I've arranged to meet some chaps at my club this afternoon,' Perry said, conspicuously changing the subject.

Amelie glared at him. Trust Perry. He could always be relied on to suck up to whoever was likely to be the most useful to him.

'Not too long, I trust. I have calls to make,' Winifred said.

'How terrible for you both to have to give up an hour or so to the store. I do hope it won't stop you from spending the profits,' Amelie said, with heavy sarcasm.

Perry just laughed. 'Nothing stops me from spending. Just think, if nobody spent, there would be no customers for the store, would there?'

The fact that there was a grain of truth in this made Amelie crosser than ever. At that moment, she hated all her family, even her beloved grandfather.

'Don't you ever get tired of being so frivolous, Perry?' she asked.

'No, never,' Perry said, quite unmoved.

'I really think you should stop being so childish, Mel,' Edward said.

'Yes, you're a married woman now. You should start to behave like one,' Winifred agreed.

At three o'clock on the dot, Thomas entered the room to complete the family gathering.

'Well, well, here you all are. Good and prompt, I see,' he said, apparently oblivious to the seething atmosphere. 'Sit down, sit down. Archer will bring in the tea.'

He took his place at the head of the table, and Archer served tea with his usual quiet efficiency.

'Now then,' Thomas said, when they were all sipping in

silence, 'I expect you all have some idea as to why I've asked you to come here today.'

He paused, and there were nods and murmurs of agreement round the table.

'So I shan't waste any time in telling you that as from the end of this month, I intend to retire from active participation in the running of the store.'

This time he did not allow any comment.

'It's a move I've been contemplating for some time now, but it not something that can be done without a great deal of thought and planning. Before relinquishing the reins, I have to ensure that the store will continue not just to flourish, but to keep the principles on which I built it.' He glanced at Edward as he said this, then went on. 'So a certain amount of change is needed in the structure of the firm.'

Perry shifted in his seat, clearly bored already. Thomas shot him a look of barely suppressed irritation.

'As you all know, up till now I have run everything myself. Several of my colleagues, especially those whose stores are now public companies, think that this is a quite ridiculous way to run an organisation as large as Packards. My reply was always that it worked, so there was no point in altering it. However, we must change with the times. From now on executive power will pass to a board of directors.'

Amelie sat up straight. So, Edward would not have total control. She looked across the table at him, but his expression was carefully neutral.

'The directors will be drawn from the senior managers, namely the head of finance, the head of staffing and the chief buyer. They will be answerable to the managing director, who will have the overall responsibility for the running of the store. This managing director needs to be a member of the family – Edward.'

So that was it. Effectively, Edward was in charge. This time it was Amelie who had to try hard to keep her face impassive, as she saw Edward's smile. Not a big grin of triumph, just a small smug tugging at the corners of his mouth, to show that he knew all along that he was going to get his way. Amelie felt like hitting him.

'Thank you, Grandfather. I very much appreciate your trust in me. I can assure you that I will put every effort into maintaining the high standards for which you have made Packards famous,' he said.

'Congratulations, old chap,' Perry said, shaking his hand. 'I'm sure you'll make a jolly good job of it.'

Toady, Amelie thought.

'An excellent decision, Father,' Winifred declared. 'We all agree that Edward will be a worthy successor to you.'

'I don't.'

There was a moment's stunned silence as everyone stared at Amelie. For a second or so, she was almost as astonished as they were at her outburst. She had not meant to speak her thoughts out loud. Then everyone spoke at once.

'I say, old girl –'

'Really, Amelie, this is hardly the time nor the place to be –'

'I rather think you might want to withdraw that statement.'

Thomas cut through them all.

'Let the girl speak.'

Amelie took a deep breath. There was a very dangerous look in Edward's eyes. The wisest course was to take his advice and back down. But if she did so, then she would always regret it.

'We all know what I'm talking about,' she said. She looked round the table at them all. Her grandfather nodded faintly, a forbidding expression settling round his mouth, Winifred looked disapproving, Edward furious, Perry – she came back to Perry, for she could have sworn there was sadness in his face. But there was no time now to think about it.

'Quite apart from the rights and wrongs of the matter, it doesn't do Packards' reputation any good to have a managing director who is known to seduce his own shopgirls. Society might not care very much,' she glared at Winifred, 'but most of our customers are not from Society, they're respectable middle class people and they don't hold with that sort of behaviour.'

'William Whiteley –' Perry began.

'Yes, William Whiteley was notorious for it, and look what happened to him: he was shot by one of his own illegitimate sons.' Amelie snapped.

'I don't think that Edward will make the same mistake again,' Thomas said, addressing his successor.

'No,' Edward agreed, staring down at his hand as he gripped the pen in front of him.

'Mistake!' Amelie cried. 'Mistake is hardly the term I would use –'

'So I shall move on to the next matter: the distribution of shares.'

It was no use trying her usual way of getting round her grandfather here. This was a business meeting. Amelie held her tongue, though inside she was still seething. Her mother, she noticed, was listening with sharpened interest. Shares meant income.

'As you all know, at the moment only two of you have shares in Packards. Winifred has a ten per cent holding, and Edward five per cent. Then there are various settlements and allowances. I propose to change all this. From now on, there will be no allowances. Edward, naturally, will have a salary commensurate with his responsibilities as managing director, and you will each have a twelve per cent holding of Packards shares, with the exception of Perry, who will have six per cent now and the rest when he makes a suitable marriage. These shares are not transferable.'

Thomas paused, while they all took in the implications of this announcement. Winifred looked moderately pleased, Perry obviously had not quite figured out whether or not he was better off. Amelie did a quick sum in her head. She glanced at Edward, and saw that he was asking himself the same question: what about the other fifty-two per cent? Slowly, she smiled, as she realised what was happening.

'The remaining shares I shall retain, as chairman of the company,' Thomas stated.

Amelie bit back a chuckle. Good old Grandpa. She might have known that he would never really let go. Edward would have to justify his every decision at the board meetings.

'Do these shares entitle us to a vote on company matters?' she asked.

Edward shot her a look of pure venom.

'Certainly, if you wish to exercise it,' Thomas agreed.

'Oh, I think I might well do,' Amelie said.

'There is one more change to announce. An advisory position to the board,' Thomas said. 'The store needs someone who is in touch with what the customers want and what is going on in other stores, both here and abroad. We may be a well-established firm, but we need to keep up with the times. To this end, I propose that this position, with an appropriate fee and the title Head of Innovation, should be given to Amelie.'

'Oh –'

Amelie was deaf to the exclamations and mutterings around her. She gazed at Thomas.

'Oh Grandfather, thank you! That's wonderful – I – I shall work so hard, you'll see. You won't regret it for a moment. We'll make Packards more successful than all the rest of Oxford Street put together.'

'I'm sure we shall, my dear. Now if there are any questions – ?'

The rest of the meeting passed for Amelie in a dream. She heard not a word of her mother or Perry complaining about their percentage of the shares. Her head was already buzzing with things she wanted to present to the new board. Opposite her, Edward glowered but said nothing. He would, she knew, fight her every inch of the way, but she did not care. She had a real place at last, and she was going to make it count.

Archer came in with the legal documents and witnessed their signature. Thomas declared the meeting closed. Still in a daze, Amelie wandered along the fifth floor corridor and down into the store. Really her store now. Or at least, twelve per cent of it was. She watched the flow of customers, the floorwalkers directing operations, goods being shown and sold, money whizzing over the wires to the counting house.

Packards, the most prestigious department store in London. From now on, she would have a hand in shaping its future.

KEEP SAFE FOR ME

Patricia Burns

Winter, 1941, and London is in the Blitz. Rita Johnson, like many thousands of Londoners, is struggling to keep up something like a normal life. But even war can have some advantages. Rita is earning good money in a factory, and all the dangers and difficulties push her loveless marriage to Ron into the background. Rita longs to get away, to join the forces, to escape from the restrictions surrounding her, but she is bound by her family ties.

Then her younger sister Lily arrives home with Jack Wilkinson, a bomber navigator, and Rita's life takes on a new meaning. Jack is all that Ron is not, and Rita is immediately attracted to him. But he is her sister's man, and she is a married woman . . .

'The authentic flavour of the East End . . . compelling'
Harry Bowling